GABRIELLE'S DISCIPLINE

BOOK 2 IN THE BRIDAL DISCIPLINE SERIES

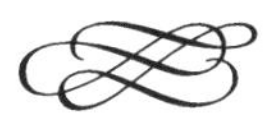

GOLDEN ANGEL

Printed in the United States of America

Cover art by RaineyCloud9

Edited by MJ Edits

Formatted by Raisa Greywood

Thank you so much for picking up my book!

Would you like to receive two free romances from me as well? Join the Angel Legion and sign up for my newsletter! You'll immediately receive a free Stronghold Doms holiday story from the Stronghold in a welcome message as well as a link to pick up book 1.5 of my Bridal Discipline series!

As part of the Angel Legion you'll also receive one newsletter a month with teasers, sneak peeks, news about upcoming releases, and well as what I'm reading now.

ACKNOWLEDGMENTS

I have a lot of people to thank for helping me with this book. My Maries, my power houses: Marie #1 for all her help with editing, catching small errors, and the continuity issues that I occasionally struggle with (I swear, she remembers all the things that I can't). Marie #2 for her incredibly close attention to detail, especially when it comes to commas, mixed-up words and my excessive use of the word "that". Katherine, for her ever-lasting support, encouragement and suggestions. Michelle for her comments and suppositions, which always end up changing the way the plot and character development flows. Sir Nick, for providing the much-needed male perspective. And RaineyCloud9, for the gorgeous cover art and promotional posters that I've been sharing.

As always, a big thank you to all my fans, for buying and reading my work... if you love it, please leave a review!

A LISTING OF CHARACTERS, TITLES AND RELATIONSHIPS

Philip Stanley the Marquess of Dunbury married Cordelia Astley, the Dowager-Baroness of Hastings

Lady Gabrielle Astley – stepdaughter to Cordelia Astley, now ward of the Marquess of Dunbury

Hugh Stanley, Viscount Petersham, married to Irene, cousin to Philip Stanley

Edwin Villiers, Lord Hyde, married to Eleanor (sister to Hugh)

Thomas Hood, eldest son of Viscount Hood

Walter Hood, second son of Viscount Hood

Felix Hood, youngest son of Viscount Hood

Isaac Windham, Duke of Manchester

Benedict Windham, brother to the Duke of Manchester

Arabella Windham, sister to the Duke of Manchester

Christopher Irving, Earl of Irving, married to Marjorie Irving

Wesley Spencer, Earl of Spencer, married to Cynthia

Alex Brooke, Lord Brook – heir to the Marquess of Warwick, married to Grace

CHAPTER 1

It was not the smallest wedding ever conducted in London but it was certainly among them.

Dressed in a new gown of white and silver, a borrowed veil upon her head, silk stockings with blue garters, and an old family heirloom diamond necklace around her throat (a gift from the Marquess of Dunbury, her guardian), Gabrielle looked every inch the bride at her hasty wedding. Of course, the reason the gown was new was because this was her first Season in London and she just hadn't had the chance to wear it yet. The blue garters on her stockings were worn at the insistence of Cordelia, Gabrielle's stepmother and the Marchesse of Dunbury. The Marquess was Cordelia's second husband; her first had been Baron Hastings, Gabrielle's father. She and her stepmother were only a few years apart in age, and Gabrielle still couldn't decide whether she detested or adored Cordelia. Sometimes it was both. When Cordelia had first arrived in Gabrielle's life, she'd been hopeful at Cordelia's friendliness, but at the same time wary after the ill treatment of her first stepmother. It didn't help that she knew her father desperately wanted a son. Gabrielle's mother and first stepmother had both died in the attempt to give him one, and, despite Cordelia's youth, Gabrielle hadn't been sure her second stepmother would fare any better. Instead, Cordelia had ended up outlasting Gabrielle's father.

Since Cordelia's second wedding - was it really only a little over a month ago? - Gabrielle's life had changed completely. The Marquess of Dunbury had become her guardian and he had paid more attention to her than her own father ever had. Although, that attention had not always been positive.

Gabrielle could admit that she was not always the nicest person, particularly when it came to her stepmother, and the Marquess was very protective of Cordelia. That had led to several clashes, which had resulted in Gabrielle's very first spanking since childhood. And her second.

Her emotions about being spanked were mixed. Although she'd hated being treated as a child, hated the humiliation of the exercise, and the pain, she'd also been comforted and coddled following her punishments - even praised. There was a part of her that yearned for that recognition, even though her father was gone (and had never shown any particular interest in her person, no matter what she did to garner his attention).

Before Cordelia had remarried, all of her attention had been focused on Gabrielle, and Gabrielle had loved it. She had taken Cordelia's attempts at finding a second husband rather badly, and her successful marriage to the Marquess even worse. At the time, she'd thought she'd be shoved aside and ignored again... instead, she'd been given her first Season in London. She'd had suitors, she'd made friends, and then she'd botched it all because she'd fallen in love with the wrong man.

It wasn't that Mr. Felix Hood was unsuitable - completely the opposite, he was the Marquess' best friend, third son of a Viscount, and wealthy in his own right. He was charming, elegant, sophisticated, well-read, and incredibly handsome. Unfortunately, he was also in love with Gabrielle's stepmother.

At first, Gabrielle had thought he might be interested in her, but she'd quickly been disabused of that notion. He had seemed to show interest, but he'd never made any formal move to court her - he was the *only* man she'd danced with at her come-out ball whom she didn't receive flowers from the following day, the only one who hadn't sent her a single bouquet since, never written her a poem, or even taken her for a short drive in the park - and she'd overheard a conversation between him and the Marquess where the Marquess had actually asked him to keep an eye on her and he'd agreed to the duty. The revelation had been humiliating, despite the fact that she'd never dared show a preference for him anyway (thankfully). She'd been foolish to think that he would dance attendance on her for her sake, but it had still hurt.

After that, she'd quickly tired of London, as she'd realized she had no idea whether or not any of her suitors were truly interested in her, or her dowry, or her connections. She'd known Mr. Hood had no need of her dowry and he already had a connection to the Marquess, but when she'd realized his attentions had been due to duty, not desire, she'd truly lost hope. It wasn't her lot in life to have a marriage like the Marquess and Cordelia's; one that was loving, a true partnership, and very passionate.

Being in London, living with the perfect couple, and having to see Mr. Hood on a regular basis had caused her to act rashly in her desire to escape all the reminders that she would never have what her stepmother did. For some reason, no one ever wanted Gabrielle. She as herself, was never enough to satisfy anyone - not her own father, not Cordelia, and not her suitors. The best solution to ease the ache in her heart seemed to be to return to the country, where at least she didn't have to stand witness to everyone else's happy, perfect lives.

The thought of being in London when Mr. Hood finally did search out a bride, rather than having to stand guard duty over her, had made her feel ill.

The fastest way to escape had been to encourage a rather desperate Viscount Fenworth (whose urgent need for her dowry made him the perfect match, as long as her main goal was to quit London as soon as possible) to elope with her. The Viscount had been more than willing, agreeable to letting her retire to the country to rusticate at his main estate, and was, at least, not entirely repellent to her.

Last night she was supposed to have eloped with him, but they'd been caught. The entire *ton* had been witness to her attempt to elope with the Viscount, who had made their attempt entirely clear in his haste to secure her as his bride, and then Mr. Hood had actually punched the Viscount when he wouldn't be quiet. It was too late though; the damage was done and by this morning Gabrielle was already known as a flighty creature who had attempted to elope with a man.... who knew what else she might have done with him?

No one could be certain that she'd allowed Fenworth liberties, but they all assumed.

Ironically, Gabrielle was practically pure as the driven snow. Her first kiss - her only kiss - had been interrupted by Mr. Hood, and had been the beginning of her disillusionment with gentlemen of the *ton*. Mr. Pressen, the suitor in question, had disappeared after that, and if he'd truly had feelings for her, then Gabrielle didn't believe he would have kept away. He hadn't even attempted to fight for her. Not even for her large dowry.

She knew much more than kisses went on between a husband and wife, in large part because the Marquess and Cordelia... well, suffice to say, they did not always confine their activities to the bedroom and Gabrielle had gotten quite an education one afternoon in the library. So she was well aware she wasn't anywhere close to ruined, but the truth didn't matter as much as appearances when it came to the *ton*.

The Marquess and Cordelia had informed her when she first awoke that she was to marry Mr. Hood straightaway, thus saving her reputation. The wedding and breakfast had already been arranged and the guests would be arriving in a little more than an hour, giving her just enough time to dress and prepare herself. Their words. They expected her to be grateful - and truly, if they had chosen any other husband for her, she would have been.

Really, she would have preferred to have received another spanking, or even a series of them, and have that be the end of it, but she knew that such a punishment would not restore her reputation. Only marriage could do that, and Mr. Hood had left last night to procure a special license. The hasty wedding would stem most of the talk amongst the *ton* about last night's events - or so the Marquess and Cordelia seemed to think.

When Arabella, Gabrielle's best friend and the sister of the Duke of Manchester with much more experience in Society, had arrived this morning, ready to play bridesmaid, she'd concurred with their conclusion. Which meant Gabrielle was stuck, in a mire of her own making.

She looked up at Mr. Hood, his dark hair brushed back from his forward, his dark eyes burning with intensity as he looked down at her while the minister droned on. Behind him, Mr. Hood's eldest brother, the Viscount, was standing up for him as best man. Behind her, Arabella was acting as her maid-of-honor. Their audience included the Marquess - who had given her away - and Cordelia, the Marquess' cousins Lady Hyde, Viscount Petersham, and their spouses, Arabella's brothers, and Mr. Hood's middle brother. There was no escape.

Gabrielle lowered her eyes as she made her vows in a low, husky voice, pressing back the urge to cry as she pledged herself to a man who would probably treat her kindly, because that was what her stepmother would want, and whose kindness would break her heart. There was nothing to be done, although she hoped she might be able to convince him that she should be allowed to leave London. Perhaps stay at his family's estate. At least that way she wouldn't have to watch her husband fawn over her stepmother, while pretending affection for Gabrielle in order to impress Cordelia.

Mr. Hood made his vows in much louder tones, his voice sure and confident, and she knew that he truly meant them. Well, all except the love part. But Mr. Hood was an honorable man, a dutiful man as he'd already proved, and she had no doubt that he would keep his vows. After all, despite his reputation as a rake, the only woman he'd paid any attention to, other than Gabrielle, had a striking resemblance to Cordelia. Obviously he could only admire Cordelia from afar, and Cordelia had made it clear that she cared for Gabrielle, so now he would care for Gabrielle for Cordelia.

Bitter, bitter, bitter...

She shoved such thoughts to the side, choosing to concentrate on the pink rosebuds in her bouquet. They reminded her of her come out ball, when Mr. Hood had been so attentive, so charming, and she'd thought he actually had a passing interest in her. No bouquet had been forthcoming the next morning and she'd realized she was wrong, but that evening had proven to her that they could rub along well enough together. That was all she had to do for now, until she could persuade him that she'd be happier away from London - and, not so incidentally, him.

"I now pronounce you husband and wife. You may kiss the bride."

Gabrielle's breath caught at her throat as Mr. Hood stepped forward, his fingers under her chin, tilting her head up. She blinked at him, surprised by the intensity of his gaze as he looked down at her and very gently lowered his mouth.

This was... this was nothing like her first kiss. Mr. Pressen had been attractive, but even at the time she'd realized that his kiss had left her breathless because she had *wanted* to be left breathless by her first kiss. This kiss left her breathless because of the way her entire body warmed at Mr. Hood's touch, the yearning that poured through her, and the utterly shocking way he held it for far too long, considering their audience.

Her entire body flushed as his lips moved over hers. Was he always this passionate? Was he just a very good kisser because he was so experienced? The questions swirled about her mind as the sensation of his lips on hers sent her senses rioting.

When he pulled away, she blinked up at him, dazed and confused, inwardly cursing her body's reactions. Her only hope of surviving marriage to him was to keep her emotions in check, to hold herself away from him, but how could she do that when a mere kiss sent her spinning?

MARRIED. Not quite happily yet, but Felix was determined to get there, if he had to drag Gabrielle kicking and screaming to do it. Mostly, his new bride seemed confused and withdrawn, not at all like the fiery young woman he'd gotten to know - or even the kinder version of her that he'd witnessed on occasion. The only time she smiled during the entire wedding breakfast was at the servants - although he supposed that wasn't too surprising. He'd noted that Gabrielle had a very sweet way with the servants; it was with her guardians and himself that she acquired a waspish tongue.

The very first time he'd seen her had been on Philip and Cordelia's wedding day, when he'd witnessed her gifting two servants' children a gorgeous pair of dresses for their dolls. It had made a rather lasting impression, especially as it was quite contrary to the disdainful and disrespectful way she had spoken of her stepmother mere hours after he'd witnessed that kindness to the children. Although, since then, her relationship with her stepmother did seem to have become less fraught. Felix was aware that Gabrielle had been disciplined by her guardian, and from what he'd seen, benefited greatly from it.

Which he was glad of. He firmly believed in spanking a badly behaving wife. In fact, he'd actually threatened to spank Gabrielle before, which had not gone over well, considering that at the time he'd had no real right to do so. Now he did, but he wasn't going to hold any of her past transgressions against her.

It didn't look like she'd be making any new ones anytime soon, however. She was practically silent at the breakfast table, her focus entirely on her food, although she'd sent a few longing glances down the table to where Arabella was sitting. Felix regretted that her friend had to be seated so far away, but family came first. He'd never quite understood Gabrielle's animosity towards Cordelia in the past, and he certainly didn't understand why Gabrielle would barely even look at her stepmother today. While it was obviously distressing Cordelia, Gabrielle wasn't actually being impolite, so there wasn't much he could do about her behavior. She seemed to be in a kind of shock at the hasty wedding, rather than purposefully ignoring Cordelia at the moment anyway.

Instead, he applied himself to keeping the conversation going, allowing Gabrielle to sit silently since it appeared that was what she wanted. He and Philip combined their efforts to keep Cordelia entertained. Part of him wanted to spark Gabrielle's ire, the way he always had in the past, just to get a reaction from her, but that would be ungentlemanly. She just looked so pale and unlike herself, and he could practically feel the tension emanating off of her, growing as each minute ticked by.

Finally, he decided that they'd been there long enough that they could take their leave without being rude.

Taking Gabrielle's hand, he looked around the table, catching everyone's eyes. "I believe it might be time for Gabrielle and I to quit the table, we both need to change and then we have quite a bit of traveling to do."

"Traveling?" Gabrielle asked, stirring beside him. He could feel her fingers stiffening against his.

Felix shot a glance at Cordelia and Philip.

"Oh yes," Cordelia said, her hands fluttering. "I forgot to mention in all the excitement this morning, that Felix sent a message asking for your things to be packed for a trip. I had Molly put them together."

The frost coming off of Gabrielle was enough to chill the warmth in the room, as everyone eyed her, almost waiting for an outburst. She avoided his eyes, but he saw Philip's catch hers, and he raised his eyebrow at her, as if asking if she truly wanted to throw a fit here and now.

"I see," Gabrielle said finally, her voice still frosty but polite enough to pass muster. She was still avoiding Felix's eyes and the paleness in her cheeks was so severe that she nearly looked translucent. "Thank you."

"I didn't realize you didn't know. We'll be going to the main estate," Felix said quietly, squeezing her fingers gently. "My parents will be excited to meet you." If anything, Gabrielle somehow managed to look even paler at his pronouncement.

"Molly will be going with you, as your lady's maid," Cordelia said in a rush, she glanced at Felix and smiled. "And Felix has agreed to take her and Robert onto his staff once you're settled." He'd agreed after Cordelia had told him that Gabrielle had taken a special liking to her maid Molly and her daughters, and they to her.

Apparently Molly wasn't the only member of the staff that had an interest in Gabrielle; Philip's housekeeper also had a soft spot for his bride - he'd seen the woman surreptitiously watching them from the doorway throughout the meal. He'd thought some familiar faces would benefit her during the transition, and that seemed validated by the fact that they'd - finally! - been able to say something that didn't make her even paler.

"Thank you," Gabrielle said, her green eyes flicking so briefly to Felix that he didn't even have time to smile at her before she looked away again.

For a moment he regretted the necessity of taking her away from her stepmother and friends and out to the estates where she would know no one, but he had already made his decision. She needed to meet his parents - his mother would already be beside herself that he was wed without so much as notifying her - and they needed time away from London and its busy schedule to... connect. Their hasty disappearance would not go unremarked; he was sure rumors were already spreading this morning that Gabrielle had attempted to run off with Fenworth last night. It would be up to their friends to spread the word, far and wide, that Felix and Gabrielle had married immediately and that he'd swept her off on a honeymoon.

After last night's events, such gossip would actually benefit Gabrielle's reputation and make for an easier return to Society in a few weeks. They couldn't miss the entire rest of the Season after all, they would need to put in an appearance before the capital emptied of the most influential members of the *ton*. By that time, he was sure that his friends and family would have everyone convinced that Felix had been interested in Gabrielle all along, but had chosen to stand back for her first Season, only to erupt in a violently jealous rage when Fenworth tried to turn her head, and had immediately staked his claim in the most legally binding way possible.

It was close enough to the truth after all, although Felix's hesitation in making Gabrielle his wife had more to do with his confusion over whether or not she was interested in him. He wanted a faithful, loving wife... as a rake, he knew very well how bored matrons of the *ton* would cavort. It was not the kind of relationship he wanted to have with his own wife, especially not after seeing the successes of a love match.

So he had three weeks to whisk Gabrielle away and try to build the kind of relationship he wanted with his wife. Since she had actually been living with a successful love match, he was hoping that she'd see the benefits of such. That she'd tried to run away with Fenworth didn't bolster his confidence on the matter, since Fenworth obviously didn't love her, but he couldn't help but think she was running scared.

Cordelia had confessed to him that she rather thought Gabrielle did have some regard for him, and that was why she tried so hard to push him away. The poor dear was used to being ignored or devalued by the men in her life, and he had done a particularly poor job in courting her before now.

LEAVING Dunbury house was much harder than Gabrielle had anticipated. She'd already said farewell to Arabella after the wedding breakfast, hugging her friend tightly and exchanging promises to write. Arabella had mourned the loss of Gabrielle at her side for the Season.

"Now I'll be trapped with all the ninnies who just want to speak with me in hopes of an introduction to him," she pouted, jerking her head at her brother, the Duke. The Duke just raised an eyebrow at her and turned back to the Marquess and Cordelia to say something. "Stodgy bore," Arabella muttered. She pulled Gabrielle in for another tight hug. "When you get back, you must tell me all about *it*. Perhaps you should take notes so that you don't forget anything important."

Trust Arabella to make her laugh, even at a moment such as this! Gabrielle clung just as tightly to her friend.

"Maybe *it* won't be very impressive," Gabrielle murmured back, hiding her real fear, which was that Mr. Hood wouldn't be interested in doing *it* with her. Although, from what she'd heard, men didn't need to feel any emotion with the woman they did *it* with. Otherwise, they wouldn't go through so many mistresses. And Mr. Hood was a rake. He must have done *it* with countless women.

Which just made her feel sick and sad again. She really must push past these emotions that bubbled up when it came to him.

Giggling, Arabella whispered back. "Well then you must tell me all about how disappointing *it* was."

"What are you two talking about?" The Duke of Manchester's voice was full of suspicion - as well it should be - as he loomed over them. They broke apart, Gabrielle now giggling as well, a nervous burble of laughter that felt perilously close to hysterics. Arabella's brother was an imposing figure with his meticulously styled dark brown hair and brooding eyes; every inch of him was pressed, starched, and - as Arabella would say - stodgy. Although he was certainly handsome enough to be a rake, and had the supreme confidence of one, he lacked the air of danger. There was something very safe about him, as if he exuded honor from his every pore.

It was a sad joke on him that he was responsible for a high-spirited, mischievous, little imp like Arabella. While they looked very alike in facial features and coloring, they were nothing alike in temperament or spirit. Arabella had been an eager accomplice to Gabrielle's romantic misadventures since her come-out, just for the delight of making mischief and so that she could badger Gabrielle for the details at a later date. She was very cynical about her own suitors and their supposed romantic interest in her.

"I was just wishing Gabrielle well on her journey," Arabella said, batting her eyes up at her brother in a way that she probably thought made her look innocent. Gabrielle had discovered very early on that Arabella was a terrible liar. However, she was stubborn enough to just keep silent about a secret once it was told to her, no matter what dire threats her brother might rain down upon her head. Arabella shook her brown curls at the Duke. "You have no faith in me, brother."

"I have no reason to, sister," the Duke said dryly. His gaze moved to Gabrielle's face and his stern countenance softened. "Do have a good journey though, Mrs. Hood."

Gabrielle jerked, a kind of shock going through her as she was addressed by her new name for the first time.

"Oh that does sound strange!" Walter Hood, her new brother-in-law jostled in to give Gabrielle a buss on the cheek. She smiled at him, although weakly. She got along quite well with both of her new brothers-in-law; they were just as charming and handsome as Felix was, although for some reason they'd never made her heart race like her new husband did. "Mrs. Hood, my sister-in-law. Who'd have thought Felix would be the first to tie the knot?"

"Anyone who's met us knows that I'm the mature one," her Mr. Hood said, stepping up beside Gabrielle and putting his arm around her, tugging her against him. She looked up at him in a kind of shock; the movement had been strangely akin to one she'd seen the Marquess use on Cordelia when one of his friends was flirting with her.

He was giving his brother a dark glare, the way Arabella often did when challenging her brother. Gabrielle had watched the way the sibling relationships worked and she could tell when they were teasing each other and when they were in earnest. This was teasing but... with an edge that wasn't normally present.

Perhaps now that she was his wife, he felt possessive of her?

It shouldn't make her feel happy, but it did. Just a little. At least he wanted her in some way, considered her to be his, and put a small importance on her person. That was more than she'd expected.

"It's time we were off," he announced, tugging her towards the front door of Dunbury house where the carriage was waiting outside. Arabella had been her last - and longest - farewell. "We have a ways to go today, but we can be there before nightfall if we make good time."

"I sent a runner ahead to inform mother that you're coming," the eldest Mr. Hood said with a grin. He was the most serious of the three brothers, probably because he was the heir to the Viscountcy, so Gabrielle was unsurprised he'd taken responsibility for such an important chore. "I wish I could be there to see how you're received."

"I'll just bet you do," Mr. Hood muttered as he escorted Gabrielle out of the door.

She almost balked at the precipice, but there was really nothing to do but allow him to lead her to the carriage and help her in. For all that she'd hated Dunbury House when she'd first arrived, hated how out of place she'd felt, how alone, now all she wanted to do was turn round and barricade herself behind the door.

Why hadn't she thought through the wider implications of what might happen if her plan failed? Although, even when her thoughts had touched on it - during those few times she'd allowed herself to think of failure - she had never imagined that Mr. Hood might put himself forward to save her. At worst, she thought she'd be dismissed to the countryside, to live out her days in seclusion. It would mean giving up the excitement and events in London, but she'd quickly found that such things didn't mean as much to her as she'd thought they would.

While she'd enjoyed having suitors, loved the flowers and poems showered upon her, especially appreciated her friendship with Arabella, and had even begun to value her relationship with Cordelia and the Marquess, it had all paled when she'd realized that her suitors were probably more interested in her dowry and connections than in her, and that her... attraction to Mr. Hood was not reciprocated. The situation had become intolerable when she'd realized that his regard was for Cordelia, and that living in Dunbury House meant being forced to watch him fawn over her stepmother constantly.

And now he was her husband.

Gabrielle's pace slowed as they neared the carriage; she felt as though the air was made of molasses. Of all the changes her life had gone through, this had to be the most frightening. Her breath caught in her throat as panic welled.

Her new husband relinquished her hand to wrap his arm around her waist, driving her inexorably forward.

"It's too late to change your mind," he whispered in her ear, his voice harsh. Gabrielle blinked back tears that threatened, unable to reply, because she knew that if she tried to speak she'd burst into tears and she certainly wasn't willing to let him see her do that. "Into the carriage."

His arm tightened about her waist, his fingers almost caressing her hip and Gabrielle made a strangled sound as she went from dragging her feet to practically bolting for the perceived safety of the carriage. It was a gorgeous conveyance, boldly decorated on either side with the family's coat of arms to make it quite clear who was inside. The heavy maroon velvet curtains had been drawn back so that it would be easy to look inside.

Gabrielle supposed that it was so anyone who wanted to look would be able to see her and Mr. Hood; another tactic in dispelling the rumors that were surely already winging their way around town. Anyone who saw them would immediately want to know *why* they were together in the carriage, and *where* they were going. By mid-afternoon, the gossip-mongers would have descended *en masse* upon Dunbury House, and Cordelia and the Marquess would be ready for them.

All for her.

Their efforts warmed her while simultaneously filling her with guilt and remorse.

Settling into the middle of the seat, Gabrielle hesitated. She didn't know if she wanted Mr. Hood sitting across from her or next to her. Both had their pitfalls.

He made the choice for her when he climbed in and sat on the other bench, facing her. Unwilling to face him just yet, Gabrielle looked back out the window. Cordelia was smiling at her, in a hopeful kind of way, and Gabrielle managed to smile back at her step-mother. She was doing as best she could for Gabrielle; this situation was not her fault. It was not lost on Gabrielle that mere months ago she would have found a way to blame Cordelia for it anyway. Waving at Arabella, Gabrielle drew out the time until she would finally have to sit back in her seat with her new husband facing her.

CHAPTER 2

As London began to roll by, Felix cleared his throat. His bride peeked at him through her lashes. The subdued, passive figure that she made irked him. In a pale pink muslin dress to travel, her hair still styled as it had been for their wedding, her hands folded in her lap, she looked nothing like the fiery, flirtatious, sometimes bratty young woman that she often presented to her suitors. She also showed no sign of the compassionate, sweet, and charming face that he'd glimpsed on occasion.

Instead she seemed almost submissive.

While Felix liked his women submissive in very particular circumstances, a carriage ride following his wedding was definitely not one of them. Truth be told, he'd expected Gabrielle's inner spark to flare up once they were alone; he'd rather been looking forward to having her vent her feelings upon him. He wanted that clash, that *truth* from her. Instead she'd withdrawn inside of herself and he felt as though he was farther away from the true Gabrielle than ever.

The carriage rocked as they began to move down the London streets. It was late enough in the day that a closed carriage with open curtains would certainly draw attention, although the picture that he and Gabrielle currently painted was not what he wanted portrayed.

Felix cleared his throat. "My parents' estate is about a four hour journey from London." Looking at him from underneath her lashes, Gabrielle dropped her gaze again when she saw him looking directly at her. Sighing inwardly, Felix reached out to take her hand. He felt the small jerk of response when they touched, as if she wanted to pull away, but didn't dare.

"I think you'll enjoy the visit," he said, leaning forward, his voice gentle. "My mother will harangue me for marrying without her presence, probably continuously for the first few days." A tremor of a smile curved Gabrielle's lips, heartening him. "My father will just shake his head and let my mother have at me, while sneaking you off to the kitchen for treats. His favorite are Cook's blueberry tarts, which should be in season now." Her smile grew a little bit.

Encouraged, despite her silence, Felix began to slide his thumb over her gloved hand, wishing that he could touch her bare skin. Soon enough.

Still leaning forward, he started to describe the estate to her - the manor house, the summerhouse where they would stay during their visit, the fields of hops that his father grew, the small but well-bred kennel of hunting hounds, the nearby town of Brentwood with its array of local shops and assembly rooms. By the time he got round to telling her about the creek where he and his brothers had played pirates in their childhood, the carriage had left London and Gabrielle's smile was still hovering about her pink lips.

As much as he longed to lean forward and kiss her again, he'd noted how she'd slowly relaxed as they'd traveled and he'd talked, but how she'd tense again whenever he changed how he was holding her hand. Despite her sneaking off to kiss Mr. Pressen during a ball, Felix was quite sure that she had little to no other experience at intimacy with a man. Which both relieved him and made him feel even more possessive than he already had.

After her rendezvous with Pressen, Felix had wondered whether she'd had true feelings for the man or if she'd just been in search of excitement and passion. Both he and Cordelia had noted her need for attention, and he'd decided that she just wasn't very discriminating about the kind of attention. It had been part of why he'd been so indecisive about actually courting her - he wanted a relationship like Philip and Cordelia's, and he knew all too well how easily it was for wives of the *ton* to arrange affairs outside of their marriages. Felix was determined his own wife should never need to.

Hopefully removing Gabrielle from London would assist him in focusing her attention. London was full of distractions by way of its entertainments and her large circle of suitors. By the time they returned, Felix was determined to have his wife's attention fixed upon him. He needed to show her that she had no need of distractions outside of their marriage, and he was certain of his ability to fulfill her passions and desires... once he was given a chance to.

As he extolled the virtues of his family's estate, he could see her interest, even if she didn't respond. It wasn't until he changed the subject to their stables that she finally spoke.

"I don't ride very well." Her green eyes flicked up to meet his, full of wariness, before she looked away again.

This wasn't a surprise to him, as Cordelia had already mentioned it before. Gabrielle's father hadn't encouraged Gabrielle to do much of anything other than shop, embroider, and manage the servants in between stepmothers. He simply smiled and squeezed her hand.

"You can certainly learn to, if you like," he said. "Some of the horses will be too big or too spirited for you, but my parents always keep at least one or two on hand for learning purposes." Of course, anyone in their family learned how to ride when they were small children - Felix had been riding almost before he could walk - but they always kept a few gentle horses in the stable for the less experienced. His mother loved to have guests, and not all of them were able to handle the steeds he and the rest of his family preferred.

Gabrielle just nodded, almost shyly, and glanced out the window.

Frustration built as he realized that was the end of the interaction for her. Keeping his hold on her hand, Felix got up from his seat and slid in beside her, making her scoot across the carriage bench as she stared at him with wide eyes. The sudden rise in anxiety made the atmosphere quite tense as he settled in beside her.

Ignoring the alarm in her eyes, he turned his focus out the window and began pointing out some of the sights with his free hand. Slowly, he felt her hand in his begin to relax again, and her shoulder pressed against his arm as she leaned against him to see where he was pointing. A little surge of triumph pulsed through him.

For some reason, Gabrielle was behaving very much like a skittish horse. He supposed he could understand, as she had been thrust into a new environment and a new relationship very quickly, and he doubted she'd ever been alone with another man. Inwardly he frowned as he suddenly wondered if Cordelia had even had time to speak to Gabrielle about what went on between a husband and a wife. If she hadn't... well, no wonder Gabrielle was a bit skittish. Then again, if she had, that might also make Gabrielle skittish.

Allowing his voice to gentle even further, Felix allowed himself to celebrate the small victories, as he felt Gabrielle's fingers curl very slightly around his own. Not much later, her head dipped onto his shoulder and he grinned to himself as he heard her even breathing. At least he could be sure she trusted him not to ravish her in her sleep.

Relinquishing her hand, he wrapped his arm around her and pulled her head against his chest, closing his own eyes. It had been an exhausting twenty four hours, what with last night's dramatics, his rush to secure a special license, and then this morning's wedding. Enjoying the feel of her head nestled into his shoulder, one small hand pressing against his chest, Felix let himself drift off to sleep as well.

THE SHIFTING of her cushion woke her, but she was reluctant to awake. With a soft mutter, Gabrielle snuggled deeper into what should be the softness of her pillow, only to realize that she was pressing her face against something quite hard... and strangely hot. There was an arm about her shoulders, fingers stroking her upper arm, which meant that the warm she felt beneath her cheek and hand was -

Alertness came swiftly with the sharp shock of realization, and she sat up abruptly, eyes wide, and a muffled shriek vibrating in her throat.

The lazy, self-satisfied, rake's smile that her new husband bestowed upon her did nothing to settle her mind. Gabrielle's heart was beating frantically, between realizing that she'd be cuddled up against him in her sleep and the way he was looking at her now. She could only imagine that she looked afright, but the expression on his face said anything but. His eyes raked over her hair and rumpled skirts with a strange kind of smugness that made her skin tingle, and she narrowed her eyes as her temper sparked.

Seeing her expression, his smile actually widened.

"We're here, my lady." The overly polite tones struck a chord within her; the same tones he'd used to needle her with when they'd first met and she'd felt as though he was mocking her with his superior knowledge of the *ton* and town life.

Deciding to ignore him while she calmed herself, Gabrielle peered past him, out the carriage window. The sun was setting as the carriage rocked along, but she could see plenty of the manor house that they were approaching. It was a very large country house, three stories high and quite imposing as the front of it was fully lit, the lights in the windows shining out like beacons in the waning light. A row of trees followed the lane, which wended its way up to the main entrance. Larger than the house she'd grown up in, it still felt familiarly like home.

Not exciting or sophisticated like London, but comfortable and warm. To her surprise, she truly was glad to be back in the country.

"It's beautiful," she said, carefully sitting back and scooting away from the large male body next to hers. The sudden loss of warmth was only physical, she told herself.

Even in the dim light of the carriage, she could see him looking at her out of the corner of her eye. Both of his hands rested on his thighs, one long finger tapping against the muscle. Gabrielle tried not to think about how nice it had felt to be nestled up against his body with his hands resting on her. She especially tried not to think about the marital acts she'd witnessed between the Marquess and Cordelia back in London. That just made her think about the times she'd wickedly experimented in self-pleasure following her first accidental role as a peeping-tom, and that made her think about the face she'd pictured every time she'd indulged in such perverse activities.

A blush rose in her cheeks at that man's nearness, but fortunately it was too dark in the carriage for him to be able to see that.

She heard the groom call out the halt, and the stamp of the horses' feet, as the carriage slowed and then stopped.

Despite her desire to escape the close confines of the carriage, she still hesitated when Felix stepped down and held out his hand. She wanted to escape the carriage in part to escape being forced into such close proximity to him. Waking up on his chest like that... her skin still felt like it was too tight and tingling. The thought of touching him again made anxiety rise in her, but she didn't truly have a choice.

Barely touching her fingertips to his, Gabrielle scrambled out of the carriage, only to see him frown down at her.

"Gabrielle - "

Whatever he was about to say was cut off as the door to the Manor flew open and a woman came rushing out, followed by a more slowly moving gentleman.

"Felix!" The lady was graceful even in her hurry, her blue skirts swirling around her as she moved. She was clearly dressed for dinner, but, as they were out in the country, she lacked the more elaborate accessories that adorned the ladies of the ton. The dress she was wearing was of very fine material and gorgeously cut, but was much simpler than the finery of London. Gabrielle found herself relieved to see it; something else that felt familiar and comforting.

Turning to meet her, Felix smiled and shook his head as he opened his arms to greet his mother with a hug. She had the same dark hair and eyes as her son, although her hair was liberally streaked with white, the contrast somehow exotic rather than aging. Her sons obviously got their height, broad shoulders, and calm demeanors from their father, who was following his wife at a much more sedate pace.

Just as tall as Felix, he had kind brown eyes that alighted on Gabrielle as he smiled. Dressed as a country gentleman, he obviously favored browns and earth tones over the stark blacks and whites his sons tended to dress in. His brown hair was sprinkled with grey, and he'd gone fully grey at his temples. Despite the lines on his face, he was still a very handsome man, and obviously doted on his wife going by the look he threw her, full of amusement, resignation, and exasperation.

"And you must be my new daughter-in-law!"

To her shock, Gabrielle found herself drawn into an embrace by the other woman. Although she didn't know what Felix or his brother had written to their parents, she hadn't imagined a warm welcome, considering the circumstances and hastiness of their wedding. But Viscountess Hood had her in a crushing hug, and she didn't seem at all upset.

Unsure of how to respond, Gabrielle threw a panicked look at Felix. The bloody useless fool was just standing there, shaking his head and grinning.

"Good grief, Lizzie, let the gel breathe," the Viscount chuckled as he drew closer. "You'll scare her off and then where will Felix be?"

"Absolutely not, you're not scared are you?" The Viscountess pull back to meet Gabrielle's eyes. They were close enough in height, the older woman just a touch shorter. Smiling delightedly, the Viscountess wreathed her arm through Gabrielle's, leading her towards the house. "She's probably just tired and overwhelmed. It's been a very long day after all. We've been waiting for you to arrive before we ate our meal."

"Mother, aren't you going to allow me to introduce you?" Felix said, his voice sounding somewhat plaintive. Gabrielle had to stifle a giggle, and the Viscountess gave her an encouraging look, while somehow simultaneously giving her soon a repressive one.

"I don't need to be introduced to my new daughter, thank you Felix. We'll just move straight to the getting-to-know-each-other part."

"Hello dear," the Viscount said as she passed. Lady Hood paused just long enough for the Viscount to lean forward and give Gabrielle a buss on the cheek. "Welcome to the family."

The warmth and obvious parental approval that both of them were brimming with as they looked at her left Gabrielle perilously close to tears. In a daze, she allowed Lady Hood to pull her along, up and into the house, pointing out various aspects of the architecture and artwork all along the way.

~

SIGHING, Felix rubbed his hand over his face. He should have realized his mother would take over the moment they arrived. After all, she'd been waiting years for one of her brood to show even the slightest interest in marriage. While Thomas had had several long-term mistresses, he seemed to have no interest in actually settling down with one (to his mother's dismay - she'd had high hopes of a widow that Thomas had been attached to for about a year), and Walter gallivanted about the ladies of the *ton* without ever showing a preference for any of them. Walter loved all ladies, of all hair colors, of all sizes, and all stations of life as far as Felix could tell. But he only loved them for a few days and then he moved on. The only ladies he absolutely avoided were the young innocents in the marriage mart.

Since no one expected Felix, as the youngest, to have married first, his mother was justifiably quite excited. She was always lamenting the lack of feminine company - as if her bosom friends and many connections at home weren't enough. The woman wanted daughters. Felix was actually rather surprised that she and his father hadn't come into town for the wedding, despite the incredibly short notice. Still, she didn't seem upset with him, so either the note informing her of the ceremony had been enough to placate her, she considered meeting Gabrielle on the same day to be just as good, or she was just so happy to have a daughter-in-law that he could have gotten away with murder if he'd wanted to. Knowing his mother, she was probably motivated by some combination of all three.

"Hello, son." Ever cheerful, his father clapped him on the shoulder. "I hope you realize that you've made your mother the happiest woman on the face of the earth. Although, once she calms down you'll probably have to listen to a diatribe about having the wedding without her."

"Unfortunately time was of the essence," Felix said, giving his father a wane smile and brief embrace. He always marveled at the difference between his solid, methodical father and his impulsive, flighty mother, but they balanced each other out. "I was actually expecting the lecture immediately."

"Oh no," his father said chuckling, as they made their way into the house. Felix couldn't help but smile as the familiar scent of home - and Cook's blueberry tarts - surrounded him. "She's far too excited about the prospect of another female in the house. The fact that she's entirely suitable, disregarding the scandal which you've taken care of by marrying her, and that Thomas described her as delightful company and quite bright in his note to us, has your mother in alt. She's spent all day getting the rooms ready."

Rooms? Immediately Felix was distracted from wondering what, exactly, Thomas had written in his note. "I'd planned on us staying in the summer house."

"Unfortunately we had a small incident in the summer house," his father said with a sigh. "Two of Patrick's boys decided to sneak out and spend the night there, as part of a dare, I'm told. They fell asleep and one of their candles tipped over. Fortunately they both escaped without injury, but the house's current condition is not livable."

The dismay on Felix's face didn't abate even when they walked into the dining room, where his mother already had Gabrielle sitting and held captive in conversation. She glanced up at her son, beaming, and then blinked at his expression.

"Oh, did your father tell you about the summer house?" she asked, and then, without waiting for an answer, turned to explain to Gabrielle. "There was a small fire, so it's uninhabitable at the moment, but don't worry, you two will be quite comfortable. We set up the East Wing for you to sleep in and have some privacy, although of course we'd be thrilled if you would join us for supper each evening, and perhaps some breakfasts? We do keep country hours here, if you don't mind making the adjustment."

"Of course," Gabrielle said, smiling back at his mother.

Felix wanted to grump, but he couldn't. The smile on Gabrielle's face was full of warmth, and she was looking at his mother like she was some kind of deity that Gabrielle had decided to worship. It was not an expression he'd seen on Gabrielle's face before, but she looked more open and more content than he'd ever seen her and if taking meals with his mother made her respond so... well, he wasn't going to take that away.

He wasn't going to take his bad mood out on Gabrielle either, that would be counterproductive. It was no one's fault that they couldn't use the summer house. And, as his parents resided in the West Wing of the house with all the family's rooms, and the East was rarely opened except for important visiting guests, he couldn't very well complain that they'd been anything but accommodating. His plans for having Gabrielle to himself, to begin a strong relationship, had been scuppered but he could make new ones.

Ones, he realized with resignation as he sat down opposite his bride, which were probably going to have to include his parents. She was gazing at his father with a kind of wary hopefulness that turned into bright joy when his father sat down, smiling at her, and immediately declared how pleased he was with Felix's choice of bride.

Why did Gabrielle like everyone else in his family better than him?

With a wave of her hand, his mother summoned the soup course, and it quickly became clear that both of his parents were intent on prying as much information from Gabrielle as they could. After a moment, Felix realized many of her answers were also new to him, and perhaps his parents' presence wasn't such a bad thing. His mother could pry and he could learn, without any effort on his part.

In ballrooms and at dinners, conversation was, by necessity, kept to more superficial avenues. His parents were much more interested in Gabrielle personally and, as she was now related to them and they were in the privacy of their own home, they were free to question her much more purposefully.

"So, you're used to country life?" his mother asked, shooting Felix a delighted glance, as if picturing her wayward son visiting more often to please his bride.

"This Season was my first time in town," Gabrielle said, almost shyly, looking to his mother for approval before continuing. "My father..." She cleared her throat. "My father was quite focused on his estate, the only time he went to town was when he was searching for a bride, and so of course he never took me."

"Well there's certainly nothing wrong with that," Felix's mother said, patting Gabrielle's hand. Felix frowned as tension melted away from Gabrielle at the reassurance, unsure of why she'd needed it in the first place. He was still trying to figure out her behavior, as he'd never seen her behave like this. It was like watching a puppy doing tricks for its master, but unsure of whether it would receive a reward or a kick at the end of it. "As you can see, Henry and I don't spend every Season in town. London can be quite gaudy and entertaining, but it tires me out so quickly."

Probably because, when in town, she had a tendency to attend as many balls as she could possibly squeeze into an evening - every evening - and follow it with as many at-homes and teas the next day. His father never allowed her to visit for long, because she wore herself out every time with her incessant socializing. It didn't matter how long their stay was either, she would keep up that schedule until they left, claiming the entire time that she wasn't tired.

It was rather amusing to watch her subvert that into approval of Gabrielle. He had a feeling that no matter what his bride said, his mother would find some way to approve. She'd probably even cheer Gabrielle sneaking off from the balls to seek out some excitement, claiming that young ladies were deserving of adventures.

"I did enjoy the balls and the dancing, but coming out here..." Gabrielle smiled, taking a deep breath. "I'd forgotten how lovely the country is, and how fresh the air."

"Exactly," Felix's father said, giving her an approving look.

Felix could swear he actual saw Gabrielle blossom, her eyes sparkling as she preened back at his father. This was definitely a side he'd never seen of her before.

The soup tureen and bowls were taken away and replaced with roast pork, potatoes, and, if he smelled correctly, plum sauce.

His mother smiled, seeing his look. "Yes dear, that's your plum sauce." She turned her smile to Gabrielle. "Felix has such a passion for plum sauce, it's always been his favorite."

"Mine too," Gabrielle said, looking surprised. Felix couldn't hide his own reaction of surprise; he hadn't known they'd had that in common either. Seeing his expression, his mother's eyes narrowed, her lips pursing, before she turned her attention back to Gabrielle. Guessing what had perturbed his mother, Felix did the same.

AT THE END OF DINNER, when her new mother-in-law took Gabrielle off to the drawing room so that the men could have their port and cigars, Gabrielle went quite willingly. She already adored the older woman, who was so blatant in her approval and easy in her immediate affection. At first it had made Gabrielle nervous, as she'd realized it had very little to do with herself as a person and everything to do with her new position in the Viscountess' life, but she could tell that the liking was becoming real.

Both of Felix's parents seemed to like her, immediately and without reservation, and they were both already doting on her. The Viscount had plied her with food and compliments, while the Viscountess had posed question after question in her desire to know Gabrielle better. Along the way they'd imparted quite a few stories, all of which seemed to feature Felix in various scrapes, which made him seem quite a bit less imposing.

To her surprise, he'd seemed very approving during dinner as well, in a general sort of way. For once, he hadn't made any of the comments that got her back up around him. He hadn't behaved like a sophisticated London gentleman with his parents there, or regaled them with stories about exciting adventures or important endeavors; he'd actually been rather quiet and it seemed like he'd been listening... like his interest was truly in her.

Several times he'd made comments that had stirred her temper, but only because she'd realized that he must have been talking to Cordelia about her. That or Cordelia had talked to Philip, who had talked to Felix, but Gabrielle had trouble imagining Philip and Felix gossiping about her father's household. Even though, her temper hadn't stirred very far, she'd been too busy enjoying the warm attentions of his parents, basking in their patent approval, and their sincere interest in her. She knew they were interested because she was now part of their family, but she hadn't truly expected them to treat her as family.

"Well then, dear," the Viscountess said, sitting down on a settee as gesturing for Gabrielle to join her. The drawing room was quite cozy, decorated in soothing green and pale yellow with hints of blue and cream sprinkled throughout in the form of cushions and small decorations. On the mantle was a small collection of tiny figurines, all country figures - Gabrielle easily recognized a pretty shepherdess dressed in pink and her flock. The Viscountess' eyes sparkled as Gabrielle settled down next to her. "Now we may truly talk with the menfolk otherwise occupied. I want to hear all about your and Felix's courtship."

"My lady..." Gabrielle floundered, immediately at a loss for words. She knew that Felix and Thomas had both written ahead, had neither of them explained? Or had the Viscount read the note and then kept some of the pertinent details from his wife? Fear flashed through her as she suddenly realized that the Viscountess' warmth might be based upon a false impression.

"Please, call me Lizzie," the Viscountess said cutting her off.

"Oh no, I couldn't," Gabrielle protested without thinking, diverted from the original topic - with a bit of relief.

"You call your stepmother Cordelia."

"Cordelia is... we are very close to the same age." And she'd never seen Cordelia as a mothering figure. How could she when Cordelia had married her father when Gabrielle was fifteen and Cordelia was eighteen? Though she hadn't thought of Cordelia as an older sister until very recently.

"I see." The Viscountess hummed as she tapped her finger against her skirts, obviously thinking. "Well then, you may call me Mother or mama or whatever variant you please, as long as you don't call me 'my lady.'"

"Yes- yes, Mother."

The Viscountess - Mother - beamed and Gabrielle practically floated at how easy it was to please her. She could not call her mother-in-law 'mama,' for that had been what she'd called her own mother before she'd passed, but it felt very good to have someone want to take that position in her life. Her father's second wife had shown very little interest in Gabrielle, other than wanting her to be seen and not heard, and preferably not seen very often, while Cordelia had been far too young and Gabrielle far too prickly for them to develop anything like that relationship.

"Now then, about your courtship."

Tension seized Gabrielle again, but the Viscountess was already speaking again, airily brushing away Gabrielle's concern that she didn't *know*.

"I realize that the wedding came about a bit hastily because of the possible scandal, but Thomas indicated that Felix had been seeing you for weeks before that," Mother said, her dark eyes dancing merrily. "Tell me all about that."

Gabrielle hesitated again. No matter what she'd thought about Felix, she didn't want to denigrate him to his own mother. While the woman seemed to like her quite a bit now, she wouldn't if Gabrielle insulted her son. However, Gabrielle was also not very good at lying and she knew it; what she was good at was sliding around the truth in such a way that most people didn't even realize she wasn't being entirely honest.

"Well, he is good friends with the Marquess, of course, so we met at the wedding. We were seated next to each other for the meal and we had quite a bit of time to converse." Which was true. It had devolved when Felix had begun spouting off his admiration for Cordelia, prompting her jealousy and some ill-tempered remarks on her part, which in turn had him threatening to spank her. But she certainly wasn't going to mention any of that. Smiling serenely to cover her emotions, Gabrielle thought quickly. "At my come-out, he was the first gentleman to ask me to dance, and he claimed two. We've danced many times together since then, and he was very quick to come to my rescue after the... um... incident."

Blushing, she looked down at her hands, hoping that she'd fulfilled her new Mother's requests well enough.

"I see," the other woman said thoughtfully. Just then the door opened to admit the tea tray, distracting both of them. Once they were situated with their tea cups, Gabrielle took advantage of the break in conversation to ask a question about the estate, hoping to distract Mother from any further questions about her and Felix's 'courtship.'

CHAPTER 3

Coming into the drawing room, Felix couldn't help but smile at how happy both his mother and his bride looked. Unfortunately, the happiness in Gabrielle's green eyes dimmed the moment she saw him, a wary tension seeping into her posture. At the same time, that wariness was tinged with a certain anticipation.

Seeing her in his family's house, looking so vulnerable and beautiful, certainly had an effect on him and his libido.

Entering the room, he gave his mother a kiss on the cheek.

"If you don't mind excusing us, Mother, I'd like to show Gabrielle to our rooms. It's been a rather long day."

His mother blinked in surprise. "Oh yes, I suppose that's for the best."

Felix and his father exchanged a look. While they'd been enjoying their port and catching up, his father had pointed out that unless he wanted his wedding night completely monopolized, he should remove himself and Gabrielle from the social situation as soon as possible. Not that his mother would mean to keep him; she just got excited and wanted to spend all night talking. There would be plenty of time for them to become acquainted with Gabrielle, however, especially now that they had to stay in the main house and not the summer house.

The wariness and anticipation in Gabrielle's big green eyes seemed to grow as he offered her his arm, but she put her fingers delicately on his wrist and wished his parents a good night.

Hoping to calm her nerves, Felix made sure to point out all sorts of markers she could use to find her way around the house as he escorted her to the East Wing. Their rooms were adjoining, and he took her into hers first.

The room was a dusky rose and cream, very feminine and flowery. The furniture was all a light maple and intricately carved and Gabrielle seemed quite pleased by it, although it made Felix want to shudder. Her things had already been unpacked and her toilette was laid out on the vanity.

Keeping her hand on his arm, Felix led her over to the door leading into his room.

"And this is where I'll be staying."

Because of their touch, he could feel her fingers stiffen between his arm and his hand as she realized the arrangement of their rooms. His room was much more masculine, decorated in a deep forest green and darker, sturdier wood than the furniture in her room. The maroon and navy curtains on the four poster bed guaranteed a dark haven for sleeping, as all the rooms in the East Wing could become quite sunny.

"Thank you for showing me," Gabrielle murmured, her fingers tugging to get away from him.

Well now, he couldn't allow that, could he?

Adroitly, Felix shifted and tugged on her hand, skillfully turning her right into his arms. Her small gasp made him grin as he lowered his head to hers, taking advantage of her parted lips to immediately slide his tongue into her mouth as he kissed her for the second time. This was how he discovered that, despite how he'd found her with Mr. Pressen, she certainly had very little experience in kissing.

She was stiff in his arms, her hands pressed against his chest -

although not yet pushing, and her kiss was tentative. Hesitant. Stroking one hand down her back, Felix coaxed her tongue with his, inviting a response, being as gentle as he could while his arousal roared inside of him. To his delight, she began to follow his movements, learning from him how to kiss, how to use her tongue to dance with his.

Her back arched instinctively, pressing her breasts against his chest, and Felix savored the triumph as she became pliant against him. Their kiss deepened as she relaxed, as he aroused her passion, and his hand came around her body and up to cup her breasts.

Immediately she gasped into his mouth, her stiffness returning, and then she was shoving him away. In shock, Felix stumbled back, unable to stop her from turning and fleeing, the door between their rooms slamming behind her. He'd only taken one step when he heard the ominous sound of the lock sliding shut on her side.

"Gabrielle!"

"Go away!"

The door did little to muffle her order; the panic in her voice was clear and Felix cursed himself. Closing his eyes, he clenched his fists, trying to decide what to do. Should he break down the door? He doubted that would help ease her panic. Approaching it, he knocked gently.

"Gabrielle, are you alright? I didn't mean to frighten you... did Cordelia tell you what to expect?"

"I know... I know what you want to do, I just... Not tonight. Please." If he hadn't heard the fear and true pleading in her voice, he might have pressed. Instead, he sighed, his body still throbbing with need for her... but he also wanted to demonstrate that he was sensitive to her needs as well. Pressing his forehead against the cool wood of the door, he took a deep breath.

"Very well. I will see you tomorrow. Sleep well."

Another long pause and then he heard her, her voice barely above a whisper.

"Sleep well."

Very doubtful but he appreciated the sentiment.

Knowing that his parents would still be awake and in the drawing room, Felix decided a retreat was in order. He needed some space between him and his bride, seeing as their wedding night was not going to be what he hoped. The walk to the drawing room should give him time to compose himself... and then he could ask for advice. Undoubtedly, his mother would have some insights.

HEART POUNDING, Gabrielle stood by the door adjoining her room to Felix's. Hearing the other door close, she rushed to the door to the hall and locked that as well. Pressing her ear against it, she heard his footsteps moving away and closed her eyes in both relief and disappointment.

While part of her had wanted him to chase after her, or to stay and at least attempt to convince her to unlock the door, at the same time she didn't know how she could bear the intimacy with him.

Her fingers drifted up to touch her lips as she moved towards the vanity, her shaky knees in need of a place to sit. That kiss had... it had completely discombobulated her. The kiss in the church this morning had been a mere cipher to tonight's kiss.

It had sparked something deep in her belly - a wanting, a needing, that had her emotions rioting and made her skin feel tight while the rest of her felt swollen. Between her legs, she knew that she was slick and wet, while her nipples throbbed mercilessly. Closing her eyes, so that she didn't have to see herself in the mirror, she brought her hands up to her breasts and squeezed. A small gasp escaped her lips at how good it felt, a ghostly sensation of his fingers over one mound making her reaction more intense.

She'd been so caught up in the kiss that she'd almost forgotten what came after. It had confused her. After all, she hadn't expected Felix to truly act as though he wanted her. He'd married her for Cordelia and Philip... but his manhood had been as swollen as Philip's had been for Cordelia when she'd accidentally spied upon them. Gabrielle had felt it pressing into her, had yearned to feel it actually pressing inside of her.

Only the unfamiliar sensation of a man's hand touching her breast had brought her back to herself... In a flash, she'd wondered *why* Felix was so eager for her. Had he been picturing Cordelia? Fantasizing about her while he was kissing Gabrielle? Their eyes had been closed while they were kissing after all. Was that why he'd been so intent on kissing her?

She'd panicked, as the thoughts had flown through her mind. Unable to deal with both the physical and emotional confusion, she'd pushed him away and run. Although she'd meant to be a good bride, to accept the marital duty, she hadn't realized how much it would affect her.

How much she would want it.

She sniffed away a tear, and then jerked in surprise as someone knocked on her bedroom door.

"My lady? It's Molly - do you need my assistance?"

"Y-yes," Gabrielle managed to creak out, before clearing her throat and speaking with more volume. "Yes Molly." Getting up, she swiftly crossed the room and pulled open the door.

Molly bobbed a curtsy as she entered. "Mr. Hood said you would need assistance with your toilette this evening."

"Yes, thank you." Gabrielle smiled as Molly came in and began bustling around to get things ready for Gabrielle's nightly routine. Moving back to the chair at her vanity, Gabrielle sighed and relaxed as Molly began the familiar task of taking down Gabrielle's hair. For just a few minutes, she could almost pretend she was back at Dunbury House, and forget her current troubles.

WHEN FELIX RETURNED to the drawing room, he wasn't surprised to see both of his parents' eyebrows rise in surprise and query. Fortunately, he'd had plenty of time to think about what he was going to say as he'd traversed the halls.

"Gabrielle was a bit more tired than anticipated, she's going straight to bed." No need for them to fret about their son's relationship with his new wife, or to inadvertently shame Gabrielle for not attending to her wifely duties. His parents would say nothing, of course, but the excuse needed to be made.

His father's expression smoothed out, although his mother's just turned thoughtful. Part of him wanted to groan; on the other hand, perhaps that meant she knew something that he didn't. And he had come here for her insight after all. If he'd wanted time alone to think, he could have taken a walk through the gardens.

"Well why don't you sit and catch up with us," his mother said, waving a hand. Felix settled into the arm chair before she hit him with the heavy guns, her thoughtful expression not changing a hair. "I so wanted to hear about your courtship of Gabrielle."

Felix coughed, scrambling. "Well, ah, it was a bit of a rushed marriage."

"Yes, of course, but you knew her beforehand, did you not?" The one arched eyebrow his mother treated him to might as well have been a pistol. "Thomas seemed to think that you had an interest in her, and I must say, I can't imagine you marrying a woman you had *no* interest in. While you're a good friend and a good man, you're not that selfless."

"Well..." He coughed again, looking to his father for help, but his father just shrugged; he looked too interested in the inquisition to intervene. Felix sighed. "I didn't precisely court her, per se. Although, of course, we encountered each other quite often, and of course I tried to dance with her as often as I could."

"As often as you could..." His mother repeated, skeptically. Felix bristled defensively.

"Well, she did have quite a few suitors. Her dance card was often quite full."

"And you did nothing to set yourself apart from or above these suitors?" The dry way in which his mother asked the question had Felix squirming. He was quite sure his mother didn't mean the way he'd occasionally antagonized Gabrielle, and she certainly did mean the time that he threatened to spank her, although he was sure that none of her other suitors had done so.

"I wasn't sure I wanted to marry her yet," he said grumpily. His mother's eyes narrowed as she scowled at him, her temper obviously rising.

"Lizzie," his father said warningly, recognizing the look on his wife's face. Immediately, Felix's mother settled back into her chair, a serene mask back over her face. Felix's lips quirked. This was the kind of relationship he wanted with Gabrielle. All of the family was aware that his father would take the Viscountess in hand when he felt she needed it, as she had the propensity to meddle without invitation. It was something his father worked hard at keeping her from doing, especially when it came to her sons, since her desire to meddle in their lives was without limit.

Giving his father a dazzling smile, his mother turned her attention back to Felix. She stayed silent, still smiling. Inviting. Coaxing without a word.

Felix sighed again.

"I need your advice, Mother."

"Of course I'm always happy to offer my advice when asked," she cooed, giving his father a triumphant look. His father just chuckled.

"I admit, I was not the most ardent of suitors, but Gabrielle and I have married now and I don't wish her to be unhappy with me as a husband. I was wondering if you had any insight to smoothing my road, as it were."

"You should court her," his mother said succinctly.

Felix's brows drew together. "Court her?"

"Yes, court her." Now she sounded exasperated. "When I asked her about your courtship, I heard nothing of her receiving flowers, being read poetry, written notes, or indeed anything smacking of any romance. You treated her as a family friend, not without reason, but now you've married her. The poor thing deserves some romance."

"She received plenty of romance from others," Felix said, a bit sourly.

His mother's sharp eyes pinned him to his seat. "She deserves some from her husband. If you want to have a successful marriage, act like it."

"Your mother's right, son," his father said, making Felix slump. His father rarely weighed on in his mother's advice; if he was doing so now, it was because he thought she was right and that it was important. "Marriage doesn't mean the courtship is over." His parents smiled at each other, the kind of special smile that he'd shared between them through all the years. The kind of smile that said they were speaking volumes without sharing a word. "In the best marriages, the courtship never ends."

"Unless, of course, your only interest in your marriage was saving Gabrielle's reputation," his mother said tartly, returning her attention back to her son. "In which case, I shall have to revise my opinion of your intelligence, character, and judgment, because she's worth much more than that."

A smile quirked Felix's lips again at his mother's staunch defense. Apparently Gabrielle had made quite an impression. As much as his mother was dying for a daughter-in-law, she wouldn't be such a champion for her unless she truly liked the young woman.

"It's not the only reason I married her," he admitted. "But I've never been able to charm her and she seems to like everyone else in our family more than she likes me, including you two and she just met you today."

"We might be a special case," his mother said, exchanging another glance with his father. "Gabrielle seems... longing for parental attention and guidance. At least, that was the impression I received."

"Really?" Felix had trouble wrapping his head around that notion. "I think Philip provided her with quite a bit of guidance, and Cordelia did almost nothing but pay attention to her. In fact, the amount of attention Cordelia paid Gabrielle caused quite a few problems between her and Philip in the first weeks of their marriage."

His mother waved her hand dismissively. "Yes, Gabrielle told me about Cordelia. Do you not find it significant that *she* calls her stepmother by her first name? She also said they are very near in age, which makes them more like rivals; having a true mother and daughter relationship would be very difficult. And from the very little she said about her childhood, it's quite obvious that her father was not very involved."

"Yes, Cordelia said the Baron could be very neglectful of Gabrielle," Felix said, his mind turning over his mother's opinion. "She received just about anything she wanted materially, but she was often ignored unless she threw a tantrum."

"Oh the poor thing," his mother said, almost gushing. She threw another look at her husband. "Well, Henry here will certainly provide her with a fatherly presence."

"Of course, of course," his father muttered, looking amused at his wife's ordering of his life.

Pursing her lips, his mother focused on Felix, her dark eyes intent. She pointed at her son. "You will woo that girl, do you hear me Felix Francis Hood? You will treat her to romance. You will show her that you didn't just marry her to save her. And you will allow her to retire early as many times as you need to."

Standing up, she swept over and gave him a kiss on the cheek. "You're a good son. I know you'll be a good husband."

As long as he followed her advice, was the unheard message. On the other hand, Felix couldn't really argue the point. Smiling, she gave her husband an inviting glance over her shoulder before gliding out of the room. Standing up, Felix's father began to follow after her, pausing to rest his hand on Felix's shoulder.

"And if she's anything like your mother, don't hesitate to bend her over your knee when she needs it."

Sitting alone in the room, Felix stared at the complex, swirling design of the carpet while he thought over his parents' advice. As far as he could see, they'd shared their own secrets to a happy marriage. His father still brought his mother flowers from the field or ordered them from a shop, even though she had her own gardens. His mother still ensured that his father always had his favorite liquors and ales in the house, and that he ate at least one of his favorite foods at least once a week. They still flirted with each other, especially when they thought no one was looking, and he'd once seen them waltzing under the moonlight, out on the patio, with no music.

Courting his wife seemed like a novel idea, considering that he'd always thought the courting was a means to an end but... it worked for his parents. Why not try to make it work for him? And, if Gabrielle became too spoiled from being showered with gifts and affection, then he could always take his father's advice and turn her over his knee.

TOSSING RESTLESSLY, Gabrielle scissored her legs together. The bed was incredibly comfortable, the countryside was wonderfully silent (unlike London, which could be quite noisy even late at night), and she should have fallen asleep quite easily. Her nightgown tangled around her limbs and she kicked at the covers.

Under the sheets she was too hot, with them off, she was to cool.

But that wasn't really the problem. The problem was that every time she closed her eyes, she could feel Felix's lips on hers. His hand on her breast. His tongue in her mouth. His hard body pressed against her. His manhood, his desire, digging into her soft belly.

Since the day she'd accidentally spied upon Cordelia and the Marquess, Gabrielle had occasionally indulged in pleasuring herself, touching herself between her legs until she reached that ecstatic peak. It always left her feeling limp and satiated afterwards, but she hadn't wanted to do that here. She knew it was wicked - it *felt* wicked - and her room in Dunbury House hadn't adjoined anyone else's. There had been no one to hear her there.

And there, her imagination had always given her a nameless, faceless lover, whom she fantasized about touching her and entering her the way the Marquess had done to Cordelia. That imaginary lover always had a resemblance to Felix, but tonight she knew that she would be able to picture him and only him. There would be no pretending otherwise.

But her body ached. Her womanhood was throbbing again. Would she be able to sleep if she didn't?

Clenching her jaw, Gabrielle cupped her breasts and squeezed -

hard. The pain and pleasure flashed through her, making her scissor her legs again. Her nightgown rode up her thighs, the silky material wisping over her skin, as if teasing her.

Frustrated, exhausted, she'd reached the end of her rope.

Pinching her nipples through her nightgown, she moaned as the lace over them scratched against the sensitive nubs. Her body arched, her thighs spreading as she tormented the little buds, tugging and pinching on them so roughly that they stung. She liked it, almost as if she was punishing herself.

The idea of punishment made her think of the Marquess spanking her... Felix had threatened to do that once. The thought should have enraged her - it certainly had at the time - but instead her body just throbbed again. It was all too easy to imagine bending over in front of Felix, her belly resting against a chair's arm, her bottom high in the air for him to swat.

Disturbed, Gabrielle forced those thoughts away, instead picturing herself leaning back on a window seat - just like Cordelia had - while Felix kissed his way down her neck, his hand squeezing her breast. One of her own hands took care of that, while the other moved down between her legs, pulling the hem of her nightgown up so that she could touch herself. She was wet, slick, and it felt so good as she dragged her fingers through her sensitive folds, circling the little nub of pleasure at the apex of her womanhood.

Her fingers pressed into her body as she remembered what the Marquess had looked like, thrusting his manhood into Cordelia's womanhood, picturing Felix above her, doing the same. She whimpered, her hips jerking as her fingers moved inside of her, her body clenching around them. Abandoning her breasts, she moved her other hand down to her swollen folds, using one to pump her fingers in and out of her while the other rubbed against her pleasure button, making her gasp and pant for air as her passion spiraled, her body straining for completion.

Felix's dark eyes flashed into her mind, the heat of his body, the hardness...

"Oh... Oh!" Ecstasy exploded inside of her as she sobbed out her relieved rapture, her fingers pressing against her sensitive spots, circling them, soothing them as they tingled and sparked. Her last exhalation came out as a sigh. "Felix..."

BLOODY BUGGERING HELL.

Gripping his cock, it was all Felix could do not to try and break down the door separating himself from his wife. His wife who, if he wasn't mistaken, was quite familiar with self-pleasure and was thinking of him while she did it.

He hadn't meant to listen, he'd just been unable to stay away from their adjoining door, and when he'd laid his forehead against it, wishing he were on the other side, he'd heard the unmistakable sound of a lady panting with pleasure. Soft, barely audible moans... slowly rising. Little, muffled whimpers. And then those last sounds, the ecstatic cries and, finally, his name.

Stumbling back from the door, he jerked his cock several times, grabbing up a handkerchief from his dresser. Wrapping the silky material around the fat head of his cock, he pumped his fist, groaning as his seed spilled into the fabric, his body throbbing with need.

Panting for breath, and from the effort of keeping himself quieter than Gabrielle had, he braced his arm against the edge of the dresser and leaned his head against it. His thoughts whirled. Of all the things he might have expected to hear from Gabrielle's room, those soft moans and his name said in such a manner would certainly have never made his list. It had been hotly erotic, damnably frustrating, and had given rise to hope.

Perhaps his wife was not as averse to him as he'd thought.

CHAPTER 4

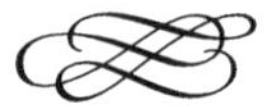

When Gabrielle came down to breakfast the next morning, she couldn't help but be a bit nervous. Molly had come to wake her and get her ready for the day, along with the message that Felix was already up and would meet her in the dining room. Although she wasn't so eager to face him, she did hope that his parents would be there. Not just as a buffer, but because she truly did quite like both of them. And because they seemed to quite like her.

So she went into the dining room with quite a few emotions colliding inside of her. She was a bit embarrassed about her fantasies from last night and her activities before she'd been able to fall asleep - even though no one knew about them, she'd still done it in their house. Even more unnerving, she had no idea what Felix's reception of her might be after she'd denied him his wedding night. On the other hand, she was hopeful and anxious to see his parents, hoping that they would like her just as much in the light of day as they had in the evening.

To that end, she'd put on a pretty pink day gown with a gently scooped neckline, quite modest and flattering, that had a pale yellow ribbon trim. Very fashionable, yet perfectly fitting for the country. Her hair was done up in a simple chignon with just a few tendrils falling to frame her face. Nothing too fancy, but she knew she looked well... she wanted to look as presentable as possible. If it were just Felix, she was honest enough to admit to herself that she might not have made the effort, but she did want to impress his parents. She certainly didn't want to do anything that might change their positive opinion of her.

"Good morning, dear!" Lady Hood - Mother - said as Gabrielle came into the room. She was sitting to the left of her husband, who was seated at the head of the table with Felix on his other side. Both Felix and his father were reading different sections of the newspaper, just as Philip did at breakfast. Mother had a small section next to her as well, although she didn't even glance at it again once she saw Gabrielle.

"Good morning," Gabrielle responded, smiling. Her smile faltered for just a moment as Felix rose, but he just gave her a little half bow and pulled out the chair next to him.

"Good morning," he and his father said, although the Viscount's salutation was much more absent-minded, whereas Felix's was said directly to her, with a rather rakish smile.

Well he didn't look upset about last night.

Gabrielle didn't know whether to be relieved or disappointed. Shouldn't he be at least a little aggrieved about the events of last night? What kind of man didn't care that he'd been denied his marital rights?

On the other hand, did she truly want him to be angry at her on their first day of marriage?

Taking her seat, Gabrielle blinked as she looked at the gorgeous bouquet of wildflowers in a vase that had been placed above her plate. A quick glance confirmed that they were not part of the central arrangement, and her place setting was the only one thus adorned.

"Those are for you," Felix said as he sat back down, nodding towards the flowers.

"For me?"

"I got up early this morning and picked them myself."

"Oh..." Gabrielle reached out to touch the petals of a particularly pretty white and pink flower. They were so soft under her hand. Her voice caught in her throat. These were her first flowers from him and they were beautiful... and he'd picked them himself! Somehow that made them even more special than if he'd just ordered an arrangement. Gabrielle had seen quite a few arrangements delivered to her door and she'd known that, even though the gentlemen might have chosen the flowers, they'd done very little beyond that other than pay. Felix had taken the time to get up and pick out each one of these flowers and then to arrange them in a vase for her. "Thank you."

THE ABSOLUTE WONDER in Gabrielle's voice hit Felix like a lightning strike to the chest. Her fingers stroked the petals of the flowers, brushing over them like she was touching them to see if they were quite real. Across the table, watching her, his mother blinked back a couple of tears. Even his father was peering over his newspaper, a look of astonishment on his face.

The utterly heartfelt sincerity in Gabrielle's thanks was almost humbling.

When Cordelia had told him that Gabrielle had been quite thrilled to receive flowers from so many suitors, he'd been under the impression that she'd taken them as her due. That she'd been thrilled to see the money spent on her. He'd been under the impression that Gabrielle coveted worshipful male attention, preferably in the form of expensive fripperies. Cordelia had talked quite a bit about Gabrielle's material acquisitiveness, even as she'd explained that was how Gabrielle's father showed his affection, but this looked like something different.

After all, Felix hadn't spent a dime on these flowers, and yet the expression on Gabrielle's face was almost reverent.

"You're welcome," he said, a bit roughly. When he'd gotten up early to pick the flowers, he had to admit, he'd done it because his mother had told him to. He certainly hadn't expected such a reaction on Gabrielle's part, or on his. Now, he felt as though the early morning and the effort of tramping through the nearby wildflower fields was more than worth it when, five minutes ago, he'd considered it almost a penance.

Hell, if it made Gabrielle that happy, he'd be out in the fields every morning.

"They're beautiful," she said, and he received the kind of smile he'd been craving from her for weeks. The one he'd rarely seen her bestow, but which was open and sweet and completely without guile.

Across from him, his mother smugly sipped her tea.

A footman came in with a plate for Gabrielle, and she smiled and thanked him prettily, before turning her attention back to the flowers. Felix kept watching her, the newspaper forgotten on the table. Gabrielle was much more interesting as she inspected each flower, as if she didn't want to accidentally miss seeing a single one.

"Do you enjoy gardening?" he asked, suddenly curious.

"I've never really had the opportunity," she said, a bit wistfully. "We didn't have much in the way of gardens, and none of my stepmothers were very interested."

"Well you may join me in my garden at any time," Felix's mother said, smiling encouragingly at Gabrielle, who immediately perked up. "Do you have a favorite flower?"

Gabrielle's fingers lingered over the petals of the pink and white flower that he'd noticed she seemed to touch the most. "I love all flowers, although I will admit, I do have a bit of a preference for anything pink." She glanced down at the dress she was wearing and smiled.

It occurred to Felix that he'd never even though to ask what her favorite flower might be. Or her favorite color. Bugger it all.

At least now he had the answer to two of those questions.

"Well, perhaps you shall pick one eventually," his mother said breezily. She beamed at them. "I have a wonderful idea! Felix, why don't you show Gabrielle around the gardens this morning? It's a glorious day out and Gabrielle can familiarize herself with what we have to offer."

Giving him a completely unsubtle significant look, his mother nodded her head decisively.

Fortunately, Felix was not adverse to her suggestion. The weather was shaping up to be sunny and quite glorious, the gardens were fairly private and romantic, and it would give him the opportunity to get to know Gabrielle better.

"I think that's a wonderful suggestion, Mother."

OUT IN THE COUNTRY, Felix was dressed very differently than when he was in London. His breeches were more worn and softer looking, the color a faded dark brown, his cravat was also soft looking and tied simply, and it was obvious no one had bothered to stiffen his collar. Even his hair was a bit different, the dark strands flopping into his eyes until he brushed them back again.

Gabrielle found this version of him just as attractive as the more sophisticated side he had shown in London. It didn't hurt that he'd taken hold of her hand when they'd entered the gardens and hadn't let it go yet. Not put her hand on his arm, as a gentleman would, but actually had his fingers looped through hers.

Even when she pulled away, he'd be there a few moments later, his fingers pressed against her lower back or brushing a strand of hair off of her shoulder, before eventually searching out her hand again. The little touches were making her feel quite breathless.

In London, there had been times when she'd wanted to be the center of his attention - had yearned for it in fact. Now, she barely knew what to do with it.

"Oh, this is beautiful," she said, near to gasping as they stepped out from the path into a small glade. Weeping willows hung around an ornamental pond and fountain, marble benches laid out in the shade, and small bushes dotting the scenery. It was quite the loveliest setting she'd ever seen.

"There are gardens very like this on Philip's estates," Felix said, following her to the fountain. She trailed her fingers through the water, shrugging.

"I've never see the estates, and we had nothing like this at home." Her lip curled. "My father was not an outdoorsmen and none of my stepmothers were particularly interested in gardening. I hope the Marquess doesn't expect Cordelia to manage his."

Out of the corner of her eye, she saw Felix frown at her, and she felt like biting her tongue. Why had she even had to mention Cordelia's name? She didn't want to talk about Cordelia. She certainly didn't want to hear Felix go into his usual raptures about how perfect and wonderful Cordelia was.

To her relief, other than frowning, Felix didn't respond to the comment. Perhaps he realized it would do no good. Certainly, if he had said something in Cordelia's defense, their conversation would have taken a swift turn for the worse. Gabrielle just couldn't help the bitterness that welled up in her sometimes, even though at other times she actually liked and appreciated her stepmother.

When it came to the relationship between her Cordelia and Felix, though, the bitterness that welled up seemed to be endless and overwhelming.

"There's a rather pretty folly, just a bit further into the gardens," Felix said, his voice determinedly affable, but she could hear the strain that was now in it, and she silently vowed not to bring up Cordelia again.

Perhaps there was a chance that she could make Felix care for her at least as much as he did for Cordelia. After all, she was here and Cordelia was not. With some space, maybe Felix would decide that he liked her better. Just the thought, just the glimmer of hope, made her heart ache a little because she knew - *she knew* – how unlikely such a venture would be. Had anyone ever preferred her over anyone else? Felix's parents liked her well enough for now, which was probably where this tiny well of hope sprang from... and he seemed as though he wanted to try and be a husband to her. It was a start.

At worst, she might fail and then he would return to London and she could stay here with his parents. Hopefully wouldn't change their minds about her even if she couldn't inspire some kind of affection from their son.

"What kind of folly?" she asked, with a genuine smile.

"My mother has an obsession for all things Greek," he said, relaxing, and he reached for her hand again. Her fingers tingled in response as his palm enclosed them. The way he smiled at her made her glad that she hadn't pursued talking about Cordelia.

If he kept touching her like this, that little kernel of hope inside of her heart would start to grow.

THE FOLLY WAS a small structure meant to mimic a Greek temple, but on a much smaller scale. The marble columns were very pretty though, as were the exotic plants his mother had in pots around it. During the winter those pots would be moved into the greenhouse, but he'd known they would be out now. Only the olive tree stayed in position year-round, and it had never been known to actually produce any olives. England's climate just wasn't right, unfortunately.

Moving amongst the gardens, Gabrielle looked like a pretty pink rose in her soft dress. It clung to her curves, especially her bottom whenever she bent over to admire a flower or bush, and he couldn't help but the think of the first time he'd ever seen her - when she'd been bending over talking to some children. Her bottom was rapidly becoming an obsession for him, because he finally had the right to touch it, but he didn't feel as though he could yet.

Keeping his mother's advice about courting firmly in mind, Felix planned to woo his wife, and he also planned to seduce her. Sadly, neither effort included running his hands over her bottom at this time, no matter how much he might want to.

He did feel as though he was making progress, however. Not only had Gabrielle started reaching for his hand without thinking twice, but more than once he'd seen her giving him that contemplative, wondering look a woman got when she realized a man's interest in her. She was thinking about him, about his touch, and - hopefully - about last night's kiss.

This time he wouldn't press her too far too fast though. Little touches. Seductive touches.

And he wasn't going to argue with her. Time enough for that later, when their relationship was more firm.

Which was why he'd bitten his tongue when she'd slighted Cordelia. That and the fact that something his mother had said had made an impression on him. She and her stepmother were only a few years apart in age, so despite the relationship, perhaps Gabrielle did see Cordelia as a kind of rival. Cordelia had already been married twice - the second time reaching quite high socially - and had a multitude of feminine skills, many of which Gabrielle seemed to lack.

As he tried to find out more about her, he discovered that she didn't sketch, didn't play a musical instrument, and didn't ride very well, all skills which a young lady normally had by the time she debuted. Felix had assumed that Philip and Cordelia just couldn't countenance going to the musicales, he hadn't realized it was because Gabrielle would not have been able to perform. Just about every young woman in London was trained in some kind of musical instrument, whether she had talent or not.

Gabrielle didn't say outright, but he received the impression that her education had been left largely up to her governess, and her governess had found it easiest to let Gabrielle do very little. He was surprised it hadn't occurred to Cordelia to try and educate Gabrielle in some of those areas, but then again, he doubted Gabrielle would have been very receptive to the idea. Still, Cordelia hadn't even mentioned trying to correct the deficiencies in Gabrielle's education.

Not that he thought they were deficiencies (except perhaps Gabrielle's indifference to riding), but there were those among the *ton* who certainly would if they'd known. It occurred to him that there were quite a few things Cordelia had left out when speaking to him about Gabrielle. The view she had of her stepdaughter and the view that Felix was seeing now were very different.

The Gabrielle that Cordelia had described to him was spoiled, prone to tantrums, materialistic, grasping, and a figure to be pitied for the emotional neglect of her father. The Gabrielle that he'd encountered in London had seemed to back Cordelia's description, but tempered with bouts of charm, kindness to servants and children, and an improving attitude under Philip's guidance. Gabrielle here on the estate was eager to please his parents, glowed with the slightest hint of approval or appreciation, and had been delighted by handpicked flowers.

Part of him missed the feisty brat from London, but at the same time he was intrigued by this softer side to Gabrielle. He liked seeing her eyes light up in excitement at the beauty of the folly, enjoyed her wonder at the smooth, marble columns.

"Is this what the temples in Greece actually look like?" she asked, circling one of the columns, while Felix leaned against another one, watching her.

"So I'm told, I've never been. My parents went, years ago, and my mother certainly has a fondness. You should ask her about the trip sometime." He'd noted Gabrielle's desire to travel and her interest in far off places before; it was one of the few things that he did know about her. Too bad he couldn't have taken her on a romantic honeymoon on the Continent... he'd plan one for her eventually though. France, Greece, Italy, Spain... Felix enjoyed traveling, but he'd never experienced the exuberance that Gabrielle did at just speaking of exotic locations.

"Perhaps," she murmured, looking wistful.

The expression on her face drew him to her, his hands settling on her waist. She looked up at him, startled, thick lashes framing her wide eyes.

"I'll take you to Greece, if you like."

"You will?" The utter astonishment in her voice, the blatant disbelief he would even want to, made him nod his head without hesitation.

"Anywhere you want to go," he said firmly, and lowered his mouth to hers.

Excitement whirled, along with suspicion and the memory of one too many broken promises. Her father had always said they'd travel - once he'd had his heir. But the heir had never come. Her first stepmother had promised to take her to London, but that trip had never materialized. Even Cordelia, who had promised to take her to the ocean, had never managed to fulfill that commitment. Although, Cordelia had taken her to London, so Gabrielle supposed that she could supplant one location with the other.

There was an intensity in the way Felix stated his offer that made her feel like perhaps he meant it.

The kiss felt like a token of agreement, his lips gentle and coaxing, filled with promise. She opened her mouth to his, taking him in, caught up in the romance of the moment.

The beauty of the gardens and the folly, the growing optimism she had for being able to build a relationship with her husband, and her budding hope for the promise of travel and adventure made her more than a little receptive to his advances. She kissed him back, as best she could, her hands pressed against his chest. The firm hold he had on her hips meant that their bodies did not press against each other, and Gabrielle found herself leaning forward, yearning for the contact.

Her breasts brushed against him, her nipples hardening, but his hands didn't move.

Instead, he took his time, exploring her mouth, his thumb caressing her waist, keeping her distant... but connected. She leaned into the kiss even more, the sunlight warming them as they kissed, and kissed, and kissed.

When he finally pulled away, her lips felt swollen, and her body felt as though it was tingling all over. She blinked up at him, taking in the lazy, rakish smile, and the pleasure in his eyes.

"Come on, beautiful. Let's keep walking," he said, taking her hand and tugging her along.

Gabrielle felt a small flush of hopeful happiness at the compliment. It was the first time she felt like he actually meant the praise, rather than just saying it because it was expected. Her lips still tingling from the kiss, she followed obediently after him, curious to see where he would lead her next.

They returned to the house at midday for tea and to rest. During the afternoon, Felix took her on a tour of the manor house, so that she could find her way around on her own. It was a beautiful house, filled with all sorts of artwork and various strange pieces of decor, most of which had some story behind them.

When it was time to change for dinner, Gabrielle chose her green silks, with the low neckline. This time, she was dressing for Felix as well as her in-laws. Today had given rise to her hopes that their marriage might not be awful. That he might actually come to care for her.

For herself, today had also confirmed that she was in love with him. He was everything she'd ever wanted in a husband; he was the kind of man that girlish dreams were made of. Tall, dark, handsome, brooding on occasion, but charming and witty most of the time. Today he had been solicitous with her, interested in her conversation, and she'd truly enjoyed herself with him. Her hand felt almost strange without his wrapped around it.

They'd chatted, even laughed, flirted... and Gabrielle had decided that she absolutely would make him care for her. He could fall out of love with Cordelia and in love with her!

Besides, whatever he felt for Cordelia, it couldn't be very strong, not with the way he was acting with Gabrielle now. Back in London, Gabrielle had thought she loved him, but now she thought she might have just been being dramatic. What she felt for him now was much deeper and based on a much more substantial understanding of his personality. On actual conversations, jokes, long glances, and very sweet, soft kisses. The emotions she'd been feeling for him in London had bloomed, and she could only think that she would become deeper ensnared the more time they spent together… could the same possibly be true for him as well? He certainly was more attentive, more interested in her than he'd ever been in London. That tiny well of hope was swelling, burbling inside of her and pushing her forward.

He'd stolen kisses from her throughout the day, leaving her aching and wanting. Between her legs, her womanhood was wet and tingly in anticipation. Tonight, she wouldn't run from him. Tonight she would become his wife in truth and Cordelia could go suck eggs for all she cared.

A small flash of guilt ran through her, rounding her shoulders, as soon as she had the thought. Her bottom tingled. She knew quite a bit of her antipathy towards Cordelia was unwarranted, but sometimes its ugly head rose anyway. In the Marquess' household that had resulted in spankings when she hadn't been able to hold her tongue.

Here, she didn't have to speak to Cordelia and she'd certainly prefer *not* to speak of her. No point in reminding Felix of the rival for his affections.

When she joined the family in the drawing room, the look in Felix's eyes when he saw her made her hope rise up again. He actually forgot to stand immediately when she walked into the room, but she knew that he hadn't done it out of disrespect. The sincere admiration on his face as he took in her attire, her low neckline and clinging skirts, was everything she'd hoped for.

He came to her, bowing low and taking her hand to kiss. "You look ravishing, sweetheart."

Gabrielle couldn't help but smile. Earlier he'd called her beautiful, and now sweetheart! He even sounded as though he meant it.

"Just lovely," Mother said approvingly, waving her hand for Gabrielle to come closer. Felix led her over, his eyes sliding over Gabrielle's figure in a way that almost made her wish they were alone; but at the same time, she was glad of his parents' presence to help give her time to bolster her courage. "That shade of green suits you wonderfully. No wonder you were such a hit in the London ballrooms."

She preened under their attentions, happily joining in the conversation as it turned to the local social events and fashions, asking as many questions as she could. Eventually, she would be attending them. It was an exciting proposition. Her father had rarely allowed her to attend any of the local events, even once she'd come of age, although they'd gone to a few as a family once he'd married Cordelia. He'd wanted to show off his young bride.

When Felix escorted her into dinner, his arm kept brushing against her side, against her breast, and she could feel her nipples tingling and hardening in response. Knowing that tonight she was going to do it, she was going to become his wife completely, made her breathlessly excited and incredibly anxious. The scene she'd witnessed between the Marquess and Cordelia kept running through her mind, but this time it wasn't because she was aroused, but because she was trying to remember everything Cordelia had done. Tonight, with *her* husband, she wanted to ensure that she did everything right.

Her nerves made her miss bits and pieces of the conversation, and she had trouble looking at her husband without blushing, but no one seemed to mind. She noticed that he was also having trouble with distraction, and more than once she looked at him to see him staring at her. Being seated across from him made it difficult not to look at him, but she was also immensely grateful that he wasn't right next to her. It would have been much harder not to be completely distracted if he'd kept touching her the way that he had been all day.

TONIGHT, when Gabrielle suggested they return to their rooms early, Felix jumped at the suggestion. He'd been surprised when she'd appeared at dinner tonight in a ravishing dress, no fichu to cover the pale mounds of her breasts, and a blush on her cheeks every time she looked at him. Although he'd set himself upon a course to seduce her, to be perfectly frank he hadn't expected her to respond so openly, so quickly.

He wasn't going to repeat his mistakes, however, just because she seemed willing to be seduced. After frightening her last night, he would keep himself in check. Move slowly. Remember what his mother told him about wooing her. It also occurred to him that Gabrielle might see this as her duty - something that he'd realized was actually quite important to her. Tonight she'd constantly steered the conversation, always to what his parents would expect of her as his wife, listening intently to their answers.

A dutiful wife was not Felix's goal.

It concerned him when he realized she'd never had any other example. If her father had loved her mother or her stepmothers, Gabrielle didn't mention. Cordelia had certainly married him for nothing other than duty, and then had immediately done her duty again by finding a suitable husband to be a guardian for Gabrielle. While Philip had married out of affection and it had turned into a love match, that wasn't exactly how it had started.

Despite her occasional antagonism towards Cordelia, he got the impression that Gabrielle also tried to emulate her stepmother in some ways. The idea that she might consider their wedding night part of that... well he couldn't stomach it. Felix had never taken a woman to his bed that hadn't been eager for it.

He was sure that he could make Gabrielle eager. Today's kisses had proved that. She'd stopped shying away from his touch and had willingly held his hand, willingly kissed him back, but he'd also kept himself firmly in line. No wandering hands, no pressing his body against her, and certainly no kissing her anywhere but her lips. He'd been able to feel her pressing against him, wanting more.

Which was exactly what he wanted. He wanted her to want more, specifically more from him and no one else.

As they walked towards their bed chamber, his eyes drifted down again to her creamy breasts and the pretty pink flush of her cheeks.

"You truly do look lovely this evening. I don't think I've seen you in that dress before."

The pink in her cheeks deepened as she beamed up at him, apparently pleased that he remembered she'd never worn it. Most women did appreciate the small details being noticed, especially about their fashion, he thought smugly. "I did not have occasion to wear it in London. The color is a bit dark for a debutante, but it was so pretty that we bought it anyway. Cordelia thought I could wear it later in the Season."

"I will never understand the fashion for dressing the poor debs in pale colors," he said, shaking his head. "It makes most of them fade right into the walls. Although you always chose your colors well. The pinks in particular. I should have guessed that was your favorite color."

"I love pink," she said, almost a little wistfully, as they reached the door to his bedroom. Felix opened it and led her in, already noting that she was much easier in his company than she had been the night before. "It's such a happy color."

While he wasn't quite sure what she meant by that, Felix knew better than to argue. Instead he just closed the door gently behind them and turned to her, where she was standing in the center of the room, hands folded over each other and looking at him expectantly. Her stance was definitely one of duty, which made his cock protest, because he knew that he was going to have to abstain tonight again. He would awaken her passion, but he would take his time, to ensure that she came to him out of more than obligation.

So tonight, when he stepped forward to kiss her, he was just as gentle as he had been during the day. She tilted her head back, offering up her lips, and making his cock ache as it hardened. He wanted to groan, knowing that it seemed like she was offering up so much more, but that he wasn't going to partake tonight.

Tonight... he would show her pleasure. Spark her passion. Let her feel what he could do for her. Begin the seduction. An innocent like herself wouldn't know what the stopping points were, but he certainly did. He would take each slow step, ensuring that he didn't frighten her again, and binding her to him in this manner. He was going to make her his - heart, body, and soul.

CHAPTER 5

The slow, drugging kisses were both frustrating and wonderful. Gabrielle clung to him, squirming closer as he tried to hold her away. She didn't understand his reticence now, when last night he'd practically crushed her against him, and it only made her more determined to press herself against his body. She needed to know if he still desired her, if his manhood still grew hard.

Finally his arms twined around her, allowing her to close the space between him, and she smiled against his lips as she felt the proof of his desire against her body. Between her legs, she felt more wet and swollen than ever before, and the urge to press her fingers there, to ease that throbbing need, had her kissing him back more fervently than ever. She would die of shame if he ever knew that she did such a thing, so, without that recourse, all she could do was distract herself with touching his body, hoping he would touch hers.

Her hands slid into his jacket, his hard muscles moving under her fingers as she stroked his chest. As if encouraged by her own explorations, his hand very carefully slid up to her breast.

This time she didn't panic. This time she just let the pleasure of the foreign sensation wash over her. It felt so strange, but so good to have someone else touching her there. His finger ran over the hard bud of her nipple and she whimpered into his mouth, her knees weakening, as her entire body responded. It felt like a fire was moving through her, starting at her center and spreading through her limbs, making her more needy than she'd ever felt before.

She was rewarded as his hand tightened on her, his body pressing against hers, and they began moving towards the bed. Excitement spiraled inside of her as his hand slipped into the front of her bodice, touching the bare skin of her breast and intensifying the sensation. She shuddered, her hands clutching at him as she was dimly aware of the bed coming up behind her.

Pushing his jacket off of his shoulders, she mourned the loss of his hands on her for the moment it took to shake the garment from his arms, and then moaned as he wrapped her even more tightly within them. The physical sensations were so sharp, so intense, and so much more than she'd ever imagined. Her body was being swept away by these unfamiliar caresses, her inexperience making her mindless as she processed the novel surge of passion that was driving her.

When Felix's mouth left her lips, leaving them swollen and aching, and moved to her neck, she gasped aloud as he feathered kisses over her sensitive skin. Nothing she'd heard, nothing she'd seen, could have prepared her for how it felt. There was something intensely intimate about it, making her knees quake even more, as she realized that his arms were truly the only thing holding her upright.

She had the sensation of being lost in a whirlwind, and her dominate thought was joy at his desire... at his interest.

Experienced rake that he was, she didn't even notice that he'd undone the buttons on her dress until it suddenly gaped and fell, leaving her in her corset and chemise. Heat rose in her cheeks as his mouth trailed down her collarbone, her gown in a puddle at her feet. Not wanting to be the only one unclothed, she insisted on tugging his waistcoat and shirt from him.

He raised his eyebrow as she helped pull his shirt over his head. "Are you sure you know what you're doing, sweetheart?"

"I know enough," she replied tartly, her body still thrumming as she stepped back into his arms. She looked up at him, her chin lifting in challenge. "Am I doing anything wrong?"

The smile she received in return was wicked. "Absolutely not."

His lips fell to hers again as he began the work of removing her corset, and Gabrielle's body thrilled to the touch. With his chest bare, she could run her fingers through the wiry hair there, exploring the differences between his hard, muscular body and her own much softer one. The flat discs of his nipples had tiny, sensitive bumps at their center, and he groaned when she brushed them with her fingertips. A strange rush of power swept through her, making her explorations even more earnest.

THE EAGERNESS with which Gabrielle had undressed him threatened his resolve. He knew she was an innocent. Her gasps and trembles at his touch, the way she seemed unsure about exactly how to touch him, her blushes as he kissed and undressed her was proof enough of that, but he hadn't expected her to reciprocate. The passion that she was showing both pleased and concerned him.

If he couldn't bind her to him by something more than duty, would she eventually turn to someone else to share this passion? Would her affections one day be lavished on another man? Felix couldn't bear the thought.

He wanted all of this, all of her, focused on him, for the rest of their lives. So he used every trick he'd ever learned, dragging his mouth and fingers over her skin as he removed her corset and chemise. When he picked her up and placed her on the bed, completely nude, and paused to admire her form, she blushed bright pink.

The swell of her breasts were tipped with dark pink nipples, begging to be suckled and touched. The cream of her skin was unblemished, save for an adorable trio of tiny moles at her hip, mere inches from the enticing thatch of dark brown curls on her mound.

She pressed her legs together as her blushed deepened, one of her hands moving to cover her breasts.

"No, sweetheart, don't hide from me," he said, leaning down and placing his knee on the bed, leaning forward to press his hand against the mattress on the other side of her body so that he was hovering over her. "I want to see every beautiful inch of you."

Hell, he wanted to touch every inch of her, worship every inch of her. Gabrielle blushed again as he very slowly lowered his mouth to hers, adjusting himself so that he was straddling her thighs, but keeping his weight well away from her. Inside his breeches, his cock was fit to burst, and it didn't help when her delicate fingers reached up to stroke his bare chest again, her fingers seeking out those spots that she'd already discovered.

Felix had never bedded a virgin before, but he hadn't imagined her being quite so brazen - especially after the night before. Had his efforts today really changed her that much? Or had she just had enough time to resign herself to being his wife?

Although she didn't feel resigned... but her inexperience also meant she possibly didn't quite understand what he was doing to her body. As an accomplished rake, Felix had dallied with quite a few ladies who had never experienced passion or pleasure in the bedroom and he knew that they found their first experiences with it to be overwhelming. Was Gabrielle simply responding physically because he was her first?

The questions whirling in his brain were the only things holding his lust in check as he caressed the soft curves of her body, his teeth nipping at her lower lip, his tongue pressing inside of her mouth. Beneath him, Gabrielle shuddered and arched, moaning into his mouth as he stoked the fires of her passion higher. She was incredibly responsive. When her nails dragged down his chest, the sharp sensation left him shuddering.

Moving one hand down between them, he felt her belly quiver as he traced a pattern over her silky skin, moving ever lower to the juncture of her legs. Shifting his weight, he slid one knee between her thighs, parting them. Gabrielle's body stiffened and then softened, and then stiffened again as he slid his fingers through her curls. She whimpered, her hips arching - which was not quite the reaction he had expected, but which he was quite pleased by.

The delicate folds of her pussy were dripping with her arousal, the stiff bud of her clit swollen and hard under the pads of his fingers as he dragged them around the sensitive nubbin. The startled cry she let out had him grinning. The sensation of self-pleasure was very different from having someone else touching such intimate areas. There was no way to predict how they might touch, how they might move.

He let his finger slide lower, ignoring the way her hips lifted, searching for more contact with the tiny bud, and move lower to her virginal hole. One finger pressed inward and he groaned at the tightness as she clamped down around him. The incredible slick heat made his cock ache to be inside of her, to feel that tightness wrapped around him. Gently he pumped his finger, stretching her opening, using his thumb to tease the swollen bud of her clitoris, making her gasp and arch with pleasure. The barrier of her virginity was still intact and he nearly groaned at the thought of being her first and only. Gabrielle was his.

Having her writhing beneath him tested his self-control more than anything else he'd ever experienced. He focused on pleasuring her, on her every gasp, her every shudder, finding her most sensitive spots, anything to district himself from the urges of his own body. This was about her... about pleasuring her, showing her what he could do for her, showing her what their marriage could be.

Curling his finger inside of her, he stroked, and she screamed against his lips, his mouth muffling the sound of her ecstasy. His cock pulsed, fluid leaking from the tip and rubbing uncomfortably against his breeches. Her body spasmed around his finger as he stirred it inside of her, expertly drawing out her pleasure as the heel of his hand pressed against her swollen pleasure nub.

ECSTASY RIOTED through Gabrielle's body, more intense and more powerful than she'd ever experienced before. Felix's fingers on her, inside of her, were a revelation. The man was wickedly sinful, making her melt with his kiss, making her explode with his touch. She sobbed against his lips, tears leaking from her eyes at the sheer intensity of the pleasure ripping through her.

She could feel him inside of her, stroking and pressing, as the rest of his hand circled against her sensitive flesh. The sensations sent her soaring, making her writhe with abandon beneath him, clutching at his shoulders, until the climax finally ebbed and she began to breathe more freely again. Her grip on him loosened as his movements slowed, and she rubbed her palms against his skin, luxuriating in the strangeness of touching a man totally bare.

As his finger slid out of her, she smiled up at him, ready for the next part.

But his kiss was gentle, not passionate, and when he sat up on his knees it was with an air of finality about it. He shifted to the side, removing himself from between her legs and sat beside her instead. Gabrielle watched him, confusion rising, as he trailed his fingers down her stomach and her leg, a gentle caress, but not the kind she was looking for. There were marks on his broad shoulders from her own passion, reddened crescents where she'd dug her nails into his flesh, but they didn't mar the perfection of his body at all. Those lean muscles, decorated with dark hair that trickled from his chest down to his stomach, shifted as he moved, leaning his weight onto one hand as he looked down at her. She lay frozen, unsure of what to do now and feeling strangely vulnerable.

"Did you enjoy that sweetheart?"

Gabrielle narrowed her eyes at him. The wry tone in which he'd asked that question...

"It's not over." She rolled onto her side to face him, stifling the urge to cover herself up. With the way he was looking at her, covering her body would not help her cause. There was a hunger in his dark eyes, one that she recognized, and she could see the stiff, full shape of his manhood even though he was still half dressed. He wanted to do the rest of it, so what was stopping him? She didn't like the way he'd just pulled away.

"It is for tonight." The gentle way he said it did nothing to assuage the fury and hurt that suddenly lanced through her. The languid satisfaction in her muscles vanished, all of them tensing as she realized he was rejecting her. That he didn't want to do what she'd seen the Marquess and Cordelia doing.

"Get out." The ice that was sliding through her veins was clear in her voice. She rolled away from him, grabbing for a pillow, wanting nothing more than to cover herself now. Whatever had caused the hungry look in his eyes, it obviously wasn't what she'd thought. She'd been wrong about him again.

The corner of his lip quirked upwards, infuriating her further. Did he think this was funny?

"We're in my room," he said.

Sliding off the side of the bed, still hugging the pillow to her front, Gabrielle sidled around the large piece of furniture, refusing to meet his eyes. She felt so humiliated and stupid for thinking that he wanted her. For thinking that she should try to be his wife. Bleakness rose up inside of her, making her chest tight, and she beat it down, because she wouldn't let him see her cry.

"Gabrielle," he said, sighing, as he moved to block her way. She stared at a fixed point in the middle of the chest she'd been admiring only a few minutes earlier. It wasn't that nice a chest now that she thought about it. Since she had nothing to compare it to, it was quite likely that there were much nicer chests out there in the world. "What's wrong?"

"Wrong?" she spat the word at him. The pent-up emotions in her chest seemed harder to contain than usual. The passion she'd just shared with him, the openness, left her feeling raw and unshielded. His words scraped at her emotions; rejection and fury welled in response. In fact, she hadn't felt quite so emotionally undone since Cordelia's wedding, when she thought he'd been threatening to beat her. Now she knew the difference between a spanking and a beating, but at the time she'd been frightened, miserable and alone. Furious, miserable and alone didn't feel much better. "What could possibly be wrong? I'm married, but not a wife. I let you... let you do *that* to me, but you still don't want to, to..."

Her voice ran out, and she felt her cheeks turning even pinker, now from embarrassment instead of the wave of anger she'd been riding.

Felix crossed his arms over his chest. Gabrielle gripped the pillow she was holding tighter, leaning against the bedpost, shifting her gaze to his shoulder.

"Exactly what don't I want to do?" he asked, his voice deceptively mild. There was a hardness underneath it that she recognized from her encounters with the Marquess. Somehow, for some reason, he thought she'd done something wrong.

Her anger boiled over.

"The marriage act."

"How much do you know about the marriage act?"

The heat bloomed in her face, and this time she couldn't tell if it was embarrassment or her ire. "I know *that* wasn't it."

"And how do you know that?" His voice was hard now, uncompromising.

Gabrielle's gaze dropped to his bare feet. It was definitely embarrassment coloring her face now. Somehow she'd ended up on the defensive... guilt suffused her. She knew she shouldn't have spied on the Marquess and Cordelia the way she had... but she'd been too enthralled by what she'd witnessed - too excited by it to try and sneak away. It hadn't just been educational, it had been fascinating. Arousing.

"Gabrielle. Tell me, now."

She'd rather die than tell him. Because if she did tell him, she might die anyway - of embarrassment. What if he told the Marquess and Cordelia? The Marquess couldn't punish her anymore... could he? Would Felix let him?

Thinking about the possible consequences of confession made Gabrielle's lips tighten, and she shook her head, unable to lift her head to look him in the eye.

Making a noise rather like a growl, Felix stepped forward and grabbed her so quickly that Gabrielle squeaked in surprise and dropped the pillow she'd been clinging to. The next thing she knew, Felix was sitting on the edge of the bed and she was over his lap, his hard member digging into her side and one hand holding her securely in place.

"What are you doing?!" She squirmed, trying to get away; she splayed her hands on the floor as her balance teetered.

Her husband's hand rubbed her bottom and Gabrielle sucked in a breath as the vulnerability of her current position hit her. She was naked, with her bottom tilted up - the same position the Marquess' chair had put her in for spankings, but so much more intimate and so much more terrifying.

"Gabrielle," he said, his voice soft but somehow even more threatening than before. "Tell me how you know about the marital act, or I will spank you until you do."

This was the second time Felix had threatened her with a spanking, and unlike the first time she wasn't terrified by the mere prospect. Discipline in the Marquess' household had taught her the difference between a spanking and what she'd thought a beating would be. Gabrielle's bottom had paid the price for misbehavior more than once in the past few months - with a wooden paddle and Cordelia looking on, no less. She was sure that she could take whatever her husband would mete out; deep down, she knew that he wouldn't ever *really* hurt her. It made his threat less effective.

Especially because she didn't see a paddle anywhere in sight.

Clamping her lips together, Gabrielle shook her head and wriggled, trying to get away... but his hand held her tightly against him, his arm like a bar across her lower back as his fingers curved into her opposite hip. There was no escaping, which meant that she would just have to bear it.

SLAP!

SLAP!

Ouch! It stung, but at the same time, Gabrielle felt almost like laughing. Her husband's hand was no match for the paddle the

Marquess had wielded. There was no deep, throbbing burn; it was lighter, sharper, but much more bearable than the spankings she'd received before.

Almost as if he'd heard her thoughts, Felix's hand came down harder, on exactly the same spot he'd already spanked on each cheek - the very center.

SMACK!

SMACK!

Gabrielle gritted her teeth. Those two had hurt more than she'd expected after the first smacks, but certainly still not enough to make her confess her sins. She could only imagine how much worse the punishment would be for spying on her guardians! Besides, this still didn't hurt as badly as the paddle.

SMACK!

SMACK!

"You can make this stop at any time, you know," her husband said, his voice silky and coaxing. "Just tell me how much you know about the marital act and how you came by your education."

Gabrielle couldn't help it. She laughed. "You think a few swats to my bottom will make any difference to me?"

THERE WAS HIS FEISTY BRIDE. Felix couldn't help but grin at her challenge. He wondered if she realized how much she was enjoying her current predicament. While she'd made a few half-hearted moves to escape his hold, she hadn't truly struggled. And despite her taunting words, he didn't think she was looking for release - it was more like she was testing him. Trying to find her boundaries, prodding him to react. If he let her go now, she would never respect him or his dominance over her.

Not that he had any intention of doing so anyway, but it made his resolve to tame his bride even firmer.

"Very well then," he murmured, tipping her forward even more.

She shrieked as her legs kicked involuntarily, her bottom raising even higher in the air than it had before. "A spanking it is."

While she may have been disciplined under Philip's hand, that was a very different thing from being disciplined by a lover or a husband, as she was about to find out. Felix didn't waste anytime; he immediately aimed his hand for her sensitive sit-spot; the crease between the delicious curve of her bottom and her thighs. The first four swats he'd landed on the center of her cheeks, which now carried two bright pink splotches on the creamy mounds. His cock was hard as steel, pressed against the soft curve of her body, as he admired his handiwork.

His recalcitrant wife shrieked her outrage as he peppered her sit spots with sharp, short swats, much faster than the initial strikes he'd landed on her curvy posterior. Obviously, she'd never had a focused spanking on this area, and he was seeing the effects now as her legs kicked and her squirming to escape began in earnest. Her soft, creamy skin turned bright pink very quickly under his hand, while the delicate shell of her pussy continued to leak cream. She might be protesting, but her body was responding in a way that made it even harder for him not to turn her onto her back and plunge into her softness.

"Stop it! Let me go!"

Felix paused, pressing his hand against the wet heat between her legs and making her gasp. Her body went rigid as he massaged his palm against her swollen, sensitive lips, the tips of his fingers seeking out her little pleasure bud.

"Are you ready to answer my questions?" he asked softly, massaging her clit in a slow circle with his fingers. Gabrielle whimpered, her hips bucking slightly. He could feel the warmth of her skin where he'd been spanking her and knew that she was probably confused by the sudden combination of pain mixed with pleasure. It was a sensual assault that she couldn't possibly have any experience with.

"I-" Her voice cut off as if she was trying to decide whether or not to tell him.

Pinching her clit, he let her shriek before he began spanking her again.

SMACK!

SMACK!

SMACK!

SMACK!

She cried out, kicking and thrashing, as he kept his aim focused on her sit spots, which were already burning. When he aimed a swat directly on her pussy, she howled, her hips bucking, but he saw how her arousal only increased. Her skin had turned a dark pink now, with her creamy cheeks above and ivory thighs below. Between her pussy lips, her little clitty was hard and swollen, easily visible, as if begging to be smacked again. With every swat, her flesh rippled and bounced, and his cock jerked in response.

"Please!"

He paused again. "Please what, Gabrielle?"

"Please stop, it hurts." She twisted, turning her tear-stained face to him, her eyes red-rimmed and cheeks wet, she looked quite pitiful. Felix hardened his heart.

"I've told you, sweetheart, this ends when you answer my questions."

Stubbornly, her lips pressed together in a thin line before she turned her face away, looking back at the floor. Felix almost sighed. As much as he was enjoying spanking her, he wanted her to talk to him as well.

SMACK!

SMACK!

SMACK!

For every two that he landed on a sit spot, he slapped another swat against her pussy, nearly as hard. Gabrielle choked back a scream when he did so, but the burning swats didn't stop her arousal from growing. His hand came away from her pussy wet after every slap, and her movements had changed so she was practically rubbing herself against his thigh. Did she realize what she was doing?

Felix hefted her weight, pushing her back slightly so that she couldn't find purchase with her mound on his leg. The combination of a painful spanking and the building need for an orgasm would be more torturous than either would be singularly. Moaning, she kicked again, but her struggles were becoming more half-hearted.

SMACK!

SMACK!

SPLAT!

She screamed as his hand impacted against her pussy, jerking and lifting her hips up to meet the blow. Felix paused, pressing his fingers against her again, enjoying the way her honey drenched his hand as he did nothing more than rest it against her opening.

"Are you ready to talk to me Gabrielle?"

The tension drained out of her body and she slumped over his lap, the fight spanked out of her, submission practically emanating from her. He'd always known she wouldn't be the type to just give in; it would take a strong man to earn her trust and respect. The spanking proved to her that he couldn't be manipulated, that he would insist on being the head of their household, and what would happen if she were to defy him.

Of course, he knew this wouldn't be the last time she would require a spanking. After all, he hadn't broken her spirit and he didn't want to. He liked her fiery and argumentative, but only one of them could lead in their relationship and it was going to be him.

"Gabrielle?" he asked again, his voice low and soothing as he gently stroked her pussy, enough to keep her aroused and distract her from the roasting he'd just given her, but not enough to bring her to climax. "Tell me what you know of the marital act."

"Do you promise not to punish me more?"

He only hesitated a moment. Whatever it was, it must be bad, but he would keep his word. It was a risk, however he knew this would be an integral moment in earning her trust. "No more punishment, as long as you tell me the truth."

CHAPTER 6

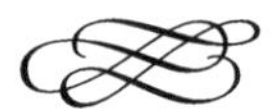

Whimpering, Gabrielle tried to push herself up, wanting a moment to compose herself, but her husband kept her held securely in place over his leg. Her skin where he'd spanked her felt like it was on fire. The spankings the Marquess had given her had been spread out over her entire bottom, not concentrated on two single spots... well three, if she counted the slaps that Felix had begun giving to her womanhood.

The entire situation had her completely off-kilter. Not only was she naked and over her husband's lap, with his erect rod pressing into her and indicating how aroused he was by spanking her, but she was aroused too! The combination of her roasted rump and his intimate massages had her mind whirling at the complicated mix of sensations. She could barely tell if she was on fire or about to tip into ecstasy. This was entirely different from the spankings she'd received from the Marquess, not just in terms of how painful it was, but also in how helpless she felt.

She'd been so close, pressing herself against Felix's leg, but then he'd moved away and no matter how she'd moved, she hadn't been able to reconnect that delicious pressure. It felt like she was burning inside and out, and she just wanted the spanking to stop. Even without the paddle, she could tell that she was going to have trouble sitting tomorrow. The spots where Felix had focused his blows were much more tender than she'd realized, and sensitive enough to have her regretting laughing and taunting him over a spanking.

His hand rubbed over her sore bottom, making her whimper again. There was something soothing about the caress, even as it sparked little stinging pricks of pain against her sensitive skin.

"Tell me, sweetheart."

"I... I..." She closed her eyes, squeezing them shut, as if she could hide her shame that way. Her voice dropped to a hoarse whisper. "I saw the Marquess and Cordelia."

Felix's hand stopped, frozen on her sore bottom. "You what?"

She couldn't tell if he was shocked or horrified or both or something else entirely. The words spilled out of her, much more easily now, as she tried to explain herself. Even though he'd promised not to punish her, she didn't want him rethinking that decision.

"They came into the library; they didn't know I was there and - I didn't know what they were going to do! But then they started doing, well, *that,* and I... I watched." Her voice dropped again in embarrassment, and she kept her eyes closed. Not that she could see anything but the floor in her current position, but for some nonsensical reason, it truly did help her feel less humiliated. "I saw everything they did."

Her body, which had been slumped and loose, tensed again as she waited for his reaction. Waiting for the spanking and the pain to start again. Whatever arousal she'd been feeling had died during her confession, in anticipation of his reaction.

To her shock, her husband pulled her up and swiftly arranged her on his lap, her burning bottom pressing against his thighs and manhood, her head against his chest, and his arms around her. Gabrielle clung to him. She had never been able to explain just why she'd responded to being cuddled and praised by Cordelia and the Marquess after a spanking, just that she had. Now, the relief she felt as Felix held her close - and not just because it was obvious that no more punishment was forthcoming - had tears sliding down her cheeks again.

"Good girl," he murmured into her hair, his hands gently massaging her shoulder and hip. More tears slid down her cheeks as she tried to sniff them back, her entire being warming to his caresses and comfort.

Gabrielle nuzzled against him, not even questioning why she should desire this closeness to the man who had just set her bottom afire. She actually felt calmer than she had in days, as if her tears and cries had wrung out all the anxiety from her body and left her empty; a blank emotional state that was ready for whatever came next.

Closing her eyes, she leaned into Felix as he pressed his lips against her hair, then her forehead. His arm behind her shoulders adjusted, reclining her body and she allowed her head to tip back as his lips moved across her cheeks, kissing away the tears that lingered there. She kept her eyes closed, lashes fluttering slightly as his kisses moved over her face. The burning of her bottom made her wince as she shifted on his lap, but didn't stop the slow heat that was swirling in her core.

Finally his lips found his way to hers, a gentle kiss that quickly deepened as she opened her mouth beneath his, hands sliding around his neck, as she opened for him. He'd kept his promise. There would be no more punishment, no more spanking, despite what she'd admitted. He was true to his word, and something sparked inside of her, feeding the hope that this was the right course of action. There was something between them now that hadn't been there before, a promise kept, and her emotions flared wildly, her body opening and submitting to him in a way she hadn't been able to before.

Gabrielle felt almost desperate to have him touch her, to finish what they'd started - if he changed his mind now, she'd wait until he was asleep and then she'd find something to beat him with, she swore she would. She was his wife and she was determined that he would treat her as such. It was the only way she could think of to change his feelings about her and about her stepmother. To give him what Cordelia never would or could.

He was going to be hers.

She kissed him more fiercely, writhing in his arms, no longer caring about the pain in her bottom. It was already hurting less and less as the need within her welled. When his hand slid from her hip to her bottom, squeezing the tender flesh, she moaned into his mouth as sparks tingled through her body. Her fingers dug into his shoulders as she shifted on his lap, turning to face him more fully.

The stinging of her bottom no longer felt painful; his hands on the tender flesh ignited her senses, and she gasped as he lifted her so that she was straddling his thighs and she could feel his manhood pressing against her through his breeches. Rubbing her breasts against his hard chest, she rocked slightly, shuddering at the pleasure that shot through her as her swollen nether lips parted and her womanhood spasmed with aching need.

Felix groaned as she rocked on top of him, his hands tightening on her soft cheeks, his body jerking slightly beneath hers, and a sense of feminine power welled in her breast. Fiercely, Gabrielle kissed him harder, rubbing herself against him, frantic with need and at the same time, cataloging his every reaction. She would learn everything that he liked, that he desired, and she would give it to him, and then, perhaps, he would love her. Perhaps she could earn from him what she'd never been able to secure from anyone else. That she would finally be able to supplant Cordelia in someone's affections would only be the icing on the cake...

It was easier to think in terms of finally beating Cordelia than it was to admit that she wanted Felix to love her because she was quite sure that she was already falling in love with him.

THE EAGER PASSION of his wife had completely undone Felix. This was not at all how he'd expected tonight to conclude, but he was astute enough to realize that insisting on waiting to consummate their marriage would do more damage to his relationship with Gabrielle than giving in to her demand. He would not have her feeling rejected by him, especially not in the bedroom, and it would hard to couch waiting to become intimate in any other terms, even though rejection would not be his intent.

She was leaving him no choice...

The worry that she was so insistent because she knew it was her duty still nagged at the back of his mind. Especially now that he knew where she'd gained her knowledge of the marital act. After his mother had pointed out that Gabrielle must feel more of a sisterly rivalry with Cordelia than a mother-daughter relationship, he couldn't help but cringe at the idea that perhaps Gabrielle was only intent on sleeping with him in order to be on equal footing as a wife.

The intensity of her passion helped to assuage a good portion of that concern, however. Her small gasps, her slick arousal that was seeping through his breeches, her hard nipples rubbing against his chest, and her desperate kisses made it clear her arousal was completely unfeigned. Despite the spanking - or perhaps because of it? Jealousy roused at the thought that perhaps she'd enjoyed being spanked by Philip too... but he quickly pushed that away.

There was no way Philip had spanked her in the same way that Felix just had, or even in a manner that would be anywhere near as intimate. Still, it was obvious she was at least a little masochistic, and - in some ways - very submissive despite her fairly aggressive behavior now.

Twisting, Felix maneuvered her onto her back, her legs splayed to reveal the pink shell of her sex, glossy and wet petals that were swollen with arousal, open and ready for him to breach her. The dark hair on her mound and outer lips framed her pink, inner flesh perfectly and he slid his hands up her legs, wanting - needing - to touch her. His lips curled into a smile as she gasped and arched, her hands clutching at the bed sheets, her creamy breasts jiggling in response.

Perhaps duty did motivate her, but passion did as well and he could use that. Eventually, it would not be duty that brought her to his bed, but the promise of pleasure, the need for his hands, his mouth and his cock. If she wanted their wedding night tonight, then he would give her one that she would never forget. Then he would make sure she was far too busy, far too satisfied, to ever seek such pleasures with any other man.

Pressing her thighs further apart, Felix lowered his mouth to her pouting lips.

"*Felix*!" Her cry was a half-strangled shout of shock as the tart-sweet taste of her honey exploded on his tongue, and a small burst of triumph flowed through him. Apparently Gabrielle's knowledge of bedroom activities was not entirely complete.

Her thighs tried to close around his head and he nearly growled. Sliding his arms beneath her legs, he used his shoulders to spread her wider, as his arms wrapped around her thighs and pulled them open, baring her pussy to him completely. The slick lips parted beneath his tongue as he licked the center of her body, ending with the swollen nub of her clit at the apex.

"Oh!" Gabrielle's fingers tangled in his hair, her head falling back from where she'd lifted it to see what he was doing. While he had enjoyed seeing her wide, green eyes staring at him, he enjoyed seeing her writhe with pleasure even more. The cherry tipped mounds of her breasts moved with her body as he feasted and she squirmed against his mouth, gasping at the intensity of his oral assault. "Please... oh... I can't... I didn't know..."

Pressing her back further, Felix moved his mouth down to lick at the hot cheeks of her bottom, tonguing the spots he'd spanked so deliberately and harshly, as he used the position to run little circles around her clit with his fingers. Her pink flesh was hot against his face, and Gabrielle's moans became more ardent as he nuzzled her chastised bottom while simultaneously pleasuring her.

His cock felt like it was going to explode as he realized how completely she'd given herself over to his ministrations. There were no protests, no pleas, just her impassioned moans and cries, her glorious writhing, and her acceptance of his touch, no matter what he wanted to do to her. So Felix did something he'd always wanted to do, and pressed his tongue against the crinkled star of her bottom hole, pinching her clit at the same time.

Gabrielle screamed as her climax hit her. Her tiny hole clenched against his tongue, which tasted of her honey as her juices were dripping down her body. Felix thought he might actually pass out from his own need for release as he performed this forbidden act. No matter how adventurous, none of his other lovers had permitted him to attempt this on them.

But then, he hadn't asked Gabrielle either, he'd merely taken... and she'd climaxed.

He laved the tiny hole, his fingers still moving on her clit, pinching and rubbing the little bud as she thrashed against his strong hold, sobbing as the intense pleasure was drawn out.

The cessation of her orgasm left her limp, satiated. Felix rose above her, letting her legs drop to the bed. She blinked at him slowly, through heavy-lidded eyes as he knelt between her listless thighs. Her pussy was swollen, gleaming from his attentions. Wetness coated her cheeks from the tears she'd shed at the unaccustomed rapture and her expression was one of dazed surprise, as well as satisfaction.

Using one hand to undo his breeches, Felix pressed the fingers of his other hand to her wet sheath, stretching her virgin channel.

"Oh..." Gabrielle practically mouthed the word, her eyelashes fluttering as his fingers probed the warm channel. It flexed and clenched around him, like hot silk, making him groan as his cock throbbed in response. He wanted to be inside of her, to feel her muscles spasming around him, massaging him, milking him.

Pumping his fingers, he fisted his cock tightly, so hard that it hurt, and beat back his urges. He needed patience. He needed to go slowly. Even with just his fingers her pussy was tight, despite the orgasm she'd just had, and he was not a small man in any sense of the word.

Sliding his fingers out of her, he pressed the blunt head of his cock at the virgin entrance of her body, her slick heat coating his most sensitive skin. Braced on his forearms, poised above her, he looked down into her bright green eyes, which were feverish with arousal.

"Are you sure, sweetheart?"

She didn't answer verbally, instead she pressed her hands against his chest and slid them up, winding her arms around his neck as she drew him down for a kiss. Her lips parted on a cry as his body lowered and his cock began to slide inside of her. Gabrielle wriggled beneath him as he entered her, his blunt rod parting her slick flesh, stretching her wide and filling her. The tiny scrap of virginity guarding her entrance was no match for the thick length of his cock as it pressed deeper, and he swallowed her short cry of pain.

Kissing her distracted him enough to keep from thrusting into her quick and hard, the way his body wanted to, but he couldn't stop the slow glide to fill her, even when he'd felt her stiffen as he'd broken her barrier. He needed to be inside her too much, every instinct in his body screaming to claim her, fill her, and make her his. The heat surrounding his cock was incredible, a silken vise that gripped him and massaged him as he buried himself inside of her.

Her whimpers as she clung to him, kissing him back fiercely, helped him reign in his passion.

Slowly... he had to move slowly... and hope that he didn't completely unman himself and spill his seed in the first few minutes of coitus, as if he were himself an untried youth rather than one of the *ton*'s most accomplished rakes.

Oh my... oh my, oh my, oh my....

Larger, more descriptive words were impossible as sensation swamped Gabrielle. While she'd witnessed the marital act and she'd imagined the marital act, nothing had quite prepared her for the reality of the intimate invasiveness, the shocking vulnerability, or the sharp shock of pain. Pain that didn't come from her still tender backside, but instead from deep inside of her as her husband's staff moved inside of her in a way her fingers never had. Deeper than her fingers ever had. Stretching her wider, making her hurt wonderfully - at least, it was wonderful after that initial tearing sensation that had surprised her.

He was moving inside of her, filling her, while simultaneously surrounding her with his body. His arms were on either side of her, his fingers in her hair, one hand sliding down her thigh and pulling her leg open wider as his body joined with hers. Gabrielle was gasping at the incredible sensations, her sore bottom completely forgotten in the wonderment of these new, shocking physical revelations.

It felt like he was almost too big for her, and yet she stretched until she felt breathless, as though his invasion had pushed all the air out of her lungs. When his body finally pressed against hers, warm and hard between her thighs and against her womanhood, and she realized that he was fully inside of her, she felt a moment of relief that he wasn't any larger. Already she felt overly full, and yet fully wonderful.

This was what it felt like to be a married woman. To be joined with her husband. She could feel his heart pounding in his chest, his kiss delving deep into her mouth, his hard rigidity holding her open... and then he began to move.

She gasped as the sensation of him inside of her receded, and then thrust in again, making her tingle from head to toe as her body arched in reaction. It was the strangest feeling, and yet incredibly pleasurable too. The gentle but firm thrusts, moving his manhood in and out of her, were so much more intense than anything she'd ever managed to do to herself, so much more pleasurable than she'd ever imagined.

The initial pain was forgotten, the tenderness of her bottom was forgotten even as the sensitive skin was pressed against the bed sheets - everything felt like pleasure as his body rocked against the little bud of her clitoris. She could feel her climax building inside of her, but it felt different.

Fuller.

Bigger.

More encompassing.

With every slow drag of his hips, Felix sent her soaring higher and she dug her fingers into his shoulders, clinging to him like he was her port in the storm of sensations that threatened to drown her. She was lost and he was her anchor to reality. His lips feathered over her face and she realized he was kissing away the tears that were leaking from her eyes, which were squeezed shut. She hadn't even realized she was crying; her rising ecstasy was so intense that it was like her body was falling apart at the seams.

A rushing noise filled her ears as Felix ground his body against hers, trapping her pleasure button between their bodies and rubbing it with his own, his manhood jolting inside of her, and Gabrielle cried out as pure rapture rolled through her. She sobbed at the intense rush of passionate bliss that burst inside of her, tingling along her limbs, making her shake as if her body was a vessel for pure sexual energy that had no release - it just bounced around inside of her skin, sending her higher and higher into ecstasy, until she screamed from the sheer need to release it.

Heat pulsed inside of her and she felt her body clamping down around Felix, making him feel even larger as she shuddered in heavenly gratification.

Her limbs suddenly felt heavy, and Felix's weight settled on top of her as he panted for breath, his lips brushing against her hairline. Even though it was harder to breath with him lying on her, she realized that she liked the sensation. Liked having him so close to her. At the same time, underneath her muzzy satisfaction, there was a small kernel of panic as she wondered whether or not he felt the same striking closeness to her that she now felt to him.

"Bloody hell." His voice was so low that she could barely make out the words. "My cock's done knackered."

"Your cock?"

Coughing, her husband moved, propping himself up on his forearms and taking some of the pressure off her chest and belly. Gabrielle almost missed it, but she had to admit, the sight of his face so close to hers, hovering above her, wasn't bad either. Especially because he was looking at her with an expression remarkably similar to the way he often looked at Cordelia.

Like he actually liked her now.

She smiled up at him. "Your cock?"

"My ah..." His hips shifted and she gasped as a ripple of sensation slid through her body, like a shadow of the glorious climax that she'd just experienced. "The part of me that's inside you right now."

"Oh! Your manhood."

An amused smile lifted the corners of his lips. "If that's what you'd like to call it."

"You call it a cock?"

A curious expression crossed his face at her question, and she actually felt the part in question jerk inside of her. "Yes, although perhaps you should refrain from using that word at the moment... you're going to be sore enough tomorrow as it is."

Rolling off of her, and taking all that wonderful, heavy, body heat with him, he pulled her to his side. Gabrielle winced as she rolled, her legs moving. It wasn't just her bottom that was tender now, between her legs felt quite almost bruised, completely distracting her from the questions she'd had.

"Ow."

Suddenly frowning, Felix moved his arm out from underneath her as he got up. "Stay there."

She watched him curiously as he wet a cloth in his water basin and returned to the bed. When he began to clean her off, very gently, between her legs, she blushed and closed her eyes but didn't protest his ministrations. They felt rather nice actually; the water was cool on her swollen flesh, wiping away the stickiness on her womanhood and her thighs.

Even better was when Felix slid back into bed, his dark eyes studying her intently as if looking for anything he'd missed, as he drew her into his arms.

"Are you alright?" he asked.

"Yes, of course," she said, her temper stirring a little. Did he think that there was something wrong with her, that she was somehow deficient as his wife? That she shouldn't have been able to do her duty for some reason? He had resisted performing the act after all...

"Don't be tart when I'm ascertaining your wellbeing," he said, pulling her into his side so that her head was tucked into his shoulder as she was laying on her side, one hand on his broad chest. His hand slid down to her hip, and then sliding to her rump, patting it gently and awakening the soreness from her spanking earlier. "I don't want to have to give you a second spanking tonight."

For a moment she thought about arguing, and then she thought the better of it. She had taken his question the wrong way, apparently. Still, she wasn't going to deign to reply to his threat.

"What now?" she asked, after a long moment when he seemed content to just lay there on the bed. She felt incredibly relaxed - despite the threat - and she didn't particularly feel like moving... but this was his room after all. As nice as it felt to lay on his shoulder, with his hand proprietorially resting on her hip, she wasn't sure what came next.

"What do you mean what now?" he asked, opening one eye and peering down at her. "Now we go to sleep."

"Oh." Disappointment and a sense of loneliness flashed through her, but she started to push up from the bed, only to squeak as he yanked her back down again.

"Where do you think you're going?"

"To my bed," she said, completely confused, although rather enjoying the way he was now on his side with both his arms around her. One bicep was providing a pillow for her head while that same hand curved around her mid-back, holding her in place while his other hand was wrapped around her lower back and resting on her bottom cheek. "You said we were to sleep."

"You sleep here from now on," he said, pulling her into him.

Joy flared in her chest as her nose was pressed against his, the wiry hair tickling her face. There was something about the way he'd made the demand that sent warm happiness fizzing through her. Gabrielle snuggled into him, completely willing to comply with that particular order. The last time she'd slept beside someone was when she'd run to her mother's room after a nightmare, as a child. Her mother and the Baron hadn't slept in the same room, that she knew, but Felix wanted her in his.

It wasn't something she'd thought about before, but now that he'd made the demand, she found that liked it. Especially if he was going to hold her all night.

Apparently, attending to her marital duty had been just as beneficial to their relationship as she'd hoped. After all, he hadn't been interested in sleeping beside her before this. Now he was.

Now, she was *wanted.*

CHAPTER 7

Bedding his wife had rewards above and beyond the obvious, Felix thought smugly over breakfast the next morning. Apparently all Gabrielle had needed was a good tumble to tame her - at least temporarily. He doubted her fiery temper would be completely eradicated, but at least it helped. He didn't want her spirit to completely disappear, after all, he just didn't want a temperamental wife *all* the time. Granted, her mood had been much more even tempered ever since she'd met his parents, but this morning she was milder than he'd ever seen her. There was an air of happy softness about her, as if her expression was now more geared towards a smile than a frown, and that smile might appear at any moment, given the slightest provocation. The opposite, as it were, of her usual mien.

Unfortunately he hadn't been able to repeat the experience, as Gabrielle *had* been rather sore this morning. Although that hadn't stopped Felix from burying his tongue between her legs and soothing her that way. She'd been both shocked and gratified by his attentions, while he'd been left smug and frustrated. If she wasn't feeling better by tonight, perhaps he'd educated her on how to pleasure him with her tongue. She'd seemed amiable to staying abed this morning, but Felix hadn't wanted to push things too quickly.

After all, last night had advanced their physical relationship much further than he'd intended.

"So what are your plans for the day?" his mother asked, interrupting his thoughts. He smiled at Gabrielle, who had been caught with a mouth full of bacon when his mother asked the question. Her green eyes sparkled back at him, full of mirth.

This was the kind of relationship he'd wanted with her, from the very beginning. It was easy to see Gabrielle's innate sweetness now, her sense of humor. Some ladies might be embarrassed or even resentful at being caught out with her mouth full - if they even took a large enough bite to call it that - but Gabrielle just shared an amused look with him.

"I thought I might take Gabrielle down to the creek," he said easily. The creek was a long walk from the house, but one with many pleasant views, including a wishing well and a blackberry patch. It would be cool and private. His brothers and he had passed many a day there, enjoying playing away from wandering eyes. The perfect place to continue his seduction (or wooing, as his mother would insist on calling it) of his wife.

Despite the soreness of her bottom (which she was at least somewhat used to) and the soreness between her thighs (which was new and strangely delicious), Gabrielle felt wonderful this morning. It was as though last night's spanking had allowed her pent-up emotions to spill over and drain out of her, leaving her feeling wonderfully light. He'd spanked her, but it had been a much more intimate spanking that the Marquess had ever given her - for which she was grateful. The aftermath had been a shocking revelation. Certainly much more effective at comforting her than mere praise and cuddling.

It didn't hurt that her husband had held her all night long. She'd awoken, several times, unused to sleeping beside someone, only to have his arms tighten around her when she'd wriggled into a new position. Of course, he was asleep and she couldn't be sure that it was *her* he held in his dreams, but she could pretend. Maybe even hope, a little. When he'd awoken in the morning, he'd certainly been eager to get between her thighs, with no reward for himself.

She still blushed to remember how shockingly depraved he'd been, his mouth and tongue licking over her flesh, soothing away some of the tenderness of her womanhood. As she'd pressed her bottom into the mattress, the lingering soreness of her spanking had only enhanced her pleasure.

And now he wanted to spend more time with her! And he was smiling at her the way he'd smiled at other ladies, the way he'd smiled at Cordelia.

The smile on her own face was a force that couldn't be hidden away, even if she'd wanted to. She couldn't remember the last time she'd felt this unequivocally happy.

"Oh well that sounds lovely, dear," Mother said, although she looked a bit disappointed. "I'll be out in the gardens this afternoon. If you're back in enough time before supper, perhaps you'll join me?" Her entreaty was addressed directly to Felix, but her eyes quickly moved to Gabrielle and stayed there, including her in the request with a look of hopefulness.

"Of course, I'm sure we can make it back in plenty of time," Gabrielle said immediately, delighted that the older woman so obviously wanted to spend time with her. Besides which, she had a bit of a lonely air about her, which Gabrielle could certainly sympathize with.

"Yes, that should be no problem," Felix said, a little reluctantly. Gabrielle's heart leapt. He almost sounded as though he didn't want to return early, as if he wanted to spend the whole day with her! She'd assumed he'd want to be back in the house by the afternoon... she couldn't remember the last time someone had actually wanted to spend so much time by her side. Especially without seeing it as a duty.

He didn't see it as a duty, did he?

Of course not... his duty would have been fulfilled after last night. There was no need for them to spend all day together. In fact, his duty might be better fulfilled by working or helping his father. Instead, he wanted to spend his day at leisure with her.

The hope that was thumping inside of her breast was almost painful.

THE CREEK WAS JUST as Felix remembered it.

Cool water burbling over rocks; small, deeper, pools filled with tiny creatures; heavy branches shading the full width of water; a few deeper chasms that he wouldn't want to wade into in breeches; and, unfortunately, it still had children playing in it. That had been a surprise. When he'd been younger, the creek had only drawn him and his brothers, as far as he knew.

When he and Gabrielle had entered the small, sandy clearing he and his brothers had used as children, Felix had been rather discombobulated to find that it had been invaded. Not only that, but as soon as Gabrielle had recognized two of the young girls playing there, he'd known there would be no drawing her away to a less used section of the creek. The two little girls had come with her from London, after all, and they were eager to show her all the discoveries they'd made since arriving and to introduce her to their new friends among his servants' children.

Still, it wasn't a total loss.

Gabrielle's laughter was as free and joyous as the girls she was currently wading through the shallowest part of the creek with. Holding up her skirts so the hem brushed her knees, she followed the two little girls around as they pointed out all the fishes swimming around their feet, giggling as they danced away to keep their toes from being nibbled on.

"They're too little to be our supper, but your little toes are apparently just big enough to be theirs!" Gabrielle teased the girls, who squealed and clung to her.

"They arn' gunna eat yer toes!" One of the boys standing next to Felix called out. "Silly twits." Trevor was the leader of the little band as far as Felix could tell; he was the oldest at nine years old and would probably be apprenticed the next year, but for now he was free to play with the rest of the kids. Felix was showing him and the other boys how to catch toads, although so far none of them had been successful (including Felix).

While he would have rather been teaching his wife to do much less innocent things, he did at least get to enjoy watching her capering like a water nymph, obviously enjoying playing with all of the children. In return, they flocked to her almost instinctively. When Felix and Gabrielle had first appeared in the clearing, the children had all stiffened, recognizing their betters immediately and obviously quite intimidated by them. Within five minutes of asking a few questions and distributing her sweet smile, Gabrielle had the small band in the palm of her hand. Trevor had taken quite a bit of pride in showing her the rope swing they'd set up, which Gabrielle had declined to try, although she'd enjoyed watching the boys running and jumping to grab it with their hands, swinging wildly back and forth as she cheered them on.

And now Trevor felt comfortable enough to call Gabrielle and the little girls 'twits,' Felix thought, his mouth quirking.

As popular as Gabrielle had been with the *ton* after her debut, Felix hadn't realized how uncomfortable she'd also been among them. She'd held herself well, and she'd definitely enjoyed the parties and balls from what he'd seen, but she hadn't truly been able to indulge in unfettered enjoyment. It was here, with the children, acting like a child herself, that he felt like he was finally seeing the true Gabrielle.

She took true enjoyment in every one of their endeavors. No passive observer, she didn't just watch them, she included herself in their games and play. Enthusiastically. Joyously. It made Felix wonder what kind of childhood she'd had, because she seemed far too happy to indulge in childish antics and games, all with the wonderment of a newcomer to them. He could only guess that it had been an even more repressive childhood than she'd hinted at when she spoke of her father.

Eventually Gabrielle looked up at the sky and sighed. "We should be getting back," she called out to Felix. "Otherwise I won't be able to spend any time in the garden with your mother."

This was met by a chorus of disappointment by the children, and led to promises by both Gabrielle and Felix to come play with them again.

As they walked back across the fields, Felix took Gabrielle's hand in his. Despite the interruption to his plan of seduction, he'd enjoyed his morning with her and the children. It was hard not to think about what kind of mother she'd make and how she might play with their children. Which, of course, led him to thinking about the act of creating those children, which made the lack of privacy all the worse. He couldn't even try to seduce her here in the fields, just in case the children decided to follow them back to the manor house.

"Thank you for taking me to your creek," Gabrielle said, sounding almost shy as she peeked at him through her thick lashes. The pretty pink flush in her cheeks and her loose, disheveled hair from playing made her look younger than she was, and much more innocent. "I enjoyed playing with the children."

"I could tell," he said, smiling down at her and squeezing her fingers, enjoying the shared moment of pleasure. "Did you have a creek when you were growing up?"

A shadow crossed her face and he was immediately sorry that he'd asked the question as her expression became more closed, like a cloud had suddenly obscured some of her joy.

"I was not able to explore much of my father's estate."

"That might not be such a bad thing," Felix said, with false cheer, trying to recover the moment they'd had. "I spent far too much time in that creek, often fully clothed after one of my brothers pushed me in."

Just as he'd hoped, Gabrielle laughed and the shadow of her past lifted. "Did you push them back?"

"Well, I tried, but being the youngest I was also the smallest," he said, happy to doll out embarrassing stories about himself if she would just keep laughing and smiling like that. "Mostly my attempts just ended with me being tossed in again - unless, of course, I could convince one of them to team up with me."

Felix found himself dominating the conversation the entire walk back, much as he had on the walk there, but it seemed to be how Gabrielle was most comfortable. He thought he was starting to get the hang of keeping her pleasant and happy - romance her with meaningful gestures, find children for her to play with, and don't talk about her past.

ALTHOUGH GABRIELLE WAS a bit reluctant to end her morning playing with Molly's daughters and some of the other servants' children, as well as watching Felix engage with them, she enjoyed her afternoon in the garden with Felix's mother just as much. The older woman shooed her son off and then plied Gabrielle with tea and a small luncheon in the gardens, happy to be able to chatter with Gabrielle and share all the country gossip and then listen to Gabrielle's tales from London. She was obviously thrilled to have Gabrielle's company and, it occurred to Gabrielle, that she must be a bit lonely.

From the Viscountess' talk, it became clear that the Viscount was not fond of the hectic fervor of the London Season. Apparently they often alternated years – one in the country and one in London – or made short trips to London for the Season. This particular Season they'd opted to stay in the country because last Season they'd spent the entire time in town and the Viscountess had been quite exhausted by the end of it. She obviously kept up with quite a bit of gossip through letters, but visits during the Season would be few and far between, and country life was always a little slower.

"Perhaps we could have a ball," Mother said, tapping her lips thoughtfully. "Just a small gathering to celebrate your and Felix's marriage. Or a house party..." She sighed then, looking a bit regretful. "Of course, I keep forgetting that this is supposed to be your honeymoon. We'll have to hold off on any celebrations until the end of the

Season, I suppose. Just because you came here for your honeymoon doesn't mean it should be interrupted."

"What about a dinner?" Gabrielle asked, immediately wanting to find a way to please the older woman. "It would be lovely to meet some of your neighbors."

Truthfully, she would prefer to get to know her new in-laws better, and spend her time figuring out how to make her husband fall in love with her, but Mother looked so resigned that she wanted to make the offer. And it worked. Mother immediately brightened, her countenance matching the cheery, yellow, cambric dress she was wearing.

"What a wonderful idea," Mother said, beaming. "I'll speak with my husband and Felix about it. You're such a generous sweetheart."

A dinner was a small price to pay for her new Mother's happiness. Gabrielle beamed back at her.

They took a walk around the gardens, with Mother going into detail on the care of her flowers. The rose garden in particular was a thing of beauty, and Gabrielle listened to Mother's careful directions to the gardeners on exactly how she wanted each bush cut. She even let Gabrielle make a small bouquet of the roses, one in each color, with the thorns carefully trimmed. Tying a ribbon around the stems, Gabrielle already knew she would carefully dry and press each flower before it wilted, as a reminder of this wonderful day. They could go in the same book that she'd put the flower Felix had given her.

Both women soaked up each other's attention, delighted to be in one another's company. Gabrielle was surprised at how interesting she found every aspect of gardening - or perhaps Mother's enthusiasm was just catching, as she enjoyed having an eager, female student.

By the time they came in to change for dinner, Gabrielle felt as though her head had been stuffed with useful knowledge. She wondered where she and Felix would live during the year... something they'd never talked about. Wherever it was, she hoped it would have a garden. Gabrielle would love to be able to put some of Mother's advice to good use, and then be able to show her how well she had followed all of it.

Molly was in her room, ready to help her change for dinner.

"I'd like these in a vase, by my bed," she said, placing the small bouquet down and went over to her basin to wash off her face and hands. She dampened a cloth and wiped away the dirt and dust from her exposed skin. Unfortunately there wasn't enough time for a full bath.

"Absolutely, my lady," Molly said smiling. She held up two dresses from Gabrielle's closet, a russet silk and a blue and ivory jonquil. "Which would you like to wear for dinner this evening?"

"The russet, please," she said, undoing the buttons of her day dress. The russet would look well against her skin, which was still flushed from being outdoors all day. She really should have taken a parasol, or worn a bonnet, but being back out in the country she'd forgotten. On her father's estate, she'd rarely needed either accessory, since she'd been unable to spend much time outside.

Putting the jonquil away, Molly helped her into the russet silk, the skirts whispering as they swept into place. Gabrielle looked at herself in the mirror as Molly laced her up. The bold color made her skin look paler and creamier by comparison, so that the effects of the sun didn't show as much, just as she'd hoped.

"The girls were so happy to spend some time with you today," Molly said. "It sounds like your new husband is a kind man. They said he was a right one."

"Yes... he surprised me," Gabrielle confessed as Molly led her over to her vanity and began to drag a brush through Gabrielle's tangled locks. While country life was not as formal as in the city, she still needed to be presentable for meal times. Hearing movement in the room next to hers, she smiled. Felix was in there, also getting ready for dinner. She'd missed his presence this afternoon, although she'd enjoyed the time spent with his mother. "He said he played there quite frequently as a child, although I hadn't expected to see him playing today."

Despite the circumstances, he'd still managed to look quite masculine and formidable, even with his jacket off, his trousers and shirt-sleeves rolled up, and wading through the creek pointing out the various insect and wildlife to the rambunctious young boys that had followed him around like he was the Pied Piper. It had been wholly adorable, a word she'd never thought to use to describe Felix. Since they'd left the city, she'd seen several sides to him that she'd never seen before. She couldn't help but feel a bit smug that by now, surely, she must know him better than Cordelia did, no matter how close they'd been in London.

It had also heartened her to see how well he managed with the boys and the girls. He'd been open and indulgent, firm when he needed to be, and he never mocked any of them - in fact, he'd swiftly stopped any teasing that veered towards cruelty. Every single child had merited his attention at one point or another, and they'd all ended up practically worshiping him for it. Gabrielle didn't even think he'd realized how they'd regarded him, but she certainly had. Felix would make a wonderful father.

Even if he was a bit strict. Look at how he'd dealt with her after all. Still, as long as a spanking was followed by comforting, discipline was surely not a bad thing. She could only wonder how differently she might have felt about her childhood if someone had cared enough to spank her when she'd warranted it. But, once her nurse had been replaced by her governess, no one had. Her governess had always allowed Gabrielle to do as she pleased, which had been satisfying at the time but it certainly hadn't made her feel cared about.

Cordelia had.

The Marquess ultimately had.

And now Felix was.

"There you go, my lady," Molly said, her voice filled with satisfaction. "You look lovely."

Blinking, Gabrielle focused on the mirror. She hadn't realized how lost in thought she'd been.

"Oh..." Gabrielle reached up to touch her hair. Molly had done it a bit differently than usual, leaving about half of it loose and long, hanging down her back in soft waves. The front had been pulled away from her face and piled into curls at the back of her head, tumbling down from there. While Gabrielle would never have worn her hair like this in London, she rather liked the effect for her. The lack of formality made her appear softer, more approachable, and yet still gave her an air of grace that she appreciated.

"Do you like it?" A touch of anxiety tinged Molly's voice.

"Oh yes," Gabrielle said, smiling in reassurance. "I love it. I'm sorry, I was wool gathering and then I was just taken aback and how different I look."

"You look happy, if you don't mind my saying so," Molly said. "I think the country suits you better than the city... or perhaps it's the company that suits you so well." That last was said with a sly look that made Gabrielle giggle.

"It might be both," she said a bit ruefully. "I always dreamed of balls and excitement, but I didn't realize how exhausting they could be. And the company there can be quite wonderful or quite tedious. I certainly wouldn't want to spend all my time in the country, but I believe this break from the Season has already been quite beneficial."

"And a new husband doesn't hurt," Molly said cheerfully. Gabrielle had the sneaking suspicion that Molly had decided she liked her new employer and so was encouraging her mistress to be happy with the situation as well.

Surprisingly, she was finding that she was.

DINNER WAS AN INTERMINABLE AFFAIR. Felix was truly wishing he'd made some kind of alternate arrangements to the summer house, but he hadn't thought he'd need some kind of back up. It wasn't that he didn't enjoy his parents' company, he just hadn't wanted it on his honeymoon. Especially since this was not the usual situation for a honeymoon.

When he'd had the thought that he could use his parents to help turn Gabrielle to his side and make her more compliant to the idea of being his wife, he hadn't realized that they might actually distract

Gabrielle from him. It was a strange situation to be jealous of his mother in regards to his wife, and yet there it was. The two of them had obviously bonded during the afternoon and as they chatted about flowers and fauna, the best times to plant certain breeds, and how much sunlight roses needed, he found himself feeling rather left out.

So when his mother suggested having a small dinner with the neighbors, he felt as though he had to put his foot down. Bad enough that he'd spent today sharing his new wife with children and his mother, he wasn't going to spend an evening conversing with neighbors when he should be using that time to seduce Gabrielle. Fortunately, his father backed him up.

"You should plan a celebration for after the Season is over, when more of our neighbors are in residence anyway," his father said amiably, quite a concession for him considering that would swell the guest list numbers. However, it also made his pouting mother perk up, which was all for the good. Gabrielle had looked worried, but she smiled when his mother seemed happy with the proposed solution.

Was she hoping for more socializing? Or did she just want to make his mother happy?

Felix fervently hoped the latter. The idea that Gabrielle was already eager to have others' company, specifically, other men's company, had him grinding his teeth. At least his father had squashed his mother's notion for a dinner party. He was determined that by the time their 'honeymoon' was over that he would have Gabrielle bound to him, emotionally and sexually.

After dinner, his mother played on the pianoforte while he danced with Gabrielle. His father was content to listen to his mother play and watch the younger couple dance, smiling as his foot tapped in rhythm on the floor. He'd never been much of a dancer, although he indulged his wife on occasion, but he'd always had a love of music.

Gabrielle's face was wreathed in smiles as Felix danced with her, her eyes alight. He realized that he'd seen this expression on her face many times in the ballroom, although rarely when she'd danced with him. It was a bit of a relief to realize that it was because she loved dancing, not because she loved the attention, as he'd always assumed.

After all, there was no reason for her to show him a false demeanor, they were already married. And there was no other audience here, so she wasn't playing to anyone else.

She was just happy when she danced, and it showed.

Since the room was otherwise empty except his parents, the dancing was much more intimate, and he didn't have to hand her off to anyone else. Of course, it also meant that his parents were watching their every move, which meant that he didn't feel comfortable trying to actually seduce her. He supposed this would be what his mother called wooing, which he wasn't as comfortable with, but going by the expression on Gabrielle's face, he was doing well enough.

"I like your hair like this," he said as they spun across the floor, her waist tucked neatly into his arm as his mother played a gay waltz. Tendrils of hair brushed against him, swaying behind her as they moved. "It looks beautiful."

A pleased pink flush spread across her cheeks. "My maid likes to try out new styles on my hair. I rather like this one myself."

Giving her his most rakish smile, Felix pulled her a little closer, so that her breasts brushed against his chest. Not close enough for his parents to think anything untoward, but just that little brush of their bodies made Gabrielle blush even harder and almost stumble.

"It puts me in mind of how beautiful it looked last night, spilling across my bed."

"Felix!" She hissed, turning as red as her bottom had last night. "Your parents are right there!"

"They can't hear what I'm saying."

Her little nose went up in the air, making her look both saucy and haughty at the same time. Felix couldn't help but chuckle, but he desisted. Time enough for that as soon as he could sweep her away to his bedroom. A few more dances should satisfy his parents, and then Gabrielle would finally be all his again.

CHAPTER 8

Nervousness made Gabrielle fidget as Felix showed her into his room again, rather than taking her to her own. She didn't know why she should be nervous; last night had been wonderful, but she didn't know what to expect now.

Fortunately, Felix didn't give her very much time to think. As soon as he'd locked the door behind them, he was standing in front of her, pulling her into his arms and lowering his mouth to hers. Gabrielle's lips parted immediately, welcoming him in as she pressed herself against him. Dancing with him had been almost torturous. He'd flirted and charmed, giving her small caresses as they moved, and all Gabrielle had been able to think about was whether or not he'd want to indulge in the marital act again.

She'd certainly hoped so.

It looked as though that wish was coming true. He truly wanted her! Happiness rushed through her as she kissed him back. Last night she had been a bit worried that he'd only been aroused because perhaps it had been a while since he'd been with a woman. Or from spanking her, which he'd obviously enjoyed. Or just because he felt like he needed to do his duty and consummate their marriage.

But his desire seemed to have increased, not waned, and he

showed no interest in spanking her now, and with his duty done there was no burden on him to consummate with her again tonight. Not unless he wanted to. Her heart fluttered, her lower belly filling with warmth and need in response to his ardent kiss.

Nimble fingers divested her of her dress quickly and efficiently as his hands expertly caressed her, fingers sliding against her skin and setting her afire. This was so much better than last night, when she'd been desperate, anxious, and then spanked. Now she was starting to feel a bit desperate, but only physically. Desperate to have him closer to her, to feel his skin against hers, to have his weight pressing down on her... now that she knew how wonderful it felt.

Gabrielle did her best to help him undress, fumbling a bit with unfamiliar garments, but Felix just smiled at her and kissed her, distracting her even more as they slowly moved towards the bed.

The difference between last night and tonight was marked; tonight their movements were slower, more luxurious, and Gabrielle was delighted to be able to explore her husband's body in a way she'd been unable to the night before. She pressed kisses against his chest and shoulders, giggling as he shuddered and groaned, moving her more swiftly towards the bed in response.

Tonight, he fell down on the bed on his back, completely naked and pulled her atop him.

"What are you doing?" she asked, as he arranged her so that he lay back with his head on a pillow while she straddled his waist. She blushed as he looked up at her, his lascivious eyes roaming over her body and drinking in the sight of her. Her loose hair swayed against her bare back, adding to the sensations, and she wondered if Molly had intended the hairstyle to be quite so sensuous or if it was a happy accident.

Strangely, she felt very vulnerable in this position. Her legs were splayed wide over his body, her breasts hanging down without anything covering them, and when he reached up to cup them, her blush burned even brighter.

"You might be a bit sore after last night, so I'm going to let you take charge this evening."

"Take charge?" The surprise and wonderment that filled her voice was unfeigned, and a little uncertain. She wasn't sure she wanted to be in charge; despite spying on the Marquess and Cordelia, not to mention the revelations of the night before, she still didn't feel like she knew what she was doing.

"Well, a bit." The rakish grin he gave her as he rolled her nipples between his fingers had her shivering as heat and need shot through her. She leaned forward into his touch, placing her hands on his chest to keep her balance as she gasped with pleasure. "I'm going to teach you how to ride me, princess."

"Alright," she said softly, meeting his gaze as he fondled her, feeling rather bold and yet shy at the same time. The hungry desire she saw in his dark eyes sent a surge of happiness through her. He wanted her.

Tugging on her nipples, he used them to force her to bend forward more, pulling her lips down to his. Gabrielle moaned with the mix of pleasure and pain emanating from her tiny buds, whimpering against his lips as her lower body met his and she rubbed her slick folds against his hard cock. They didn't feel too sore. In fact, she shifted her hips, feeling the blunt head slide through her wetness, seeking out the entrance to her body.

Feeling needy, she shifted again, pressing down and gasping into Felix's mouth as she finally found just the right spot and he began to stretch her open again. He groaned, one of his hands sliding away from her breast and around to her back, holding her in place as his hips surged upwards, pushing him deeper.

Now she understood what he meant by being sore...

Her insides burned as they stretched again, even though he wasn't fully inside of her, and Gabrielle moaned. Immediately, Felix released his hold on her, moving both of his hands to her hips and pushing her up.

Dark eyes regarded her with constrained patience, his fingers tense on her lower back. "Ride me, sweetheart, just like you would a horse. You control how fast we go."

"I believe I told you I'm not very good at riding," she muttered, making him chuckle. His manhood moved inside of her and she clenched around him, leaning forward a little to keep herself from sliding down completely on him.

"I'll help," he said, his voice full of mischief and erotic promise.

Before she could question just how he meant to do that, his hands were lifting her up and then, just as he was about to slide out of her body, began to pull her back down. Gabrielle gasped, her head falling back at the sensation of sinking down onto him. When she whimpered and tightened, the feeling of being filled, of her body stretching to receive him becoming almost painful, Felix immediately reversed direction and began to lift her up again.

While she hadn't much experience riding a horse, she still immediately understood what he was about and her body relaxed into it. Her thighs strained as she rose and fell, lowering herself a little more fully onto him each time. Even as her inner channel burned, pleasure bubbled along her senses; and she found that she truly enjoyed watching Felix strain and groan as she moved over him. His eyes were mostly fixed on her breasts as they bounced, although sometimes he looked up to watch her face as well, as interested in her expressions as she was in his.

Once she was finally seated fully upon him, his cock thick and pulsing inside of her body, Felix moved his hands from her waist back up to her breasts, cupping and squeezing them gently.

"Ride me, princess," he said throatily, lifting his hips as if to help her start.

He pinched her nipples and Gabrielle moaned as she began to move again, sliding up and down on his cock, shuddering at the sheer pleasure of it. The discomfort and burning was fading away, making space for her growing passion as her honey coated his rod, making each thrust easier, more pleasurable.

There was power in being on top, and yet not for one second did she forget that Felix could wrest away this illusion of control with very little effort on his part. She was riding him because he wanted her to, and if he wanted to roll her on her back, there would be nothing she could do to stop him, even if she wanted to.

This position was very different from last night. She was able to press her sensitive folds down against his body, rubbing her pleasure bud on his groin as her muscles tightened around his cock, increasing her ecstasy. Felix's hands were free to roam and he took full advantage of it, caressing every inch of her that he could reach, returning again and again to torment and arouse her breasts and nipples. When his hand slid down her stomach and between her thighs, the pads of his fingers rubbing against her swollen bud, she nearly screamed at the intense sensation.

Her thighs trembled and then collapsed as she rubbed herself against his finger.

POOR, tired beauty... Felix had enjoyed watching Gabrielle moving above him, pleasuring herself with his body, but it was clear that she was running out of energy. They would certainly have to turn her into more of a horsewoman, so that she would have more stamina for this position. Still, it had accomplished what he'd wanted... she'd realized some of her own sexual power, he'd introduced her to another avenue of pleasure, and he'd been able to enjoy watching her while also ensuring they moved at a pace she could handle.

Flexing his stomach muscles, Felix sat up, curling his arms around Gabrielle and flipping her over onto her back with him above her, his cock still embedded deeply inside of her. Gabrielle shrieked with surprise, her green eyes wide with excitement as he reversed their positions. She arched beneath him, squirming into a more comfortable position as she pulled her hair out from under her back. It flowed across the pillow and sheets like a dark curtain.

Bloody hell.

As much as he liked seeing the bounty of her hair, she'd better never wear it like this anywhere outside of the house. Felix was feeling strangely jealous over it... he didn't want any other men seeing even a single lock of her unbound hair.

"I'm sorry."

The quiet apology brought him out of his jealous seething. "What?" He looked down at her, confused.

"I'm sorry that I couldn't keep um, riding you." Gabrielle's gaze flitted away uncomfortably, a blush staining her cheeks.

"Oh sweetheart," he said with a wicked chuckle. "I'm not. Now it's my turn to ride you."

And then he started to move.

One day she'd have the muscles to ride him with abandon for as long as it took her to climax. That she didn't currently didn't bother him at all. It just meant that he was able to take his preferred place - atop her.

She whimpered and gasped as he thrust with long, slow strokes, designed to tantalize her passions and draw out her pleasure. Although she'd been close when she'd been atop him, she hadn't quite managed to reach her own peak... the delay would actually increase her pleasure now that he'd taken control.

Taking her hands, he wound his fingers through hers as he pinned them down to the bed on either side of her head, lowering his mouth to her breast to take one pert nipple between his lips. Gabrielle keened at the loss of the control, the swell of pleasure. Just as he'd thought, her pussy tightened around him immediately, clenching rhythmically as her climax neared. His feisty, spirited girl liked to be dominated. Last night had not been a fluke. Even without the spanking, she responded to his control, his sensual authority over her.

It was enough to make a man lose his head.

Groaning, Felix thrust hard and fast, releasing her nipple with a pop as he began to move too quickly to keep hold of it in his mouth. Gabrielle's legs wrapped around him, spreading her thighs wide as her hips canted upwards and she writhed beneath him. Her struggles to move her arms only aroused them both as she screamed out her orgasm and he pounded into her, feeling her spasming around him.

With a choked cry, Felix thrust in hard and deep, burying himself inside the hot clasp of her body and letting his own pleasure spill. She clenched around, milking his throbbing cock and draining him of every ounce of seed as they shuddered together in ecstasy.

He panted as he rested his weight on his forearms, placing them on the outside of hers, his grip on her hands softening. Tenderness flowed through him as he pressed kissed to her hairline, moving his lips down the side of her face and over to her mouth. Her eyes were closed, lashes fluttering slightly as he kissed her. Beneath him, he could feel her breasts heaving, pressing against his chest as she caught her breath.

Pressing his lips to hers, he kissed her, slowly and softly, without the urgency that had plagued him before. This was pure enjoyment as his tongue explored her mouth, a kiss for the sake of a kiss, and not something that he'd ever done with any other woman. But with Gabrielle, even though their passion was spent, he still couldn't get enough of her. And she kissed him back, sweetly and submissively, pliant beneath his touch.

When he pulled away, those brilliant green eyes opened again and looked up at him, filled with feminine softness. "Did I do it right?"

It took him a moment to realize that she was speaking of riding him. Chuckling, he rolled off of her and onto his back, wrapping his arm around her shoulder and pulling her against him so that he could cuddle her close. This submissive side of hers that he'd tapped into was eager for praise and Felix found her to be utterly adorable and completely irresistible. A fiery spirit and submissive eagerness? He was a hell of a lucky man.

"Sweetheart, you were perfect."

THE SPLASH DIDN'T GET Felix's immediate attention, but the sharp cry of pain certainly did.

He'd taken Gabrielle out to the creek again, figuring he could stand to share her for the morning as long as he could take the afternoon. He wanted to spend some time teaching her how to ride a horse. She'd been hesitant but willing when he'd suggested his plan for the day. Felix hoped that being on horseback would mean they could go a bit farther afield and he would have some time to woo her in the light of day.

Not that he was unhappy with their time together at night, but his mother had pulled him aside and suggested he find more ways to romance Gabrielle during the day. Exactly how she'd expected him to do that yesterday when she'd claimed Gabrielle's company for the afternoon, he wasn't entirely sure, but the contradiction didn't seem to bother his mother. When he'd suggested riding, she'd nodded approvingly and then whispered a suggestion to bring a small picnic with him before she'd left the dining room.

Gabrielle had been delighted to return to the creek and the children, as he'd expected. He'd rather been enjoying himself as well, especially since it was much cooler by the water than it was at the house.

"My lord!" One of the little girls squealed as he spun around to see what the commotion was. Little Beth was standing beside Gabrielle, who was sitting in the water, her skirts around her knees and her face pale as a ghost. "My Lord, she fell!"

The little girl looked ready to cry, her small hands tugging on Gabrielle's sleeve, blonde ringlets hanging damply from being splashed when Gabrielle had fallen.

"I'm alright, Beth," Gabrielle said, gasping slightly. "I just need a moment."

As Felix approached, he could see the pain in her bright eyes. They were shining like emeralds, awash with a glistening sheen of tears that she was attempting to blink back. Beth's older sister had come running up and was now holding Beth's hand in support, giving Felix a look of apology.

"Put your arms around my neck," he instructed his wife, sliding his hands into the water beneath her. She squeaked, sucking in a breath as he lifted her.

"It's my ankle," she whispered as he straightened, her voice filled with pain that she was obviously trying to hide from the children. "I set down my foot wrong and it caught..."

"Is she alright, my Lord?" Trevor asked. He was standing in the middle of a semi-circle of the boys, all of them watching Felix and Gabrielle with concern. The girls, other than Beth and her sister, were standing on the creek bank, watching in silence. Some of the older ones were looking at him with admiration as he carefully secured Gabrielle in his grip.

"Just a little slip," Gabrielle said, forcing cheer into her voice, before Felix could respond. "Nothing to worry about."

Except, even without inspecting her legs, Felix could tell she'd hurt her left ankle. It was pinker and already a little swollen compared to the right.

"I'm going to take her back to the house," he told the children, their little faces solemn with concern. "Be careful playing out here, we don't want anyone else getting hurt."

They shook their heads, promising to be careful, and Felix started off towards the house. As soon as they were out of sight of the clearing, Gabrielle let out a little whimper of pain, leaning into his shoulder as if drawing on him for strength.

"Just hold on, sweetheart," he murmured, lengthening his stride and trying not to jostle her too much as he hurried back towards the house.

THE THROBBING PAIN in her ankle flared every few steps that Felix took as her leg jiggled. Gabrielle clung to him, biting her lip to keep from crying out. She was already causing him enough trouble, falling and twisting her ankle, and now he had to carry her all the way back to the house. He'd started out moving quickly enough, and while his speed hadn't slowed, she could feel his body straining at the exertion, and he was breathing much more heavily.

She kept waiting for him to yell at her for being so clumsy, but instead he just kept murmuring reassurances, telling her that they were almost at the house. Maybe he'd yell at her there? Part of her couldn't believe that he was still carrying her the whole way. Even through her pain, she admired his strength and chivalry.

Someone must have seen them from the window, because the housekeeper met them at the back door, opening it so that Felix could carry her inside.

"I've sent a maid to fetch your mother," Mrs. Wainwright said, waving her hand at Felix and directing him towards the closest chaise. "And another for some ice. Do we need to call for a doctor?"

"No," Gabrielle said immediately, her anxiety spiking. She squeaked as Felix set her down on the chaise and she realized she was still quite damp. "Oh dear, my skirts are still all wet!"

Immediately she tried to stand, before she ruined the piece of furniture, but then cried out and fell back. Her ankle felt like a sharp spike had been thrust through it when she tried to stand.

"Sit, don't move," Felix ordered, in a hard voice. Gabrielle blinked through her tears, staring up at him. She'd never heard him speak in quite that manner, even when he'd bossed her around before... even when he'd threatened to spank her.

"But I'll get the chair all wet," she protested, not completely cowed, despite the strange note in his voice. She could only imagine what such a piece of furniture cost and how upset his parents might be if she ruined it with damp.

Felix ignored her, kneeling down to pick up her foot as the housekeeper went to get some towels. His hands were surprisingly gentle as he lifted her foot onto his knee and inspected her ankle. It was a bright pink color now and very swollen. Gabrielle bit her lip as she looked at her injured limb. The throbbing pain went all the way up to her knee, making her whimper as Felix very gently removed her walking boot and then cupped her ankle, pressing very gently with his fingers and testing its movement.

"Definitely not broken, just sprained," he said, his voice soothing, running his fingers up and down her calf. "You'll need to stay off it for a while."

Nodding her head, Gabrielle braced herself for the censure and scolding, possibly yelling, that she'd been waiting for. At least Felix didn't seem inclined to summon the doctor. Knowing that her clumsiness actually cost money always worsened the reaction her father had to any of her injuries.

"What's wrong? What happened?" Mother practically flew into the room, a look of worry on her face. Gabrielle cringed, wishing she could slide off of the chaise before Mother saw the wet skirts draped over the expensive damask fabric, but since Felix wasn't moving and he still had Gabrielle's foot on his knee, there was nowhere for her to go. The housekeeper followed, with some towels, and a maid with ice.

"Gabrielle took a bit of a fall," Felix said, looking up at his mother, taking the ice from the maid and packing it into a towel. Gabrielle started in surprise at the complete lack of irritation in his voice. Now that he knew she hadn't broken anything, and considering the distance he'd had to carry her back to the household, his lack of ire was a bit shocking to her. "She'll need to stay off her feet for at least a week."

"Oh you poor dear," Mother said, leaning over to inspect Gabrielle's ankle as Felix pressed the towel-wrapped ice to it. Gabrielle hissed out a low breath of pain and relief as the heat in her ankle subsided.

Next to the Viscountess' spotless appearance in a lilac muslin day dress, her hair braided and secured around her head, Gabrielle felt a bit like a wet goose, but no one seemed perturbed. No one yelled or even scolded. Not even when Felix lifted her up from the chaise to carry her up to her rooms and it was obvious that a large, slightly muddy wet spot had been left on the chaise by her skirts.

It was one of the most surreal afternoons of Gabrielle's life. She was undressed, given a quick wipe down, and redressed, before being comfortably set up in the morning room, where everyone went out of their way to see to her needs.

Felix didn't leave her side for a moment, while his mother flitted in and out of the room as she thought of more items which might make Gabrielle more comfortable or which she was sure Gabrielle would want for entertainment. Even Felix's father stopped by to check in on her, bringing with him a book that he thought she might like to read.

Gabrielle nearly cried at his quiet but heartfelt concern.

HIS WIFE WAS BREAKING his heart.

It wasn't her injury - although he felt helpless and aggrieved every time her forehead wrinkled and her eyes betrayed her pain. It was her surprise, her confusion, at the attention she was receiving. The wonder on her face when his father stopped by to see her, and the reverent way she held the book he proffered up. She practically hugged the damned thing to her like a child holding a stuffed animal.

She also kept eyeing him warily, as if she expected him to bite off her head any moment.

Felix was losing his temper, but not with her. Definitely not with her. He just couldn't countenance what her reactions said about the kind of treatment she was used to.

Not once did she make a complaint. Not a single demand.

It was completely unexpected, especially after the behavior he'd seen in London and the things Cordelia had told him. As he watched his mother fuss over his injured wife, he frowned, trying to figure out what had changed between London and here.

As he thought about it, it occurred to him that he'd actually never seen Gabrielle be demanding in London. She'd been waspish, bitter, and sharp-tongued, and both Philip and Cordelia had told him about a shopping trip where she'd overspent and snuck in a few more items... but looking at Gabrielle's behavior now, he couldn't help but wonder if that had been more of a call for attention than anything else. From what Cordelia had told him, Gabrielle had always been spoiled materially by her father. It was clear from what he'd learned since then that he definitely hadn't spoiled her in any other way.

Cordelia had always been sympathetic to Gabrielle, and insisted that there was a good heart despite her behavior, but now he wondered... was Cordelia too close to the situation? Had she neglected Gabrielle in a different way? After all, she wasn't Gabrielle's mother. She was barely older than Gabrielle herself. Both she and

Philip had mentioned that Gabrielle set herself up as a rival for Cordelia when it came to suitors... could that have influenced Cordelia's behavior with her?

As often as Cordelia had spoken of placating Gabrielle, she'd done so with a kind of martyrish air that had seemed all too understandable at the time. Had Cordelia always seen herself as a martyr when it came to her relationship with Gabrielle? It would be hard to give Gabrielle the kind of acceptance and yet firm guidance that Gabrielle needed if the authority figure saw Gabrielle as a burden that they were resigned to.

Although Cordelia surely had had the best of intentions, Felix was coming to the conclusion that she had not always had the best attitude towards Gabrielle or the best way of handling her stepdaughter.

Just look at the worshipful way that Gabrielle responded to his own mother, who had welcomed her with open arms and immediately assumed her to be wonderful. Perhaps the Baron's attitudes towards his daughter had still been passed on, in slightly altered form, to Cordelia, whereas Felix's mother met Gabrielle with no preconceptions or judgment, despite the hasty wedding.

This was all conjecture, but he swore to himself that when they returned to London, he would keep a closer eye on the relationship between Cordelia and Gabrielle. In London, he'd been rather wishy-washy about whether or not he wanted to court Gabrielle, in large part because her behavior and attitudes were so mercurial, but he'd always been drawn to the side of her that had become fully realized over the past few days. Now that he was certain this was her true self, he didn't want her to fall back into her old, brittle, waspish habits. Part of that would be her own responsibility, of course, but he would protect her from any outside influences that might cause her to revert, even if it came from a friend.

His protective side was irrevocably stirred, and he realized that, even as his heart was breaking for her, he was absolutely in love with his wife. Which would be wonderful if she felt the same for him... he felt as though he'd made some headway in that regard, but it also seemed as though she was just trying to make the best of the situation. Understandable, but he wanted more. He wanted her fiery spirit submitting to him joyfully, he wanted to be the one to bolster her, support her, to shower her with time and attention, love and care, and to protect her and guide her to the happiest life possible. A life with him.

It occurred to him, as he watched his mother and wife, that this injury was actually going to be detrimental to those plans. After all, with an immobile wife, trying to find the privacy to be intimate with her and to seduce her was going to be even more difficult than with a mobile one. And he hadn't been doing a very good job with the latter already.

So when Gabrielle's eyes fluttered in tiredness, and she lay down on the daybed - after allowing Felix to prop up her wrapped ankle on a cushion - and fell asleep, Felix went in search of his father. His mother opted to stay and watch over Gabrielle in case she awoke needing anything. Which was exactly what Felix wanted to speak to his father about.

He found his father in his study, which brought back all sorts of memories from childhood. There had been many times that he'd gone in search of his father, needing or wanting something, and ended up in this room with its familiar faint smell of brandy, musk, wood, and cigar smoke. It seemed much smaller now than it had when he was a child, of course.

"What can I do for you, son? Does Gabrielle need something?" Affection flashed in the Viscount's hazel eyes at his daughter-in-law's name. Felix couldn't help but grin, both because of how easily Gabrielle had captured his parents' hearts and at how well his father knew him.

"No, mother has her well in hand, even if she wasn't napping right now." Although he tried to keep his pique out of his voice, his father caught it anyway.

Setting down his fountain pen, the older man leaned back in his chair, his lips quirking with amusement. "I take that to mean that your mother has Gabrielle so well in hand that you've been rendered unnecessary?"

"Yes," Felix said shortly, coming forward to sit down across from his father in one of the comfortable leather chairs. "I appreciate Mother's concern, and it's not that I don't love you both dearly but..." He paused, trying to think of the least offensive way to phrase his issue.

"But your honeymoon would be much easier without your parents around," his father said, chuckling. He'd never been one to mince words for politeness sake, a trait the Viscountess despaired of.

"More so now that Gabrielle will have to stay off of her feet for at least a week, if not more," Felix said, giving his father a lopsided grin.

"Immobility does make escaping your mother more difficult," his father said, returning the grin, making them look very alike despite the age difference. Then his father sighed. "I suppose I could take her to London for a few weeks."

The resignation in his voice made it sound as though he was facing the hangman's noose. Felix's grin widened.

"I appreciate your sacrifice, sir."

"You should," his father grumbled. "You'll be enjoying the country-side and your new wife, while I'll be surrounded by a bunch of blath-ering twits, when I'm not being harassed by those dragons your mother calls friends."

"You can always escape to Thomas'," Felix suggested. He tilted his head as a thought passed through his mind. "Or you could send Mother there, with her friends. Now that I'm married, I'm sure she'll be feeling rather... motivated when it comes to my brothers."

His father looked a bit cheerier. "That's true. And if she's focused on him then she won't notice if I miss a few events."

Somehow Felix doubted that, but he also know his mother wouldn't put up as much of a fuss about his father's absence if she had something else to focus on. Poor Thomas. Unfortunately for him, Felix was perfectly willing to throw his brother to the wolves - or the young misses in this case - if it meant he would have Gabrielle to himself.

CHAPTER 9

Sending off her in-laws made Gabrielle's eyes well up with tears. She'd rather enjoyed being fussed over by Mother, and she couldn't imagine how she was going to spend her days now. Last night, for the first time, she'd slept (rather poorly) in her own bed. While Felix had said it was because he didn't want to accidentally hurt her ankle, she'd still felt rather abandoned. Then Mother had appeared first thing in the morning with a breakfast tray, plenty of attention to shower down on Gabrielle, and the unhappy news that she and the Viscount would be going to London as soon as they were packed.

"I'll write to you as soon as we arrive," Mother said kindly, leaning down to air kiss Gabrielle's cheeks.

The morning had been spent with the household in an uproar as they hastily packed the Viscount and Vicountess' trunks, but even through that, Mother had taken the time to check in on Gabrielle and entertain her.

Gabrielle pouted, feeling some of her old sulkiness creeping back into her heart. "I don't understand why *you* have to go."

"A wife belongs with her husband," Mother said, her voice

comforting, although her gaze slid to her son instead, where he was hovering in the doorway of the morning room. Just past him in the hall, Papa was coming down the stairs, shouting for his valet to attend him. "And I have things to do in London as well."

"I thought you were staying here this Season, though." Gabrielle knew she sounded petulant. Her father had often given in to her when she'd used this tone of voice, that or sent her away. Cordelia had always attempted to placate her, and the Marquess had just given her a stern look that meant she should be quiet.

Mother kissed her forehead, which just caused more tears to spark in the back of Gabrielle's eyes, her nose feeling as though it was swelling as she tried to sniff away her roiling emotions.

"Lizzie! We need to go."

"We'll see each other again before you know it," she said, instead of answering the question in Gabrielle's voice. As she stood, Gabrielle saw the Viscountess shoot a dark look at Felix.

The Viscount came in to say goodbye to Gabrielle, while she pondered the look that Mother had given Felix. The older man admonished Gabrielle to take care of herself, before repeating that order to Felix. A little smile worked its way onto her lips as she realized that neither parent had told her to look after Felix, only the other way around.

Was it her imagination, or did Mother seem irritated with Felix? Her farewell to her son was not as warm as Gabrielle would have imagined.

"I'll return in a moment," Felix said to her, before following his parents from the room.

She could hear them leaving out the front door, and the clatter as the carriage and baggage train moved away from the house. Frowning, she carefully considered everything she'd seen this morning. Every gesture of the Viscountess', everything she'd said - and everything she hadn't. There was only one conclusion Gabrielle could come to.

So when her handsome husband returned to the room, looking sinfully attractive in his breeches and muslin shirt, with just a vest over it rather than a full jacket, Gabrielle ignored the reaction of her body to being totally alone with him and narrowed her eyes. Unfortunately she couldn't stand up - her ankle was still quite swollen and painful - but she could glare with the best of them no matter her position.

"Did you tell your parents to go to London?"

He stopped immediately, standing in the center of the room, an expression of guilt on his face. It only lasted a moment, but that was all Gabrielle needed.

"How could you?!"

"It's our honeymoon, Gabrielle, we weren't supposed to be spending it with them anyway." His voice was soothing, placating, and he held out his hands in supplication as he started moving towards her again. "You can't possibly have wanted to spend our honeymoon with my parents."

Gabrielle snatched up one of the many cushions on the day bed - not the one holding up her ankle of course - and launched it at him.

He caught it, his dark eyes blazing as his forward momentum ground to a halt. The look in his eyes did not bode well for her, but she was too upset with him to care.

SHE'D THROWN a cushion at him! Felix couldn't believe it. He started towards her again, intent on putting her over his knee. "Gabrielle!"

"Don't come near me!" she shouted at him, her voice rising until it was near to hysteria at the end. Immediately he stopped moving forward. Not because she was going to get her way necessarily, but because he was legitimately confused by the deepness of her distress. "How could you just send your parents away? Just when I was beginning to know them?! You never asked me what I wanted, you just decided and sent them away. So now who is to keep me company when you're busy? Am I just going to be trapped in this room, alone and without anyone to speak with?"

"You'll speak with me, of course, I'm not going to leave you alone on our honeymoon!" Felix protested. He decided to forgive her the thrown cushion. Although she was behaving a bit hysterically, and over-dramatically - making him sound like some villain from a Gothic novel, keeping her trapped in a high tower - she did also make a good point. He had not spoken with her about removing his parents from the household. While he'd realized his mother would be upset, it had not occurred to him that their leaving might have such an effect on Gabrielle.

"I don't want to talk to you, I want to talk to Mother!"

And that was the telling sentence. She hadn't said "your" mother, she'd just said Mother. Felix sighed, remorse filling him. Dammit. He hadn't thought about that aspect of the situation. He'd been so eager to have Gabrielle all to himself that, even knowing how she felt about his parents and his mother in particular, he'd been rather thoughtless. It was not well done of him.

"I'm sorry, sweetheart," he said, holding the cushion she'd thrown at him in front of him like a shield against the tears that were glimmering in her emerald eyes. "You're right, I shouldn't have asked them to leave without asking your feelings on the subject."

The expression on Gabrielle's face was almost amusing. At least, it would have been if he hadn't been feeling both guilty and like a bit of a reprobate - not to mention what it revealed about her life. She was completely taken aback by his apology, almost as if she didn't understand that she was receiving one. There was a kind of shock in her eyes and she was barely breathing. The tears had dissipated as she blinked in confusion. All in all, she looked as though she was struggling to comprehend exactly what he was saying. The suspicion that filled her expression after a few moments only made him feel worse.

"I meant it," he said, keeping his voice soft and imbuing as much sincerity into as he could. "I was only thinking about what I wanted, and I did not mean to, but regardless, that is what happened and it was not well done of me."

"No it wasn't." She said the words tartly, but without the same kind of hysterical passion that she'd used before. In fact, she said them almost defiantly, as if testing him.

Felix raised an eyebrow at her. "That does not, however, excuse your reaction." He held up the cushion. "There will be no more tantrums and certainly no more throwing things if you're unhappy with me. I am always willing to talk, but not if you're behaving like a child."

"Then perhaps you shouldn't treat me like one, and *you* should talk to me, before making assumptions about what I would and wouldn't like!" The hysterical edge to her voice was rising again, the defiant tilt of her chin becoming even more pronounced. "You can't dictate to me how you expect me to feel!"

She threw another cushion at him.

Felix caught it with his other hand and immediately tossed both on the floor, advancing on her with implacable sternness. It was obvious to him that Gabrielle was no longer truly feeling put out, she was throwing the tantrum for the sake of throwing a tantrum. Testing her boundaries. The way a child might, but also the way a submissive woman might when faced with a new situation. They were all alone here now, she was immobile, and she might have seen his apology as weakness. Truthfully, he should have expected this.

"Stop! Stop!" Gabrielle's shrieks went ignored as Felix gently but firmly took her wrists in hand and maneuvered her over his knee, careful to keep her injured ankle on its cushion. "You can't do this! I'm injured!"

"And if you injure yourself more by thrashing around, you will only add to the tally of spanks I'm going to give you," he said, pressing down on her back to hold her in place over his lap. Both her upper and lower body were supported by the day bed, which meant that her rump wasn't as high in the air as he might have liked, but it would do.

"You can't spank me until I feel the way you want me to feel!"

"I said nothing about dictating your feelings, that was your interpretation. I will respect your feelings, and you will respect mine, but I will not tolerate you behaving like a child and throwing tantrums because of those feelings," he lectured as he pulled her skirts up and pushed open the center of her drawers. The white silk framed her bottom nicely, showing off quite a bit of her thighs as well, making his cock stir. Staying away from her last night had been torturous, and he was regretting it a bit now. He bet if she'd been given a good tumble last night, she wouldn't be half so feisty with him today.

WHAT WAS WRONG WITH HER?

There must be something, because she was feeling something strangely like relief as Felix pressed her down over his thighs. Why would she be relieved? Why did some part of her relax as he pulled her skirts up?

She still squirmed, trying to get away, half in shock that he would spank her while her ankle was still injured when he wouldn't even go to bed with her last night, and yet she couldn't get away from the sense of satisfaction that crowded in next to her other emotions... the inexplicable alleviation of her anxiety and unhappiness now that she was over his lap with her bottom bared.

SMACK! SMACK! SMACK! SMACK!

Gabrielle shrieked, squirming harder as her husband's hard hand began to quickly pepper her bottom with short, sharp strikes. There was no measured pause between swats, the way he'd done the last time he'd spanked her or the way the Marquess had always done. In fact, there was barely enough time for her to draw breath as his hand marched down one side of her rump and back up the other, covering her cheeks from crest to the sensitive spots where her bottom met her thighs.

SMACK! SMACK! SMACK! SMACK!

"Ow! Please, Felix, stop!" she managed to gasp out, feeling as though she had to shout to make herself heard over the sound of his palm cracking against her flesh. "I'm sorry!"

"You certainly will be," he said grimly.

SMACK! SMACK! SMACK! SMACK!

Tears were starting to roll down Gabrielle's face as she gripped the fabric covering the day bed. The lingering soreness in her ankle didn't even impinge on her consciousness now that her bottom was starting to burn so hot.

Without pausing the spanking, Felix began to lecture her, his voice loud and droning over the sound of his hand impacting her roasted cheeks.

"You will not throw things at me. If you are upset you will talk to me about it like an adult, without throwing a tantrum. I had apologized, and I don't think you were even upset anymore. I think you just wanted to cause some drama. You don't need to do that to get my attention, wife, and I intend to see to it that you don't enjoy the attention that you do get with that tactic."

Gabrielle shrieked as his hand came down hard on her two sensitive sit spots, as if to emphasis his words and just how much she wouldn't like the result. Tears were rolling down her cheeks as he continued to spank her, his voice aggrieved as he told her how disappointed he was in the way she'd decided to behave. The tears weren't just because of the spanking, they were also because she was sad that his parents had left, and - worst of all - because he was right.

His apology had been sincere and she'd seen that. But she'd still been annoyed with him. Had still been afraid that she'd be neglected now that his mother was gone. She was honest enough to admit to herself that she also hadn't known how to accept his apology... having rarely been offered one that came without conditions. Gabrielle was used to throwing tantrums to get her way, she wasn't used to being told that she was right or that her upset was valid... she usually had to scream and cry and kick up a fuss, and even then people just gave in to placate her. Felix's apology didn't follow the usual script of her life and she'd been at a loss, so she'd just done what she always did and continued pressing her grievance.

She still wasn't sure what reaction she'd expected from him. Part of her was appalled that he'd spank her while her ankle was injured. Another part of her had noted the care he'd taken to see that she was comfortably positioned for her spanking - as comfortable as she could be while her bottom was set ablaze anyway - and was thrilled that he hadn't just walked out of the room. After all, she couldn't follow him if he had. He could have just deserted her and left her alone as a punishment, and honestly she would have felt much worse if he had.

Instead, he was taking the time to spank her because he wanted to correct her behavior. Not stifle her emotions or punish her because he was angry, but because he wanted to have a better relationship with her. Even Gabrielle could recognize that talking things out instead of continuing to screech at him, much less throw a second cushion at him, would have been a better avenue to take. She wouldn't have blamed him if he had walked away. In fact, it was what she'd been expecting. She didn't know why she'd tried to push him away, but she knew she was relieved that he hadn't gone.

With that, Gabrielle slumped against his legs, sobbing piteously but no longer trying to wriggle away from the punishing hand that was still blistering her cheeks. She deserved it. Of course, her body still bucked and squirmed in reaction to the pain, but she wasn't fighting against it anymore.

A few moments later, the spanking stopped, and Gabrielle immediately tensed, crying more now because she was sure that this was the point when Felix would walk away too.

Instead, she was very gently lifted and turned, her burning bottom pressing against his thighs, her skirts still around her hips, and cradled in Felix's arms. He only used one arm at first, as he carefully re-positioned the cushion under her ankle, before wrapping both of them around her and tucking her head into his shoulder. The warmth of his body, the strength of his arms, the comfort that enveloped her, made her cry even harder.

"Shhh, shhh, it's over now," Felix murmured, holding his weeping wife tightly against him. The spanking he'd given her shouldn't have made her cry this much and he was concerned. Concerned enough that even her bare, flaming bottom hadn't been enough to hold his arousal. In fact, the more he'd spanked her and the more she'd reacted, the less aroused he'd been. This was very different from any spanking he'd ever given a woman before. He had to admit, when he'd married Gabrielle, he certainly hadn't expected this much weeping. The fiery spirit that he'd admired covered up quite a bit of unexpected deep misery. Not that it changed how he felt about her, if anything it made him more protective of her. And happy to be her protector, to be needed by her. "You took your spanking very well, sweetheart, and now it's over."

"I'm so-so-so-sorry," she wailed out onto his shoulder. "I do-do-don't kno-o-o-w what's wro-o-o-o-ng with me-e-e-e-e."

"Nothing's wrong with you," he crooned, rubbing her back. "It's over and you're forgiven, Gabrielle, and next time you'll just talk to me and accept my apology, instead of tossing fluffy cushions at my head." Recalling a story that Lord Hyde had once told Felix about his own wife, Felix thought he might be lucky that a couple of cushions were the only things he had to dodge. Even if he hadn't caught them, it wasn't as though they'd do much damage.

Feeling rather helpless, he let her cry herself out, offering up his handkerchief for her to blow her nose when he realized she wasn't going to be able to get control of herself quickly. He winced internally, wondering if some of her sobbing was about the loss of his parents' company. Dammit. He really had messed up a bit on that one. He couldn't bring himself to regret the decision, because this was even more proof that he needed the time to bond with Gabrielle, but he should have at least talked with her beforehand. Prepared her. Reassured her that she wouldn't need their company because she would have his.

Slowly her sobs subsided, leaving her with hiccups and a few whimpers that became softer and softer as she leaned against him. He could feel the utter laxness in her body as she slumped against him, drifting into much needed rest.

Very gently, he stood up and turned around, laying her down on the daybed and pulling her skirts down over her limbs. She snuffled and winced, even in her sleep, as her bottom pressed against the daybed, scooting to find a more comfortable position. Felix didn't let her go very far, because she needed to keep her ankle elevated. Tenderly, he undid the wrappings on it to make sure there hadn't been any further injury to her limb. It didn't look any more swollen than it had earlier, so he was reassured by that.

Re-wrapping her ankle and patting her skirts back down, he sighed. Her lips and eyes were pink and swollen from crying, making her look even younger and more vulnerable than ever. Warm affection slid through him and he leaned over to brush a strand of hair off of her cheek.

Immediately, her hand came up to grasp his wrist, her eyelashes fluttering open, hazy for a moment as she looked at him, and then suddenly filling with alarm.

"Don't leave me alone," she begged, her green eyes opening as wide as he'd ever seen them.

"I won't sweetheart, I was just going to get-"

"No, don't leave," she insisted, sounding a bit panicked as she started to sit up, reaching for him with her other hand, her fingers digging into his wrist.

"Hush," he said firmly, pushing her back down with a hand on her shoulder and seating himself beside her. "I'll stay."

The simple assurance seemed to be enough for her and she settled back down, her eyes fluttering shut again. Her grip on his wrist loosened and he slid his hand into hers, winding their fingers together. The very edges of her lips curled up, not quite into a smile, but close. Felix sat there watching her until her breathing evened out and he was quite sure that she was asleep. Only then did he very gently take her hand out of his so that he could ring for a maid.

He waited at the door, to keep the maid from knocking and accidentally awakening Gabrielle, and asked for food, a water basin, and more handkerchiefs. Just in case. When his wife awoke, she would find him there with her, but he would also have anything that she might need on hand.

Felix was determined that she wouldn't have even a moment to miss his mother.

IT WAS the sore throbbing in her bottom that woke her eventually. Gabrielle winced as she clawed her way up out of sleep. The cheeks of her bottom no longer felt like they were one fire, more like they'd been slow-roasted until well done. It didn't help that her weight was pressing down on them. She started to roll to her side, but was stopped when pain shot up her leg from her ankle to her knee, and she whimpered.

Instantly, hands pressed her back onto her back, and she groaned as her bottom throbbed beneath her, even as the ache in her leg subsided. Her eyes felt gritty as she opened them, and the memories came rushing back. The tantrum, the spanking, the sobbing... her pathetic pleading with Felix to not leave her alone and his shocking acquiescence. The words had come from somewhere deep inside of her; words that she would have never spoken if he hadn't broken down her walls so thoroughly just before.

"Careful, sweetheart," he said. Something cool pressed against her face, wiping her eyes and cheeks. It felt good against her hot skin as he washed away the leftovers of her tears.

Gabrielle was almost afraid to open her eyes again; afraid that she was dreaming, or that when she looked at her husband he would be angry with her over her dramatics. Would he believe that she had truly meant her plea for him to stay?

"Look at me," he said, his voice calmly hypnotic, almost as though he'd read her thoughts.

Unable to ignore the compulsion to please him that surged inside of her, Gabrielle opened her eyes again and met his gaze. He was staring at her with such a tender expression on his face that she had to blink twice to be sure that she was seeing correctly.

"How are you feeling?" he asked.

"Thi-" She practically choked on her dry throat and had to cough several times before she could get the word out. By then, of course, he was already holding a glass of water up for her. Gabrielle winced as she pushed herself up, putting more weight onto her sore bottom. "Thirsty. Thank you."

Taking the glass from him, she practically gulped the water down, eyeing him as he watched her. Just past him, on the table, was a wash basin where she assumed he'd dipped the cloth he'd used to dry her face, a pitcher of water, and a small tray of fruit and biscuits.

"How is your ankle?"

"Fine, thank you," she said, disliking the formality of their conversation, but she felt awkward. Unsure of how she was to behave at this moment. After all, her bottom was still sore and throbbing, but she wasn't angry or resentful - in fact, she wanted nothing more than to curl up in his arms again. Although the way he was looking at her was changing that desire just slightly, to being in his arms.

The way he watched her drink the water made it clear that, despite his absence from her bed last night, he still wanted her. Was still aroused by her. Gabrielle flicked out her tongue to catch a droplet of water on her lips and her husband's pupils dilated, making his eyes seem even darker than usual.

Gabrielle pressed her thighs together, which amplified the ache in her bottom and her womanhood simultaneously. One hurt, the other didn't but it fed off of the first.

As if he knew exactly what she was thinking, Felix's mouth curved into that familiar, rakish grin.

"Don't," she said.

"Don't what?" he asked, leaning closer as her breath came more shallowly.

"It's the middle of the day and you spanked me," she whispered furiously. "Don't... you know." She waved the empty glass at him and he plucked it from her hand, putting it on the table behind him without even looking. Gabrielle leaned back away from him, which did nothing but put her flat on her back with Felix looming over her, his hands coming down on either side of her body. She flushed, all over it felt like, her nipples pebbling at the starkly hungry expression on his face.

"Is your bottom still sore?" he asked, with false solicitousness.

"Yes," she hissed at him. The arousal in his eyes flared again, making her suck in a breath. The ache between her legs was growing. Pressing her hands to his chest did absolutely nothing but make her more aware of how close he was to her, remind her how hard his body was compared to hers.

"Good," he murmured, and his lips dropped to hers.

Gabrielle made a muffled sound of outrage against his mouth, but that didn't stop him. He just used the opportunity to slide his tongue into her mouth, his chest lowering towards hers despite the press of her hands. Shifting above her, he put all the weight of his body onto one arm, freeing one of his hands to cup her breast. The soft mound felt swollen and achy to his touch, and when he pinched her nipple she moaned with the satisfaction of his rough caress.

The throbbing in her bottom was quickly transmuting into a mix of pain and pleasure, of heat and need. Her hands stopped pushing against his chest and began to rub it, sliding her fingers beneath his vest and the thin material of his shirt, teasing him back as he deepened their kiss. Gabrielle had missed him last night. Missed this. She'd felt so alone and bereft that she hadn't even been interested in pleasuring herself in his absence.

His hand went back and forth between her breasts, making them feel even more swollen and achy under his attentions, her nipples becoming turgid little points that rubbed deliciously against the fabric of her dress. Even though the fabric was soft, the sensitivity of the small buds made it feel almost wonderfully scratchy. Gabrielle had begun to cling to him as her hips moved of their own accord, lifting up to reach for contact that was unavailable in their current positions. She kissed him more frantically, her need growing as he played her body like a maestro, creating a crescendo of passion within her.

When he finally began to pull up her skirts, she was practically mindless - which is why she forgot her hurt ankle and tried to lift her hips up to help him, using her feet to brace, and ended up crying out in pain.

Immediately Felix pulled away, leaving her lips feeling swollen and well-used, as he looked down at her sternly.

"Don't move, sweetheart. I've got this. You just keep your leg where it's supposed to be."

"I'm fine," she said, a bit irritably, as she reached for him again.

"You hurt your ankle because you're moving too much, and you'll be getting another spanking before anything else," he murmured as he leaned down to drop another kiss to her lips.

A shudder went through her body at the threat - or maybe it was his fingers trailing up her bare thigh. Either way, Gabrielle was much more careful about how she arched her body when his fingers pressed against her wet folds, delving between them and sliding her cream up to the sensitive bud at the apex of her womanhood. Pleasure sizzled through her as he circled the tiny nub, rubbing against it and then drifting away, teasing her and making it incredibly hard not to writhe the way she wanted to. Her bottom pressed against the daybed, adding to the mixture of sensations as she reveled in the dichotomy of pleasure and pain.

His fingers slid inside of her and Gabrielle nearly bucked as she clamped down around him in needy excitement. Her lips were molded to his, and she moved one of her hands down his chest to the hard shaft pressing against the front of his breeches. Felix groaned against her lips, his fingers twitching inside of her as she palmed the thick length of his cock, rubbing her hand over it despite the barrier. Inside of her, his fingers swirled, pressing against a most sensitive spot and making her gasp along with him.

Then he was moving away, leaving her lips cold and her hand empty, spreading her thighs apart so he could settle between them. Ever the mindful husband, he was extremely careful with her injured leg, moving it with the cushion as he spread her wide.

"Don't move," he reminded her, sliding one hand underneath her to squeeze her bottom and awaken a ghost of the flames that had burnt her there during the spanking. She didn't doubt he would spank her if she hurt herself, even on accident. Gabrielle mewled as his mouth pressed against her slick, sensitive folds a moment after his warning had been issued, licking up the center of her wetness all the way to her pleasure bud.

His fingers, still slick with her arousal, moved lower than their previous position and Gabrielle gasped as they pressed against the sensitive opening of her most intimate orifice.

"Felix!"

"Don't. Move." The implacable command left her quivering as one slick digit pressed into the tight opening, and Gabrielle squeezed her eyes shut, obeying him but unable to face him as he probed the tiny hole. There was a slight burning sensation as her tissues stretched to accommodate him, but it felt good too... strange... full... and even better when his mouth resumed licking and caressing the sensitive flesh above his perverse incursion into her body.

"Oh... oh!" Gabrielle's fingers dug into the daybed as Felix began to thrust his finger back and forth in her anus, stretching the narrow cavity, his tongue sliding into his more usual aperture, and driving her wild with the new sensations that were overwhelming her.

There were no secrets to be left on her body; he was exploring her thoroughly and completely, even those parts of her she'd always thought of as forbidden. His mouth, his fingers, his tongue... he licked down around the thrusting digit into her back entrance and Gabrielle nearly screamed at the perverse pleasure of it. It was all she could do not to buck away, not to wriggle, but she didn't want to hurt her ankle and she certainly didn't want to give Felix an excuse to stop and spank her, when she was so close to the pinnacle that her body craved.

Then his mouth moved back up again, latching onto her swollen clitoris and he sucked hard as his finger mimicked the sex act inside of her bottom. The ecstasy crested and Gabrielle fair screamed as her orgasm blazed through her. Her virgin muscles tightened around Felix's finger, making it feel even larger, increasing the burn as he continued to force the thrusting movement, and sending her to higher heights of rapture. It was decadently wicked and strangely satisfying.

Long licks of his tongue laved her sensitive tissues as she came down from her blissful high, his finger easily sliding out of her barely stretched rosebud and leaving her empty. Gabrielle took a deep, shuddering breath as her eyes opened again, bringing her back to earth and the smug gaze of her husband.

He moved back up to press a kiss to her lips, letting her taste her honey. The sweet, musky flavor wasn't bad, although she couldn't help but make a small face. Still, she opened her mouth for his tongue and she could practically feel his pleasure that she didn't protest.

When he pulled away and began to push down her skirts, she frowned. "What about you?"

"Later," was all he said, before bringing her the tray of fruit and biscuits and hand feeding her.

She felt incredibly spoiled by the attention, even as she was a little perturbed that he wasn't going to slake his own lust, despite the fact that she could see his cock tenting his breeches. He wouldn't even talk with her about it, changing the subject and pushing away her hand when she tried to reach for his manhood, telling her that she was tempting him to put her over his knee again. Exasperated, Gabrielle gave up and let him do what he wanted, which was apparently to indulge her every whim except that one.

Once she resigned herself to that, they passed a pleasant afternoon together. Felix pulled out a book of Shakespeare and they took turns reading from *A Midsummer Night's Dream,* making her giggle as he used different voices for each of the characters. Once both of them wanted to rest their voices, Felix produced a checkerboard and challenged her to a match. Dinner was an intimate affair with just the two of them, and Gabrielle found herself telling Felix about some of the places she'd always wanted to visit. Not just the usual amusements for the English that could be found in France and Italy, but she'd always wanted to see the pyramids and the Great Sphinx of Egypt - which wasn't very ladylike but Felix didn't disparage or attempt to deter her, and Gabrielle felt hope rise in her as he listened with interest.

It wasn't until that night in bed that he finally indulged himself, showing her a new way to make love in the process. Gabrielle lay on her side, her bad ankle on top with a cushion between her feet, while

Felix pressed into her from behind. His cock felt huge in that position, his groin rubbing against her still slightly tender buttocks, his fingers rubbing her clit and squeezing her breast, moving slowly back and forth as he penetrated her from behind until they both cried out in ecstasy.

They fell asleep in that position, Gabrielle finally deciding that perhaps his parents' absence wasn't the worst thing in the world.

CHAPTER 10

"Mail from London, Mr. Hood," Mr. Taylor, Felix's parents' under butler said in a solemn tone, practically bowing as he handed them over to Felix. Everything about him was impeccably correct, upright, and starched. Felix managed to keep from smiling in amusement as he accepted the offering.

Since his parents had taken Mr. Appleby, their head butler, with them to London, Felix and Gabrielle had been left in Mr. Taylor's care and it was obvious he took his responsibilities seriously. In his late twenties and having been in the household for fifteen years, this would probably be his first time running the household in the absence of Mr. Appleby. Felix couldn't remember himself or his brothers ever having been in residence on the estate when his parents weren't. Skinny as a stick, with a rather large Adam's apple, and straw-like hair, he somewhat resembled a very stern looking scarecrow.

Well, until he turned to Gabrielle, who was propped up on the daybed again, with utter worship in his eyes. "Mrs. Hood."

"Thank you, Mr. Taylor," she said, accepting her letters with a sweet smile. The man gulped, bowed again, and retreated. Now Felix really couldn't hide his amusement, although neither his wife nor the under butler seemed to notice, which was probably for the best.

Not that he blamed the man for his obvious adoration. Gabrielle had that effect on the staff, and the young men in particular were susceptible to her genuine sweetness towards them, not to mention her beauty. She was looking particularly lovely today, in a bright green day gown that just matched her eyes, trimmed with ivory ribbon, and her hair braided and pinned up to keep it off of her shoulders, revealing the long line of her neck. She was practically glowing with an inner light, which Felix smugly attributed to himself.

With his parents out of the way, he'd made it his mission to keep his wife entertained and happy - and well sated. This morning he'd woken her by kissing her all over, ending with the tender flesh between her legs while she'd moaned and cried out in ecstasy. The more he indulged her, the more submissive she seemed to become, at least in bed. There wasn't a single part of her that she denied him, not even when he renewed his interest in her virgin bottom hole, first with his finger again and then with his mouth. In fact, she'd rather seemed to like it once she got into it.

Felix grinned down at his kippers, feeling wonderfully smug. So their marriage had gotten off to a rocky start; Gabrielle was even more than he'd realized, and their compatibility in the bedroom even more than he could have hoped for.

"Cynthia, Arabella, and Cordelia all wrote me," Gabrielle said, looking delighted. "And one from your mother." She held up a thin envelope, turning her head to beam at him, obviously thrilled that his mother had written so quickly. "Do you think I should have written the others sooner?"

"No, we're on our honeymoon and they understand that," Felix said, reassuring her as her brow puckered in thought. "That's why they waited several days to write."

"I see," she said, her expression clearing. He couldn't help but feel happy at her complete lack of suspicion and her willingness to accept his explanation. It was all true, of course, but he was fairly certain that Gabrielle in London would have met his explanation with cynicism, and she certainly wouldn't have taken him at his word or let herself be guided by him.

Glancing through his own correspondence, mostly business, a note from Walter, one from Thomas, another from Manchester (Arabella's eldest brother), and one unexpected one...

"I have a note from Cordelia as well," he said in surprise, and immediately wished he hadn't.

Gabrielle's entire body froze in the middle of unfolding one of her own letters, her expression going completely blank and still, like a statue. He wanted to curse as he could practically watch her personality and happiness withdraw.

Only two things managed to do that so completely - trying to talk about her past and anything to do with Cordelia. Although, she'd seemed perfectly happy to have Cordelia write a note to her, she just didn't seem to know how to react to Cordelia writing a note to Felix as well. Truth be told, Felix wasn't entirely certain how to react to it. Why hadn't Cordelia just written them one note, together? That was the usual thing to do when writing to a couple.

But more importantly, what did he do now to fix this?

Ignore it? Read it later when Gabrielle wasn't around? Or read it now and hope that she didn't attach undue importance to it?

For his own peace of mind, Felix decided to read it immediately. He didn't think he could take a morning of Gabrielle being withdrawn from him; drawing things out would just be torture for them both. Better to get it over with.

"Perhaps Philip had something to say," he said, as casually as he could, picking up the letter and opening it. Gabrielle didn't respond and kept her eyes averted, focused on the letter that she was now finishing opening with very slow, deliberate movements. Something inside his chest clenched as he felt like there was now an icy barricade between them, despite the fact that she was sitting beside him. If someone could be said to be reading furiously, that's what Gabrielle was doing, with her cheeks pinked and her forehead furrowed.

Felix looked down at Cordelia's flawless handwriting. The letter wasn't very long, nor was there anything of great import in it or anything that couldn't have been said to Gabrielle. At the end was a post script from Philip, saying that he looked forward to seeing Felix and Gabrielle and hoped that they would be as happy as he and Cordelia, which made Felix smile. He already felt quite happy with Gabrielle, despite her prickles and tantrums, and despite the uphill battle into her affections.

After all, anything of value was worth fighting for.

Feeling her eyes on him, Felix handed the letter over to her as she blinked at him with astonishment cracking open the social mask she'd had covering her emotions. "Here, sweetheart, you can write back for both of us and I'll just add a post script at the end as Philip has. There's no point in both of us sending letters."

Gabrielle's slim fingers held the letter gingerly, her wide eyes blinking in confusion and - did he dare hope? - relief. "Are you certain?"

"Oh yes," he said dismissively, turning his attention to the other letters at his elbow. Picking up the one from Manchester, he peeked over the edge of it at Gabrielle who was now studying the letter Cordelia had sent to him as if it held some kind of vast secret.

That didn't bother him. He was too happy that the icy barricade had melted just as swiftly as it had appeared. Apparently he had reacted correctly to soothe Gabrielle. Hopefully Cordelia's letters wouldn't exacerbate the situation. Perhaps Gabrielle was jealous that he was receiving attention from her stepmother as well? She hadn't exhibited any of that when his mother doted on him, but after all, his mother was his. Perhaps she didn't like sharing Cordelia's attention with him because Cordelia was hers, even she didn't exactly see Cordelia as a mother figure.

She had very few people that were hers, after all.

"Thomas and Walter sends their regards," he said to her, after he was done scanning their letters. Both were very short and said much the same as Manchester's - reassurance that everything that could be done was being done to clear up any lingering rumors from Gabrielle trying to elope with Fenworth, and that Fenworth himself had fled to the countryside to rusticate for the rest of the Season. Of course, he was fleeing his debts, not the scandal he'd tried to cause, but without him in town any gossip would blow over much more quickly. They reassured him that people were much more interested in some other scandal that had cropped up the day after he and Gabrielle had married.

"Send them mine back, please," she said, smiling.

There was still a bit of tension in her demeanor, but it didn't seem to have anything to do with him, to his relief. Still, he would read the letter that Cordelia had sent to Gabrielle later, when he got a chance. He didn't want to ask to read it, since it was such a sore topic with his wife, but he wanted to know why Cordelia had sent them separate letters.

THE FLUSH of excitement over receiving mail from London had faded the moment Felix had announced that he'd received his own letter from Cordelia. A hard little knot had formed in her stomach at the look of surprise and pleasure on his face. He hadn't expected or asked for the letter, that much was clear, but he'd been pleased to see it. Gabrielle had gone numb inside, because the other option was to cry.

And she wouldn't do that.

When he scanned the letter and passed it over to her, seemingly uninterested in responding to it, most of that knot dissolved. Most of it. She still couldn't quite get past that look of pleasure... why had he become disinterested? Was it because the letter hadn't contained the kind of missive that he'd desired? Or was it because he'd noticed Gabrielle's distress?

The latter would be the most desirable reason, in her opinion. After all, even if he was pleased that Cordelia had written him, he'd then chosen Gabrielle's feelings over her stepmother's.

To keep from completely coming apart at the seams over breakfast, Gabrielle focused steadfastly on the letters she'd received. Viscountess Hood sent a very short missive to say that they'd arrived safely in London, she was very happy to be in the city although she missed Gabrielle's company already and looked forward to when they could enjoy the Season together as mother and daughter. She sent her love to Felix and wished them a happy honeymoon. Smiling, Gabrielle set the letter aside for Felix to read if he wished.

Cynthia's letter was longer and much more newsy.

Dear, naughty Gabrielle,

You scandalous chit, how I adore you! I wish I hadn't missed all the fun, but I've been a bit naughty myself this Season and have missed out on several events due to it. Wesley seems to think that getting me with child will slow me down and has bent his efforts to that effect.

Blushing, Gabrielle giggled at Cynthia's indelicate references, as well as her unabashed enjoyment of misbehavior.

Fenworth has fled, so any gossip around you has died down very quickly, though of course I've heard quite a bit from Eleanor (before she and Edwin left town) and Arabella. Arabella and I have formed a bit of an alliance, now that you're absent from the scene... I don't believe her brothers approve, but as long as my Wesley is on hand to keep me in line they don't quite disapprove either. Manchester is even more of a stuffed shirt than my own husband! I pity the woman who ends up with his scowling demeanor in her bed. Although, truthfully, Wesley is not much of a stuffed shirt except when it comes to my *behavior, whereas Manchester is one all of the time. Poor Arabella! I do believe she wouldn't be having any fun without my presence, so I am endeavoring to keep her entertained until you return.*

Everyone is agog that you've so quickly reformed Mr. Hood. You've garnered quite a few admirers among the men, as well as the old dragons, for such a feat. The debutantes all think you're a hero and hope to duplicate your feat, the silly things. I try to tell them that catching a rake is a very different thing from reforming one.

The key, of course, is to keep him entertained, addicted, and ever unsure of what you're going to do next. Wesley has no time to look at other women, even if he desired to, because he's too worried about what might happen if he takes his eyes off me. Although I don't worry overly much about it as I know he loves me, but I don't intend to ever let his interest wane, either. He shall spend his entire life trying to catch me and I will spend mine trying to keep him, and that suits us admirably. Of course, Eleanor, Irene, and Grace handle their husbands a bit differently in practice, but I believe the basis precepts are the same. That's my bit of marital advice!

More salacious tidbits of gossip followed, including an account of how Lady Winchester - a widow with a remarkable resemblance to Cordelia, and an unfortunate interest in Felix - had taken up with Felix's middle brother, Walter, after the news of Felix's wedding to Gabrielle. That was a relief. It seemed that the lady hadn't truly had an interest in Felix, just in a man - or perhaps in a rake. So there should be no ill feeling from that end and hopefully one less person that Gabrielle would have to eventually deal with.

She was also sure to mention that no one seemed very interested in Gabrielle and Felix's hasty wedding, in large part because the very day *after* their wedding, the Marquess of Butte's daughter, who had been engaged to the Duke of Cornwall's second son, eloped with his first son and heir. There was nothing to brush away interest in a scandal like another, much larger, much more obviously scandalous scandal.

Cynthia's letter was entertaining reading, and it was with a light heart that she moved into Arabella's. She didn't put Cynthia's letter where Felix could read it; she wasn't sure she wanted him seeing Cynthia's advice about marriage. If she was going to take it, and entice Felix to chase her for the rest of their lives, then it was better he not know about it. Rakes did like a chase, she'd once heard. And, unlike Cynthia, she didn't have her husband's love to bind him to her. Although he obviously cared, at least a little.

Glancing at him under her eyelashes as she unfolded Arabella's letter, she smiled a little to see him completely engrossed in his own correspondence. His fork stabbed his plate several times as he tried to eat without taking his eyes from the letter. No feminine handwriting on that one, so she assumed it was business. His pile of letters was much larger than hers, but he was plowing through them at a much faster rate. Perhaps they were shorter. Or not as interesting.

My dear Gabrielle,

I miss you so already! Just a few days without your company and this Season is already a dreadful bore. Although, of course, the scandals never stop, Isaac and Benedict have taken it upon themselves to make sure that not even a hint of such comes near me again. They've chased off any interesting suitors and I'm left with a pack of the dullest, most strait-laced men in all of England. They can't possibly think I'll actually choose my husband from such an assemblage! I'd rather drown myself in the Thames first!

Lady Spencer has been my only solace in these dreary times, although she's hardly a stalwart companion. Not a ball goes by that she and the Earl don't disappear for at least an hour. Off doing that, *I expect, because she always returns just a little mussed and her skirts rumpled. Not that she'll tell me anything about* that. *What is the point of having married friends if they won't divulge important information?*

Oh dear... Gabrielle pursed her lips in amusement. Poor Arabella. Stifled by her brothers and not even Cynthia would talk to her about bedroom matters. Not that Gabrielle would be much better. She'd known enough before, but she'd always pretended ignorance to Arabella. It wasn't exactly the easiest topic. Well, at least now she had some time to think of what she would say to her friend.

Like Cynthia, Arabella reassured her that any scandal had been quickly swept under the rug, and cited the shocking elopement as the final nail the in coffin. With the Hood brothers, the Marquess of Dunbury, the Duke of Manchester, Lord Hyde, and the Earl of Spencer circling the wagons and protecting Felix and Gabrielle from undue gossip, no one wanted to speculate on the circumstances of their marriage, not when there was much juicier meat to be had. The way Arabella told it, her brother glared away anyone who so much as hinted that perhaps there was something amiss with the hasty wedding. Gabrielle could picture that - the Duke of Manchester was a very large, very imposing, and very stern man. His glares made quite an impression on everyone except Arabella and, to some extent, Gabrielle. Despite his demeanor, he was actually quite kind, especially to his sister, despite the trials she put him through.

The silly chits chasing my brothers have gotten worse now that you're away and married. I do believe they thought that one or the other must have been courting you. Now we're assaulted from all sides, and I'm fair buried in compliments. I wore a new dress last night and I could scarcely greet anyone without being told how utterly fantastic I looked - as if I needed their brown-nosing to be aware - and what a smashing hit my dress was. I swear, I could dress in a barrel and these twits would declare it a new fashion, if only I'd introduce them to poor Isaac. As if I'd ever let some silly hen get her claws in him that way! Not that he appreciates it, since his response is to send me onto the dance floor with the latest bore.

Arabella's entire letter was like that - gossip and descriptions of her latest purchases interspersed with derision over her brothers' strictures and dramatic bemoaning of her life without Gabrielle. It made Gabrielle giggle, but it also made her miss her friend.

London and her life there seemed so far away and so long ago, although in reality it was only half a day's travel and she'd only been on the Hood estate for a few days. Still, she and Arabella had been nigh inseparable in London. Cynthia had spent quite a bit of time with them as well, but she'd also been distracted by her husband, often disappearing during balls for a length of time with him. Now Gabrielle had a much better idea of what they'd been doing.

She kept Cordelia's letters for last, which was truly a pity as reading them completely ruined her mood.

THE SMILE on Gabrielle's face had been strained all morning. Felix had done his best to distract her with checkers, and then began teaching her chess. Gabrielle had truly enjoyed that, her eyes coming alight as she pondered the more complex game. Since Felix was only a negligible chess player he wasn't able to explain the strategies as well as someone else might, but it also meant that it wouldn't take much for Gabrielle to reach his level. She picked up the basics very quickly and her attitude was much more competitive than it had been during checkers.

She fairly crowed with triumph when she managed to capture his queen during the third game, and Felix realized he had better apply himself more to his tactics and less to admiring his wife.

"You aren't letting me win, are you?" she asked, eyeing him suspiciously.

"No," he grumped, bringing back her smile, as she saw his irritation with himself. "You're a much faster learner than I was."

"It's fun," she said, her eyes scanning over the pieces. She was much more focused on the game than he was. "Like watching a play... or people in a ballroom. Every move has a counter, like a dance." And Gabrielle was a superb dancer.

"Perhaps we should start playing for wagers," he murmured, moving his rook out of danger of the trap she'd set. Gabrielle pouted at him, although her eyes sparkled.

"Wagers? How would one wager on chess?" she asked, moving a pawn forward.

"Like this... I take your pawn," he said, sliding his knight across the board and picking up the little white piece, "and you give me a kiss."

Gabrielle laughed as he leaned forward, cupping her chin with his hand and lowering his lips. She met his kiss with her own, their tongues sliding together, and his hand slid down to the sensitive nape of her neck, brushing it with his fingers. Since she was mostly immobile, thanks to her ankle - despite the reduction in swelling - he had to go to her, but he didn't mind. The kiss was eager, playful, but by the end she was just as distracted as he had been.

Now when she looked down to study the board, her cheeks were flushed a pretty pink and she kept peeking under her lashes at him. "What about me? What do I receive?"

"What do you want?"

She bit down on her lower lip, her cheeks flushing even brighter, piquing Felix's interest. He raised his eyebrows at her, leaning forward to rest his forearms on his knees as he tried to meet her eyes.

"Now you must tell me," he teased, giving her his best, most charming grin. "I have to know what put that pretty pink in your cheeks."

Gabrielle tossed her head haughtily, refusing to be embarrassed, meeting his challenge head on, and arousing him more than if she'd attempted to play coy. "Very well. I wish you to remove a piece of clothing as forfeit."

Now it was her turn to laugh at his shocked expression, laughter that he joined in with after a moment. Completely unexpected, brazen, and yet somehow still very Gabrielle. She met his challenge with her own, and knocked him off balance for good measure.

"Then make your move," he said, slowly unbuttoning the front of his vest in preparation. Also as a distraction. Gabrielle was now watching his fingers as they popped each button out of its hole, rather than looking at the board. Since he wasn't more formally dressed, he needed her distracted otherwise he'd probably be completely nude very quickly.

His tactic worked well enough that he didn't lose his vest until a couple moves later, and only after collecting a second kiss. This one even deeper and more lingering than the first.

The second piece of clothing he lost was his shirt, leaving him sitting bare-chested (but for his cravat) across from Gabrielle, who was obviously having more and more trouble concentrating on the game. As he'd meant her too, which was why he'd chosen the shirt to go. Her green eyes kept flicking up to look at his exposed body, and Felix smiled like the cat who ate the canary, his gaze steady on her. Enticing. Distracting.

When he took one of her knights during his next turn, he decided he wanted more than her lips.

"Felix! What are you doing?!"

"I never specified a destination for my kisses," he said, chuckling as he nimbly unbuttoned the front of her day gown, baring her breasts. Gabrielle gasped as his lips brushed over her skin, his hands parting the opening in her dress.

"At least lock the door! What if one of the maids comes looking for us?" she whispered urgently. "Anyone could walk in!"

Doubtful, but if it would make her feel more comfortable, then he would indulge her. It was the work of a moment to hop up and lock the door, before returning to her, leaning her back to bare her throat and chest to him. The sun coming in through the window was a golden glow on her skin as his lips moved down from her neck, over her collarbone, and then to her breasts. Gabrielle whimpered as he took each tightly furled nipple in turn, tonguing each bud as he suckled, before letting them free, leaving them slightly shiny.

Then he quickly returned to his seat.

Gabrielle's green eyes flared brightly before narrowing at him, her breasts heaving as she panted for breath. Her dress gaped, framing the creamy mounds and pretty pink nipples, as if inviting Felix to return and continue his kisses and caresses. His cock was on board with that, but he was having too much fun with the game.

With a long, slow look at him, Gabrielle sniffed and then turned her attention back to the board, leaving Felix frowning, but only for a moment. The stiffness of her nipples and the color in her cheeks gave away her ardor, despite her pretense otherwise. He loved that she was pretending. He especially loved that she was pretending her open gown didn't bother her, braving her discomfort in order to distract him more fully. It was working. Seeing her so disheveled, her breasts framed so nicely, and the pretty pink flush on her cheeks made him want to study her, not the chessboard. Her shoulders rounded forward, trying to hunch a little, and revealing that she wasn't quite as confident as she would have him believe.

Lovely.

This time he took another of her pieces before she could take one of his. He wondered if she'd realized that he was no longer concerned with winning, he just wanted to decimate her troops and win as many kisses as he could.

This one started at her uninjured ankle and Gabrielle gasped and giggled as he pushed her skirts up ahead of his lips, kissing all the way to her womanhood. He could feel her tense, as if waiting for him to leave her now that he had her aroused and eager, the way he had with her breasts. Instead, he spread her thighs wide and kissed the wet, swollen flesh beneath her dark curls, licking his way up.

"Checkmate," he whispered.

"Is not!" Gabrielle protested, trying to push him away. Felix just chuckled and crawled up her body, purposefully kicking his foot out to knock over the board and send the pieces scattering across the floor. She scowled at him. "You did that on purpose."

"I have a more interesting game," he said, leering at her as found her wet folds with his hand, sliding his fingers immediately into the warmth of her body and making her moan. "It's called, how many times can I give Gabrielle pleasure in one afternoon... and I plan to win." He used his thumb to circle the bud of her clitoris, feeling the little nubbin stiff and swollen against his touch, and making her hips jerk.

"How do you win?" she asked breathlessly, her back arching as his fingers curled inside of her. She reached up to take hold of his shoulders, her nails digging into his flesh. Pumping his fingers, Felix enjoyed watching her writhe for him as he stirred her arousal, coating his fingers in her wet heat.

Instead of answering, he just chuckled and thrust his fingers again, leaning down to kiss her nipples as they thrust upwards in response. She whimpered, her hands sliding into his hair, pulling him against her, holding him in place as he suckled her nipple, her hips moving, riding his fingers. Sexual smugness filled him at how uninhibited she was, how eager.

She had her first orgasm on his fingers, squeezing them tightly as he expertly used the heel of his hand to stimulate her clit. Then he moved his mouth down to her pussy, sliding his honey-soaked fingers into her crinkled rosebud, stretching the tiny hole while he licked and sucked her to a second, sobbing completion. Her breasts jiggled, nipples pointed heavenward, as she tugged on his hair and screamed with ecstasy.

Rolling her over onto her stomach, he propped up her hips with two cushions, making sure that her injured ankle was taken care of as well, before sliding into her smoothly from behind. He wouldn't have risked this position with her injury, but she was too satiated and limp to really move back against him as he began to ride her from behind. Slow, smooth strokes of his cock into her sopping wetness, his fingers sliding easily back into her rear entrance, filling her completely as she moaned and clenched around him. He could feel his cock moving through the thin separation between her holes, and the sensation was fantastic.

Gabrielle was his dream woman... laid out in front of him, vulnerable and submissive, giving him access to her entire body - not just without protest, but with passion. She whimpered, she moaned, and she cried out in pleasure as he took her from behind, slowly at first and then moving faster and faster, slamming into her with force and watching the flesh of her ass jiggle.

Sliding his fingers from her tiny hole, as his movements began to make it difficult to keep his place, he began to swat her bottom, moving his hand all over. Not a single blow was enough to really hurt her, or even pink her skin, but her moans increased twofold in response, her pussy clenching down around his thrusting cock like a vise. Watching her flesh jiggle under his assault, the pink lips of her pussy stretched tightly around his shaft, Felix's lower back began to tingle, his balls tightening.

An extra hard smack in the middle of Gabrielle's fleshy cheek made her shriek, and then her pussy spasmed hard around him, rippling as she began to climax. He groaned using both hands now to grip her hips, slamming into her with as much force as he could, the tingling in his lower body spreading and shifting into sexual bliss as he began to empty himself into her ready body. Spurt after spurt of his seed being pulled from him by the contractions of her pussy, milking him dry.

He slumped forward, totally drained, his body draping over hers. Her head was turned to the side so that he could see her profile, her eyes closed, thick lashes resting on her pink cheeks, a small smile curving her lips.

Felix brushed a kiss over her temple, flexing slightly and enjoying the way she shuddered beneath him.

"Sweetheart? Did I win?" he asked, impishly.

"Mmmm."

He chuckled, disengaging from his exhausted wife, and set about putting her to rights. Pulling her skirts down and straightening them, rolling her onto her back with her ankle appropriately propped up, and then giving her gorgeous breasts each one last kiss before doing up the demure buttons of her gown. Through it all, Gabrielle stayed limp, only stirring occasionally, too exhausted to do anything but sleep. He'd quite worn her out, he thought smugly.

Once she was presentable again, he unlocked the door, and went back to the table, sitting where he could watch her. She lay in quiet repose, her chest moving slightly as she breathed in her sleep. Truly a sleeping beauty.

Picking up the letter Cordelia had written her, he finally indulged his curiosity, and once he had, he almost wished he hadn't.

He loved Cordelia, like a sister, but what was wrong with her? The letter that she'd sent to him had been like a letter from a sister to a brother - full of her and Philip's activities, the balls, the riding lessons, her new horse and her new friends. In stark contrast, her letter to Gabrielle was filled with gentle scolds. Gentle, except that they weren't offset by anything to make them more palatable. No news. Nothing of Cordelia's life or even light gossip. Just an accounting of the gossip that had sprung up after the wedding, a reminder to be thankful to Arabella's family, the Hoods, and Philip and his family for their support, and some rather stilted marital advice. The majority of which seemed to revolve around not causing Felix any trouble.

While he appreciated the sentiment of that last, the overall tone of the letter was one of censure. He wouldn't have thought Gabrielle particularly sensitive before marrying her, but now he knew differently. Now he'd seen firsthand exactly how Gabrielle had reacted, to both letters. The difference between them was night and day - it was obvious Cordelia enjoyed Felix's friendship and that she thought of Gabrielle as a burden, and that she didn't expect much of her as a wife.

Incensed on Gabrielle's behalf, after thinking through everything for a few minutes, he could only sigh and shake his head. He would have to read through whatever response Gabrielle wrote to Cordelia to ensure it wasn't too antagonistic, even if it would be somewhat deserved. Now that he'd seen each of their perspectives, it was obvious to him that the easing of tension in their relationship would have to come from their husbands.

Part of that would come from Cordelia only receiving one letter in return for her two. Now, even though he wished he could have kept Gabrielle from being hurt by comparing the tone of the two letters, he was glad that he'd reacted the way he had over breakfast this morning. Cordelia would know that both of her letters had been received and that he and Gabrielle were a united front. Although he appreciated her protectiveness of him, it was not her responsibility, and he was a bit annoyed that she didn't show any such consideration towards Gabrielle.

Not that Cordelia should think that Felix would harm Gabrielle in any way, but her entire letter to Gabrielle had sounded like one long assumption that Felix would be a wonderful husband to Gabrielle and that Gabrielle would have to work hard to deserve that. Nothing was further from the truth, and he couldn't fathom why Cordelia should think so. After all, she'd often been the one defending Gabrielle... although her defense was usually along the lines of Gabrielle not truly knowing better. Gabrielle as a person to pity because of the way her father had treated her. Gabrielle as a hapless victim of fate.

But she was so much more than that. It was becoming more and more clear to him that, despite her affection for Gabrielle and her defense of her, Cordelia didn't see her stepdaughter very clearly. Understandable, perhaps, but Cordelia and her feelings were not his concern. Gabrielle was.

Putting the letter back down on the table, he got up and moved over to the daybed, crawling on beside his wife and gently sliding one of his arms underneath her head as a pillow. Murmuring sleepily, she turned her face into his chest, happily snuggling in. He would keep her safe and make her happy, even if he had to face off against one of his best friends to do it, for he was quite sure that Philip felt the same way about his own wife.

CHAPTER 11

"I think I'll write a letter a day," Gabrielle said over breakfast. She hadn't had time to write yesterday. After her nap, Felix had righted their chess game and they'd finished it. He'd won, of course, but she'd come very close to beating him, she was sure of it. Today he'd promised her another match, as well as some time in the gardens, although she would have to walk with a cane, with him on her other arm. "Would it be too much trouble to send the letters that way rather than all at once?"

"Not at all," he said with a smile. "Appleby will send someone to take the post down, no matter how many or few letters we have each day."

"Wonderful. I thought I might write your mother back today, and then Arabella tomorrow, then Cynthia, and then Cordelia." She eyed Felix to see if he reacted to her proposed schedule. He just smiled, nodded, and went back to his coffee and newspaper, leaving Gabrielle feeling quite pleased that he didn't care it would be several days till she wrote Cordelia back.

Besides, she needed some time to decide what she would say to her stepmother. She was still irked by the letter Cordelia had sent to Felix. It had been overly friendly, entirely too familiar, and perhaps even a bit flirtatious. Although Gabrielle had no doubt that Cordelia loved Philip and would never betray him - it just wasn't in her stepmother's personality - it appeared that she still wanted her hooks in Felix as well. Even though he was now married to Gabrielle.

If Felix had responded positively to that, or wanted to write Cordelia back on his own, Gabrielle didn't know what she would have done. Her hope that Felix might eventually prefer her to Cordelia would certainly have dwindled. Now she dared to hope that perhaps he already was starting to prefer over her stepmother. He'd been surprised and pleased to have his own letter from Cordelia, but he hadn't been interested in writing her back. Even though her letter had been excessively friendly.

"Would you like to meet my hounds today?" Felix asked, his voice boyishly eager.

It amused Gabrielle how such a foreboding looking man could even look or sound boyish, but he did on a regular basis. Gabrielle rather liked both sides of his personality - the sweet, more boyish side, and the stern authoritarian, even if the latter did spank her. The spankings hadn't been so bad, even though they'd hurt, because of what had followed after.

Warmth. Comfort. The feeling of being loved. Even though he hadn't said it, even if he didn't yet, Gabrielle would do her best to see that he would.

So of course, there was only one answer that she could give him.

"Yes, of course."

Her husband beamed at her and she smiled back, happy with his happiness. Even if she wasn't very interested in dogs, it wouldn't hurt her to show an interest in his passions. Mentally, Gabrielle started making a list of things she could do for Felix. Visit his dogs as often as he wanted, let him teach her how to ride (not that she was disinterested, but she didn't feel a burning need), ensure that the cook made his favorite meals regularly... she was sure that Taylor would know Felix's preferences for liquor. At the very least, she could ensure whatever household they were in was well stocked.

Happy to have a plan, Gabrielle found herself smiling even more broadly as she accompanied him down to the kennel.

KEEPING an eye on Gabrielle to ensure that she wasn't putting too much weight on her ankle, Felix couldn't help but grin at the way she was cooing over the half-grown pups of his bitch's latest litter. She hadn't been adverse to coming to see his dogs, but she hadn't been particularly enthusiastic either. That had changed the moment she'd met the young litter. They were out of their puppy stage, but still awkwardly adorable with oversized paws and legs that made them look as though they were flopping about while they played. Gabrielle, leaning on the cane she was now using to assist her ankle while she walked, laughed as they gamboled around her, holding out her hand to whatever eager pup came up for attention.

"Did you ever see Philip's hounds?' he asked, a bit curious about her reaction.

Gabrielle scratched one of the pups behind his ears, making his eyes cross with pleasure as his tail thumped the ground. "No. He never brought them in the house and I didn't think to go looking for them." She laughed as one of the dogs started to chase her own tail, going round and round in circles. "I didn't realize they'd be so entertaining or I might have asked to. Well, if I'd had the time. Debuting in London was very busy."

"I can only imagine," he said, leaning back against the fencing as he watched her. Her father must not have had hounds, although he didn't want to ask her, certain that it would be the quick death of her good mood. Felix was learning. It was a bit frustrating sometimes, trying to glean information about her past without actually asking any direct questions, but she dropped plenty of hints even if she never spoke of it outright.

After a bit, he insisted they go back up to the house so she could rest her ankle, challenging her to another game of chess and promising that they could come back to visit on the morrow.

Although her ankle was healing quickly and didn't seem to pain her, he didn't want her to overdo it. She started to protest that she was fine, but desisted when he gave her a significant look, trying to express - without directly threatening her - that he was not going to take no for an answer.

He was more than a little pleased with she acquiesced without a fuss, just a sigh as she put her hand on his arm and allowed him to lead her back to the house. After all, he didn't want to have to threaten to spank her for every small thing, although he would if he had to. Fortunately she seemed to be making an effort to placate his anxieties over her recovery.

THEIR DAYS WERE slow and lazy, and filled with each other's company. Gabrielle's ankle slowly healed, under Felix's careful observation, and he made sure she received plenty of rest each day, even as she wanted to push herself further. He only had to threaten to spank her once, when she wanted to go back to the creek before he thought she was ready for such a long walk. After pouting, she'd given up on trying to force the issue and let him have his way. He more than made it up to her by showering her with affection and attention, and then bringing the servants' children to play with her inside one afternoon, so that she didn't have to go to them.

Gabrielle's letters went out and were returned, always with more news from the capital. Arabella was her most faithful correspondent, always quick to return a letter, and it was clear that she was missing her friend at the events. More and more of her letters were full of complaints about the false friendships other young ladies tried to form with her, only to immediately throw over her company or betray her confidences to the Duke. She also received letters from Lady Hyde and Viscountess Petersham, the latter was also in the country, as she had reached the time of her confinement. Although they had not been able to strike up a true friendship while in London, it appeared that the Viscountess was rather bored with confinement and waiting for her baby to be born, so she was writing anyone and everyone that she knew. From the tone of her letter, it sounded as though she hoped they could become good friends in the future.

The second letter Gabrielle received from Cordelia was very different from the first. It was addressed to both Felix and Gabrielle, and seemed rather conciliatory. Gabrielle felt a thrill of triumph that Cordelia had been forced to back away from her closeness with Felix, and he certainly didn't seem bothered by it at all. Although he'd add a post script to each of her letters to Cordelia, it was never overly familiar and it was usually addressed more to Cordelia's husband than to herself. It filled Gabrielle with smug glee every time she sent a letter to Cordelia now, knowing that the ties between her stepmother and her husband were slowly being cut away while the ties between her and Felix were growing.

Their nights were filled with loving and passion. As her ankle healed, Felix showed her more and more ways that they could find pleasure together. He introduced her to perverse decadence, setting her kneeling on a cushion while he thrust his cock in and out of her mouth, until his seed spilled on her tongue and she swallowed it. He bent her over and took her from behind, like a stallion riding a mare during breeding season. Several times he didn't bother to wait until the evening, putting her on whatever reasonably comfortable flat surface he could find and turning her into a mindless creature of need before spending both of their passions and leaving her breathless and limp.

In return, she became bolder about kissing him and touching him during the day. Teasing him and flirting with him, leaning forward to show off her bosom or lifting her skirts to reveal the pale skin of her legs. And he would leer and then she would let him chase her - not running, of course, because of her ankle, but by making him seduce her before she would give in. She didn't know if this was what Cynthia had meant by making him chase her, but she thought it might be.

Felix was delighted by his bride and the progression of their relationship. Coming to the country and sending away his parents had been the right thing to do. His only complaint was that as slow as the days were, they were still somehow going by far too quickly. He didn't want to return to reality and the social scene.

But, of course, such a thing was unavoidable. However, his desire to ignore the upcoming end to their break from the real world turned out to be his worst decision yet.

RUNNING her finger along the pink stationary with its curly handwriting, Gabrielle frowned. Reading their correspondence over breakfast had become a ritual for her and Felix, one that she normally enjoyed greatly. It was time spent in companionable silence; a time for solitary thought while still being together. She thought it was a lovely way to start the day. At least, it had been until now, because now she was thinking that perhaps there were some important discussions that they should have been having.

"Felix... why does Cordelia say that she's looking forward to seeing us next week?" Gabrielle kept her tone even, blocking out her rising anxiety as well as her anger that, if such a thing were true, she should have known about it already.

If Felix had invited Cordelia and Philip to come and visit, cracking their idyllic existence on the estate, without telling her, Gabrielle was going to be hard pressed not to throw something at him. Possibly the eggs on her plate. On the other hand, if it were the opposite, and she and Felix were returning to London next week, she was probably still going to want to throw something at him. Felix hadn't spoken of an end to their honeymoon, and Gabrielle had started to think that they would just stay here until next Season.

After all, whenever she told him how much Arabella missed her, he murmured sympathetic noises but he certainly never told her to write and reassure her friend that she would be returning soon.

"Ah, Philip must have told her," Felix said absently, his attention still on his newspaper.

Gabrielle smacked her hand against the table with a loud bang, making one of the footmen jump while Felix finally looked up in surprise, his startled eyes meeting hers.

"Philip must have told her what?" she asked, displeasure sliding through her voice, despite the extreme civility with which she asked the question. Her green eyes narrowed as the hurt and disappointment in her chest contracted. Gabrielle pushed the emotions away, packing them into a little ball and squeezing it smaller and smaller until it was all gone and the inside of her body was just a vast expanse of emptiness.

Emptiness was easily filled by other emotions. She just had to decide which one she'd prefer to feel.

Her husband blinked at her, completely baffled. Truly, throwing the eggs might be too good for him. Maybe she should just impale him on her fork tines.

"That we'll be returning to London next week."

"We will?"

Another blink. "Well, yes. We can't stay here for the entire Season." Now his tone was almost patronizing, as if she should have realized it.

Anger filled the emptiness inside of her. Anger, tantamount to fury. If there was one thing Gabrielle had perfected in her life, it was throwing a tantrum. Decorum be damned.

On the other hand, she didn't want a spanking. Not when she was wrapped in justified, perfectly righteous anger. So instead of throwing her plate at him or stabbing him with her fork, she just gripped the utensil lightly and let her eyes shoot daggers.

"Don't you think that perhaps you should have told *me* that? I had no idea that we were returning to London next week."

"There's still plenty of time to pack," he muttered, his gaze falling back down to his paper. As handsome as he was, as foreboding as he could look, right now he resembled a naughty schoolboy more than anything else.

"Yes, because of course needing to pack would be the *only* reason I would want to know where I'll be living next week. And where *will* we be living, Mr. Hood?" His eyes were back on her now and he winced. "I assume you have a residence all set up? Or shall I be kept in the dark until we arrive? Perhaps I should ask Cordelia if *she* knows, since she seems to be much more abreast of the situation than myself."

A second wince had Gabrielle in a raging fury. Cordelia did know. Cordelia knew and she, Gabrielle, his wife and the person who would actually be living there, didn't.

Standing up she looked down her nose at him as she gathered up her letters. "I see," she said, fuming.

"Gabrielle-"

Ignoring him, she swept quickly out the door, her legs moving as fast as they could because if she stayed there she was going to scream or cry or beat him about the head with the centerpiece. Thank goodness her ankle had finally fully healed, or she would have never been able to get away. As she moved down the hall she could hear his chair scraping across the floor as he realized that she wasn't going to respond.

"Gabrielle, come back here!"

Practically running, she made it all the way to her room, where she barricaded herself in, locking both locks before throwing herself face down on her bed and let herself finally cry. She didn't care if it was dramatic. The anger had only bolstered her for a few minutes and then the hurt had set in; jagged edges of pain that pushed aside her ire and made it feel like she'd physically been stabbed.

All these days together, all this time, and nothing had really changed. Somehow she still had no control over her life, and he hadn't even talked to her about it! Just like he hadn't talked to her before sending his parents away, and he'd been sorry then, and he might be sorry now, but it didn't matter if he was never going to change how he behaved, did it? She'd been trying so hard, agreeing to all his suggestions, happily indulging in their pleasurable passions, and doing everything she could to make him happy. She'd thought that his regard for her had grown. That she mattered to him.

A knock on her door had her pulling her pillow more tightly against her, using it to muffle her sobs. Gabrielle had no problem crying when throwing a tantrum or when she was using her tears to get her away, but she didn't want him to see her like this. Vulnerable. Hurt. She didn't want him to know how much she cared. To guess that she loved him. Because it would just give him more power over her... better that he not know, so that he couldn't use it.

"Gabrielle, I'm sorry," he said, sounding just as sincere as he had when he'd sent his parents away. "I should have told you. I just didn't like to think about having to go back, so I didn't want to talk about it."

She didn't respond, curling into a tighter ball and wallowing in her resentment and misery. As if his excuse mattered, or even truly made sense. Telling her wouldn't change it. All it did was make her realize that he saw her as a chess piece, to be moved where he willed, without consultation or consideration. Perhaps trying to be an agreeable bride had allowed him to think that he could take her for granted. Perhaps giving him everything he asked for made him think that he didn't need to ask. Or perhaps her need to please him had just made him think she would do whatever he wanted and there was no need to even speak to her about anything of importance.

Cynthia was right. It was better to have him chase her. At least then he wouldn't be so sure of her that he would move her about, willy-nilly, without so much as a by-your-leave.

In fact, it gave her rather savage satisfaction to listen to him pacing back and forth outside of her door, muttering to himself. She let that satisfaction and her hurt harden her heart as he started begging at her door again. This would teach him!

MAYBE HE SHOULDN'T HAVE SENT his mother away.

Felix glared at the thick wooden slab keeping him away from his wife. At least it was a different wooden slab than the one he'd spent the day glaring at. Now he could do it from the comfort of his own bedroom. His lonely, empty bedroom with his lonely, empty bed.

During one of his more manic moments during the day, he'd considered breaking down one of the doors into Gabrielle's room. Or tricking her into admitting him along with the maids who brought her meals. But that wasn't going to make her less upset with his gaffe. And he was inclined to let her anger run its course.

Eventually she'd become bored in there and have to come out and speak with him, right?

Besides, he didn't want to force his presence on her. He wanted her to want his presence. He wanted to know that he was forgiven.

All afternoon he'd paced the hallway outside of her door, except when he left to eat. He'd hoped both times that she'd come and join him. Instead, she'd run the bell for the maid and requested a tray be brought to her. So Felix had eaten his meals completely alone, feeling utterly bereft.

He'd grown used to Gabrielle's constant companionship. Her keen wit, her enthusiastic observations, even her silences. Gabrielle was not a woman who had to constantly fill the silence with chatter; she was perfectly happy to just sit with him while they attended to their own entertainments. It was strangely intimate and incredibly enjoyable, and he'd gone and ruined simply because he didn't want to have to talk about or plan returning to London until the last possible moment.

Once again, he hadn't thought about how that might upset her. Since his parents had left, she'd become so agreeable about doing whatever he wanted, when he suggested it, that he hadn't been thinking. Again. This was the second time he had done this to her.

It had been a long, long time since he'd had to consult anyone but himself about his decisions. Since his parents were always thrilled to have their offspring in the house, he didn't even have to do more than send a note that he was on his way when he wanted to visit. His mother always made room for him. When he wanted to be in London, he was, when he wanted to be in the countryside, he could go there too. If he had the hankering to up and visit the Continent, he'd only need to pack his suitcase.

He'd known that he couldn't bring Gabrielle back to Jermyn Street - it was a street full of bachelors, rakes, and other wild, young hellions. Not the kind of place any bride belonged. Philip and Felix's brothers had been keeping their ears to the ground for a house to let in a respectable neighborhood - not an easy task in the middle of the Season. Felix was incredibly lucky that Philip had learned of one, so that he and Gabrielle wouldn't have to resort to living in a hotel. Which, of course, he must have mentioned to Cordelia and he must have told her when Felix was planning on being in residence.

While it wasn't the best of excuses in the world, it was a true one. Felix was unused of having to consider anyone but himself, and he hadn't wanted to think about the end of his honeymoon, so he hadn't. Obviously he needed to change some of his habits if he was going to be a good husband. Gabrielle wasn't going to be content to just follow where he went, at least not without some conversation first.

He had a feeling he was going to learn his lesson much more soundly this time, he thought, morosely studying his empty bed. The last time he'd had to apologize, it had been subsumed by her immediate transgressions, and so the focus had shifted to Gabrielle and her need for a spanking. This time, she hadn't displayed any behavior he could spank her for. She'd behaved exactly the way a lady should.

No screaming. No throwing objects. No cursing or insults.

Maybe he shouldn't have been so insistent that she be a lady.

Sighing, Felix gave the barricade between himself and his wife one last forlorn look before crawling into his empty bed. Empty beds had never bothered him before, but he'd become used to having Gabrielle in his arms every night. Now the emptiness seemed vast and lonelier than ever.

"Good morning!" Felix blurted the greeting out, practically tripping over himself when Gabrielle suddenly emerged from her room. He'd been pacing in front of her door again, after the most unrestful night he'd ever had.

"Good morning." She barely glanced at him, cutting off the ends of the words so that they sounded clipped and barely civil, turning away and walking down the hallway.

"I'm sorry, Gabrielle," he said, quickly catching up to her with his longer stride. She looked beautiful, in a cornflower blue day gown. It was more modest than the dresses she'd been wearing since he'd awoken her passions. Not even the slightest hint of cleavage, and it was looser on her frame, rather than clinging to the curves that he adored so much. Her hair had been braided and pinned up, not a single strand escaping the coiffure, and her eyes had a slight tinge of pink around them, and he felt a stab of guilt at the evidence of her tears.

Certainly not crocodile tears.

"What could you possibly be sorry for?" she asked coolly, her gaze focused ahead. "After all, I'm only your wife. I shall go where you direct."

"That's not what I want," he said, catching her hand and tugging her to a stop. The green eyes that met his were dull, without any of the fire that he'd become so used to seeing. "I should have told you... I'm not used to having to account to anyone else, and I truly didn't want to think about the end of our honeymoon."

She blinked at him, her expression unchanged.

"Gabrielle," he murmured, putting his hand to her cheek and starting to lean down for a kiss. She whirled away, her steps moving much faster this time. Felix sighed as he followed, a little bit slower this time. Not because he didn't want to be by her side, but because he needed a moment to think - to plan. Apparently, forgiveness was not going to be easily won.

HER HUSBAND MIGHT BE AN INCONSIDERATE, unthinking, self-centered nodcock, but when he wanted to apologize, he certainly did so with a serious determination that rivaled his focus when in the midst of passion.

It was hard to hold onto self-righteous anger when he was practically oozing with sincerity, his expression laden with guilt and self-recrimination. Last night she'd convinced herself that he didn't care.

Today, she was having trouble holding onto that conviction. Everything he said, everything he did showed that he cared.

Despite her chilly demeanor, he persevered in apologizing to her yet again, explaining that he had been thinking of only himself for so long that it was a habit, and one he was determined to break, for her. It wasn't the excuse that made her pause, it was his admission that his actions had been wrong and that he was going to do differently in the future. Of course, neither of them could know that was true until such circumstances arose, but as apologies went, the promise that he would do better in the future certainly had an effect. He also apologized for hurting her feelings, again, and recognized that this was the second time he'd done so over something similar.

Which melted her heart just a little.

It was as if he somehow knew all of her thoughts, all of her doubts, recognized them as legitimate, and wanted to fix it. It was both affirming and frustrating – frustrating, because she wanted to stay mad at him a little longer and he was making it so difficult! So Gabrielle tossed her head, letting him speak as he followed her down the hallway, but not making any reply.

When they reached the dining room, she ground to a halt in the doorway. The table was awash in pink flowers. They weren't all the same variety, although she was quite certain they were all from the garden, but they were all beautifully, gloriously pink. He'd remembered. And gone to the trouble to gather them all.

"Oh..." She exhaled the word softly, almost like a sigh, as she took in the sight.

Warmth against her back let her know that her husband was pressing close behind her, and she hastily stepped forward. Her heart wanted to let him back in, to drop the walls she'd shored up overnight, but her brain was more cautious. On top of that, the more cynical side of her personality kept thinking about Cynthia's advice to make him chase her. After all, the longer she made him suffer, the more the lesson would sink in, wouldn't it?

~

HAVING Gabrielle in his bed should count as a victory, but it didn't feel like one.

A single lit candle made a soft glow on her sleeping face. He'd told her that he'd wanted to read before falling asleep, once she'd made it clear that they wouldn't be engaging in any more interesting activities that evening. Really, he'd just wanted the time to think.

After dancing attendance on her all day, he'd started to feel a great deal of misgiving as the hours wore on. At times, he was sure that she'd forgiven him. Her eyes would warm, a smile would tug at her lips, and then suddenly she'd turn away and give him the cold shoulder just as he thought he'd been making progress. It had started to seem more and more like an act.

Especially tonight, once they'd retired.

Gabrielle had agreed to sleep in his room, at his insistence, but she'd called for her maid to help her undress in her own room, and then when she'd come into his, she'd been wearing the thickest, most covering nightgown he'd ever seen on a woman. Granted, his experience was all with women who wanted him to take their garment off, but he still hadn't realized such puritanical nightgowns existed. It went from collar to wrist to ankle and he could barely even discern his wife's lovely form through the voluminous folds.

Not that he'd had much time to try; she'd practically sprinted for the bed, pulling up the covers and rolling with her back facing him.

Once she'd fallen asleep, she'd turned back towards him, her hand reaching out to land on his thigh while he sat beside her. Which allowed him to study her face, softly beautiful in her slumber. She looked much sweeter and more approachable now. It was hard not to reach out and touch her, but he didn't want her to wake and turn away from him again.

Why hadn't she forgiven him?

Not that he necessarily expected quick forgiveness, but he couldn't shake the feeling that she wasn't actually angry at him. She was just acting as though she was.

Was that it? Was she just acting?

Felix's frown deepened.

He'd had mistresses in his past, and more than one of them had played that subtle game, but he wouldn't have expected it from Gabrielle. One of them, incensed when she'd felt he was neglecting her, had gone so far as to give him the cut direct at an event. She'd wanted him to chase her, begging for forgiveness. Instead, Felix had bowed out and sent her *conge* the very next day.

Obviously, he wouldn't be doing the same with his wife.

But if that was the game she was playing, he doubted that she would appreciate the outcome any more than his mistress had.

CHAPTER 12

Fingers trailed down her legs, pulling her skirts up as her nipples puckered.

"Felix!" Gabrielle giggled, squirming on his lap, as he bared her bottom. Those questing fingers pressed against her - no, wait, they were rubbing over her cheeks.

"Gabrielle..." he murmured, much more quietly than she would have expected. "Gabrielle..."

"Aren't you going to do it?" she asked, teasing, as she looked over her shoulder at him. He was gloriously naked, his eyes filled with wicked promise.

A sharp smack against her bottom - and the world tilted. Shifted. Gabrielle blinked except... no, her eyes were closed... she was dreaming? She was dreaming. But it felt so real!

Clawing her way to consciousness, Gabrielle felt all the blood rush to her head as she realized that the reason her dream felt so real was that part of it was! She was over her husband's broad thighs, her bottom high in the air, his hand rubbing the spot he'd just whacked. The biggest difference was that he hadn't just lifted her skirts up - she was completely naked!

"Felix?" she blinked, turning to look over her shoulder at him, just as she had in her dream. Just like her dream, he was completely unclothed. Unlike her dream, he didn't smile at her roguishly; instead he looked rather stern.

"Gabrielle," he said, his expression unsmiling, his hands firm on her lower back and bottom, holding her in place.

She felt muzzy and confused, sleep still fogging her brain. And she didn't understand what was happening.

"Gabrielle," Felix repeated. "Have you forgiven me?"

Blinking, Gabrielle shook her head, trying to clear it of the fog and remember what he was talking about. Oh, yes, forgetting to tell her about their return to London next week. The thought sent a little stab of displeasure through her, but not the hurt and anger that she'd felt yesterday.

"Well, yes..." Her voice trailed off and her cheeks turned pink. Averting her eyes - her neck was getting a crick in it anyway from the awkward angle - Gabrielle coughed to give herself a moment.

"Exactly when did you forgive me, Gabrielle?" Felix's voice was low, unyielding, and Gabrielle squirmed as she finally remembered her plan from yesterday had not included letting him off the hook so easily.

"Umm...."

SMACK!

"Ow!" Gabrielle shrieked at the unexpected swat to her bottom, right in the center of her left cheek. It stung and burned, yet sadly did very little to help clear the cobwebs from her thoughts. In fact, it made it harder for her to think clearly. What she did know was answering would make him stop and then maybe they could talk. "Yesterday! I forgave you yesterday!"

He sighed, his grip on her wriggling body as firm as ever. "Then why didn't you say so yesterday?"

Gabrielle clamped her lips together as her brain fired off a warning signal. Even in her hazy state of barely wakened confusion, she knew confessing she had been enjoying watching him chasing after her was not a good idea.

Apparently her husband hadn't been expecting an answer anyway, however, as he continued without pause.

"Do you know what I think? I think you didn't want me to know you had forgiven me. I think you were playing a game, seeing how far you could push me and what I would do."

SMACK!

She squeaked as his hand came down on her right cheek, giving her a matching painful patch in the center.

"I think you would have continued that game today. In fact, I think you would have kept me swinging, pretending that you hadn't forgiven me, for quite a few days."

Slumping over his legs, Gabrielle did feel a spurt of guilt as she heard the hurt in his voice. Yes, that was exactly what she'd planned on doing.

"Have I gotten anything wrong so far?" he asked. Gabrielle shook her head, finding it too hard to open her mouth to answer him.

With another sigh, his hand left her bottom. She almost looked back over her shoulder to see why when, a moment later, something nudged at her anus. It pushed it, narrower than his finger at the tip but getting wider.

"Ow! What-?"

"Hold still, sweetheart, and try and relax," he said, his voice calm and almost soothing. "It's almost all the way in."

"What is?!" Panic was starting to build. She had no idea what he was inserting into that private area - certainly not his finger, which was the only thing that had ever touched it before, and only when she was so overcome with passion that she hadn't minded the intrusion.

This was completely different - frightening because it was unknown, and more painful because it was the only thing she could focus on. Her tiny hole burned as it stretched, feeling like it was going to tear at any moment... and then suddenly, whatever it was completed its journey and she felt it settle into place. There was still some part of it holding her slightly open, but the largest part was now snugly inside of her, still stretching her with a tingling burn that had her squirming uncomfortably. Another part of it pressed against the outside of her rosebud, which Felix twisted, making both the strangeness of the sensation and the burning increase.

"Ow, ow!" She squirmed harder, her little hole clenching, which made her gasp as tears sprang in her eyes. The burning was getting worse, not better!

"Because you told me the truth now, I'm not going to spank you very hard, but this little piece of ginger is going to help teach you a lesson," Felix said. Gabrielle's head whirled. Ginger! He'd put *ginger* in her *bottom*?! It was perverse! It was painful! And yet it was also making her pussy tingle excitedly, which made her want to groan in humiliation and resigned frustration.

SMACK!

Gabrielle clenched and then shrieked as the burning, inside and out, increased.

"I am happy to apologize and to do whatever I need to do to make things up to you when I've done something wrong, but withholding forgiveness to punish me is not acceptable."

SMACK! SMACK!

This time she tried not to clench, but it was almost involuntary. The tingling burn felt like it was fizzing inside of her. It hurt, but it didn't stop the growing ache between her legs; in fact, the burning almost encouraged it. Gabrielle whimpered, her bottom wriggling and clenching as Felix kept spanking her, making her burn inside and out.

THE SIGHT of Gabrielle's quivering bottom with the little knob of ginger between her pink cheeks had Felix hard as a rock. He'd already been aroused by the little noises she'd made as he'd pulled her over his lap, when she was still asleep. Having her sleepy and soft, obviously muzzy while he questioned her might not have been fair, but it had gotten the truth out of her pretty quickly.

She didn't argue with his assessment or protest against the spanking, or even try to escape the burn of the ginger.

Since he was still feeling a bit guilty over his high-handed ways, he'd known he wouldn't be able to give Gabrielle the spanking she truly deserved, which was why he'd decided to use the ginger finger. It added an extra element to the punishment, despite the lightness of her spanking.

A delightful element for him, watching her squirm on his lap, her bottom cheeks bouncing under his hand, squeezing around the finger of ginger and then releasing again. The peeled finger was only about two inches long and a bit thicker than his finger just before the notch that he'd carved to keep her from being able to push it back out or for it to slide all the way inside of her. Just thinking about the way it must be tingling and burning inside of her, igniting those sensitive tissues, had his cock leaking pearly fluid in anticipation.

He didn't miss her response either. Not only was she completely compliant, but her pussy was swollen and pink, glossy with her arousal, despite her cries and whimpers.

"Did you enjoy yourself yesterday?" he asked.

No answer.

SMACK! SMACK!

"Yes! I mean, no!" Gabrielle sniffled. "Maybe a little."

Since she wasn't looking at him, he didn't have to hide the amusement at her honesty from his face.

"The next time I apologize, will you tell me right away when you've forgiven me?"

SMACK! SMACK!

"Yes!" she squealed, her body bucking. "I promise!"

Good enough for him. Although her spanking hadn't been all that severe, Felix didn't truly have the heart to really punish her. He was inclined to go light on her, since he'd contributed to the issue... which was why he'd sent the maid for the ginger before Gabrielle had woken up. At the time, he hadn't been sure whether or not it would be necessary - after all, if she was still mad at him, he wouldn't have used it - but he was glad he'd been prepared. It was having a most salutary effect on his wife.

Flipping her onto her back, he ignored her shriek of protest as her bottom bounced, probably making her clench around the fiery finger in her rear entry. Her nipples were hard little points on her chest and her cunt was so soaked with honey that he could smell it.

"Felix!"

Sliding his arms under her legs, so that her knees easily fit into the crook of his elbows, he leaned forward, bending her practically in half as he lined up his cock with her needy pussy.

"Oh!"

Pink lips formed a perfect 'o' as her green eyes widened in shock, her body opening for him. He drove into her in one stroke, grunting with the pleasure of her tight wetness squeezing the hell out of his cock. The sudden stretching made her writhe underneath him - as much as she could in such a pinned position. She whimpered again as his weight pressed her sensitized buttocks into the mattress, her body clenching around him and the ginger.

Then he began to move.

The expression on Gabrielle's face was fascinating, a mix of pain and pleasure, her lips parted as she said his name over and over again, as though she couldn't think of another word to say after it. Her arms came up to wind about his neck, holding onto him for dear life as he set up a bruising rhythm, fucking her down into the bed with a need that was almost ferocious. Her eyelashes fluttered, her body submissively open to him, as her voice rose in ecstasy.

Her pussy clamped down around his cock, shocking him with the suddenness and intensity of her climax, especially considering his rough treatment and the burning finger of ginger still lodged in her arse. Felix groaned, holding her tighter, fucking her harder as she arched beneath him and screamed in ragged ecstasy.

Rapture was practically wrenched from him as his orgasm came as fast and hard as hers had. He jetted his seed into her body, his hips still moving, rubbing himself against her as she sobbed with the overwhelming sensations he was creating. Their passion wound within them, spilling over and sliding into each other, until Felix was gasping and jerking as his body spasmed even though he had no more fluid to spill.

He finally pulled away, completely spent, and fell on his side, resting for just a moment before taking his wife and pulling her atop him. She was a dead weight in his arms, limp and satisfied. As his fingers moved down to her bottom and find the finger of ginger, removing it from its haven, she made a few small noises, but she barely stirred. Holding her tightly against him, Felix found himself falling back asleep, relieved and happy that the storm had been so easily overcome.

After all, they would be returning to London in a week and he didn't fool himself into thinking their lives would be so easy there. That was, after all, why he'd been so determined to build a firm foundation for their marriage before their honeymoon ended. He could only hope it was strong enough to weather the stresses of the *ton* and the rest of the Season, otherwise they'd have to start all over again afterwards.

THE CARRIAGE RIDE back to London was much more pleasant than the ride from London, even though both journeys were filled with anxiety. During the former, Gabrielle had been bereft, angry, and lonely... she'd felt like she was being exiled and sent away from the only security she had. She'd wanted nothing more than to return to London and Dunbury House.

Now, she would be happy to stay away from Dunbury House, and she was torn between a desire to stay in the country and her excitement about returning to London. She was eager to see Arabella and Eleanor, part of her thrilled to the thought of returning to the social scene with its entertaining gossip, the music, and the glamour... but she'd also truly enjoyed the slower pace of the country and the dreamlike days with just her and Felix.

After her ill-advised attempt to punish him, and her subsequent spanking and punishment with the ginger root, the days had passed far too quickly. They'd spent all their time together, whether at the creek with the children or in the house playing other kinds of games, and Gabrielle found herself dreading being apart from him. Even though she knew they couldn't spend every minute of every day together for the rest of their lives, and that he might very well become annoying if they attempted it, at this moment it sounded like a very reassuring prospect.

Going to the city meant risking losing his attentions... it meant facing her stepmother and seeing whether or not she still had an effect on Felix... it meant that the tenuous bond between her and her husband was finally going to be tested. And Gabrielle wasn't feeling very secure in its strength. After all, it was such a fragile bond. One that had only sprung up after she'd decided to turn his head and make the best of their marriage. He'd still never said that he loved her, although she believed that he did care for her now.

But would it be enough to hold him to her side when presented with other options?

Her thoughts and anxieties marred what was an otherwise enjoyable journey. Felix sat next to her, holding her hand or tucking her under his arm to nap. They talked about the house they were going to. The Marquess of Dunbury had found it and written a description. The address wasn't far from the Duke of Manchester's house in Mayfair, and it pleased Gabrielle that Arabella would be so close by.

Of course, it wasn't very far from Dunbury House either and she was less sure how she felt about that.

"Will your parents be staying in London for the rest of the Season, or will they go home?" Gabrielle asked, as the thought occurred to her. Rather surprising that it hadn't before, but she had been rather distracted after all.

"I'm not sure," Felix said, his hand stroking down her arm. She snuggled closer to him. Since he was leaning back against the side of the carriage, she was already halfway on top of him, her head resting in the comfortable nook between his shoulder and chest, her hand on his stomach. "I'm sure my mother will want to stay and my father won't. They didn't say anything in their last letter to me, did mother say anything to you?"

"No, just that she looked forward to seeing me again." A sentiment that Gabrielle reciprocated, although she had to admit that it had been rather nice to be with just Felix the past few weeks. She hadn't expected to feel so loathe to give that up.

THE HOUSE WAS PERFECT. Small, but well outfitted, tastefully decorated, and just on the outskirts of Mayfair. The neighbors were a mix of gentry and wealthy businessmen and their families, all of whom were curiously watching from their windows as Felix and Gabrielle arrived. The hustle and bustle made it clear that they were the new occupants, and he was sure the neighbors were watching and making their own judgments.

Felix smiled as he helped his wife step down from the carriage, graceful even though she was obviously exhausted by their travel. The short naps she'd taken during the ride hadn't been very comfortable and she'd come awake with a start every time.

"Welcome to our home for the Season," he said, scooping her up in his arms as she squealed in happy alarm.

"Felix! What are you doing?" she asked, laughing as he mounted the stairs. The front door opened to reveal Mr. Taylor, his thin face even more severe than usual and Felix suspected that the somber man was fighting his own smile.

"It's traditional to carry the bride through the front door of her first home," he replied, giving her a rakish grin. "And, as this is our first place of residence together..."

"Oh..." The wonder in her voice made him look at her expression. She was staring at the house with tears glimmering in her eyes, obviously touched by the gesture. Felix cradled her closer as he maneuvered his way into the house, stopping just inside the entrance so that they could take in the view together.

To the right was a parlor, perfect for entertaining, and to the left was a musical room with a piano clearly visible from the doorway. Just ahead were stairs and a hallway leading to the other rooms.

"We should go exploring together," Felix murmured, reluctantly letting her slide from his arms. While part of him wanted to take her straight to the bedroom and lock themselves in, shutting out the world until they absolutely had to face it, they really should familiarize themselves with their home for the next month. Besides, from the way Gabrielle's head was swiveling around, she doubtless wanted to become better acquainted with the house.

They went into the parlor first, so that Gabrielle could coo over the decorations, her happy expression making it impossible for Felix not to kiss her. Which was so enjoyable that he repeated it in the musical room, the billiard room, the dining room, the kitchen (where their dinner was already being prepared), on the stairs, in each of the three guest rooms, and in their bedroom. That last kiss began to turn into something else entirely, which left Felix cursing when Taylor knocked on the door to inform them that Viscount and Viscountess Hood had arrived for a visit.

"Oh no!"

As frustrated and annoyed as Felix was at the interruption, he couldn't help but find Gabrielle's frantic panic completely enchanting. She was attractively flushed, her hair disheveled as she pushed her fingers through it, trying to create a semblance of order, her dress half hanging off of her -

"Felix! Help!"

Sighing, he complied, assisting her with putting her dress and hair in order. Maybe later he'd spank her for making him wait. Not a real spanking, of course, but ever since the explosive aftermath of her punishment a week ago, he'd included some kind of sexual torment in every single coupling, with satisfying results for both of them. Gabrielle was excited by sexual pain and his dominance, and he was happy to indulge them both. Eventually, he planned to take her last virginity and make her wholly his, although he was slowly working his way up to that. Already she could take three fingers in that tight little hole without wincing, moaning with passion the entire time.

"Felix, come on!" his wife hissed at him.

Sighing, he trotted dutifully behind her, out the door and down the hall to the stairs, his erection flagging as he heard his mother's gushing tones drifting up the stairwell as she excitedly chattered to his father.

"Such a charming little parlor! I just love the little figurines on the mantle, aren't they dear?"

A masculine grunt of response.

"Oh tosh, dear, I think they're lovely."

"Mother? Papa?" The excitement and joy in Gabrielle's voice washed away any resentment Felix had been feeling. He couldn't help but smile indulgently as his parents greeted Gabrielle, his mother fussing over her and calling for tea because she thought Gabrielle looked tired and in need of nourishment. Their greetings to him were just as affectionate, if not as effusive.

Gabrielle practically glowed at his mother's attentions, with the strangest expression on her face... it wasn't quite happiness or surprise, but more like a puppy who had been expecting to be kicked, but had been rewarded with a treat instead. They were going to need to work on her expectations from people, although he supposed that experience would probably cure her of some of her anxieties. After all, his parents were going to be just as delighted every time they saw her.

In fact, his mother insisted on Gabrielle sitting beside her on the small couch, while his father took up one of the armchairs. Felix preferred to stand after having been in the carriage all day, and leaned against the mantle near his father - the one holding the figurines his mother liked. They were rather charming; little blue and white animals made out of fine china. Maybe he'd see if he could find her one as a present. Or just buy it from the house's owner.

Plying them with questions about the estate and the remainder of their honeymoon, both of his parents beamed at him when Gabrielle began to chatter, telling them all about his efforts to care for her and entertain her. His mother's approving gaze made him smirk. Had she thought he wouldn't be able to handle himself in her absence? Granted, he'd stumbled a few times, but overall things had gone off swimmingly, and Gabrielle didn't mention any of those times.

In fact, her happiness practically flowed out of her like a fountain, making the room seem even brighter than it had before.

"Well that sounds lovely, dear, I'm glad my son took such good care of you," his mother said, giving him another approving look.

"I do have my occasional uses," he said dryly, making his father chuckle.

"Limited though they can be," his mother said with a playful sniff, before turning her attention back to Gabrielle. "Well, I know you two will need a couple of days to settle in, but I would love for you to come over for tea the day after tomorrow and meet some of my friends. I'm just dying to finally be able to show off my new daughter."

"Of course, I'd love to meet your friends," his wife said, only a tiny bit of anxiousness flickering across her face.

"They're going to love you," his mother said, crowing with delight and inadvertently reassuring Gabrielle. "I've told them all about you and they're just in alt to meet the woman who finally tamed one of my sons."

Felix's father leaned towards him. "I'll be at the White's that afternoon, if you want to come join me," he murmured, underneath the chatter of the two females, with a fairly pained expression on his face.

Somehow, Felix immediately knew that there was no way his father would be able to pry his mother out of London before the end of the Season. Not now that she was well entrenched and had a daughter-in-law to show off. He should really get his father a good bottle of brandy or something as an apology.

His parents stayed for dinner that evening, their very presence revitalizing Gabrielle, who no longer looked as worn from traveling. He sincerely hoped she maintained that energy after they left. Still, as they ate, he couldn't help but frown inwardly a bit. Gabrielle still seemed so surprised and pleased by his parents' presence, he couldn't help but feel that it made Cordelia's absence all the more conspicuous.

She'd known what day Felix and Gabrielle were going to arrive. While it might be presumptuous for friends to appear on the doorstep on the day of arrival, family certainly didn't fall under the same category. Yet, his wife didn't seem upset by Cordelia's absence, just thrilled by his parents.

Felix set aside those thoughts in favor of paying attention to the conversation, leaving them for further contemplation when there wasn't company demanding his attention.

"IT WAS SO LOVELY to see your mother again - and your father too," Gabrielle said as Felix nimbly undid the laces on her corset. The warmth that had suffused her all evening lingered, making her feel almost buoyant, like she was bubbling over with contentment. "I truly did miss them."

"I did as well," Felix said, pressing a kiss to her collarbone and making her shiver. She felt more than heard his sigh. "However, I would prefer not to talk about my parents *right now.* Not while I'm doing this to you."

His hand closed over her breast, squeezing almost harshly and making her gasp as excitement sizzled through her, straight down to her core. Gabrielle didn't know why she loved it when he made her tender parts hurt, but she did. It wasn't that he was cruel about it, although he could be very calculated, and she sensed he only did it because she wanted him to... at first she'd felt rather shocked and a bit ashamed by her responses, but Felix had taken too much delight in them for her to sustain either of those reactions for long.

They both liked it when he did perverse, sadistic things to her body. Things that she was sure her stepmother would never indulge in. Cordelia and the Marquess liked to make love in all sorts of locations, but her stepmother would never be able to give Felix what he obviously liked. Gabrielle could and would.

Not that he would abuse that. The one time he'd done something that had been too much for her - spanking her pussy after making her orgasm with his mouth, which had been far too painful on that sensitized flesh - he'd immediately stopped and apologized. Gabrielle had been worried that he'd be disappointed, worried that she wouldn't be able to fulfill his needs, but if anything he seemed more concerned that she wouldn't want to be so debauched with him again. When she told him that she could try again, if he wanted, he'd shaken his head and said it was only pleasurable for him if it was pleasurable for her.

Strange, how a man who could spank her bottom raw when she needed punishment would be so tender and concerned over one slap that had made her cry out in pain during their play. She supposed it was the difference between intentional and unintentional pain; one which he meant to cause and one which he didn't.

Her husband was an inveterate control fanatic.

Fingers pinched her nipples, definitely harshly, and Gabrielle hissed as her back arched, her head falling back and giving him access to her neck. She clung to his broad shoulders as his teeth scraped over the delicate skin of her throat, his tongue licking at her pulse. Her body throbbed.

"More," she begged, her voice a whimper, because she'd discovered that he liked to hear her plead, liked to hear her say anything.

Felix groaned, pressing against her, moving her back towards the bed as he stripped her down, his hands roughly caressing every part of her that he bared.

"More, please Felix."

His mouth moved down her body, bending her backwards, one hand in her hair to hold her securely.

It hurt. It made her muscles ache. And yet she thrilled to his control over her as his mouth closed around one tightly budded nipple, his teeth sinking in and making her cry out.

When he let it release with a pop and spun her around to face the bed, pushing her down so that her hands were resting on the mattress, making her bend over in front of him, she let out a little whimper.

"Felix, please..."

"You made me wait earlier." His hands slid down her sides, tracing her natural hourglass curves, making her skin tingle in their wake. When they reached her buttocks, he squeezed roughly, digging his fingers into the soft flesh.

"Your parents were here!"

"No excuses, sweetheart," he said in that silky, dark voice that he used when he wanted to play with her. When he wanted to do decadent and dissolute things to her body. That voice that never failed to make her cream when she heard it. "You made me wait."

SLAP!

She let out a muffled moan as his hand smacked against her splayed pussy. Unlike the last time, she hadn't just orgasmed... unlike the last time, this didn't hurt too much. It hurt just right. It hurt beautifully.

The hand that was still resting on her bottom paused in its strokes, waiting. She blushed and dropped her head, lifting her hips up and wiggling slightly, silently asking for more. Too embarrassed this time to voice the words.

His dark chuckle made her nipples pucker even more. The one that he'd sucked on felt cooler than the other in the open air, even more sensitive, and she wished that he had treated them more equitably... and yet loved the imbalance at the same time.

SLAP!

The sound was wet, muted by her arousal.

"You're such a naughty girl, sweetheart."

SLAP!

"Such a perfectly dirty girl, aren't you?"

SLAP!

Gabrielle whimpered, her hips bucking. Her pleasure bud felt like it was swollen to four times its normal size, aching and throbbing. Needing more stimulation to reach her peak.

"Please, Felix, more."

SLAP!

"You'll let me do anything I want to, wouldn't you sweetheart?"

SLAP!

"Yes!" Right now, she didn't care what he might want to do to her, she just wanted the sweet release she knew he would give her... whatever he desired to do to get her there, she was game for.

Wet fingers circled her anus and then plunged in, making her shudder and buck. Ever since he'd plugged her with the ginger root, she'd felt like that whole area was more sensitive. More pleasurable. The stretch burned as his fingers moved, but part of her wished for the ginger again. Wished for the burn that lingered and sparked.

The fullness made her empty womanhood ache in envy as her nipples grazed the mattress. She moaned as Felix pumped his fingers back and forth, stretching her, filling her, sending her closer to orgasm but not allowing her to crest over.

Then the blunt head of his cock nudged against the entrance to her body, underneath her fingers, and Gabrielle pushed back. Pleasure slid through her as she was filled, her anus clenching around his fingers as his cock thrust deeper. His free hand held her hip, holding her in place as he withdrew and then shoved back in, hard and fast.

Gabrielle moaned.

"If I wanted to put my cock in here, you'd let me wouldn't you?" His voice was a husky whisper as his fingers twisted. "You'd let me take you here, wouldn't you?"

A shudder of ecstasy rippled through her at the forbidden and depraved image that popped into her head. His cock? There? Stretching her open, stuffing her fuller than his fingers ever could? It would hurt... it would hurt so good...

She cried out as her orgasm rippled through her, clamping down on Felix... screamed again as his fingers pulled roughly from her body so that he could thrust harder and faster. His big hands moved up her torso to her breasts, squeezing them both so hard it took her breath away, the lack of air strangely increasing the sensation of ecstasy that was flowing through her. Her elbows caved and her body crashed down onto the bed, pinned between it and the hot, hard thrusting of her husband's cock.

The pleasure was so intense, so relentless that tears sprung to her eyes as Felix groaned and moved above her. She felt wonderfully helpless as she writhed in the throes of rapture, Felix's hard hands and cock wringing every last ounce of pained pleasure from her body, until he finally exploded inside of her in a wave of liquid heat.

CHAPTER 13

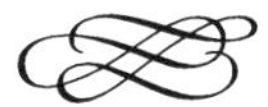

The tea was steeped impeccably to a perfect temperature. Gabrielle's blue silk dress was demure and sophisticated, her hair classically coiffed, and her manners as a hostess were supreme. Her two guests, seated across from her on the small couch, were just as elegantly attired, just as splendidly mannered, and altogether they made a tableau that appeared to be the pinnacle of London society.

Their conversation, however, completely shattered that illusion.

"He *spanks* you?!" Arabella was aghast, but her expression was one of interested horror, not true horror. "But he's your husband!"

"My husband spanks me constantly," Cynthia Spencer said, a smug little smile curving her full lips. "I drive him to it."

"But... but..." Arabella stuttered, completely at a loss for words.

"Oh dear, she has nothing to say! Do you think we should call for a doctor?" Gabrielle mock-whispered to Cynthia. Both of them laughed as Arabella shook her head.

"I don't understand this at all. Why aren't you angry?" Frowning, she turned her attention to Cynthia. "And what do you mean you drive your husband to it?"

"I like it," Cynthia said succinctly. She gave Arabella a significant look. "This is why I refused to talk to you about *it* before."

"Wait, he spanks you during *that*?!"

Laughing again, Gabrielle was so relieved that Cynthia had come with Arabella. They were her first official visitors, and she'd asked Taylor to tell anyone else who arrived that she wasn't at-home. Well, unless any other visitors were family or close friends, of course. If Felix's mother or his cousin Eleanor came by, Gabrielle would enjoy seeing them. She was rather hoping they didn't, however, as she was quite sure it would stunt the conversation that was currently occurring. Felix had reluctantly taken his leave, saying that he was going to see his brothers and murmuring something about females blathering - sounding rather like his father as he'd done so. It had been a pang to separate from him, but her friends were helping to distract her from the strangeness of his absence.

And it was wonderful to be able to talk to someone about... well, all the things she never thought she'd be able to talk about.

Arabella had been full of questions and Cynthia had been full of answers, now that she had Gabrielle to confirm everything she said. The only unmarried one in the group, Arabella had been rather skeptical of Cynthia's description of the marital act until she'd seen Gabrielle nodding her head in agreement. She thought they'd been funning her. Especially when Cynthia, apparently not embarrassed by the conversation as long as she had an ally, began to describe some of the more exotic entertainments she and the Earl of Spencer indulged in.

Like spankings.

For herself, Gabrielle had been both relieved and intrigued to know that she wasn't the only one - and even more so that she wasn't the only one who enjoyed it.

"Felix does too," she said, whispering with great daring, her eyes darting to the door as if she expected him to come through at any moment now that she'd said something.

Arabella's dark brown eyes widened in even greater shock, her cheeks blushing a deep pink that matched the ribbons on her lavender dress. She was wearing the pale colors of a debutante, which made the color in her face seem all the more bright, especially with her creamy complexion and dark brown hair to set it off. Cynthia chortled. Even with her mahogany hair swept back in a complicated coiffure, her deep burgundy dress appropriately modest despite her luxurious curves, there was such a devilish gleam in her hazel eyes that if anyone looked at her face, they would know she was up to mischief. It was part of why Arabella and Gabrielle got along with her so well.

"I knew it!" Cynthia crowed, clapping her hands together happily. "Welcome to the group of spanked wives... perhaps we should actually form one. We could be quite a merry little club."

"A club?" Gabrielle and Arabella exchanged looks of surprise.

"Oh yes. Eleanor likes it too, so does Grace although she doesn't like to talk about it," Cynthia explained with a wave of her hand. "Irene does her best to avoid being spanked, but it still happens whenever we rope her into some mischief and are caught. Actually, Eleanor and Grace don't particularly enjoy the actual disciplinary spankings, I don't think." She raised her eyebrow, looking at Gabrielle, who flushed. Cynthia laughed with delight. "I knew you'd be more like me... the harder the better."

"Really?" Gabrielle asked with relief, thankful to have found such a kindred spirit in Cynthia. She ignored Arabella, whose mouth was hanging open so wide she'd best be careful or she'd be catching flies. "You too?"

"Oh yes!" Cynthia leaned in conspiratorially, her hazel eyes sparking gold with interest. "Has he ever used the strap?"

"No!" Gabrielle shook her head in immediate denial. "He's only ever used his hand." Although, now that Cynthia had said it, Gabrielle's imagination fired. The Marquess of Dunbury had used the paddle and she'd hated it, it had hurt so much... but would it feel different if it was wielded by Felix? His hand was hard enough, but what if he used something harder? Harsher? A shiver went through her. The smug look on Cynthia's face caught her attention and fired her competitive spirit. She leaned back in towards other woman. "He did put ginger in my bottom though - it burned horribly but... I liked it."

"You did?! But it's so... humiliating!" Cynthia blurted the words out and then clapped her hand over her mouth. It was the first time Gabrielle had ever seen the brazen woman blush. Arabella looked ready to faint.

Gabrielle blushed now too, looking at her unmarried friend. "Perhaps we shouldn't be talking about this..."

"Don't you dare stop!" Arabella gulped, obviously steeling herself. "I have no mother to tell me about relations between a man and a woman, and can you imagine Isaac or Benedict attempting it? They'd leave everything out and I'd be completely ignorant!"

Especially since she hadn't even believed Cynthia and Gabrielle when they'd first told her exactly how a man and woman coupled. While she'd spent some time in the country, her brothers had obviously kept her far away from any of the breeding animals.

"Well, I must admit it's lovely to have someone to talk to about this again," Cynthia said, grinning. "Eleanor and Edwin have gone back to the Manse to spend time with their son and Edwin's parents, Irene's in the country in confinement with Hugh, and Grace doesn't like to say much about bedroom activities even though we all know she and Alex are fucking like bunnies." Cynthia rolled her eyes.

"Cynthia!" Arabella admonished. "You shouldn't use that word!"

"You didn't even know what that word meant before I told you."

"Even so! What if someone heard you using it?"

"Then I'd get a spanking."

"Or maybe some ginger up your... your..." Arabella's feisty spirit seemed to fade as she couldn't quite get the word out.

"Bottom?" Gabrielle asked, her tone innocent. "It's really not that bad... well it is, but it isn't."

Cynthia shuddered. "Has he put um, anything else there?"

"No, but..." Gabrielle glanced at Arabella, almost not wanting to say, but if anyone would be able to tell her what it was like, she was sure it was Cynthia. "He said he wants to take me there."

"Ouch..." Cynthia said making a face as Arabella gasped. "Wesley does that sometimes when I've been particularly bad. He knows I don't like it. I think that makes him like it even more."

"Does it hurt that badly?" Gabrielle asked, nerves fluttering in her stomach even as something hot and heavy coiled in her lower belly. Part of her wanted Cynthia to say yes.

"It can, if he doesn't ah, stretch you first," Cynthia said. Her lips quirked. "Wesley uses these little rubber stopper things-"

"Okay, stop!" Arabella put her hands over her ears. "I don't think I want to hear about this!"

"It's too much for her pure little mind," Gabrielle said, keeping her expression serious as Cynthia chortled and Arabella glared at her.

"My mind is *not* pure, but it can only take in so much at once!"

"Maybe we should talk about mouths instead," Cynthia mused, tapping one finger on her chin. "That's still informative but not quite so unusual."

"*Mouths*?!"

IT TURNED out that Felix's father had also escaped to the house on Jermyn Street, which Felix used to share with Walter, and which Walter apparently now shared with Thomas. Thomas usually stayed in Hood House when he was in residence, but had fled the premises with the arrival of their parents, or - more accurately - his mother and her friends and their daughters. As the heir to the Viscountancy, Thomas looked positively hunted.

"She's sending me lists - actual lists! - of females and the events they'll be attending," Thomas complained, pacing back and forth across the study. The piles of papers that were haphazardly placed on a nearby table would actual rise slightly before settling back down every time he passed, as he was pacing at a rather good clip.

Walter refused to allow anyone to clean the study, saying that they would disturb his organization system, which meant that a bit of dust rose as well. Eyeing one particularly precariously perched pile, Walter stood and went over to shove it more securely onto the table.

"Sorry," Thomas muttered as he passed by again, before turning to shoot Felix a baleful look. "This is all your fault you know."

"Don't blame your brother for having the good sense to be the first married," Felix's father said, surprising all three of his sons. Normally he stayed well out of their bickering - in fact, normally he didn't say very much at all if it wasn't on the subject of the estates, hunting, or one of the areas of history he was particularly interested in. "Your mother was already sending you a list every six months. You could have been married well before him."

"Yes, but now she's sending them every other day," Thomas griped, his dark eyes flashing as he resumed his pacing. Felix could only watch in amusement, secure in his own matrimony, but feeling some small sympathy for his older brothers. He could only imagine that without Gabrielle to keep her occupied, his mother had probably embarked on an all-out assault on his brothers.

"Well now she'll be spending her time ensuring Gabrielle's place in the *ton*," Felix said. "Perhaps she'll be distracted enough to forget your sadly unwedded state."

Walter snorted. Slumped back in his armchair, a snifter of brandy dangling from his fingers, he looked every bit the dissolute rake that he was. People were always rather surprised to discover that he was also a bit bookish; he was just as happy to spend his night in with a new book as he was out carousing about town. Although, apparently last night had been a night for carousing, going by the dark circles under his eyes and his general air of dishevelment.

"You took the only woman I could ever be interested in marrying," Walter said dramatically, putting his hand over his heart. "I couldn't possibly be interested in any woman now that I know Gabrielle is forever out of my reach."

"Don't you forget it either," Felix said, ignoring his brother's attempt to get a rise out of him.

"Perhaps if you were quicker on the draw," their father observed.

"Like a good brother, I was trying to keep from putting any undue pressure on Thomas," Walter said. Felix rolled his eyes.

"I'm nowhere near ready for marriage," Thomas said with a derisive sniff. "I doubt I will be any time soon either. The ladies on the lists mother keeps sending me..." He shook his head.

"Yes, yes, we know, you won't marry until you find the perfect woman," Walter mocked. He started ticking points off on his fingers. "She must be beautiful, well-mannered, of a social standing not too far from our own-"

"She must be good with children, an accomplished hostess, intelligent but not a blue-stocking," Felix continued.

"An excellent rider but not a hoyden, a tasteful dresser but also fashionable, a witty conversationalist but not so much that she makes you look bad-"

"She must be cultured, she must excel at, well, everything-"

Their father chimed in, "And able to put up with you."

All three of them dissolved into laughter while Thomas glowered. "I don't see what's so funny about having standards. Gabrielle met all of Felix's - if she was a better rider and a bit more experienced within the *ton*-"

"But that's just it," Felix pointed out, grinning, and feeling rather smug that he had managed to marry a woman so close to fulfilling Thomas' rather lengthy list of attributes. "She doesn't meet every one of your insane demands, and, while they're good qualities, they don't encompass the most important parts of a marriage. Besides, you've neglected to list any bad qualities that you would be willing to endure."

"Granted, Gabrielle could be a bit sharp at first, but she mellowed very nicely, especially towards us," Thomas said. "Unless you're saying she changed once you two went away."

"Gabrielle was delightful," Felix's father said stoutly, before Felix could answer. "But your brother has the right of it. You might find a woman with every single one of those qualities, but unless you care for her, it won't matter a whit."

Thomas waved his hand. "If she can meet all my qualifications than why wouldn't I fall in love with her?"

Shaking his head, Felix could only hope that when Thomas fell in love, it would be with a woman that challenged every single one of his notions about marriage. Although he'd never been quite up to Felix or Walter's reputation when it came to the ladies,Thomas had become even stodgier over the years. He needed a woman who would shake him up a bit.

"I hope you end up with a more scandalous woman than Felix did," Walter said, teasing both of them at once. Thomas growled, but the comment made Felix become more serious.

"Is there any lingering scandal?" He'd been reassured by the letters that his brothers, Manchester, and Philip had sent him, but perhaps they'd left something out.

His father shook his head. "Ignore Walter, there's not even a breath of it, or your mother would be up in arms. Any whispers were completely squashed by our arrival in town and her excitement to extol Gabrielle's virtues to her friends."

"There weren't very many whispers left anyway," Thomas said, a bit defensively. "Lady Hyde, Lady Spencer, the Dowager-Countess Spencer, and Manchester were very effective in helping us damp down the scandal."

"Helped along by a couple of eloping fools," Walter muttered.

Well that was a relief. Felix sank back into his chair, grinning as Thomas resumed his pacing, the reminder of the scandalous elopement turning him back to his original topic of complaining about their mother's machinations. Walter seemed amused as well, but as the second son he likely wasn't getting a list every other day. Just weekly.

It was rather nice to know he'd neatly avoided that little bit of motherly interference in his life.

WHEN FELIX ARRIVED BACK HOME, Gabrielle felt a bit of relief, even if it did cut off her conversation with Cynthia and Arabella. They immediately moved to more appropriate conversation topics for young ladies, so that when he peeked his head into the parlor, it was to hear an animated discussion about the current fashions for flounces. She covered her smile when he gave her a wave, made a face, and immediately retreated.

She was sure that he wouldn't have approved of their earlier conversation - especially since it included things Arabella definitely shouldn't have any knowledge of - but she didn't feel guilty at all. Conversations with her friends were something he shouldn't have any control over and she was unwilling to give it to him. Still, some part of her couldn't help but wonder what he might do if she confessed... apparently Cynthia's predilection towards actively courting a spanking was already rubbing off on her.

After Cynthia and Arabella took their leave, Gabrielle went in search of her husband. Unlike his parents' manor house, this residence was much smaller, so he wasn't very difficult to find. All she had to do was follow the sound of billiard balls woodenly clacking against each other.

Hugging the doorway, she watched her husband bending over the table, focused intently on the placement of the balls in front of him and the stick in his hands. His movements were purposeful, confident. Very like the way he did everything in life. He'd shed his jacket, and his cravat was loosened, giving him an appearance of slight dishevelment that Gabrielle found very attractive.

He struck, and the balls zoomed around the table, until one of them disappeared into the netted basket in the corner. Then he looked up at her, dark eyes pleased.

"Hello there."

"Hello." She felt strange, a little awkward with him in this new place. "Are you staying in for supper tonight?"

"Yes. I don't plan on eating elsewhere unless we're invited to a dinner." He set the end of the stick down, leaning on it as he watched her. "I'm looking forward to hearing about your day."

She smiled back at him, almost shyly. "And I yours."

"Were Cynthia and Arabella your only callers today?"

"Yes, although I told Taylor I wasn't at-home to anyone who wasn't a close friend or family."

Felix nodded, looking thoughtful. "Did you have a nice visit with them?"

"Very. It was lovely to see them again." She smiled. "I'll go tell Jacque that we'll be here for supper tonight and see what he would like to serve."

Nodding again, Felix's eyes followed her as she left, heading down the hallway and humming with happiness. The Marquess had always dined with Cordelia, unless they'd been invited to an event, but Gabrielle had heard enough gossip to know that his behavior wasn't considered fashionable. Most gentlemen ate at their clubs as often as they did at home, if not more. That Felix was apparently set to be just as unfashionable made her unaccountably happy.

So far being back in London wasn't so terrible.

She'd felt very mature today, being the hostess for her friends, and now getting the household ready for dinner. At his parents' estate, even after they'd left, she hadn't felt completely comfortable with taking over the household duties. However, she'd become rather friendly with one of the undercooks, a Frenchman named Jacques Bernard, and Felix had offered him a position with them as their main chef, which he'd taken with alacrity.

Gabrielle was very happy with the way their household was turning out. Molly had been promoted to their main housekeeper (although, in such a small house she didn't have anyone under her yet, but she would eventually), her husband Robert would be their head groom, Taylor was going to stay on as their butler, Jacques would be their chef, and hopefully she'd soon be able to find a young lady to take Molly's place as her ladies' maid. It was a warm and friendly household staff, which helped her feel more secure in her position as the lady of the house.

Her happy spirit, and her slightly amorous notions after her talk with Cynthia and Arabella during the evening, made her feel rather wanton, and she dressed in her most seductive gown for the evening. It was very low cut, and normally she would have worn a fichu with it, but since they had no guests at their table she went without, leaving the creamy white flesh of her breasts completely bare. She felt very daring, with all that dark blue silk contrasting against the paleness of her breasts, and little puff sleeves setting off her shoulders. A single sapphire drop necklace drew further attention to the amount of exposed skin she was revealing.

When Felix saw her, his eyes flared hot with desire and Gabrielle felt herself warm in response. She laughed inwardly as he rushed her through dinner, feeling a bit guilty that Jacques' efforts to please his new employers were obviously wasted. Felix couldn't be tasting a bite, he was eating so fast. In an effort to slow him, she asked plenty of questions about his day - and about his brothers once he told her that he'd spent the afternoon with them.

She was looking forward to seeing them again, although she doubted they would be present at the Viscountess' tea tomorrow, since they were doing their best to avoid further attempts at match-making. Felix seemed very pleased with himself as he described his brothers' chagrin.

As soon as she'd taken her last bite of a splendid strawberry tart with cream, Felix was already standing up and holding out his hand.

"Come here, beautiful."

Excitement kindled in her lower belly and she stood, placing her slender fingers in his. He drew her to him, placing his hand on the back of her neck and tilting her head back, cradling the back of her head and holding her in place. A secret thrill went through her at his easy handling and domination of her body.

"Did you wear this dress to drive me mad?" he asked, his eyes sliding down from her face to her exposed breasts. Pressed against him, with her breathing so heavily, she felt like the fabric might slip and her nipples would be revealed at any moment.

"Yes," she admitted, breathing the word out.

He kissed her, holding her tightly against him, his fingers sliding into her hair, his other hand pressed against her waist. Gabrielle met his kiss with her own as she slid her hands inside his jacket, leaning into him with eagerness.

Breaking off the kiss, he practically dragged her from the room as she laughed, nearly tripping to keep up with him.

"I like this house," Felix announced as he pulled her into their bedroom, his fingers already unerringly aiming for the buttons down the back of her dress. "It's small enough that the bedroom is always nearby."

"Is waiting till we reach the bedroom necessary?" Gabrielle asked innocently, fluttering her lashes. "The Marquess-"

"Philip can do what he likes, but I'm not willing to risk sharing any bit of you unintentionally," Felix said, fierce possessiveness ringing through his voice and making her heart pound a little faster. Something on the back of her dress ripped. "Dammit."

Laughing again, Gabrielle didn't protest as Felix made short work of the rest of their clothes before pressing her back to the bed. Taking his cravat, he wound it about her wrists, sending her arousal soaring as he made her helpless, tying them to one of the stout posts in the corner, dragging her body diagonally across the bed so that she was stretched out and completely vulnerable. She trembled with need, her pussy creaming with arousal as she tugged at the makeshift bonds and found them to be completely secure.

"Beautiful," Felix murmured, dark eyes glowing with an inner flame. Gabrielle blushed as he looked down at her, feeling a bit like a virginal sacrifice being offered up to a dark, erotic god. Of course, she wasn't at all virginal, but the fantasy did add a certain extra edge to her excitement.

Cupping her breasts, Felix squeezed roughly, his fingers pinching her nipples and nearly flattening them. Gabrielle cried out, her breasts arching upwards as if begging for more. The sharp pain made her body throb, the ache between her legs growing exponentially in response.

"You were naughty today, weren't you?"

For one shocked moment, Gabrielle thought that he somehow knew what she, Cynthia, and Arabella had been talking about while they'd visited, but his next words reassured her.

"You wore a dress specifically to tease me through dinner, didn't you?"

His fingers twisted and the pain in her nipples increased, making tears spring to her eyes even as her body clenched in need, the slickness between her nether lips sliding down the crack of her buttocks.

"Yes!" She didn't know whether she was answering his question or just responding to his harsh manipulation of her tender breasts and nipples.

"Such a naughty girl," he murmured, giving her nipples one last tight pinch before releasing them. The tender buds pulsed, sensitive after the abuse, but Gabrielle still felt a keen disappointment, until he turned her over so that she was face down. They pressed into the bed, exacerbating their soreness, as Felix straddled her lower thighs.

SMACK! SMACK! SMACK!

Wiggling, Gabrielle moaned. Felix wasn't spanking her hard enough to truly hurt, just hard enough to make her want him even more. Hard enough to wake up the responses in her body that knew pain came before intense pleasure. With him straddling her legs, she couldn't move very well, certainly not well enough to rub herself against the bed and find relief that way.

SMACK! SMACK! SMACK!

It was maddening and arousing, exciting and frustrating. Her nipples rubbed against the sheets as she squirmed, her bottom starting to feel quite warm under the steady, erotic assault of Felix's slaps.

"Your bottom is so pretty when it turns pink, like watching a sunset as it become rosier and rosier."

SMACK! SMACK! SMACK!

He spanked her until she was begging him to take her - not because it hurt too much, but because she was so hot that if she didn't find release soon, she thought she might explode. Felix flipped her over and spread her legs, his cock easily sliding into her wet haven, and pounding into her until she was screaming in ecstasy and he joined her in his own, explosive release.

LOOKING down at his sleeping beauty, Felix cradled her closer, trying to reconcile the conflicting emotions he had. He was planning on seeing Philip tomorrow but, for the first time, he wasn't looking forward to seeing his friend. It bothered him deeply that Cordelia hadn't come to see Gabrielle today.

His own mother had visited last night, two of Gabrielle's friends had done so today - where was her stepmother? Even if she had sometimes struggled with Gabrielle as a stepdaughter, she had a certain amount of familial obligation... or had Cordelia washed her hands of Gabrielle as soon as the ink was dry on her wedding license to Felix?

It made him angry, even more so because it was quite clear to Felix that Gabrielle hadn't expected any callers. She'd been delighted that two of her friends had cared enough to call on her and welcome her back, and she obviously hadn't expected a visit from her own step-mother or been disappointed by its lack. But she should have done. She deserved that.

There were certain social obligations that needed to be fulfilled, and even if Cordelia was busy, she should have made time. If Felix saw her tomorrow, he was going to have quite a few things to say to her regarding her treatment of Gabrielle. And if she wasn't there, he was going to have to say them to Philip.

CHAPTER 14

The Viscountess looked up as Gabrielle was shown into the gardens. Several ladies were already sipping and drinking tea, seated at little tables sprinkled throughout the patio.

The townhouse that Felix's parents were staying in was much grander than the one she and Felix had rented. Obviously the official house for the family, its foyer was expansive, with a very high vaulted ceiling and a gorgeous chandelier hanging overhead, which led to the hall Appleby had guided Gabrielle down to reach the back garden. The gardens were small but beautiful, with a marble fountain as the centerpiece to the patio.

Standing and coming to greet her, the Viscountess looked Gabrielle over and smiled approvingly. Gabrielle had chosen a pink muslin with white lace netting and fluttering sleeves to match her white and rose bonnet, giving her an appearance of being both fashionable and demure.

"You look lovely, my dear, just perfect."

"Thank you, Mother," Gabrielle said, with no small amount of relief. She certainly hadn't wanted to disappoint the Viscountess or cause her to look badly in any way.

Hooking her arm through Gabrielle's, Mother sallied forth with all the vigor of the English Navy, and just as triumphant. "Come dear, let me introduce you to my guests."

~

DUNBURY HOUSE HADN'T CHANGED a bit since Felix had left London, but somehow, he felt different walking through it. Maybe it was because he was no longer straining to hear some sign of Gabrielle's presence. Or maybe it was because he'd never entered the house simmering with resentment and disappointment in his friend.

"Felix!" Philip grinned, standing up behind his desk as Felix came into the study. The butler closed the door behind Felix, leaving them in privacy. "Welcome home."

Just seeing Philip's grinning countenance, his hazel eyes welcoming and happy, made some of Felix's more negative emotions slide away. They were still friends, even if some things needed to change, and approaching Philip in anger was surely not the best way to handle the matter.

They clasped hands and Philip waved Felix towards one of the armchairs as he went to the cabinet where he kept his best brandies and scotches, pouring them both a drink as he spoke. "How was the honeymoon? Your parents said the summerhouse was uninhabitable, so you kicked them out of their own home."

His eyes twinkled as he handed Felix a glass of scotch, seating himself in the armchair across from him.

"Well it is rather hard to honeymoon with my mother hovering," Felix said, relaxing slightly. "I feel I made the right choice in leaving the capital, however. And in asking my parents to return to it. Gabrielle and I are now on good terms. She's... wonderful."

Tilting his head slightly, Philip studied him and then nodded. "Good. I'll admit to some reservations over the hastiness of the marriage, especially because you seemed so unsure, but all's well that ends well."

Felix had almost forgotten how seriously Philip took his responsibilities towards Gabrielle, which just made him frown. His friend looked at him in surprise, obviously not expecting that response, which meant Felix had to explain.

"Why hasn't Cordelia come by to see Gabrielle yet?"

Philip blinked. "She hasn't?"

"No." Some of the tension left Felix as he realized that, whatever Cordelia's reasons, they'd had nothing to do with his friend. Animosity between the two women he could handle; if Philip had taken against Gabrielle for some reason, well it wouldn't have ended their friendship but it could hurt it. He'd felt very defensive up until this moment.

Now Philip frowned, his expression becoming foreboding. "I thought she'd gone over there yesterday afternoon."

"No, Arabella and Cynthia both came by, but not Cordelia."

Muttering something under his breath, Philip shook his head and took a long draw of scotch. Feeling much more companionable now, and trusting that his friend would take care of it, Felix did the same. Philip was protective of his wife as well, of course, but he was also a stickler for duty, and it was Cordelia's duty - both social and as Gabrielle's stepmother - to visit Gabrielle immediately. If anyone knew that she hadn't... well, they hadn't worked so hard to quell the gossip about Gabrielle's quick marriage only to have it all brought up again by the seeming disapproval of the Marchesse of Dunbury upon Gabrielle's arrival back in London.

SITTING BESIDE THE VISCOUNTESS, Gabrielle was truly enjoying herself. She'd become accustomed to the social whirl before her wedding, but now she found herself in an entirely different position altogether. No longer a debutante, she was now a wife - and not only that, a wife with several prominent allies. The Viscountess' closest friends included not one but two duchesses, several Marchesses and countesses, and one rather frightening elderly baroness who merely had to speak and everyone jumped, despite her lower position on the social scale.

Although Gabrielle was best friends with the sister of a duke, she still hadn't moved in such rarefied circles before her marriage. Now she'd been accepted with open arms and was hearing an earful. Their gossip wasn't the petty, shallow gossip of debutantes. While they talked about many of the same things - such as bachelors and marriages - their focus wasn't on how handsome a man was or whether or not his shoulders might be padded. They were interested in his finances, his reputation, and the best possible dynastic match for him. It was a whole new world that she was learning about just by keeping her ears open.

She was also learning quite a bit about being a hostess from the Viscountess, and feeling a bit guilty that she'd always been so resistant when Cordelia had tried to teach her... but Cordelia had been boring. She'd wanted Gabrielle to just sit and watch, passively learning from her example, whereas the Viscountess had Gabrielle by her side, greeting each guest along with her. The Viscountess also whispered little tidbits about each person afterwards, which helped Gabrielle remember them. Instead of feeling lost or resentful of having to observe her mentor's unattainable perfection, she felt involved and interested. Perhaps if she had made more of an effort under Cordelia's tutelage... but she hadn't been ready.

Still, her guilt and recognizing her unpleasantness made her put more effort into greeting her stepmother when she arrived than Gabrielle ever had before.

Cordelia's eyes widened slightly in surprise as Gabrielle greeted her with a sincere smile, and then even more so as she watched the Viscountess guide Gabrielle through greeting the Dowager Duchess who had followed Cordelia through the door. Gabrielle still felt guilty, but she also felt a bit smug about showing that Cordelia that she was now a mature, sophisticated wife. Not only that, but that she was worthy of being Felix's wife.

The Viscountess shooed Gabrielle away, insisting she walk with Cordelia and make any necessary introductions. "I'm sure you'll have no trouble remembering their names," she said, with an encouraging wink.

It felt strange to be in Cordelia's company again. Her stepmother was as beautiful as ever, in her jade green gown with matching ivory slippers, gloves, and bonnet. Gabrielle's emotions were what had changed... she still felt some resentment towards her stepmother, but it was colliding with this new sense of guilt, along with the stirrings of jealousy that she'd almost forgotten about, which was tangled with a deep need for Cordelia's approval.

"The country seems to have agreed with you," Cordelia said, with her usual gentle smile, her eyes searching Gabrielle's face - for what, Gabrielle didn't know. "I'm a bit surprised, as you were so eager to come to London."

"It was a very nice visit," Gabrielle said, feeling a bit off kilter. She couldn't tell if Cordelia's comment had been meant to be provoking or not. Part of her felt provoked, but another, newer, more mature part of her felt as though perhaps she should extend Cordelia the benefit of the doubt. Glancing over at the Viscountess, she decided to hold fast to the latter, as she didn't want to disappoint Mother on this very important day. "The estate is lovely. They had a creek that we played in, and a wishing well, and so many puppies I couldn't even fit them all in my lap."

Cordelia blinked at her, her hazel eyes widened in a kind of shock. "You and Felix played in the creek?"

Despite her determination to be the consummate hostess, Gabrielle felt a small knot of unpleasant emotion curl in her stomach when Cordelia called Felix by his Christian name. It felt like only something she or his mother should be able to do. Before, it had bothered her, but it hadn't felt like this - as though something intimately hers had been infringed upon. She also didn't particularly like the surprise in Cordelia's voice. It felt derisive, as though she couldn't imagine why Felix would want to do such a thing with his wife.

"Yes," Gabrielle said, lifting her chin haughtily, some of her old habits coming back to her as the need to protect herself from censure or mockery rose. "Every day that we could."

"How lovely." The confused tone of Cordelia's voice was at odds with her words, putting Gabrielle's back up even more.

"Felix enjoyed it greatly," she said sharply, emphasizing his name. Was Cordelia's confusion because he couldn't imagine Felix playing in a creek? Or because she couldn't imagine him spending time with Gabrielle? Jealous resentment pierced her stomach, emotions that had been buried since she'd gone on her honeymoon suddenly welling. She didn't even realize that her feet had ground to a halt. Their promenade had taken them to the edge of the crowd, fortunately, and no one was paying attention to their conversation. "We spent all our time together. The creek was something he wanted to share with *me*."

"Oh the creek!" The Viscountess suddenly appeared at Gabrielle's side as if by magic, beaming at Gabrielle. "Felix and his brothers played there every day. I know he enjoyed being able to share that with you, dear. I couldn't have chosen a more perfect bride for him than if I'd picked you out myself."

Like a force of nature, the Viscountess suddenly had Gabrielle and her stepmother moving again, both of them almost in a daze as they continued their stroll, Felix's mother between them, chattering away and providing a much-needed buffer. Surreptitiously glancing around, Gabrielle immediately knew that no one had even noticed that she had been about to tear into Cordelia, right there and in public. She felt ashamed that she'd failed Mother in such a way, and so grateful for the rescue. Even stranger, Mother didn't seem upset with her or Cordelia, although she did keep them apart for the rest of the tea.

As Gabrielle chatted and sipped tea, the tension that had wound itself around her spine during her conversation with Cordelia slowly relaxed. Every time Cordelia caught her eye, she would stiffen again, but only a little. Hopefully she would be able to avoid her stepmother for the rest of the Season.

"WHAT DO you mean you invited them to dinner?" Gabrielle was incensed and Felix couldn't understand why. Her nostrils flared, eyes sparking with fiery heat, and she looked so much like the hellion he'd first married that for a moment he thought he'd somehow traveled back in time. "You said you wouldn't make any more decisions without me!"

"Life altering decisions, sweetheart," Felix said, rubbing his temple. This was not the way he'd imagined spending their time before Philip and Cordelia arrived. "Not who to invite over for dinner."

"I don't want her here!" his wife shrieked. With her fists clenched at her sides, she looked as though she was contemplating throwing something at him again. Possibly a punch. When she glanced at a heavy china vase that was sitting on a nearby table, Felix frowned.

"Gabrielle!"

Her nostrils flared again and then she straightened, chin up, chest out, and eyes like lit coals. Obviously she'd caught the warning note in his voice - he wouldn't hesitate to spank her if he felt she deserved it, and then she'd have to sit through a dinner she didn't want with a roasted bottom.

"Yes, *dear*, of course, *dear*, whatever you say, *dear*." The simpering sneer in her voice made him wince before she turned and stalked towards the kitchen. Ostensibly to inform Jacques that they would have guests for the evening meal.

"Sweetheart..."

Ignoring him, she just moved fast down the hall.

For a moment, Felix contemplated following her, but he decided not to. He'd expected her to be in a good mood when she'd arrived home from his mother's tea, but instead she'd been quiet and introspective. Then he'd thought that hearing Philip and Cordelia were coming to dinner would cheer her up, or at least start a conversation... but it certainly hadn't been the one he'd aspired to. Since he'd already done nothing but make the situation worse, and she'd managed to control herself and keep from doing anything that would require punishment, he wouldn't prod her and risk pushing her into acting in such a manner that would. Instead he would let her calm down. After dinner, once Philip and Cordelia left, he could ask what was bothering her.

To his relief, his ploy seemed to have worked. Gabrielle arranged a menu with Jacques and then went to her room to dress for dinner. When she came downstairs, she looked resplendent in a silk dress made of varying shades of pink, trimmed with gold braid, and her hair done up high on her head. Small diamond earrings hung from her ears, but the simple gold chain around her throat made him frown. Tomorrow he would go to the jewelers and pick out some pieces for her. He'd noticed that her jewelry box wasn't very full, and most of what it held was appropriate for a debutante or a child, not for a woman married to a Viscount's son.

"You look beautiful," he said, bowing over her hand and giving it a kiss, allowing his admiration to show.

To his consternation, she didn't seem as thrilled as she usually did by the compliment; she seemed uncertain and appeared a little sickly. Was she not feeling well? Was that the real reason she'd come home from tea out of sorts and had been upset about their dinner guests? Concerned, Felix opened his mouth to ask, but then the doorbell rang. Immediately, Gabrielle braced herself, with all the determination of a soldier about to enter battle.

Sighing inwardly, Felix turned as Taylor opened the door, admitted the Marquess of Dunbury and his wife. Beside him, Gabrielle stiffened even further as Cordelia rushed towards them, a huge smile on her face.

"Welcome back to London!" she said, hugging Felix. He hugged her back gently, and then, just as gently, pushed her away. A frown creased her brow until he turned to Philip, holding out his hand for a greeting. Felix's lips twitched as he realized that Cordelia's navy satin dress matched Philip's waistcoat. He wondered if Philip had noticed. Cordelia turned to smile at Gabrielle. "Hello, again, Gabrielle."

Felix frowned. *Again?*

"Welcome to our home," Gabrielle said, her face looking somehow pale and wane, reminding Felix of his worry that she wasn't well. Still, she air kissed with Cordelia, and then Philip gave her a hug and a fatherly kiss on the forehead.

"You look beautiful Gabrielle, and the house is lovely," Philip said, not one iota of his expression betraying he had been the one to find it originally and knew it had come fully furnished. Gabrielle beamed up at him, looking a bit less strained.

"Thank you, sir," she said. "I hope you've been well."

"Very," he said affably, holding his arm out to her. Gabrielle took it and began to lead him down the hall to the dining room, leaving Felix and Cordelia in their wake.

Torn between his happiness at seeing his friends again, his worry over Gabrielle, and his protectiveness of her, Felix found that he couldn't quite erase his frown.

"Why didn't you welcome Gabrielle home as well?" he asked, stiffly holding out his arm.

Cordelia blinked up at him, her lovely hazel eyes looked a bit pink around the edges, now that he could see them closer. "I saw her earlier today at your mother's tea," she said. Which immediately made Felix wonder exactly what had occurred at the tea between the two women. "I don't think she was very pleased to see me."

The sadness in her tone made Felix feel even more torn between the two ladies, because he'd also seen how unhappy Gabrielle had been upon her return that afternoon. Before, he would have wondered what Gabrielle had done, sure that gentle Cordelia couldn't possibly have precipitated the event. Now, he just wondered what happened.

"Perhaps because you hadn't been to visit her on your own already?" he asked, trying to keep the censure out of his voice as he began to lead her towards the dining room, at a much slower pace.

"I did come... but..." Cordelia took a deep breath. "When I heard you weren't at home I decided to come at a different time. It's just been so... so calm and I've been feeling so wonderful, and I was afraid that without a buffer between us that, well, Gabrielle might ruin that. But I know it was wrong and cowardly, I should have visited whether you were at-home or not. Philip had a... a discussion about that this afternoon."

By the rising pink in her cheeks, Felix took that to mean that Philip had spanked his wife for neglecting her duty as a stepmother.

So he tamped down on his resentment over Cordelia's assumption that visiting Gabrielle could have ruined her happy state. It would take more than just a few weeks apart and a reunion to change the way the two women behaved with each other, and it seemed as though Philip already had his wife in hand, and Felix would have to be content with that. No matter how much he wanted to scold Cordelia.

"I think that, if you give her a chance, you'll find that Gabrielle will be a much better friend than she was a stepdaughter. Now that you don't have to live together, I'm sure you'll get along better," he said.

"I hope so," Cordelia replied, smiling up at him tremulously. Feeling as though he'd made a good start at mending the breach, Felix smiled back as they entered the dining room.

THE SMILE on Gabrielle's face felt brittle and strained, making her cheeks hurt as Felix and Cordelia finally walked into the dining room, looking at each other the way they always had.

Inside, her emotions were raging. Some were familiar, when it came to Felix and Cordelia, like jealousy, bitterness, and envy. Others were new, like the fear that was strangling her. The disappointment that nothing had changed. The well of misery that made her feel like she was falling, so much so that for just a moment she thought she was going to faint.

Glancing at the Marquess, she could see that he either suspected nothing or didn't care. Of course, he could rest easy in knowing that Cordelia was his. She might flirt or keep other men (namely Felix) hanging by a metaphorical hook, like a fish, but she would never betray the Marquess. She loved him.

Gabrielle had no such assurances.

The hope that she'd felt, the hope that had kindled out in the country, was crumbling to dust, and it tasted like ashes in her mouth.

Wrapping her old emotional armor around her like a familiar shroud, Gabrielle turned away from looking at either her stepmother or her husband, and focused on her table. The silver chargers underneath the china were gleaming, the candles were long and tapered, and the flowers in the center were full and bountiful, but not so high that it would be impossible to see over them and carry on a conversation. Perhaps that last had been a mistake. Gabrielle could have used a more potent shield than her own icy determination, even if it was made of flowers.

Because she was avoiding looking at them, she missed the adoring look that Felix gave her and the frown when he saw she didn't seem to have noticed that he entered the room. She also missed the wincing way Cordelia sat down - something she would have both understood and sympathized with.

The first few courses of the meal were pure torture as Felix and Cordelia chattered and gossiped, obviously intent on renewing their *close* friendship. It was strange - when Gabrielle wanted to summon tears, she could do so at the drop of a hat, but when she actually felt like crying, all her efforts were put towards keeping the tears at bay. Which she was grateful for, because it would have been extremely humiliating to sob into her potato and leek soup just because Felix was regaling Cordelia with some of the stories about his childhood that he had shared with Gabrielle just mere weeks ago.

They were just stories after all. Nothing significant.

So Gabrielle calmly sipped her soup and stayed silent, because who cared if Felix shared stories with Cordelia? Who cared if he showed her the parts of himself that Gabrielle had thought were hers, that she'd been so delighted by because it was something she'd known he hadn't shown Cordelia?

Chasing all the hurt and other, finer and more delicate, emotions in her heart into a little box, she closed it up tightly. This was her life. Her initial consensus had been proven correct - she had been foolish to hope for more. Foolish to think that a few weeks in the country with her husband might mean replacing Cordelia in his affections, much less fall in love with her.

The Marquess inserted his own remarks into the conversation, although he seemed happy to let Cordelia and Felix hold the reins. No one seemed to notice that Gabrielle wasn't participating. She'd become used to that living in Dunbury House, but Felix's family had included her and so it felt almost unnatural to be so quiet. Inwardly, she cursed herself for ever losing the habit.

As their soup bowls were cleared and the trout in lemon sauce and capers brought in, Felix suddenly remembered he had a wife.

"Gabrielle slipped and injured her ankle in the creek," he said. "I started teaching her chess while she recovered, to keep her entertained."

Such a simple recounting of the games they'd played shouldn't have felt like a betrayal, but it did. Was every moment of their time together going to be presented to Cordelia for her to know? Would none of the memories remain shared between them and no one else? Gabrielle's heart felt like it had been stabbed. Taking a bite of the fish, the sourness of the sauce feeling all too right, Gabrielle avoided her husband's eyes.

"She's very good at it, I've been playing for years and I struggle to beat her now," he said cheerfully.

"That's wonderful," Cordelia said, and Gabrielle could feel her stepmother's eyes on her as well. She ignored them both. "Philip's tried to teach me, but I haven't really the head for it. I'm much better at whist."

"Perhaps Gabrielle will play with me some time," the Marquess said. Gabrielle looked up to meet his eyes. The expression on his face as he looked at her was filled with curiosity, but she doubted it had anything to do with the chess game. He didn't look quite as foreboding as she would have expected; in fact, he looked almost concerned. "If you'd like a more advanced teacher than Felix, that is." The sly grin he sent in the direction of his friend made him look almost approachable.

This was the Marquess at his best, the almost fatherly way he'd been with her on the night of her come-out. Gabrielle found herself giving him a small smile back. "That would be lovely, thank you, sir."

To her right, she could practically feel Felix frowning at her as she turned her attention immediately back to her plate. Part of her was snidely delighted to have his attention on her, to know that *he* knew she was ignoring him. Another part of her wished he wasn't focusing on her, because she didn't know how well she would be able to control her temper if she was actually required to speak to him and her stepmother.

Unfortunately, now that her husband had remembered her existence, he apparently wanted her to speak as well.

"Gabrielle, sweetheart," he said, as she tried to keep her shoulders from stiffening at the endearment, "what was your favorite part of our trip?"

"The solitude," she replied, eyes on her plate as she lifted another forkful of food.

Felix coughed and she felt a tiny spike of victory.

"It must have been nice to have a break from all the noise and constant company in the capital," Cordelia said. Gabrielle wanted to sneer at her stepmother. In the past she would have. Perfect Cordelia to the rescue, attempting to spread peace and joy everywhere. Showing off what a delightful lady she was, smoothing over Gabrielle's rough edges. Which, of course, just made Gabrielle look even more like a harridan and Cordelia even more like a sweet, genteel lady. She couldn't just keep her mouth shut and let everyone pass over it and start a new topic of conversation, she had to point out by her example just how much better she was than Gabrielle.

Resentment churned and Gabrielle's jaw clenched to keep her from saying anything more. She knew it would only make her look worse and - even more lowering - probably earn her a spanking from her husband for daring to be rude to darling Cordelia.

The silence hung heavy over the table and Gabrielle knew all eyes were on her.

She lifted another portion of fish to her mouth.

"Gabrielle." Felix's tone was reproving.

Gabrielle chewed, lifting her eyebrow at him as if to say - *you answer her.* Obviously Gabrielle couldn't. Her mouth was full. Oh darn.

Sighing, Felix turned back towards Cordelia. "It was very pleasant to be away, although it's nice to be back as well. I enjoyed the break from all the social activities while it lasted. And my parents certainly enjoyed having us until they came back to London."

"Did you enjoy getting to know the Viscount and Viscountess, Gabrielle?" Cordelia asked, in that coaxing way she had. That tone that said 'see how hard I'm trying to reach out to my stepdaughter?' It grated on Gabrielle's already overtaxed nerves.

"Very much," Gabrielle said, before falling silent again. She took another bite of fish.

"My parents adored her," Felix said swiftly, filling in the gap. "They asked her to call them Mother and Poppa immediately."

Silverware clattered against china, the sound loud and surprising enough that even Gabrielle looked up to see what had happened. Cordelia's face was rather pale, her eyes huge as she stared across the table at Gabrielle.

Clearing her throat, Cordelia picked up the fork again. "How lovely."

Bitter satisfaction simmered as Gabrielle realized that her stepmother was somehow hurt by the idea of Gabrielle calling someone else mother. Although, Cordelia had admitted that she thought of Gabrielle as more of a sister, apparently some part of her still felt replaced. Rejected. It felt good, powerful, to see that something about Gabrielle could actually hurt Cordelia, rather than the other way round. And so she did exactly what she'd been telling herself not to do - she lashed out.

"Mother is the sweetest, most generous person in the world," she said smoothly, her voice laced with saccharine sweetness. "She welcomed me immediately and made me feel right at home, like I was her real daughter. We spent every afternoon together and she's already taught me so much. She's everything I ever wanted in a mother."

It was all true, but none of it needed to be said so outright, especially not to Cordelia. In her heart of hearts, Gabrielle knew that Cordelia had tried, to the best of her ability, to be a good stepmother to Gabrielle. But she had been young and inexperienced herself, in no way ready to be a stepmother to such a resentful stepdaughter and an indifferent husband. And Gabrielle knew that Cordelia's marriage to the Marquess hadn't been motivated by a desire to cause a huge upheaval to Gabrielle's life or to rub in Gabrielle's face what she would never have, and, logically, she knew that Cordelia's desire to marry Gabrielle off hadn't been purely selfishly motivated...

But knowing all of that didn't change any of how it made her feel.

Now if only she felt better looking at Cordelia's sad face. It was almost enough to make her falter and apologize, until she caught sight of Felix's expression. He looked just as condemning and angry as the Marquess - and he had no right to be! Ignoring Gabrielle all evening while dancing attendance on Cordelia, and now being just as angry at Gabrielle as Cordelia's husband? Shouldn't her own husband have some kind of faithfulness?

Of course not... not if the competition was with *darling* Cordelia.

"Gabrielle, may I speak to you outside for a minute?"

Tears pricking at the back of her eyes, Gabrielle dropped her fork so that it clattered against the plate, making Cordelia jump at the loud sound. What a ninny.

CHAPTER 15

Holding the door open for his wife, Felix gripped her arm and practically dragged her to the front parlor so that Philip and Cordelia wouldn't be able to hear any of their conversation. He had no idea what had just happened... everything had been going so well! He'd been satisfied knowing Cordelia had been punished for not attending to her duty as Gabrielle's stepmother, and while Gabrielle didn't know that, she also didn't seem to have cared that Cordelia hadn't visited before today. At first she'd been the perfect hostess, taking Philip into the dining room, and then she'd been rather quiet, but he didn't understand why she'd suddenly turned back into the sniping, biting, sharp-tongued creature she'd been when she'd first arrived in London.

Although at least they weren't in public, but she'd obviously been very aware that she had been slurring Cordelia as a stepmother, hurting Cordelia's feelings in the process, without provocation, and that was unacceptable. He couldn't allow her to think such behavior was acceptable, even in private. Give Gabrielle an inch, and she'd take a mile.

He also had to admit he was disappointed... he'd thought she'd turned over a new leaf in the country. Felix enjoyed London, and he thought Gabrielle did too, but if this was how she was going to behave then they might have to rusticate in the country more often than not. Even if she only behaved this way around Cordelia, that wasn't acceptable, as they ran in all the same circles and he wasn't going to sacrifice his friendship with Philip for Gabrielle's animosity.

"What was that?" he asked, releasing her to close the parlor door behind them. Gabrielle glided away from him, across the room to look out the front window.

"What was what?"

"Gabrielle, look at me."

Her shoulders stiffened, her chin stubbornly tilted upwards, but she did as he commanded. With the little bit of light coming in from the street, her face was shadowed, making it impossible to read her expression.

"What you said to Cordelia was uncalled for-" he started, and Gabrielle sneered so widely that even in the dim lighting he could see it.

"Oh my, well, poor *Cordelia,* I'm so sorry if *Cordelia's* feelings were hurt by nothing less than the truth-"

"Even if it was the truth-"

"It was!"

"That doesn't mean it had to be said. Did you want to hurt her?"

Crossing her arms, Gabrielle looked away again, her lips firm and stubborn in profile, her jaw clenched in determination. Felix felt like growling. What had happened to the sweet but fiery submissive wife he'd come to know? Where had this bad tempered she devil come from? The Gabrielle he'd come to know would never have been deliberately cruel... and yet he knew she had been before their marriage. It was back to the two Gabrielle's apparently.

"I can't let this slide, Gabrielle," he said, slowly. He didn't want to punish her tonight, especially when she was obviously already out of sorts and had been since this afternoon, but he had no choice. If he was going to keep her from running roughshod over him as a husband he had to put his foot down, immediately and firmly. With a stifled sigh, he moved over to sit on the couch and patted his knee. "Come here."

Even though he couldn't see her expression, he could feel her stare of astonishment. He hadn't thought her spine could get any stiffer, but now she was straighter than a poker stick. In fact, it looked liked there was one rammed up her-

"You can't!" The utter shock in her voice only strengthened his resolve. He hadn't given her a punishment spanking in quite a while now, but that didn't mean she should take it for granted that she would never get another one.

"Now, Gabrielle. You were rude and thoughtless, and if you ever say anything like that in anyone's hearing again, if I ever hear any gossip about you maligning Cordelia as a mother figure - as there would be if we'd had any other guests tonight - you'll be getting far worse than my hand. I'm not going to tolerate this kind of behavior, and we're going to nip it in the bud right now. You're better than this."

To his consternation, she stomped over and threw herself over his lap, every line of her body trembling in wounded betrayal. It wasn't the reaction he'd been expecting, to be honest. He'd thought she'd argue more, fight more, and have to be threatened more or even coaxed to place herself in position. At worst, possibly chased. Instead, she was acting like a martyr, and the expression on her face - which he'd only glimpsed - had been one of aggrieved disappointment. As if she'd expected better from *him*. Which he didn't understand at all.

Gathering himself, Felix lifted her skirts and pulled the sides of her open seam drawers apart to frame her creamy buttocks as he cleared his throat. It was a beautiful sight, but at the moment he found no joy in it. "Do you understand why you're being punished, Gabrielle?"

"Because I complimented your mother," she replied sullenly.

SMACK!

A pink print appeared in the center of her right buttock; a warning shot, despite the fact that his lips involuntarily twitched at her entirely truthful and yet incomplete statement.

"Compliments to my mother are always welcome, unless they're stated in such a way to be an insult to someone else," he said sternly. "Why are you being punished Gabrielle."

She sniffed. "Because complimenting your mother makes Cordelia look badly."

SMACK!

Gabrielle yelped. He hadn't smacked her other cheek to even her out, instead he'd hit the exact spot that he'd already spanked, turning it an even brighter shade of pink.

"Because you think I insulted Cordelia." Gabrielle sneered her stepmother's name, almost making Felix fumble at the animosity in her voice. Animosity that he definitely did not understand.

"Why are you angry at Cordelia?" he asked, resting his hand on her bottom, just over the spot where he'd spanked her, rubbing it gently. If she had a good reason, he would temper the punishment. She still needed to change how she behaved - even justified anger wasn't reason enough for veiled insults to Cordelia, which would make both ladies the talk of the *ton* if Gabrielle were indiscreet enough to air her anger in public.

"Why would I be angry at *Cordelia*?" Gabrielle asked stiffly. Felix wished that he could see her face, although he doubted it would help. He could picture her icy expression with ease, the one that gave away nothing. "What could *Cordelia* have possibly done wrong? She's *perfect*."

"If you have anything to say in your defense, I will listen," Felix said gently, still rubbing her bottom. He didn't miss the jealousy in Gabrielle's voice, and he supposed it must have something to do with the rivalry that his mother had mentioned. Both ladies were very beautiful, after all, and similar in age. While he didn't have any sisters of his own, he'd observed plenty of sisters, and had seen how jealous and competitive those relationships could be.

Stubborn silence met his offer. He couldn't imagine what excuse she would give anyway. Sighing, Felix stopped rubbing her bottom.

"Our friends have worked hard to ensure there would be no gossip about our marriage," he said sternly, lecturing her as he began to spank.

"It would be ill of us to undo their hard work by providing new fodder for the *ton,* and insulting your stepmother, a Marchesse, would certainly do that, no matter how veiled."

SMACK! SMACK! SMACK!

At least he wasn't focusing all of his attention on one spot anymore. Gabrielle squirmed as his hard hand impacted against her bottom. This wasn't fun or exciting like other spankings. She was utterly miserable, both about her behavior and Felix's attitude.

What could she have said to defend herself? Nothing. Cordelia hadn't done anything outwardly wrong. It was Felix who had given Cordelia permission to use his Christian name. Felix who was infatuated with Cordelia, not the other way round. No, Cordelia did nothing to rebuke or deter him, but Cordelia shouldn't have to tell him to attend to his own wife. He should just do it, the way the Marquess did. Gritting her teeth, she took her spanking, determined to just get through this.

Perhaps she did deserve a spanking for being intentionally cruel to Cordelia. Gabrielle had lashed out. She could have been the better person. Wasn't that part of what made her so jealous of Cordelia? So resentful? But it wasn't that Gabrielle was incapable of being a perfect lady, she just let her emotions get the better of her... she could have risen above it and been coolly polite, instead of being cruel and snappish.

"Implying that she's an unfit mother... well, that's a poor way to repay her care of you."

SMACK! SMACK! SMACK!

The skin of her bottom was becoming more and more sensitive as Felix's hand slapped against it, over and over again, turning her creamy skin bright pink as he spanked her from crest to sit-spot. Gabrielle couldn't tell if her tears were from the humiliation of being spanked while Cordelia and the Marquess were in the other room, the humiliation of needing to be spanked at all, the actual pain from the sharp slaps that were raining down without mercy, or from the pain in her chest over her broken heart.

"You don't have to love her."

SMACK! SMACK!

"You don't even have to like her."

SMACK! SMACK!

Liking Cordelia wasn't the problem. Neither was loving her. Gabrielle did both. She just also hated her sometimes. Her emotions about her stepmother were nothing that she wanted to examine closely, because they made no kind of sense.

A sob rose in Gabrielle's throat. The spanking was starting to burn like the dickens and she couldn't stop squirming, trying to get away, no matter how much she wanted to hold onto her dignity. She'd forgotten how much a punishment spanking hurt, how hot her skin could get, only to flare anew every time his hand landed. The heat in her bottom was finally more painful than any of the emotional pain she was feeling, and it didn't seem like there was an end in sight.

"If you want to make a complaint about her, you will do so *privately*, and certainly not to her or where you may be overheard."

SMACK! SMACK!

Ow... ow... he had to stop soon, didn't he? The icy, rebellious resolve to take her spanking in silence was starting to melt.

"But otherwise, you will behave civilly and politely -"

SMACK! SMACK!

Oh please...

"Whether about her or anyone else."

SMACK! SMACK!

"I won't! I won't talk about anyone, I'm sorry!" Gabrielle blurted out, her fingers digging into the couch cushion to keep from reaching behind her and covering up her roasted nates. Her dignity was shredded and she didn't care anymore, she just wanted the spanking to stop.

SMACK! SMACK! SMACK! SMACK!

Felix unleashed a small flurry of lighter, sharply stinging swats that had her crying out, before he suddenly stopped. Slumping, Gabrielle pressed her face against the couch and cried. She only stopped when Felix started to gather her up and she realized that he meant to cuddle her as he often did.

Instead, she pushed his hands away, scrambling to her feet, not even able to take satisfaction in the confusion and unhappiness of his expression. For one long moment they stared at each other, as Gabrielle's emotions churned wildly, her bottom throbbing painfully underneath her skirts. It felt like her skin had been roasted. She couldn’t go back into that other room and sit down. Not in front of Cordelia and the Marquess. Just thinking about it made her want to start sobbing again.

"Please give my excuses to our guests, I'm not feeling well," she said, forcing the words out through the thickness in her throat, before turning and fleeing the room.

Behind her, she heard Felix calling her name, but she didn't care. If she stayed, he'd hold her, and it would feel wonderful, and she'd want to stay there forever. She'd want to pretend that today hadn't happened, to pretend that he was actually hers. And it would only hurt all the more when they returned to the dining room and she'd probably have to apologize to Cordelia and then watch Felix dote on her for the rest of the night.

She just couldn't do it.

Not because of Cordelia, though.

Gabrielle finally understood.

Philip didn't care about any rivals, because he knew that Cordelia's love was his. Cordelia wasn't the problem... Felix was.

Numbly, Gabrielle changed into the thickest nightgown she owned, not caring that she'd be overheated, barely acknowledging Molly's hovering presence. Her bottom throbbed painfully, the only spot of heat in the icy coldness that seemed to have numbed her, both physically and emotionally.

Curling up in the bed, completely exhausted, Gabrielle closed her eyes, ignoring the wetness on her cheeks. She supposed that she could ask Molly to have one of the guest rooms made up and retreat there... but she didn't. From now on she was going to be just like

Cordelia, because that was obviously what Felix wanted. Dutiful, quiet, ladylike, always taking the moral high ground... Cordelia would never play in a creek or insult a guest at dinner. She was the epitome of a lady and that was what Gabrielle would aspire to be now. Maybe it wouldn't make Felix love her, but at least she wouldn't be spanked as often... and she wouldn't be as vulnerable to him.

If duty was all that was left to her in this relationship, then she would act as Felix's wife, to the very letter. He'd demanded that they share the same bed, so here she was; although, she hoped that for the sake of her heart he would take the hint from her nightgown and leave her be for tonight. She needed the time to shore up her emotional defenses. Tomorrow she could face him with her new attitude and her new standards for herself.

Perhaps she would never have a happy life, but she would follow Cordelia's example and make the best of it. After all, that's what Cordelia had done with Gabrielle's father. She was just lucky that her second marriage had turned out so well. Gabrielle was unlucky... but sometimes that was just how the dice rolled. Maybe one day she'd have a second marriage that she could find happiness in… but that would mean that Felix would be gone and that thought hurt too much for her find to any comfort at all in it.

Pressing her face to her pillow, Gabrielle told herself that she would learn to live with it, and pretended not to notice the way her tears damped the sheets.

WHEN FELIX RETURNED to the dining room, Philip and Cordelia both looked up with worry in their eyes. Well, Cordelia's worry was writ across her face, whereas only someone who knew him well would note Philip's concern.

"Where's Gabrielle?" Cordelia asked, her eyes flicking behind him as if she expected her stepdaughter to appear there at any moment.

"She... wasn't up to finishing dinner," Felix said carefully.

The scowl that Cordelia gave him was almost threatening as she started to stand. "How hard did you hit her? Why-"

"Cordelia," Philip said repressively, putting his hand on her arm and pulling her back down into her chair. His hazel eyes pinned her in place. "Felix would never hit Gabrielle. And if he spanked her, that's between the two of them. She's his wife." Still, he gave Felix a look that said he'd better not have doled out more than Gabrielle could handle, but it was more a habitual, protective response. Felix could tell that his friend wasn't truly worried that Felix was abusing Gabrielle.

Cordelia crossed her arms over her chest, her voice higher than normal but determined. "I'm not leaving here until I know Gabrielle is alright."

"Perhaps if you wanted to check in on her you should have done so when we first arrived in town, rather than making up excuses not to," Felix snapped, his temper flaring.

He hated that Gabrielle hadn't allowed him to comfort her, hated that she'd run from him. Part of him had wanted to follow after her, but not only would that have been unaccountably rude and setting a poor example for the kind of behavior he expected from her as his wife, but he wasn't sure it would make anything better. Everything about her posture had screamed that she wanted space away from him. Whatever had set her off, maybe she just needed some time to deal with it alone.

"Felix," Philip said, just as repressively and sounding remarkably like Felix's father when he was referring a fight among the siblings. "Cordelia has already been punished for her lapse and it will not be brought up again. Besides which, I'm sure you've already said your piece to her about it." He turned his eyes to his pouting wife, looking like a golden angel of judgement with the candlelight flickering off his blond hair. "Cordelia, I'm sure Gabrielle is fine and you may visit her tomorrow if you like, but tonight you will leave it be."

Both Cordelia and Felix glared at each other from across the table, neither of them totally happy with Philip's declarations. Resentment smoldered inside of Felix, which he tried to push down.

Gabrielle's behavior was *not* Cordelia's fault, he reminded himself. No matter what her problem with Cordelia was, Cordelia herself had done nothing to instigate Gabrielle's comments. And, even if she had, Gabrielle should know better than to respond that way. It was also not Cordelia's fault that Gabrielle hadn't wanted him to hold her after her discipline.

The rest of dinner was rather stilted and awkward. Although all three parties did their best to revive the camaraderie from earlier, it was obvious that none of their thoughts were focused on the conversation, and Gabrielle's empty chair felt like a hole in the company. All Felix wanted to do was go find his wife. Cordelia seemed to have the same thought, although she was beholden to her husband's dictates. Felix had no doubt that she'd be back tomorrow, however, to try and talk to Gabrielle.

Too little, too late, apparently.

He wondered if someone at the tea had said something to Gabrielle about Cordelia not visiting them sooner... but no, she would have told him. He'd even given her the time to do so.

After a rather strained goodbye, Felix hurried up the stairs to the bedroom, slowing when he was only a few feet away from the door, marshaling his arguments and defenses for not following his wife here immediately.

None of them were needed. A single candle on his side of the bed was flickering, giving him just enough light to see by. Gabrielle was a lump in the bed, her back towards the candle. She didn't even twitch when he entered, and her even, easy breathing made it clear that she wasn't feigning sleep.

Moving around to her side of the bed, he couldn't see much of her face in the darkness, but he could see that her eyes were still pink and swollen from crying, could still see the glistening tear tracks on her cheeks. The sight made his chest squeeze tightly, something like regret grabbing hold of him. Yet, he couldn't allow her to get away with bad behavior, even in a fairly private setting like tonight's dinner. Nor did he want her to think that he would ignore outright cruelty towards others.

As her husband, it was his duty to see to it that she was disciplined when she misbehaved.

Reaching out his hand, he almost touched her face before he drew it back, frowning as he realized that her brow was beaded with sweat. Tugging back the covers, he shook his head as he realized that she'd not only piled them on top of her, but that she was wearing a thick nightgown beneath, which covered her from neck to wrist to toe. No wonder she was sweating!

Shaking his head, Felix divested her of the nightgown, ignoring her sleepy protests. It was clear she wasn't fully awake, for none of her murmurs made any kind of sense. She was clearly exhausted. Baring her body made his cock stir, especially when he saw her still-pink buttocks peeping up at him, but he controlled himself.

Considering the nightgown she'd been wearing, he doubted she'd welcome any advances this evening.

Shucking off his own clothing, Felix turned his mind over the problem of his wife. Now that they were back in London, their relationship would change somewhat, he'd known that... but he thought they'd been doing rather well until today. Either he'd been wrong, or something momentous had happened today. Perhaps he'd stop by his parents' residence tomorrow and ask his mother. There had to be something he was missing.

WHEN GABRIELLE AWOKE in Felix's arms, she didn't hesitate about pulling away, mostly because she wanted to snuggle closer. Her heart rejoiced that he'd still wanted to sleep with her in his arms. Her brain noted that he'd removed her nightgown but obviously hadn't wanted to bed her. Because he'd been thinking of Cordelia? Or because he'd received the message she'd meant to send with her attire?

In sleep, he was beautiful and tempting, but Gabrielle refused to be tempted. She dressed swiftly and without help in a simple gown.

Retreat was the better part of valor, she decided, slipping quietly out of the room. It was very early for London, but she was still on country time. Calling Molly, she decided to visit the shops. Not the modiste or the milliners, but somewhere fun. A doll's shop, she decided, for Molly's daughters. Felix had given her an allowance and she didn't need any clothes.

As they walked through Mayfair, Molly a step or two behind her as befitted a maid accompanying her mistress on an outing, Gabrielle felt another stab of guilt about her treatment of Cordelia. Not for last night, surprisingly, but as she remembered Cordelia's upset over Gabrielle overspending during a shopping trip financed by the Marquess. Now that it was technically her own money that she would be spending, Gabrielle realized that she had no desire to go over the amount Felix had allowed her. She didn't want to disappoint him or give him a reason to be upset with her. Cordelia had surely felt the same about the Marquess.

After buying a new doll each for Molly's daughters, Gabrielle and Molly stepped outside to find that the streets were beginning to fill up with people. She didn't want to run into anyone she was acquainted with and have to make small talk, but at the same time, she didn't feel ready to return home yet. Chewing her lower lip for a minute, she came to a quick decision.

"I'm going to visit Arabella," she told Molly.

"Yes, ma'am," Molly said serenely. If she thought Gabrielle should return home to her husband, she was too loyal to say so.

WAKING up to an empty bed put Felix in a foul mood right from the start. He couldn't believe Gabrielle had awoken before him and managed to sneak out. Discovering that she'd left the house entirely hadn't helped any. Taylor tiptoed warily around him as he stomped through the house, muttering under his breath after he'd been told Gabrielle had gone out and not indicated when she would return.

Deciding there was no point in waiting - some inner instinct told him that she wouldn't be making a reappearance swiftly - he went directly to his parents, inadvertently interrupting their breakfast. His father was at his usual place at the head of the table, reading the daily paper, with his wife beside him, chattering without caring whether or not he was listening. Felix's mother was always more relaxed looking at breakfast, with her hair in a loose coiffure and wearing a soft grey morning dress that made her seem more approachable than she did in the evenings when she was playing her role as Viscountess to the hilt.

"Felix! How lovely, where is Gabrielle? Sit down, sit down, have you eaten yet?" His mother didn't even take a breath as she waved him to a chair, crooking her finger at a footman who immediately set a place at the table. His father gave him a nod before disappearing back behind his newspaper.

"I haven't," he admitted. He'd been too piqued at Gabrielle's disappearance, despite the fact that she'd arranged to have his breakfast made before she'd left.

"Well then you must. Coffee?" His mother waved her hand again when he nodded. "And where is Gabrielle?"

He hesitated. "She is indisposed at the moment."

To his shock, his mother's face lit up. "Indisposed?"

Oh for... Bloody hell. He realized what his mother thought and started to shake his head, before a thought caught him up fast. Was she? If she was breeding, that could explain her sudden swings in mood and temperament. Then he shook his head again, because - just in case she wasn't - they didn't need his mother hovering.

"No, mother, not in that manner." Felix smiled as his breakfast was set in front of him. It smelled delicious, especially the sausage, and his stomach was suddenly reminded that it was empty. "I actually wanted to speak with you without her... did anything happen at tea yesterday that might have upset Gabrielle?"

His mother paused, her hand on her fork, and blinked. "Well, she did have a moment with the Marchesse of Dunbury, but she didn't seem particularly upset by it."

"What kind of moment?" he asked, a hint of warning in his voice. His mother had the tendency to underplay anything that made her children look bad, and he doubted she'd change that for Gabrielle. Beside her, his father peered over the top of the newspaper again, obviously interested in anything that had to do with Gabrielle even if he didn't come right out and say it.

"It was just a moment, Felix," his mother said irritably, waving her hand at him now, as if she could dismiss him as easily as she did the footmen. "They hadn't seen each other in a while and, well, Lady Dunbury tries, but it's obvious she has no idea how to deal with Gabrielle. They're far too close in age and Lady Dunbury is far too pliable. She hasn't a clue what to do with a young lady of spirit, like Gabrielle - not that it's her fault, of course. I don't know what that father of Gabrielle's was thinking, marrying a child to take care of a child." Her superior sniff made her opinion clear on that topic.

"Well Gabrielle seemed upset when she came home yesterday, did anything else happen that might have done that?" Frustration grated on him. He needed to know what had happened so that he could fix it. He wanted his wife back. The one that he'd gotten to know in the country. The one who was fiery and funny, sweet and submissive, spirited but gentle... the one who woke up in his bed every morning, with him.

Now his mother hesitated, as if reviewing yesterday's events, a look of concern on her face. Then she frowned at him. "There was nothing of note. What did you do?"

"Me? Why do you think I did something? She was upset when she returned home." He looked at his father for help, gesturing at his mother. "Does she turn on you this easily too?"

The newspaper rose higher, effectively blocking both wife and son from the Viscount and making Felix chuckle. His mother scowled at the paper before turning her attention back to Felix.

"She and Lady Dunbury had a few words over you. I believe Gabrielle became agitated when Lady Dunbury expressed some surprise over your activities while you were away." His mother raised her eyebrows at his expression. The activities that Felix first thought of were certainly not ones that he thought Gabrielle would be sharing with anyone. "She was especially surprised to hear that you'd been playing in a creek."

"Why should that upset Gabrielle?" Felix asked, floundering. That made even less sense than if Gabrielle had, for some reason, confided in some of the more exotic activities they'd indulged in and Cordelia had expressed disapproval.

His mother gave him an exasperated look. "Gabrielle is quite sensitive to her stepmother's approval and disapproval. Playing in a creek is not proper behavior for young ladies. I believe she may also be sensitive to your and Lady Dunbury's friendship. It's hard enough to be a rival with a woman who was set up to be a maternal figure to her, much less feel as though she has to jockey for attention from her husband with that same woman."

"That's ridiculous," Felix said, shaking his head. "Not the first part, I can believe Gabrielle might have taken something Cordelia said too much to heart and become defensive or upset, but she knows that Cordelia and I are friends. We've been friends since long before Gabrielle and I were married. There's no reason for rivalry there."

His mother rolled her eyes at him. His mother! Rolling her eyes!

"How many female friends do you have, Felix?"

"Well... Cordelia, of course, and Lady Hyde and Lady Petersham -"

Raising her eyebrow expressively, his mother gave him an expression that said she thought she'd made her point. Felix made an exasperated sound.

"What?"

"You call Cordelia by her Christian name."

"Her husband is my best friend," he said defensively.

"There are none so blind as the willfully blind," she responded sagely.

"That's not a real saying, Mother, you just made that up."

"Doesn't make it any less true."

"You're wrong."

"Make note, dear," his mother said to the newspaper barrier. "I want a witness for this moment."

The newspaper rattled slightly as Felix's father let out a gusty sigh. "Yes, dear."

CHAPTER 16

Manchester House was much larger than the house that Felix and Gabrielle had rented. It had more than one parlor and sitting room, some of which afforded more privacy than the others.

When Gabrielle had first arrived, Arabella had been up for several hours already, riding in Hyde Park. Gabrielle had always wondered how Arabella managed to dance all night and then rise early in the morning to go riding. Arabella often said it was the only hour that riding there was any fun. At any rate, Gabrielle was glad for it now. Most debutantes were probably still asleep, or at least taking their time getting ready for the day, whereas Arabella was bright-eyed, bushy-tailed, and thrilled for the company.

"Are your brothers at home?" Gabrielle asked as Arabella ushered her into the morning room at the back of the house. The room was a cheerful mash of rose and yellow with bright white trim and obviously Arabella's sole domain, as both the decor and the furniture was markedly feminine.

"They're around somewhere, I'm sure," Arabella said, shrugging her shoulders. She sat in one of the armchairs, sprawling out, the heavy split-skirts of her riding habit falling apart to make her appear even more slovenly. Tendrils of hair drifted around her face, and she brushed them away impatiently, watching as Gabrielle sat across from her - rather more delicately - in another gorgeously carved chair. "What brings you here so early in the morning? You're always welcome, of course, but it is rather unexpected."

Gabrielle opened her mouth to explain, paused, and promptly burst into tears. Immediately Arabella was there, perching on the arm of the chair and pulling Gabrielle to her in a comforting embrace. It was that unthinking response that finally drew the full truth from Gabrielle, despite how humiliating it was to confess that her husband was in love with her stepmother. She held Arabella tightly, the words tumbling from her mouth, unable to stop now that she'd begun. All her pain, all her anxiety, all her broken hopes, finally unburdened onto her friend.

Cooing, Arabella rubbed Gabrielle's back soothingly, comforting her, encouraging her to continue. Finally Gabrielle recounted the events during dinner the night before, brokenly describing Felix's indifference to her once Cordelia had arrived and her subsequent behavior.

Arabella sniffed. "He's lucky you didn't toss your wine in his face. Or all over her dress."

Giggling through her tears, Gabrielle leaned her head against Arabella's soft breast, feeling calmer now. Arabella produced a handkerchief for Gabrielle to blow her nose in and dry her cheeks.

"The worst part is, he doesn't seem to even think he's doing anything wrong... or he just thinks I don't notice... or, I don't know." She swiped angrily at her cheeks. "I'm sorry. I don't mean to be so dramatic."

"Of course you do, darling, it's what I love about you," Arabella said, smiling down at her. "It's what we have in common. What's life without a little bit of drama? Dull, that's what. Do you think any of those milk-and-water misses we came out with would ever cause any drama? Of course not! They're too dull and they'll end up with dull husbands and have dull babies for the rest of their dull lives. Which is probably why very few of them have managed marriages which weren't arranged by their fathers."

Gabrielle started laughing during this derisive recitation, although her laughter felt a little hysterical. Coming to Arabella had been the correct decision. She was actually feeling better even though they hadn't solved anything.

"Well my life certainly doesn't feel dull."

"It shouldn't, it's like something out of a penny-novel! You're the lost orphan waif who comes to London and is immediately the belle of the ball, only your emotions are caught up with one man who is just out of reach, rather than all of the other men who are thronging to you! Then, after you discover his heart actually lies with your greedy stepmother, who is already married and certainly doesn't need another beau, you're forced by circumstance to marry him!" Arabella waved her arms dramatically. "If I were a writer, I could make a fortune off of you."

"Perhaps I should start," Gabrielle said dryly. "I might as well get something out of the unfortunate circumstances of my life."

"You know, most penny-novels have happy endings," Arabella said, getting up to return to her seat now that Gabrielle had her tears under control. As she sat, she frowned. "Or very tragic ones. Just promise me you won't throw yourself into the Thames. I have an appreciation for the dramatic, but not when it costs me a friend."

"I think I can promise that."

"So what are you going to do?" Arabella asked, plopping back down in her chair.

Sighing, Gabrielle wound her soggy handkerchief around her fingers. "I'm going to make the best of the situation, I suppose. I lived long enough with Cordelia, I know how she is... I can mimic her and give him what he wants."

"But what about you?"

Gabrielle shrugged. "I can hardly be unhappier than I am already. And perhaps being more like her will turn his head... if I can supplant her in his affections, then I'll have achieved my original goal."

A frown creasing her brow, Arabella mused over Gabrielle's words. "Just not as yourself."

"It's still part of myself," Gabrielle argued. "And I can be the rest of myself with you. Nothing else I've done has worked. I thought it had, but as soon as he saw Cordelia again…" She waved her hand. "Apparently whatever success I had achieved was as substantial as smoke."

"Perhaps that's not such a bad plan," Arabella said, surprising Gabrielle. Her brow had smoothed out, but her eyes still had a faraway look to them, as though she were thinking of something else. "After all, we all have different faces, do we not? Why not present the one most appealing to your desired audience?" She winked cheekily, her gaze finally focusing back on Gabrielle as she smoothed down her riding skirts. "That is why I ride when the park is deserted. My brothers have convinced me that no suitor will want a bride with a better seat than he has himself, so they've made me promise not to ride when others are around."

"A worthy suitor would have the confidence not to care," Gabrielle said, shaking her head at Arabella's brothers' folly. "Felix doesn't care a whit that I am starting to beat him at chess. Although, I confess, I am a terrible rider."

"Perhaps I should start challenging my suitors to races, to see how they react," Arabella proposed with a delighted chortle. "Sore losers receive an immediate dismissal."

"Don't you dare, sis," a deep voice from the doorway said, making both of the girls jump. The overly serious Duke of Manchester stood there, although his lips were slightly quirked in a rare smile. "I'll never get you married off if they see what a sore winner you are."

"Pish, Isaac. At least I'm fun," Arabella retorted. "How are we ever to find you a proper bride when all the young ladies think that you're a stick in the mud?"

"That doesn't seem to stop them from swarming," he said with amusement. His thoughtful dark eyes turned to Gabrielle. "Hello Mrs. Hood, welcome back to the city."

"Good morning, your grace," she said, with a small nod of her head. The Duke had told her a while ago not to bother curtsying to him, since, thanks to her close friendship with Arabella, they saw each other enough that such a formality would soon become more annoying than respectful. She still couldn't call him Isaac however, and she would never presume to suggest he should call her by her Christian name. "Thank you. And thank you for everything you and your family did in our absence."

"Our pleasure," he said. "Although I do hope you and my sister are planning to stay *out* of trouble from now on. Please don't encourage her towards horse racing, I beg of you."

Gabrielle giggled. "I'll do my best, your grace."

"Perhaps footraces?" Arabella suggested mischievously. "I'm also quite good at apple bobbing."

"I pity your poor husband," the duke muttered, shaking his head. He gave his sister a dark stare. "I hesitate to break up your tete a tete, but we have the luncheon at Lady Braden's to attend today. You agreed to be my shield against those young ladies you so disapprove of."

"Because you can do better," Arabella said with a sniff. She gave Gabrielle a regretful look. "Sorry dearest, but I did promise."

"That's fine, I should probably go home anyway and begin... my task."

As Gabrielle stood, she saw the duke cast her a somewhat suspicious glance, probably because she hadn't said exactly what her task was. Gabrielle gave him a curtsy as she passed, reminded again just how tall and imposing the man was. Even though he was young, he wore his air of authority with great poise. There was no doubting that he was a powerful man, just from looking at him.

Arabella saw her to the door and gave her a heartfelt hug. "Everything will be alright, dearest. And if it isn't, you're always welcome here."

She hugged her friend back, thankful for the unwavering love and support that Arabella had offered from the moment they'd met. Still, she hoped she would never need to take her up on that offer.

When Gabrielle returned home, she was shocked when Taylor met her at the door with the news that the Marchesse of Dunbury was in the parlor and had been waiting for her for over an hour. Taking off her gloves, she sent Molly to give the dolls to her daughters with the promise that she would visit them later to see how the presents had been received.

With some trepidation, she went to the parlor where Cordelia was waiting for her.

She felt some guilt over how she'd behaved yesterday. Cordelia's presence had struck her temper, but at the same time, she realized it wasn't Cordelia's fault. That didn't make her any more eager to see her stepmother. In fact, if she could have hidden away in her room, she would have.

But that wasn't what Cordelia would do. Cordelia would face a social situation like this as a lady. She would be cool and calm and collected. So this was the perfect time to practice being more like Cordelia. Even if it did make her heart hurt to think about why she wanted to be more like her stepmother.

"Good afternoon, Cordelia," she said, coming into the room.

Her stepmother was sitting on the chaise lounge, a pretty picture in a sapphire joplin walking dress with her hair gathered at the nape of her neck, reading a book. Quickly setting down her reading material, Cordelia stood and came towards Gabrielle, both of them clasping hands to exchange their greeting. Cordelia's hands were cool in Gabrielle's, her eyes searching Gabrielle's with concern.

"Gabrielle, are you well? I was so worried last night after... well, after."

Stiffening, Gabrielle forced a smile onto her face. That was certainly none of Cordelia's business. "I am fine, thank you for asking. I apologize for my abrupt departure from dinner. I hope you and the Marquess enjoyed the rest of your evening?"

To her surprise, instead of going along with the social pleasantries, Cordelia actually scowled! "Gabrielle, don't put me off. I was worried when you didn't come back to dinner. Did Felix... did he..."

The use of her husband's Christian name on her stepmother's lips made it even harder to keep her smile, which was starting to feel more like a snarl.

"Whatever transpired between my husband and myself is our business, although I thank you for your concern-"

"Gabrielle!" Cordelia's eyes actually flashed with temper, grinding Gabrielle's pretty speech to a halt, as the older woman's fingers tightened around her hands. It was the strangest reversal of positions - Cordelia red faced and practically stamping her foot because she wasn't getting what she wanted, while Gabrielle remained aloof and closed off. She could sympathize with Cordelia's frustration, even though part of her was enjoying it. Just a little.

As if realizing the same thing, Cordelia closed her eyes and took a deep breath, loosening her grip slightly on Gabrielle's hands. It was interesting - apparently during Gabrielle's time away, Cordelia had become more used to being a Marchesse and had finally grown a backbone. Gabrielle didn't doubt that it was the Marquess' influence. She rather wished for the old Cordelia back, however, the one who would have left Gabrielle alone the moment she met any resistance.

"Gabrielle," Cordelia said, her voice calmer. "I understand that we have not always had the best relationship, but I do care for you, and if Felix did -"

"Did what?" Gabrielle asked, now struggling to keep her own temper at Cordelia's insistence on interfering. It was as though she was accusing Felix of abusing Gabrielle while simultaneously using his given name - which made the intimacy grate all the more. Gabrielle immediately felt defensive, of both herself and Felix. Cordelia had witnessed the Marquess spanking Gabrielle, did she really think that Felix would do something worse? Or was she just trying to come between the two of them? Setting herself up as each of their allies so that she could be the one in the breach? Gabrielle snatched her hands away. "Spanked me? Like your own husband did? What would you do? Because I seem to recall you doing absolutely nothing, and you have less authority here than you did in that household." She took a deep breath, closing her eyes for a quick moment to regain her composure. Just like Cordelia had done a moment ago. She would be polite. Calm. A lady. "I appreciate your concern, but I will not discuss this with you and I think you should go."

Those big, dark brown eyes filled up with tears, and Gabrielle felt as though she'd just kicked a puppy, which made her even angrier. She turned and stalked to the parlor door, yanking it open. Ladylike… ladylike…

With the look of a martyr, Cordelia sniffed, her shoulders slumped, and she quietly proceeded into the hall and to the front door. A feeling of relief suffused Gabrielle. She just couldn't deal with Cordelia right now, and she certainly couldn't deal with Cordelia accusing Felix of... whatever. He hadn't been wrong in spanking Gabrielle for her behavior, she knew and accepted that as fact. The only thing he'd been wrong in was where his heart lay.

Taking a deep, calming breath as the front door shut, Gabrielle leaned against the parlor doorway. Cool. Calm. Collected. A real lady. Perhaps Felix would come to care for her, perhaps he would not, but either way, she would be a lady of the *ton* and she would find a way to be - if not happy - at least outwardly content.

TURNING the corner on his street, Felix nearly bowled over a young woman who was walking and sniffling with her head bent down.

"Oh! So sorry- Cordelia?"

Sniffling again, Cordelia looked up at him, her dark eyes brimming with unshed tears. "Felix... I'm sorry, I wasn't looking where I was going."

"Neither was I... are you alright?"

Cordelia nodded her head, and then shook it and then nodded again. "It's nothing I'm not used to. I went to visit Gabrielle, I just wanted to ensure she was well. I know Philip spanked her a few times, but I was always there, you see, and it's so hard to let go of the feeling of responsibility... but I don't think she appreciated my being there. I thought that maybe she and I could talk about it, maybe find it a point to bond over, but she wouldn't let me get a word in edgewise. I was just so hoping that our relationship would improve once we had some distance, but it's just as bad as ever."

Sighing, Felix pulled Cordelia into a hug, letting her sniffle against his shoulder for a few moments. He loved Cordelia like a sister, but he was starting to see what his mother meant about her not knowing how to handle Gabrielle. Despite the fact that she wasn't actually Gabrielle's mother, in a way she was a mother figure, and he doubted that Gabrielle would want to share anything about spankings - especially the kind he and she had indulged in - with her stepmother. Especially since the two were not actually very close.

"She might still be embarrassed, dear, don't feel too badly. And perhaps there are other points of married life that you two could bond over?" Felix suggested, his mouth quirking with amusement.

"I suppose," Cordelia said, stepping back and mopping up her watery eyes. Even crying she was quite a beautiful woman, although not nearly as attractive as his Gabrielle. Her tears certainly didn't affect him the same way as when his wife cried. "It was just such a revelation to me when Marjorie revealed that Christopher spanks her, and so lovely to be able to talk to someone about it, I wanted to ensure that Gabrielle had that too."

Coughing to cover his laugh, Felix just nodded his head. He hadn't realized that the Count and Countess of Irving had such a relationship, and he wasn't quite sure how to reassure Cordelia that Gabrielle had plenty of fellow-feeling from the Countess of Spencer.

"Maybe she's too embarrassed about it right now, and you can try again later. After you've bonded over other things."

"I hope so," Cordelia said. "She did seem well, and I'm sorry that last night I accused you of..." She blushed, her voice trailing off.

"I know you were just being protective of her," Felix said magnanimously. Truthfully, he was still a little hurt, but Cordelia's apology was sincere and he would be no gentleman if he didn't accept the apology. Especially since she was already in tears.

"I should be going," she said with a sniff. "Perhaps we'll see you at the Waverlys' ball?"

The ball was in two nights and was touted to be one of the highlights of the Season, in no small part because it was Lady Waverly's first as Lady Waverly. Prior to her marriage, she'd been the Dowager Duchess of Kent. Like Cordelia, her first husband had been much older.

"We'll be there," Felix said, knowing that Gabrielle had already sent their acceptance to the invitation. They already had a schedule of events set for the next three weeks. Tonight was a family dinner at his parents and tomorrow evening he was taking her to the theater, so the ball would be the first opportunity to see Philip and Cordelia again.

Hopefully by then things would be back to normal.

Saying goodbye to Cordelia, Felix continued on down the street, moving a little faster now that he knew Gabrielle was definitely in the residence - and had just had a confrontation with her stepmother. He barely gave Taylor enough time to open the door before he was sliding through it.

"Mrs. Hood is in the garden," Taylor said, not even waiting for Felix to ask the question. He nodded his thanks and headed straight there.

Sitting on a bench in the sunlight, Gabrielle was bent forward talking to Molly's girls, who were showing her their dolls. Very new looking dolls. Seeing him coming, the two little girls immediately bobbed curtsies and scampered off as Gabrielle straightened. Her expression was blank, making his insides curdle for some reason.

"Good afternoon," she said, perfectly civil and yet, the greeting was somehow empty.

"Hello, sweetheart," he said coming to a stop in front of her and holding out one hand. He expected her to refuse, or at least to hesitate, but instead she placed her hand in his immediately and came to her feet. "Having a pleasant day?"

"Very," she said, a small smile forming on her lips. It didn't quite reach her eyes. Although he would have known she was lying even if he hadn't run into Cordelia. "Would you like to walk?"

Felix accepted with alacrity. He couldn't apologize for spanking her last night, it had been deserved, but he could try to mend whatever breath had opened between them. He needed to.

Unfortunately, the walk obviously wasn't going to do it. He asked what she'd done that morning, and she'd told him about her visit to the doll shop and then Arabella's. When she told him about the dolls, she eyed him cautiously, as if expecting disapproval, but of course he didn't and she seemed to relax. It was harder than normal to read her emotions however, as if she'd somehow muted them. Muted herself.

He felt like a wall had been put up between them, one that he couldn't quantify. She didn't protest when he touched her hand, but she didn't feel right either. Frustrated, Felix tugged her between two tall hedges and pulled her into his arms.

She didn't try to pull away when he kissed her. But she didn't open to him eagerly... she was submissive and compliant, but without the joy, without the spark of passion. Holding her in his arms was like holding a shadow of herself.

Her hands rested against his chest, but didn't caress. Didn't explore.

Her lips parted for his tongue when he sought entrance, but she didn't reciprocate.

It only made Felix more wild, more determined to prove her passion. His hand went to her breast, teasing her nipple, and triumph rippled through him when he felt her finally - *finally* - respond. But when he started to pull up her skirts, she actually reacted, and not the way he wanted.

"Felix! The children might still be around!" Pulling away, she still didn't act quite like herself. Instead of giving him a dirty look or a saucy scolding, she just smoothed down her skirts, that same blank expression still on her face. "If you'll excuse me, I have some correspondence I'd like to attend to before I dress for supper."

"Of course," he said, feeling completely at a loss. He was looking at his wife, but somehow she seemed a complete stranger. This was not a side of Gabrielle that he'd seen as yet, and it was certainly not a side he favored.

~

GABRIELLE MOANED, her hips lifting as she gasped, her hands clinging to the headboard of the bed. Apparently her attempts to be more of a lady were already working in drawing her husband in - he hadn't been able to take his eyes off of her the entire evening. The more ladylike and genteel her manners, the more attentive he became.

Not that he'd been inattentive out in the country, but this was more focused attention. It had a kind of determination behind it that she'd never sensed before. Not only that, but to her delight, he hadn't spoken a word about Cordelia all day. It was as though she'd dropped from his mind. Even when his family brought up her and the Marquess for a brief moment in conversation over dinner, Felix hadn't paid any attention to it, much less contributed. He'd been too busy staring at Gabrielle.

When they'd returned home, he'd practically rushed her up to the bedroom. She'd tried to act the lady in bed at first as well, but it soon became impossible as he used his lips and hands to torment and tease her body mercilessly. There was no staying remote when he was determined to break through to her.

"Please! Felix... no more teasing!" she begged. Her pussy felt hot and swollen, the ache between them so great that it almost felt like her stomach was cramping as he licked and nibbled on her puffy lower lips. One finger pumped back and forth almost idly in her tight back hole, not enough to make her feel full, but just enough to incite her sensitive nerves and make her even hungrier for pleasure.

"Don't move your hands, sweetheart," he murmured as her arms twitched, before giving her pussy a long, lazy swipe of his tongue. Gabrielle whimpered as he circled her sensitive clitoris. The tiny button felt like it was three times its normal size and ready to explode if he would just...

She felt like howling when he pulled away, his tongue moving back to the outer lips of her womanhood, his finger receding from her tight anus.

Finally, he propped himself up between her legs, looking down at her with an expression of supreme satisfaction on his face. Gabrielle's gaze slid down the hard planes of his body to his cock, which he held fisted, pumping it back and forth. She was riveted by the view.

"Is this what you want, sweetheart?"

"Yes, please, Felix," she whispered, her throat feeling almost hoarse. She let go of the headboard to reach for him, but he barked out a reprimand immediately.

"I did not tell you that you could let go, Gabrielle."

The dark, dominant tone of voice had her body thrumming, and she quickly reached back up to hold onto the headboard, her stiff nipples bobbing with her movements. Felix reached down to pluck at them, making her writhe as the sensations increased the exquisite ache in her core.

"Please, Felix," she whispered. "Please, I need you inside me... I think I might die soon if you don't..."

A shudder went through his body and he squeezed her nipples tightly enough to make her gasp as the pain shot through her. The tiny buds throbbed even after he released them, but she'd gotten what she wanted. His hard cock pressed against her slick folds, easily pushing inside of her, filling her emptiness with pure pleasure.

"Oh yes!" She cried out, lifting her hips to take him in, already hovering on the brink of orgasm after he'd been toying with her for so long.

Gripping her hips, Felix began to thrust, hard and rough, slamming his body into hers so that she screamed with the sudden onslaught of erotic rapture. His hands were tight on her hips, holding her in place as he used her body, his cock spearing her, rubbing against her sensitive tissues with every thrust, sending her soaring higher and higher in passion. Gabrielle gripped the rungs on the headboard so tightly that it creaked as Felix wrung every last ripple of pleasure from her body, before finally being overcome with his own.

Falling asleep in his arms, she felt content... and yet slightly troubled. She would have been surprised to know that her husband was experiencing the same mix of emotions.

~

WATCHING his wife dancing with another man was not a pleasant experience. Although at least she seemed to have the same kind of reserve with Lord Braden as she did with Felix himself.

Reserve. How he hated that word. It was the perfect word to describe the way Gabrielle had been behaving for the past two days, and therefore he hated it.

She was perfectly polite, completely civil, and nothing he did had any effect. If he teased her, she just blinked and stared silently at him. If he prodded her temper, she would respond with cool complaisance. The only time he was ever able to breach the wall was in passion. Which probably explained why he'd been on her nearly nonstop, whenever they weren't in company, for the past two days.

Whenever they weren't coming together in physical pleasure, he studied her, trying to decipher a way past her reserve. There had to be one. This wasn't her, this wasn't Gabrielle. Gabrielle was fun and teasing, submissive but spicy, witty even when she was quiet... this new Gabrielle was every inch the staid and proper lady that he'd never been interested in. Except that because it was Gabrielle, he *was* interested. At least, he was interested in getting *his* Gabrielle back. Having her in the bedroom wasn't enough, he wanted her all the time.

"You don't look as though you're having much fun, Felix." Philip's drawl startled Felix, nearly causing him to jump, he'd been so focused on watching Gabrielle and Braden perform the intricate steps of the quadrille. Both of them as stiff and proper as prigs. Which Braden was, but Gabrielle certainly wasn't.

"It's a ball, who's having fun?" he drawled back, turning to his friends and giving Cordelia a wink even though his heart wasn't in it. Standing with her arm in Philip's, she was looking quite fine in a violet and silver gown, matching feathers decorating her hair. The feathers were the newest fashion. Gabrielle was wearing rose and gold ones, to match her rose silk gown with its golden net overlay and puff sleeves. Felix had bought them for her that morning, and she had thanked him so civilly and with such lady-like reserve that he'd pounced on her and licked her to completion right where she sat.

Blinking back the pleasant images in his mind, Felix straightened and bowed to Cordelia. "You look lovely this evening, my lady."

"Thank you, kind sir, and you look very handsome," she said, giggling. Twisting her head to look up at her husband she smiled broadly. "Although perhaps not quite as handsome as Philip, here."

"Philip is quite the handsome specimen," Felix said, chuckling as Philip rolled his eyes. "But has he taken you to the dance floor yet?"

Felix knew damn well that he hadn't. Since this was his and Gabrielle's first ball since they'd arrived back in town, she'd been in high demand, and Felix had spent his entire evening so far watching the dance floor and occasionally dancing with a lady here or there himself. Already he could tell that there was quite a bit of gossip circling because of his focused attention on his wife and the fact that every other lady he'd danced with thus far was a highly respectable matron. The tongues were wagging in acknowledgment that another of the *ton*'s rakes had been brought to heel and tamed.

"He has not," Cordelia replied, smiling up at Felix.

Philip gave her an apologetic look. "I'm trying to find Manchester, I need to have a word with him about that corn bill that Sussex wants to put in front of Parliament next week. Would you take her out, Felix?"

Felix held out his hand and made an exaggerated bow. "Allow me, my lady."

Laughing, Cordelia took his hand and he led her to the floor just as the previous dance was finishing.

CHAPTER 17

When Gabrielle looked over to her husband, she nearly stumbled over her own feet when she saw who he was speaking with. Damnation! Her lips tightened around the curse that she wanted to utter. Lord Braden would be shocked if she lost control of her tongue - he'd been highly complimentary about what a fine young lady she was. Personally, she thought he rather fitted Arabella's description of a dull young man, and he was patronizing to boot, but she'd still appreciated that someone recognized her efforts.

Even though Felix had been paying a great deal of attention to her the past two days, she was starting to realize that he was not as approving at the changes in herself as she'd initially thought - but, at the same time, he seemed almost obsessed with her. This seemed more like what Cynthia had said about being chased by her husband than the effort Gabrielle had made before. Not that she thought this was how Cynthia enticed her own husband to chase her, but it did seem to be working on Felix. Perhaps he didn't approve of having to seek her out constantly? In the country, they had naturally spent all their time together. Now that Gabrielle was acting as a typical *tonnish* lady, she had forced herself to those activities, which also meant that she didn't insist on her husband staying by her side.

Felix did anyway.

Of course, he'd danced with other ladies this evening, but not a single one that flirted with him. He'd ignored every flirtatious glance, every importuning invitation, and had only sought the company of his wife and other highly respectable matrons who had never had a breath of scandal whispered about their name. Gabrielle had already been congratulated - or jealously sneered at - by more than one lady about Felix's transformation from rake to devoted husband.

But that was before Cordelia had arrived.

She couldn't help but turn her head to see better, missing more than one step of the quadrille as Felix spoke to the Marques and Cordelia. As always, Cordelia looked stunning. Her violet gown enhanced all of her features, clinging to her curves, and making the most of her bosom. Next to that, Gabrielle felt almost childish in her pink and gold gown, which would be acceptable for a debutante to wear. She'd originally loved it, but now she wished she'd chosen a dress that was a more vivid color than her favorite hue... one that she wouldn't have been able to wear as a debutante, since fashion dictated they must be kept in lighter, softer shades of color.

"Are you quite all right, Mrs. Hood?" Lord Braden asked, concern on his handsome face. Their fingers were barely touching as they moved through the complicated steps.

"Oh yes, just a dizzy spell," Gabrielle said, forcing herself to smile at him. Coolly. Calmly. Collected. "I'll have some lemonade once the dance is over."

Ever the gentleman, Lord Braden escorted her to the refreshments for her drink. When she turned back to the dance floor, the lemonade turned to ashes on her tongue as she saw Felix and Cordelia dancing. What had happened to the Marquess? Where had he gone and why wasn't he dancing with his own dashed wife?!

Beside her, Lord Braden was becoming increasingly concerned. "Mrs. Hood, you're looking rather pale, would you like me to find you a seat?"

"I-" The words felt frozen in her mouth as she struggled with her emotions. Cool. Calm. Collected.

"Gabrielle, dear heart, there you are!" Arabella came through the crowd like an angel come to earth. The pale orange and yellow dress she was wearing set off her dark good looks beautifully, bringing out lighter highlights in her hair and eyes that weren't normally perceived. No feathers in her hair, she had a suitably innocent yellow ribbon threaded throughout her locks, which was all she was allowed as a debutante. She gave Lord Braden an impish smile, and the poor man smiled back helplessly. "Good evening, Lord Braden, would you mind if I steal my friend away from you?"

"Of course not, Lady Arabella, I mean -" Before the poor man could finish his sentence, Arabella was whisking Gabrielle away on her arm.

Doing her best not to spill her lemonade as Arabella tugged her through the crowd, Gabrielle caught another glimpse of the dance floor and Felix staring down adoringly at Cordelia. Her heart felt like it was being wrenched out of her chest. How many times could this happen to her? How many times could she feel this hurt, this much pain before she would become numbed to it?

By God, how she wanted to be numbed to it.

When Arabella pulled her into a small, intimate nook at the outer edge of the ballroom, Gabrielle noted with relief that the dance floor was no longer visible through the crowd. At least she wouldn't have to watch, although her imagination kept throwing up plenty of upsetting images for her to fret over.

"I'm going to murder him in his sleep!" Arabella exclaimed vehemently.

Gabrielle blinked, rather surprised by her friend's passion. She appreciated the support of course, but-

"He's going to marry some twittering nitwit," Arabella said, her dark eyes blazing with frustrated fury. "He's going to marry some milksop, because he thinks that a woman will be able to control me better!"

It occurred to Gabrielle that Arabella had not been offering to murder Felix. Which meant that she was rather confused.

"Who's marrying who?"

"Isaac! He's decided he's going to marry, as soon as possible, because I need 'feminine influence.'" She said the last two words derisively, obviously imitating her older brother. "The nodcock is going to leg shackle himself to some milk and water social climber and be miserable the rest of his life! Because he thinks I need a female figure in my life! What utter rot!"

Surprisingly, Arabella's overly dramatic devastation was actually starting to cheer Gabrielle up. Maybe it was the way she was waving her hands around like a loon, or the utter disgust on her face, or the fire in her eyes that said she was going to make whoever ended up as Isaac's bride completely miserable... but there was just something incredibly amusing about her temper tantrum. Gabrielle couldn't help but giggle.

Arabella pointed an accusing finger at her. "Don't you dare laugh at me. This is all your fault, you know. You should have thrown yourself at Isaac when you had the chance."

Gabrielle laughed harder. "I thought my lack of interest in him was why we're friends."

Making a humphing noise, Arabella swiveled away, looking out over the crowd. "So what are we going to do about your husband?"

Any mirth Gabrielle was feeling trickled away. "What do you mean?"

"I saw him and Cordelia dancing. What do you want to do? Do you want to follow through with your plan to be a lady?" Disdain dripped from Arabella's tongue as she said the word 'lady,' as though it was something nasty and unappealing. "Or do you want to get his attention?"

Given those two options, her current state of frustration, and the more spirited part of her personality that she'd kept damped down for the past two days, Gabrielle only hesitated a moment before coming to a decision.

THERE WAS a small stir on the other side of the dance floor, drawing

Felix's attention midway through the dance. He nearly knocked both himself and Cordelia over when he stumbled at the sight of his wife dancing with Lord Montague - a well-known and accomplished rake. All night she'd been dancing with proper gentlemen, meek gentlemen who would never think to flirt, much less poach another man's preserves. Now she was dancing with one of the foremost wolves of the *ton*, a man who gave both Felix and his brother Walter a run for their money when it came to reputations. Well, former reputation in Felix's case.

The bastard was holding Gabrielle much too closely. Worse, that reserve that he hated so much seemed to be gone. Gone! For Montague!

"Careful, Felix," Cordelia murmured, nimbly stepping out of his way as he made another misstep.

"Sorry, sorry," he muttered, refocusing his attention on the dance so that he didn't injure himself or anyone else. Pink and gold flicked at the corner of his eye, trying to draw his gaze again.

"She can handle herself," Cordelia said, although her expression had turned slightly worried, her lips a little thinner than they had been before. "It's just a dance."

"It's what he might try after the dance that concerns me," Felix growled.

Cordelia made an exasperated noise and turned her attention to keeping them from running into anyone else, as Felix's focus was decidedly diverted for the rest of the dance. Returning to the side-lines, they managed to find Philip talking with Manchester in short order, but not before the next dance had started up. When Felix turned back to the dance floor, he was incensed to see Gabrielle smiling prettily at yet another well-known rake, Lord Carter. To add to Felix's consternation, the dance was a waltz. Slightly older than Montague, he was inherently more dangerous as well, and he looked far too intimately entwined with Gabrielle as she fluttered her lashes at him.

Where the hell had her reserve gone? If it kept her away from rakes then he loved that damned reserve!

Possessive fury made Felix's limbs stiff as he stalked to the edge of the dance floor.

"Mr. Hood! How delightful." Lady Arabella suddenly inserted himself into his path, halting him, her cool tones making it clear that she actually wasn't all that delighted at all.

"None of your tricks tonight, Arabella," he said in a tight voice. "I'll get your brothers if I have to."

"Tricks? What tricks?" Her dark eyes widened in an unconvincing display of innocence. Her skill at lying hadn't improved any, something her brothers must be grateful for.

Trying to step around her only drew the attention of those standing around them, as there wasn't much room to maneuver. Grinding his teeth, because he didn't want to draw the scrutiny of the gossips, he realized that he was not going to be allowed to reach the dance floor without doing so. At least, not without Arabella in tow.

"Lady Arabella," he said, loudly enough to be overheard. "I apologize for my tardiness, this is my dance, I believe?"

She scowled as she took his hand, finding herself outmaneuvered. If she refused him, she would have had to let him by. That or create a scene herself, something which he'd been fairly certain she didn't want to do - she'd just been relying on his reluctance to do so as well.

So he wouldn't be able to cut in on Gabrielle and Carter; at least he'd be close by and next dance he could take with his wife. Or at least ensure that her next partner wasn't a lascivious rake.

"Ouch, watch where you're going and stop glaring at Gabrielle." Arabella's voice was tart.

"She's dancing with a rake, and I know you had something to do with it, so if I were you, I'd keep quiet," Felix said, low and lethal. Unfortunately he didn't intimidate Arabella in the slightest. Not surprising considering that her eldest brother was even taller and broader than he was, not to mention a Duke and one of the most powerful men in the country. She barely heeded him, so why on earth would she heed Felix?

"Perhaps if you'd been choosier in your own dance partners,

Gabrielle would have been more circumspect in hers," she said with a derisive sniff.

Felix narrowed his eyes, suddenly changing his focus to the young woman he was dancing with. He hadn't realized that Gabrielle's sudden change in behavior was reactionary to him. Once Arabella had planted herself in front of him, he'd thought the two of them were up to some mischief again. Other than feeling insanely protective and possessive, he realized some part of him had been slightly relieved to know that Gabrielle was getting into trouble with her friend again. It would have at least been a sign that she was acting like herself. Now he realized there was something even deeper going on.

"What do you mean?"

"I think I was quite clear, Mr. Hood."

"My dance partners this evening haven't been objectionable in the slightest. Not like that bounder she's dancing with now.

The disdainful look Arabella gave him was a thing of beauty, making him feel smaller than an ant despite his innocence in whatever she was implying. "Not objectionable to you perhaps."

With a suddenness that nearly made him stumble, clues came together in his head with a great jolt - the rivalry between Cordelia and Gabrielle, the timing of Gabrielle's sudden change in dance partners and the loss of her reserve, and Arabella's heavy handed hints. Felix felt a headache coming on.

"I don't suppose you feel like explaining to me why dancing with Cordelia might be a problem? It's nothing I haven't done before. And I've danced with Gabrielle several times tonight already. I was only dancing with Cordelia as a favor to Philip while he looked for your brother."

The haughty expression on Arabella's face slowly melted away into real puzzlement as she studied his face, apparently confused by what she saw there. Which was fair, considering how confused he was by this entire situation. "You really don't know, do you?"

"Know what?" He could feel himself becoming more frustrated with this nonsensical conversation.

She sighed in exasperation. "You should speak with your wife.

And perhaps try to pay more attention to her and less to other men's wives. Especially those who have already been linked to you by gossip on multiple occasions."

Silently dancing for a moment, Felix reviewed his evening in his head.

"Are we still talking about Cordelia?"

"Yes!"

Arabella muttered something under her breath that sounded suspiciously like 'you twit.'

It took him a moment to realize that the music was ending and that he and Arabella had ended up on the opposite side of the dance floor from Gabrielle. When he finally managed to find his pink and gold clad wife among the rainbow of colors all the ball gowns made and saw the company she was with, pure male fury slid through him. Handing Arabella off to her brother the duke - who didn't look all that happy to see her as she practically bowled through the bevy of young beauties vying for his attention - Felix stalked back towards his wife.

Time to get to the bottom of this, and he didn't care if he had to spank her to kingdom come to do so.

DISCOVERING Mr. Pressen in the Waverly's ballroom had been a bit of a shock to Gabrielle. After all, she hadn't seen the man since he'd kissed her and then been punched by Felix when they'd been caught. It had been her first kiss and a very nice first kiss until Felix interrupted. However, she could now say that it paled in comparison to the kisses that Felix gave her. Not through any fault of Mr. Pressen's, but she just didn't feel the same way for him that she did for Felix.

Although, she could do with a little less feeling for Felix currently.

To her surprise and consternation, Mr. Pressen didn't seem at all daunted by her newly married state. In fact, he seemed more interested than before. Gabrielle, although becoming used to the ways of Society, didn't realize that married young ladies were actually quite a bit more in the way of a rake's taste than the young debutantes. Debutantes were risky - especially if they had a powerful father or guardian who might insist on a wedding. Of course, Mr. Pressen had been willing to risk that at the time because Gabrielle had also come with a large dowry.

Now the dowry was no longer available, but, as a married woman, Gabrielle was riper for plucking than ever. At least, that was how the rakes saw it, especially since it seemed she might be searching for a lover... she'd gone from dancing with the prigs to more dangerous fare, which they were taking as open invitation.

Attracted to her lush figure, pretty pink lips, and classic beauty, they were more than happy to circle, offering up their own flirtations and blandishments in hopes that she might pick one of them to dally with.

Completely naive of the dangerous waters she'd walked into - since neither she nor Arabella had the experience to fully understand what they'd started - Gabrielle simply smiled and stated how glad she was to see Mr. Pressen again. When he asked her to dance, she said yes immediately, making Lord Carter sigh before he nodded his head and handed her off to his rival. Not that he ceded the floor entirely; like the other ballroom predators, he waited on the sidelines, watching.

As they approached the dance floor, trepidation made Gabrielle's heart race. She'd seen Felix waltzing with Arabella and had immediately known that her friend had probably kept him from cutting in. At least, she hoped so. If Felix hadn't cared who she was dancing with and had asked Arabella of his own accord, that would be rather lowering. She knew she was poking a tiger with a stick, trying to make her husband jealous, but if he was jealous wouldn't that mean something? If nothing else, she would like to inspire some of the same emotions in him that she experienced when she'd seen him talking with Cordelia and the Marquess.

Of course he would have to care for that to happen...

Which was why she felt rather gratified when Felix cut into her dance with Mr. Pressen after a mere minute. Gratified, but wary, because the storm clouds in Felix's expression made it clear that if Mr.

Pressen didn't desert the field post haste, Felix would be more than happy to plant him another facer. Not that Mr. Pressen resisted - he very quickly handed Gabrielle over and made himself scarce.

Looking up at the fury dancing in her husband's eyes, which were so dark right now that they looked black, Gabrielle's trepidation returned full force and her bottom started to tingle as if in anticipation of the spanking that she could already sense was coming her way.

"What were you thinking, dancing with that man?" Felix asked, whirling her away from the little court of rakes and blades that she and Arabella had gathered around her.

"I was thinking that I wanted to dance and he asked," she retorted before remembering that she was supposed to acting like a lady. Cool. Calm. Collected. To her surprise, though, she saw a little flash of something that looked almost like pleasure in her husband's eyes at her sassy response, but she had to be imagining that.

"And Carter? And Montague? What happened to Braden and the others?" The dangerous gleam was back in Felix's eye, his hold on her tightening, and Gabrielle couldn't help the shiver of pleasure that went down her spine.

Her lips pressed together. She knew she wasn't very good at lying straight out, she was much better at sliding around the truth, but right now she was finding it hard to think. She was torn between pleasure that Felix seemed jealous and wariness over his scowling mood, as well as the humming need that was beginning between her legs and the phantom throbbing in her bottom as it anticipated a spanking.

Rather than snapping back at him and asking him what about Cordelia, she just turned her face away. Composed. Cool. Calm. Collected.

"Lord Braden's dance had ended and I accepted the next invitation I received."

The cool, calm, and collected pose she'd adopted abandoned her when she was suddenly being dragged off of the dance floor, Felix's firm grip around her upper arm. She couldn't see his expression because he was walking too quickly, leaving her stumbling behind him.

"Felix!" she hissed, trying to keep up. "Felix, you're causing a scene!"

She tried to say the words quietly enough that only he would be able to hear them, but everyone was looking at them now, so she didn't know if it worked or not. Completely ignoring her, he pulled her out into the front hall where he gave the butler his name and requested their carriage. The fingers on her arm were unrelenting and now that she could finally look up and see his face, her bravado deserted her, leaving her quailing.

Her husband looked like a man who had finally reached the end of his rope, and Gabrielle had no idea what was going to happen now.

FELIX HAD REACHED the end of his rope. In fact, he'd reached the end, tossed it away, and burned the damned thing.

He was sick of his wife treating him like a stranger unless she was naked and in his bed. Sick of vainly looking for the spark of her personality in this reserved marble version of her. Sick of not understanding what she was doing or why. And he was definitely sick of watching her dance with men he didn't want within ten feet of her, much less holding her! Granted, it wasn't as if he'd had to do very much of that last, but apparently even a little was enough to send him over the edge.

Beside him, he could feel Gabrielle shifting her weight back and forth nervously, and felt a tiny flicker of satisfaction that he'd managed to chip away at her walls just a little. His grip around her arm was as much as he'd allow himself to touch her, otherwise he didn't know if he'd be able to keep from flipping her over his lap and spanking the living daylights out of her - or just lifting her skirts and marking her as his in the most primal manner available to him.

None of which he wanted to do when he could practically feel the stares of the other guests at his and Gabrielle's backs.

Fortunately, it only took a few moments for Felix's carriage to be brought round – after all, no one else was trying to leave the ball this early – and he was able to hustle Gabrielle into it very quickly. Climbing in afterwards, he sat across from her, staring at her in the moonlight.

There was a pink flush high in her cheeks and her fists were little balls in her lap, her chin lifted proudly as if she didn't care that she'd just been dragged out of a ballroom. Didn't care that they'd just given the *ton* something to talk about, only days after their return to London. Didn't care that her husband was glowering at her from mere inches away.

The ride home was silent. Because once this conversation started, Felix intended to see it through to the very end. No interruptions. Which was why he renewed his grip on her arm as soon as they descended from the carriage, waving off the coachman, and pulling her into the house.

"Felix – "

"Not yet," he growled, throwing open the front door before Taylor could reach it and dragging Gabrielle up the stairs to their bedroom. Yes, dragging, because she was starting to actively try and escape from him. She wasn't struggling, just trying to pull away. Trying to twist her arm out of his grip.

"Felix, please, let go of my arm."

"We're going to our room. We're going to have a discussion. And we are not leaving our room until I'm satisfied."

With exasperation in her voice, she stopped fighting him and allowed him to drag her the last few feet into the room. "Satisfied with what?"

"Your answers."

Felix slammed the door shut behind him.

CHAPTER 18

Crossing his arms over his chest, Felix glared at his wife, blocking the doorway with his muscled frame. A little pale, but still defiant, Gabrielle lifted her chin and gave him the haughty, distant look that he hated so much.

"What-"

"Take off your clothes."

She blinked, her hands going immediately to her bosom, as if to cover it, despite the fact that she was still wearing her dress. *"What?!"*

Felix started towards her. "Take off your clothes. I'll assist."

"But... but why?" She tried to clutch the fabric to her as he spun her around and started swiftly undoing her buttons, accidentally ripping a few in his haste.

"It will make things easier." Because he wanted her to feel vulnerable. Naked. It would also effectively keep her trapped in the room with him. And make it a hell of a lot easier to spank her once he started asking questions.

Gabrielle seemed almost shell shocked as he stripped her out of the dress, his cock swelling as her body was bared to him. It didn't matter that he was frustrated, that the spanking he was planning had nothing to do with sex - his cock responded.

Her skin was like cream satin under his fingers as he pushed the fabric off of her body, cream satin he was going to turn rosy - in certain areas.

"Wait!" she said, her fingers curling around her chemise. Not that it afforded her any real coverage, but she clutched it to her chest anyway. "You can't... you can't do whatever *this* is because I danced with a few men!"

"That's not why I'm doing this," he said with a growl, taking her by the arm again and pulling her over to the bed. He let her hold the chemise against her breasts. It wasn't on her anymore anyway; if she wanted to cuddle it, he wasn't going to wrest it from her. "I want to know what's gotten into you. Not just the dancing with those... those scoundrels, but the way you've been with me."

"What about the way I've been with you?" Her chin went up, eyes flashing. Apparently he'd sparked a nerve.

Well, too bad, she'd sparked one of his too. More than one. "You haven't been you."

Gabrielle shrieked as he pulled her over his knee, letting go of her chemise as her hands flung out to give her support. The flimsy fabric fell to the floor beside Felix's foot, followed swiftly by Gabrielle's hands as he positioned her with her gorgeous ass high in the air. "You've been distant. You haven't talked to me. You accused me of making decisions that effected your life without discussing it with you, but it seems that now you've done the same - you've started acting like a stranger and I don't know why! Not only that, but I want an explanation as to why Arabella seems to think that my dancing with Cordelia is somehow more objectionable than your choice in dance partners!"

He'd been holding Gabrielle in place as she squirmed and wriggled on his lap - although she hadn't truly been trying to escape - but at his last words she froze and Felix knew that he'd hit upon the crux of the matter. Although frustrated, he was grateful to Arabella for pointing him in the correct direction. On his own, he would have never even thought to put his dance with Cordelia together with Gabrielle's increasingly confusing behavior.

"I don't know what you're talking about."

"You're a terrible liar. And you also know I don't tolerate lying."

SMACK! SMACK!

Felix rested his hand on her rump. The two swats to the center of each cheek had been sharp and firm, but they weren't enough to truly punish Gabrielle. Just enough to warn her of what was coming if she didn't start opening up.

"Why have you been so distant since we've returned to London? You haven't been acting like yourself at all."

"I've been trying to be a lady!"

That reply actually had the ring of truth to it. As a reward, Felix rubbed the pink splotches on her bottom gently. He wasn't totally oblivious to her growing arousal when he did so, which only made the reward better.

"I can understand that in public, although I hope you know it's not necessary. You are a lady and there's no scandal from our wedding, so there's nothing to make up for. Why do you continue to act like that in private, when it's just you and me?"

Silence.

SMACK! SMACK!

"You can't spank me until I answer you!"

"Watch me," Felix muttered.

SMACK! SMACK! SMACK! SMACK!

He let his hand fall where it would, not taking particular care to aim, which meant some parts of her bottom were chastised more thoroughly than others. The uncertainty of where his hand would land and the growing pain had her wriggling again. Felix hoisted her up further to keep her bottom completely open to him. He wasn't holding back or giving her any warm-up swats; with every impact of his hand against her soft flesh he left a dark pink print which quickly started to turn red if he happened to smack an already inflicted area.

SMACK! SMACK! SMACK! SMACK!

"I'm sorry! I'm sorry, I won't do it anymore!"

That had actually taken less time than anticipated, although it wasn't quite what he'd wanted.

"I appreciate that Gabrielle, but what's more important to me is knowing why you've been doing it."

Silence.

Felix sighed. "Let's try something more specific. Are you upset that I danced with Cordelia?"

With her body across his thighs, it was impossible for him to miss the way she stiffened at the question. Felix rubbed the pink cheeks of her buttocks, holding her firmly in place with his other hand as he gave her a moment.

"Yes."

She said it so quietly that he almost missed it, and that one, sad little word made him feel like a heel even though he didn't know why she would have such a reaction.

"Why are you upset that I danced with Cordelia?"

Silence.

"Gabrielle, I will spank you until I get some real answers from you."

To his shock, his submissive, slightly aroused wife suddenly disappeared and was replaced by a virago. Gabrielle wrenched herself from his lap with a hard movement that was too quick for him to be prepared for and it sent her sprawling onto the floor, her breasts heaving, her legs splayed. It was an incredibly ungraceful movement, and he lunged, trying to catch her, but was far too late. She squeaked as her bottom landed on the hard carpet, her face almost as pink as her buttocks were, with tear streaks already on her cheeks. Her eyes were wild and furious.

"Fine then! Spank me! You can spank me as much as you want, as hard as you want! It's not going to change anything! I'm never going to want to watch you dancing with the woman you actually love, and I don't care if you punish me for how I choose to deal with it."

On his knees, one hand reaching out for her, Felix froze.

"The- the woman I actually love?"

As quickly as she'd appeared, the virago vanished, leaving him with a weepy-looking Gabrielle who quickly huddled in on herself, hiding her body from him behind a wall of limbs. Her eyes averted, she curled up in a ball, retreating from him even as he reached for her.

The notion was so foreign to him that it actually took him a few moments to understand exactly what Gabrielle thought.

She thought that he was in love with Cordelia. Her stepmother. Good grief... Felix closed his eyes and swallowed, rubbing his forehead. Where on earth had she gotten that notion?

Sitting back on his heels, Felix opened his eyes to find his wife still curled in a protective ball, her gaze flicking to him and then away again. Seeing her in such a protective stance... hell, had he thought she'd broken his heart before? He couldn't bear it.

Fortunately, he didn't have to.

Standing up, Felix stepped forward and abruptly swept her up into his arms.

"Stop it!" Her tiny fist hit his chest bone and made him grunt, although he just tightened his grip on her. "Put me down!"

"No."

Her arm stilled, half way on its way to his chest again. "What?"

"No, I will not put you down, you're going to stay right here, in my arms, and we're going to talk about this."

As he sat on the bed, Gabrielle ducked her head, and he got the impression that she was trying to hide behind her hair. Unfortunately for her, all of her hair was on top of her head, and so he could see the profile of her miserable expression.

"What is there to talk about?" she asked dully.

"Well, to begin with, why on earth do you think I'm in love with Cordelia? I mean, yes I love her, the way I would a sister if I had one, and Cordelia's annoying enough as it is so I'm glad I haven't had her plaguing me all my life, but that is the only kind of love I feel for her."

"It is?" The soft, almost hopeful tone Gabrielle used had Felix's heart swelling, feeling some hope as well. This sounded more like the Gabrielle he knew. The Gabrielle that he *had* fallen in love with. "But everyone was saying... everyone saw how much attention you paid her after she and Philip married. Everyone said you were acting like a man in love."

"Well, princess, she is my best friend's wife. I wanted to befriend her immediately, for that reason alone, and then I found that I enjoyed her company. It was easy to be friends with her. If I was in love with her or even just attracted to her, believe me, that friendship would not have been nearly as easy. Besides, I had another reason for wanting to spend time around her." He gave Gabrielle his best roguish grin, but she wasn't looking at him.

"What?"

Felix made an exasperated sound. "You, princess."

To his surprise, she scowled, pushing away from him so that she could see his expression - but at least she was finally looking at him again. "That's not true."

"Yes it is. More than half of my conversations with Cordelia have revolved around you. I've been drawn to you from the very beginning, and you know I'm telling the truth because unlike my friendship with Cordelia, *our* relationship has never been easy."

"You were just watching over me because Philip asked you to. I was nothing more than a duty to you. One that you eventually ended up having to marry, because... to save me, for them. Because they wanted you to." The bitterness in her voice actually made him feel happy - because it was quite clear that Gabrielle didn't want to be a duty to him. She didn't want him to have married her out of duty. And she was jealous of his relationship to Cordelia. To him, that all added up to one glorious conclusion - Gabrielle cared for him. Maybe even loved him. And she was just as irrational and unreasonable about it as he was, which explained her hot and cold behavior.

Hell, perhaps he deserved it, because he knew his behavior towards her had been fairly similar when they'd first met. Hot and cold and completely inexplicable at times. He had not done a very good job of courting her and perhaps he was paying for that now.

Which meant it was the time for the truth, and hopefully hers would match his and they could move past this. He was terrible at courting, as he'd discovered, and he wasn't much better at being a husband, but he could learn and he was going to prove it. Now. Because one thing he did know very well was when a woman was coming to the end of her patience with him. In the past, that was usually when he would end an affair or give his mistress her *conge.* On occasion, he'd taken that moment to turn things around, to make the relationship last longer if that's what he'd desired at the time, and that was what he had to do here. Because he wanted *his* Gabrielle back and he knew he would desire her forever.

"Yes, Philip asked me to help watch over you, but I would have even if he hadn't," he said, brushing the hair back from her face, hoping that she could feel the tenderness in his touch. The almost confused expression she wore gave him hope that she hadn't completely given up on him. She wasn't totally closed off from him. "I'm also certainly not the only one who was willing to marry you to save your reputation. Thomas would have stepped up in a heartbeat if he'd felt that he needed to, and I'm not sure Walter wouldn't have done the same. Manchester was already on the verge of offering himself as a groom, but there was no way I was going to let anyone else have you. I'm just glad I didn't have to fight any of them for it, because I would have."

HOPE WAS CLINGING to her like a limpet, refusing to let go, clogging her airways, making it impossible for her to speak. She wanted to believe him. She so, so badly wanted to believe his sweet, gentle words, accompanied by tender caresses, and the most utterly sincere look on his face. But... could she?

Confusion bubbled inside of her as Felix pulled her in for a kiss, his lips coaxing and firm, insisting that she yield her mouth to him. So she did. She let herself sink into his kiss, let him turn her on his lap, let him run his hands up and down and over her body. She so badly wanted to believe him, but she was afraid.

And just like that, it was suddenly clear.

It wasn't just Felix's behavior that had driven a wedge between them - it was her fear. Even though she'd hoped, she'd been afraid to really give into that emotion. She'd been afraid to allow it to grow. So she'd taken every excuse she could find, every contrived reason she could manufacture, to try and keep herself safe from her own emotions. Even when she'd been determined to make Felix hers, she hadn't given herself over totally to the effort, and she'd abandoned it at the first justification she came across.

Somehow, it was easier to think that he was in love with Cordelia than it was to allow herself to be emotionally vulnerable to him. It was easier to feel heartbroken over and over again than it was to be happy with him. It was less frightening to look a life of misery than it was to face that she might have everything she ever wanted.

Because if she could just convince herself that she could never have it, then she could never be disappointed. She could never be let down.

But it was a self-fulfilling prophecy, because if she never took the chance, then she would never get the prize either. She couldn't have the reward without the risk.

No wonder she was terrified. Her life had been one long lesson that risks were met with pain. That lesson had been ground in long before Cordelia had ever become her stepmother. Which, Gabrielle now realized, was why she'd never truly given Cordelia a chance either.

Felix suddenly turned her, laying her back on the bed. Her bottom was a little sore and protested as it pressed against the sheets - he hadn't spanked her for very long, but every swat had been very intense and very painful. Braced above her, he stared down at her, and for the first time, Gabrielle let herself really see how he looked at her. See not just the desire, but the emotions behind them.

"I love you, Gabrielle," he said, his voice low and husky. "I chose you for my wife, not out of duty or for a friend, but because I wanted you for me. Do you believe me?"

She licked her lips, which suddenly felt dry, as the compression in her chest became almost unbearable. "I think so," she whispered.

Her husband grinned. That roguish, devilish grin that made her heart race and said he was about to do awful, wonderful, perverted things to you.

"I love that you can already beat me at chess."

He kissed her lips again, but moved away after an all-too-brief moment.

"I love when you're sassy."

A kiss on her throat.

"I love how you fully embrace joy when you feel it, as if it encompasses your entire being."

A kiss on her shoulder. Gabrielle arched a little, reaching up to wrap her arms around his neck, but Felix wouldn't come down further.

"I love the way you have with children."

A kiss between her breasts.

"I love that you're just as happy in the countryside as you are in the city, that we can have fun no matter where we are or what we're doing."

He kissed her nipple, sucking it into his mouth and making her whimper. The little bud ached when he released it, the cool air suddenly much more intense against the wet nub.

"I love when you react in a way I could never have anticipated, keeping me on my toes."

He kissed her other nipple and this time Gabrielle tried to hold his head against her breast, making him chuckle. Plucking her hands from his head, he pressed them down on either side of her body, making her shiver as he took over.

"Do you trust me?" he rasped, looking down at her with such emotion, such *love* shining in his dark eyes that she didn't know how she'd managed to avoid seeing it before.

"Yes," she whispered, feeling incredibly brave at the admission.

"Do you love me?"

"Yes." This affirmation was said even softer, felt even braver, and yet she didn't regret it even when it felt like all the air had left her lungs, because the expression on Felix's face was everything she could have wanted.

"Do you believe I love you?"

This time she hesitated, but she didn't shy away from the answer. "Yes."

He kissed her.

Deeply. Thoroughly. With so much heady emotion that she felt dizzy from it. She was vulnerable, stripped bare, and yet she felt more safe and secure than she ever had before. Felix wouldn't let her fall.

When he released her wrists, easing more of his body onto hers, she immediately reached for him, clinging to his shoulders as he stripped off his shirt, helping him to push the garment off of his body. He was hot and hard on top of her, making her senses sing. The utter freedom she felt was both shocking and exhilarating.

Her secret had been laid bare, her confession had been heard, and instead of being rejected or mocked, she had been met with nothing but love and acceptance. It was everything she'd ever been too afraid to hope for.

Felix's hands roamed over her body, one sliding between them to slip into her wet folds, expertly circling her swollen clit. Moaning, Gabrielle lifted her hips, rubbing herself against his probing fingers as his mouth returned to her breasts, suckling on her nipples. It was as though he was rewarding her honesty with pleasure, touching her in all the ways that he'd learned sent her soaring highest with ecstasy.

His teeth tugged at her tender nipples, making her writhe as two fingers slid into her body, curving to find her most sensitive spot. Gabrielle cried out as he pumped his fingers, rubbing over that exquisite point, relentlessly, until she screamed with pleasure. Her climax rippled through her as he stroked his fingers, nibbling and pulling on her nipples, driving her through the ecstasy until she was limp and moaning.

Only then did he turn her over, pulling her onto her hands and knees, and slide into her from behind. His cock stretched her wonderfully, pressing against her sensitive tissues, making her feel weak with the pleasure of it. When his fingers pressed inside of her anus, making her feel so incredibly full, Gabrielle felt her elbows give out.

Pink bottom up in the air, fingers thrusting in that most private hole as her husband's cock thrust in her pussy, Gabrielle fisted the sheets as she tried to keep from screaming all over again. The sensations were swamping her in the most incredible way, but she felt like if she started screaming, she might never be able to stop. Her pleasure was already building again, her body quivering like a fine tuned instrument as Felix played her masterfully.

She was on the edge of climax again when Felix suddenly pulled away and she cried out in protest.

"Don't worry, sweetheart, I'm not going anywhere."

Something slick and huge nudged at her back entrance, which was slightly opened from his fingers. Gabrielle sucked in a shocked breath. Yes, she'd realized that his forays into this territory were all leading up to this moment, but now that it was here she couldn't quite believe it. Fear, arousal, excitement, a sense of utter wickedness it was all bundled together as Felix pressed his cock to her slick rosebud and began to push in.

Gabrielle began to pant as her muscles stretched, feeling the burn like a sharp ache in her backside. It hurt, but it hurt so good... she almost wanted to tell him to stop, but yet she didn't want to disappoint him either. This was trust... it was submission... it was the last yielding of her body to him. If she didn't trust him, if she didn't love him, she would never be able to take this.

Still... "Ow... ow... slower, please..."

The forward movement stopped and he pulled back slightly. She whimpered at the strange sensation, tensing and relaxing.

A hand smoothed over her back, caressing her, comforting her. "I'll go slowly, sweetheart, just tell me when you're ready. I've... never done this before."

But he'd always wanted to. Somehow she just knew that without him saying the words. It made this even more important to her. It was something they would share, that was just theirs.

Gabrielle rocked, experimenting, and couldn't help but smile at the groan it elicited from her husband, even as it caused a deep ache in her body. She couldn't tell if the ache was from pain or pleasure, it was so intense, but she wasn't going to allow that to stop her now.

Moving slowly, she began to back herself onto her husband's cock, surging forward every time she went a little too fast, panting and moaning as she worked herself back. All the while, Felix caressed her back and ass, groaning and occasionally tightening his fingers as she impaled herself.

By the time her cheeks were pressed against his groin, she felt almost completely spent. The passageway he was filling burned from being stretched so wide and so deep, her inner muscles felt acutely sensitive, and she'd never felt more powerful or more submissive in her life.

"I think I'm ready," she whispered.

THE TIGHT GRIP of Gabrielle's anus around his cock was like a heated vise, almost too much pressure to bear and yet intimately exquisite. Her little pink rosebud was practically white, all the wrinkles smoothed out from being stretched around his cock, her dripping pussy pink and swollen beneath it. He could feel her arousal coating his sack as the two rubbed against each other.

Felix's breath caught in his throat from the sheer sensual beauty and intimacy of the situation. All his... every part of her was now, finally, all his. He had her trust, her love, and her belief in him, and there wasn't a single part of her that he hadn't explored, touched and now claimed.

Well, almost claimed.

Very, very gently, Felix began to withdraw from that humid haven, groaning at the sensation of her gripping him and flexing around him as he moved. The little whimpers she was making in the back of her throat were like nothing he'd heard before - so caught between pleasure and pain that it was like waving a red flag at a bull. It took all his willpower not to just thrust back into her with force and ride her roughly... knowing that some part of her would enjoy it.

But he wanted this first time to be special. Gentler. There would be plenty of time later to indulge in more exotic flavors of this particular perversion.

He rubbed his hand over her bottom as he slowly pushed back in, giving her rosy cheeks little slaps to help his entry. As her inner muscles clamped and pulled him inward with every swat to her pink mounds, Felix could actually feel his balls practically churning with the need to empty. Gabrielle moved, backing into him, taking him more deeply much swifter than he would have done.

"Ohhhh... yeeeess..."

That was all the invitation he needed.

He didn't pound her roughly, but he did take a grip on her hips and began to move with much more fervor, his thrusts coming faster and firmer than before. It was like heaven and hell, plunging into that tight, formerly virgin orifice, all the while trying to keep himself from taking her too roughly. Beneath him, Gabrielle bucked and moaned, sometimes pressing back against him, sometimes trying to pull away.

The occasional whimper of pain between her moans of pleasure only spurred him onwards. He could feel her convulsions every time it happened, feel her shudder, and he knew that she was taking that pain to please him. To *pleasure* him. It was a gift and a responsibility, and not one that he would reject or abuse.

Leaning forward, which pressed his dick more firmly into her crevice, he slid his hand between her legs and felt her clamp down around him as his fingers reached her swollen pleasure bud. Gabrielle gasped as he pinched the little nubbin, rubbing it roughly in the way he knew she loved. She couldn't handle it right away, but this far into love-play when she was this aroused? It was a surefire way to send her screaming headlong into ecstasy.

"Oh... oh god... Oh Felix..." She began bucking beneath him as his fingers expertly pulled and pinched, pushing his cock and in and out of her tight hole as she moved. There was a touch of something like devastation in her voice, as though she was too overwhelmed to feel pure pleasure, and yet she wanted it too.

Felix thrust harder, his fingers working, as he felt the familiar tingle at the base of his spine. He wanted her to join him in ecstasy, but he knew he couldn't hold on much longer.

TOO MUCH... it was all too much...

Gabrielle felt like she was about to explode. She felt so impossibly full, so wonderfully crowded, so horribly overstimulated. Every rasp of Felix's cock in and out of her body was a devastating mash of pain and pleasure - it felt like burning, but in a different kind of way, the way ice burned, except that wasn't quite right either. If rapture could burn, that was what it felt like.

She was raw inside and part of her just wanted it to be over, but another part of her was luxuriating in the sensations... in her emotions. She loved feeling Felix's cock so hard and thick in the most forbidden part of her, loved feeling so submissive beneath him, loved giving this to him. When he began toying with her swollen clitoris, she thought she might die from the overwhelming sensations, as if her heart might actually pound out of her chest from it all.

Every time her muscles clamped down around him, he felt even bigger, the movement of his cock felt even rougher, and she soared a little higher. Her fingers dug into the mattress, her nipples rubbing against the sheets as he took her in the basest manner possible, and she was loving every minute of it. Loving every minute of giving herself to him fully, finally.

The thrusts were pain and pleasure, light and darkness, heat and ice, and she was riding a tsunami wave of sensation that threatened to knock her out. Gabrielle clung to consciousness, not wanting to miss a second of Felix inside of her, not one of his groans or a single moment of his grip on her body.

"Oh please... oh Felix... oh Felix.... please... please..." She was begging, chanting his name over and over again, and she didn't know why or what she was asking for, she just knew she couldn't stop.

When she heard him groan her name, his voice full of erotic desperation, it was all she needed to go over the edge. Her ass clamped down around him, spasming as she thrust her hips back, fully impaling herself on his staff. She cried out as his fingers pinched her clit and screamed his name as the second wave of utter rapturous climax slammed into her. It was as though every part of her body sparked at the same moment and then exploded in glorious ecstasy.

Felix was shouting her name, over and over, the same way she had called his, and she could feel the hot jet of fluid coating her inside. She could feel every pulse of his cock inside of her, every spasm that heralded another spurt of his seed. She could feel her body milking him, as if hungry for every drop of him that she could take in.

When the ecstasy finally rolled on, Felix lay draped over her, his damp body pressing against hers. Gabrielle whimpered when he rolled, pulling her with him so that they were on their sides. Her hole felt incredibly tender as he slipped from her body. Tender and almost bruised, but at the same time, she felt utterly fulfilled.

Manhandling her, Felix turned her in his arms. She looked up at him, one hand on his chest, as he carefully brushed tendrils of hair off her face. Her coiffure hadn't held up to their exertions, but it didn't matter. All that mattered was his expression. His adoring, loving expression.

"So, are you going to tell me everything you love about me now?" he asked.

Gabrielle slapped her palm against his chest. "This house is barely big enough for your ego as it is."

"I'm not sure if that's a judgment upon me or a hint that we need a bigger house," he said thoughtfully, his eyes sparkling with mischief. Gabrielle couldn't help but giggle.

"Maybe a little of both." She leaned into him, pressing her nose against his chest hair and breathing in that wonderful scent that was uniquely him. "Felix?"

"Mmm?"

"I love almost everything about you."

"Almost?"

"Don't worry. We're married. We have the rest of our lives to work on it," she reassured him sleepily.

A sharp smack to her ass had her squealing and then giggling as she snuggled into him.

"Minx."

FELIX COULD TELL when she drifted off to sleep. His precious wife. His precious, wonderful, adventurous, mischievous, and all-too-tenuous wife.

They'd overcome this hurdle, but what about the next? Or the next? What could he do to reassure her that he truly loved her, only her, and that he wanted to be married to her?

Holding her close, Felix thought about everything he'd learned since being married to her. He thought about all the advice his mother had given him, all of Cordelia's observations, and Arabella's hints. And he came up with a plan.

CHAPTER 19

Gabrielle woke up naked, alone and...
surrounded by pink rose petals?

She rubbed her eyes blearily. Last night felt like a dream come true, this morning... was not what she expected. For starters, she was much sorer than she'd expected. Very, very sore. Yet very satisfied too.

However, she was also a bit peeved to find herself alone in bed. That was definitely not expected. Usually Felix was there, either cuddling her or waking her up to do much less civilized things to her. Alone was unexpected. Although... rose petals. That must mean something.

Looking around, she could see that the rose petals were also strewn across the floor, but in a decisive path to the door.

Curiosity pricked, Gabrielle got up, only wincing slightly at her poor, bruised bottom. Not the cheeks, but the inner part. It was only marginally less uncomfortable than the morning after he'd punished her with a figging.

Deciding she was too impatient to wait for Molly, Gabrielle pulled on a simple morning dress. Pink, of course, and one that she could easily put on herself. It was loose but flattering and needed no corset beneath it. A corset would take too long.

Going to the door, she opened it and found that the trail of petals continued out into the hallway. So she followed them.

As much as she liked waking up to have Felix beside her - or on top of her - and she'd expected to have that today, she had to admit that she was rather enjoying this too. A sense of romantic excitement was bubbling up inside of her, and, for the first time in a long time, she didn't try to talk herself out of it. She didn't try to brace herself for disappointment. Whatever Felix had planned at the end of this trail of rose petals, she was sure it was something wonderful.

The trail took her down the hall, down the stairs, and through the main hallway of the house. Out of the corner of her eye, she saw Molly's daughters peering around the door to the servants' quarters, both of them giggling with their hands over their mouths. As soon as they saw her looking, they squeaked and hid, pulling the door shut. Gabrielle couldn't help but smile. Apparently the whole household was in on the secret.

Following the petals into the dining room, she came to an abrupt halt.

The dining room was awash in all shades of pink. Not a rose in sight, but every other kind of flower imaginable that came in pink, decorating every surface in the room. The centerpiece on the dining room table was an elaborate array of gorgeous pink orchids and lilies, the fragrance almost overwhelming as she stepped into the room. It reminiscent of the first truly romantic gesture he'd ever made, the pink flowers he'd covered the dining room table with for her back at his parents' estate, but on a much grander, much larger scale. Every table was covered. They were hanging from the wall sconces, from the curtains over the windows, and even from the chandelier. Vines were wrapped around the chairs, adding extra ornamentation. Breakfast was served on the buffet, but in between every culinary display there were more flowers. The floor was awash in rose petals.

Beside the completely covered dining room table, Felix was standing, looking almost nervous.

"What is all this?" Gabrielle asked as wonder washed over her, slowly stepping towards him on the carpet of pink petals as her head swiveled, taking in the incredible decorations. As she approached, Felix held out his hand and she took it, her fingers wrapping around his, and then she squeaked in shock as he went down on one knee.

"This is the proposal I should have given you, the one you deserved," he said, his dark eyes serious. It didn't matter that they were already married, that the wedding had happened and they'd been man and wife for weeks, Gabrielle's heart started pounding madly, her eyes watering up as this man knelt before her. "Gabrielle, I love you. I love your fiery spirit, I love your sweet inner core, I love the way you challenge me and the way you fulfill me. My life would not be complete without you. Will you accept this proposal, to be my wife - my true wife, in every sense of the word - for me to love and to cherish for all the days of our lives?"

Too choked up to respond, tears sliding down cheeks which hurt from smiling too hard, Gabrielle nodded her head and threw herself at him.

CHUCKLING, Felix wrapped his arms around his wife, wavering a bit as her ecstatic assault nearly knocked him off balance.

This was the way things should have been done - the way they would have been done if he had courted her properly the first time. Granted, he was sure he would have gotten there eventually if she hadn't been so impetuous and impulsive, attempting to elope with a fortune hunter, but either way she deserved it.

Gently lowering himself to the floor to save his poor knee, Felix kept her cradled in his arms as she covered his face with kisses, ending with his lips. They pressed together, her tongue seeking his, her utter joy contagious.

When she pulled away, her eyes were still glistening with unshed tears, but there was no mistaking the happiness that practically emanated from her body.

"How on earth did you do all this?" she asked, waving her hand at the room.

"I called in a few favors," he said smugly. Fortunately for him, his wife was a heavy sleeper and his mother was extremely efficient. Despite the late hour that he'd sent his request, she'd rallied her favorite florists overnight to put this together - sending the bill to Felix of course. He'd been the one to arrange everything once it arrived, getting up at the crack of dawn to do so. His mother had also sent along a note saying could he please refrain from any further excessive public outbursts in the future. It wasn't too surprising that she'd already heard about last night, but he certainly hoped that would be the last time he had to drag his wife out of an event.

"It's... incredible," she said, looking up and around, seeming not to mind that she was seated on his lap on the floor. Felix didn't mind either, he was just enjoying watching the awe and wonder in her expression, seeing the way she was lit up from within. Then she looked back at him, an openness in her eyes that hadn't been there before, one that was shining with love. "Thank you."

"I just wish I'd done it sooner," he said. "I can be a bit slow. You'll have to learn to live with that."

Gabrielle giggled and kissed him. Pulling away again, she tilted her head to the side. "Does this mean you won't be spanking me anymore?"

"Of course not," he said, huffing a bit. His hands slid down her back and hips to cup her bottom. "If you're naughty, I will not hesitate to discipline you. And sometimes even when you're not, just because you like it." He leered at her, enjoying the blush on her cheeks as she sniffed haughtily and looked away from him again. Felix squeezed her bottom, making her squeal.

She lowered her lashes, peeking at him through them coquettishly. "Perhaps we should follow the petal trail back to the beginning."

"Perhaps we should." Grinning, Felix managed to get to his feet without relinquishing his grip on his wife. She wrapped her arms around his neck as he carried her back up the stairs. Catching Taylor's eye on the way out of the dining room, Felix cleared his throat. "Taylor, could you please send our regrets to Lady Chambers, we'll be unable to make it to her ball this evening. Also, we're not at home. To anyone."

"Understood, sir," Taylor said, nodding his head. Despite himself, a grin kept breaking out on his narrow face as he watched the master carrying the mistress up to the bedchamber.

GABRIELLE GASPED with mock indignation as Felix pulled her over his lap. "You can't mean to spank me now!"

"Of course I can," said her irrepressible husband. "You and I both know very well that you like it."

Smack!

It was a light tap compared to the swats he'd given her last night, just enough to sting a bit before feeling more pleasurable. Gabrielle moaned, lifting her hips as he rubbed the spot immediately, making her feel hot and aroused in response.

Smack!

Rub.

She arched, practically purring like a cat in heat as Felix began to pepper her bottom with light swats, turning her creamy skin a blushing pink as he spanked and caressed her upturned bottom, teasing both of them. When his fingers rubbed over her little rosebud, she tensed.

"Sore, sweetheart?" he asked gently.

"Very," she said a bit ruefully. And then giggled as she felt him lean down and kiss her bottom cheek. "But I'm not sore all over..."

Felix chuckled. "I'm sure."

His fingers slid down to her pussy and pressed in, making her moan as he probed her wet haven.

Smack!

Smack!

The spanking started up again, this time as he continued to thrust his fingers in and out of her ready pussy, making her buck and wriggle as her passion grew, the sensations heightened by the heady mix. Gabrielle rubbed herself against him, feeling his hard cock slide against her stomach, and she pressed harder against it, urging him onward.

Her bottom was rosy and hot, but in a good way, her body aching to have more of him inside of her. Gabrielle reached back - not to cover her bottom, but to grip Felix's cock through his clothes. He groaned at the contact and suddenly she found herself being lifted up.

It was the work of a few moments to be rid of her simple dress, and only a few more moments before Felix was just as gloriously bare. He lay back on the bed, his cock jutting upwards out of its nest of dark curls, a single pearl of liquid on its tip. Feeling excessively naughty, Gabrielle leaned forward and licked it, making her husband growl as his hips jerks and he pulled her up towards him, arranging her so she straddled his body, her pussy hovering above his rampant erection.

Gabrielle moaned as she lowered herself onto him. This was only the second time he'd put her in this position and she'd forgotten how it made him feel almost impossibly large, as though he was stretching her to capacity. Although Felix liked to change their positions quite often, they rarely involved Gabrielle being on top of him in any manner. Today he seemed to content to let her move up and down his cock, playing idly with her breasts as she shuddered and rode him. His fingers pinched and twisted her nipples, giving her that little burst of pain that she craved and making her gasp as she thrust her breasts towards him.

Beneath her, his hips rolled, lifting her and grinding against her. He tormented her nipples, using them to direct her when he desired, and otherwise just rousing her excitement even higher. But it wasn't until she rode herself to her own orgasm that he truly took control. As Gabrielle cried out in ecstasy

, Felix flipped her onto her back and began to pound into her, making her scream as the intense assault overloaded her senses and sent her reeling. He took her hard and fast, leaving her sobbing as her orgasm went on longer and took her much higher than she could manage.

When he finally thrust home, emptying himself into her, Gabrielle clung to him, her legs wrapping around his body and holding him there as he pulsed inside of her, leaving her body humming in breathless perfection.

THEY DIDN'T LEAVE the house for two days. They talked, made love, ate, made love again, planned a trip around the Continent – including Greece in their itinerary – for after the Season was over, made love yet again, and barely left their room. In fact, he was fairly sure that the staff were placing bets as to when they would finally make their way downstairs again. Even their meals were sent up on trays, which Molly ferried back and forth for them. They pleasured each other in every way imaginable and shut out the world.

Felix would have happily kept them barricaded away for longer, but Gabrielle wanted to go to the ball at the Manchesters'. If he'd thought about it, he'd have realized there was no question of her attending their ball; Arabella was playing hostess for her brother and she would desire her friends' attendance. It was just as well, Taylor's stalwart defense of the front door was starting to crumble under Felix's mother's insistence. The butler had passed on the message that she was going to come in the house sooner or later if Felix and Gabrielle didn't come out.

For the sake of Taylor's nerves, they would have had to leave soon anyway.

Gabrielle had dressed carefully for the evening in a dark green gown trimmed with dark pink. The clean lines of the dress made her look very modest and ladylike, which should help to counter any gossip that they'd created two days ago. Although, he wouldn't be leaving that to chance. Nothing short of a stampede of horses would pry him from her side tonight, and even that might not do the trick.

Whispers followed them into the ballroom, but Felix ignored

them. He smiled down at Gabrielle, happy to see that she didn't appear to be paying them any attention either. Of course, the besotted look he gave her only increased the whispers. The *ton* did love to talk. The most hidebound and influential were pleased to see that the youngest Hood son had his wife well under control. Such a scene they'd caused, but considering her dance partners, no one could blame his reaction. Then again, they were quite smugly sure that it had all been a ploy on her part - after all, even tamed rakes were notoriously hard to manage. But see how he watched over her now? See how possessively he behaved? They nodded their heads sagely, pleased to see that the two were a good match. The Viscountess' youngest had done well, and they hoped her other two sons would follow their brother's lead.

Philip and Cordelia arrived not long after, and Felix felt himself tense a little. He tried to keep it hidden as his friends made their way to them, but at his side he could feel Gabrielle stiffen slightly as well as her stepmother approached. Cordelia was lovely in an amber gown decorated with bronze lace, garnets in gold at her throat and in her hair. As they approached, Felix put his fingers atop Gabrielle's on his forearm and squeezed them gently. When she looked up at him, he gave her a reassuring smile, trying to show her with his eyes that she had nothing to feel concerned about.

The greetings were a little stilted, Felix feeling rather awkward as he tried to keep his friendly tone with Cordelia without it becoming overly friendly in his wife's eyes. He felt Gabrielle relax as he settled back at her side, taking her hand and wrapping it back around his arm, then holding it there. If he could keep her content with such small gestures and touches then he would concentrate on that.

"I'm so glad you've ventured out again," Cordelia said, smiling at both of them, although her gaze eventually landed on Felix. He smiled back a little uncomfortably. Now that he was more aware, he could understand Gabrielle's jealousy. While he realized that Gabrielle herself made Cordelia feel uncomfortable and so she tended to focus her gaze on him instead of her stepdaughter, such an action could be interpreted incorrectly. "I hope neither of you were ill."

"No, just taking some time to ourselves," he said, looking away from Cordelia and back down at his wife. Gabrielle beamed up at him as he lifted her hand to his lips to kiss it, before securing her fingers on his arm again. "Being out in the country I grew far too used to having Gabrielle's attention all day every day, I'm afraid the adjustment to London has been rather hard to bear."

Philip chuckled, his blue eyes sparkling. "Don't let him monopolize all your time," he said to Gabrielle, his tone serious. "His ego doesn't need daily feeding. Once a week is more than often enough."

"We take turns," Gabrielle said impishly, smiling up at Philip.

A crease appeared on Cordelia's face as she looked back and forth between Felix and Gabrielle, before she smiled again, but a question remained in her eyes.

The conversation shifted as Cordelia complimented Gabrielle's dress. Smiling serenely, Gabrielle did the same in return. By the time the orchestra was tuning up, preparing for a waltz if Felix's ears were correct, Cordelia seemed satisfied but confused with the change in her stepdaughter. A few times Felix had to stop himself from being overly familiar with Cordelia, but he focused on Gabrielle and her growing confidence in the conversation and practiced being a better husband. He and Philip also handily intercepted remarks both ladies made that could have instigated a disagreement without their intervention.

Still, it gave him hope that eventually the ladies would find a way to have a relationship without any acrimony. Tonight was a good start.

The first strains of the waltz began.

"If you'll excuse us," he said to Philip and Cordelia before turning to Gabrielle. "My love, would you like to dance?"

Ignoring Cordelia's murmur of surprise and approval at his endearment for Gabrielle, Felix bowed over his wife's hand. She smiled at him, cheeks flushed with pleasure.

"Yes, please."

~

GABRIELLE WAS SO happy they'd come out tonight. Not just to support Arabella - who was dancing with Lord Braden and looking patently bored by it in between glaring daggers at her eldest brother, who was dancing with the rather shrill Miss Clara Daringwell - but because she could now see that Felix had meant every word that he'd said. His friendship with her stepmother was still intact, but with a slight barrier that hadn't been there before.

Part of her felt a little guilty, knowing she was the cause of the barrier, but she was also relieved.

It wasn't as though his personality had undergone a huge change, an outside observer probably wouldn't notice a thing, but to her the difference was tangible. His focus was on her. Even when he wasn't looking at her, she could feel how attuned he was to her rather than Cordelia. And when he spoke with Cordelia, he no longer seemed quite so adoring. Just friendly. She could live with that.

He pulled her close as they waltzed, his hand almost scandalously low on her back, his thigh deftly parting hers with every whirling step. Looking up at him with shining eyes, Gabrielle felt her heart soar.

"Thank you," she whispered, just loudly enough to be heard over the music.

Felix raised one dark eyebrow. "For what?"

"For everything."

A smile quirked his lips and she got the distinct impression that he desperately wanted to kiss her, middle of the dance floor or not.

"No, thank you, sweetheart."

She giggled. "For what?"

"For being my everything."

It was no surprise to their friends when they left the Manchester ball early, although in a much more dignified fashion then they'd departed the Waverlys'. Cuddled up to her husband in the carriage, Gabrielle could only smile as she reflected on the strange turns of her life, and the joyful realization of her own unanticipated, personal, happily ever after.

EPILOGUE

"Are you trying to hide behind a fern?"

Benedict's amused voice made Isaac wince.

Isaac was the Duke of Manchester, one of the most influential voices in the government, an imposing figure in any room due to his great height and broad shoulders, and yes... he had been reduced to hiding behind a fern at a house party.

"Possibly," he muttered, turning to face his brother. Impeccably clothed although slightly rumpled, Benedict smirked at him. They'd been at the house party for two days and, as far as Isaac knew, his brother had already found a feminine distraction in the person of Lady Wallis, who was attending the party without her husband. No doubt that explained the state of Benedict's attire, since normally he was as perfectly pressed and presentable as Isaac was.

A house party was normally the kind of locale where one could relax, where societal standards weren't quite as strict. Isaac had decided it was the perfect locale to finally decide on a wife. As a Duke, he needed a Duchess. Sooner, rather than later, Isaac had decided. He'd hoped that one of the young ladies invited would stand out in such surrounds, or at least be more tolerable than they were during the Season, when they and their mothers were hunting for bachelors.

Because of that, Isaac wasn't particularly relaxed, despite the locale. Benedict obviously was, but Benedict wasn't the Duke. He didn't have the same duties, the same responsibilities and burdens that Isaac did. Benedict was also the biggest supporter of Isaac obtaining a wife and, hopefully, an heir soon to follow, because until that time, Benedict was the first in line for the Dukedom. Not a position he found very comfortable.

On the other side of the equation, Isaac's sister Arabella was trenchantly opposed to him marrying and had spent most of the house party further thwarting any success. Although, he'd had more than one occasion to be grateful for her interference when certain young ladies became too importuning... or shrill... or dull...

"You're not going to find a wife in the ferns." His brother's mocking grin made Isaac want to give him a facer.

"I know."

"You said that's why we came here," he waved his hand expansively, to indicate the general expanse of the Marquess of Chester's estate. "Because you wanted a wife."

"I do."

"Well, I don't think you're currently looking in the right place." Benedict's cheeky grin didn't waver as Isaac glared at him.

He was plagued with cheeky younger siblings. No proper respect for his high status either. Most days he preferred to be treated like a regular member of the family. Other days, he wished his siblings would do a little more kowtowing.

Isaac sighed. "I suppose it doesn't really matter which one I choose."

"It doesn't?" The grin faded from Benedict's face, replaced by surprise and a touch of concern.

"I need an heir. Therefore I need a Duchess. At this point, I'm not sure I care who takes that place."

His brother frowned at him. "You've been remarkably picky for someone who doesn't care."

"I'm just ready to throw in the towel," Isaac said with a grimace. "The Season is over. I'm not sure I can endure another one unwed."

This Season had been bad enough, juggling his unmarried young sister and his own search for a bride. The young misses that filled the marriage mart were not to his taste, but it seemed they only came in one flavor and he would just have to adjust his expectations. Besides, he was tired. Tired of looking, tired of feeling the burden weighing heavily on him, tired of knowing that Benedict held his breath every time Isaac went for a gallop or a hunt or anything marginally dangerous. He needed an heir, so he needed a wife, and he would prefer one that was a good example to Arabella, his hellion of a sister.

He and Benedict tried, but they weren't very good at reigning her in. Isaac had concluded that a more feminine touch was needed, as she'd calmed down after befriending some of the *ton*'s ladies this Season, although she wasn't a very good influence on some of them (namely her best friend the recently married Mrs. Hood). Granted, she still got into plenty of trouble, but she was actually much easier to deal with. Unfortunately, Mrs. Hood was currently in Greece with her husband, Lady Hyde was at home with her young son, and the Earl of Spencer had refused to attend the house party with his delightful wife, divesting Arabella of her bosom companions. She needed company. Female company. Female company that wasn't distracted by their husband. Instead, he could let Arabella distract his wife from him.

Isaac nodded his head decisively. "I'll look over the herd tonight. Tomorrow I'll make a final decision and propose by sunset."

After a hesitant moment, Benedict clapped him on the shoulder. "It's your wedding," he said, but from his tone he might as well have substituted 'funeral' for wedding.

As the two brothers walked away to throw themselves back into the fray, neither of them noticed a pair of determined grey eyes peeking out from yet another set of nearby ferns, watching them go.

Book 3 in the Bridal Discipline Series, *Lydia's Penance, will be out in Winter 2016.*

DID you enjoy Gabrielle's Discipline? Would you like to receive a free story from me? Join the Angel Legion and sign up for my newsletter! You'll immediately receive a free story from my Stronghold series in a welcome message, and as part of the Angel Legion you'll also receive one newsletter a month with teasers, sneak peeks, and news about upcoming releases, as well as what I'm reading now!

ABOUT THE AUTHOR

About me? Right… I'm a writer, I should be able to do that, right?

I'm a happily married young woman and I like tater tots, small fuzzy animals, naming my plants, hiking, reading, writing, sexy time, naked time, shirtless o'clock, anything sparkly or shiny, and weirding people out with my OCD food habits.

I believe in Happy Endings. And fairies. And Santa Claus. Because without a little magic, what's the point of living?

I write because I must. I live in several different worlds at any given moment. And I wouldn't have it any other way.

I also write erotica, fetish romance, and dark offerings under the pen name Sinistre Ange.

Want to know more about my other books and stories? Sign up for my newsletter! Come visit my website! I also update my blog at least a couple times a month.

You can also come hang out with me on Facebook in my private Facebook group!

Thank you so much for reading, I hope you enjoyed the story… and don't forget, the best thing you can do in return for any author is to leave them feedback!

Stay sassy.

www.goldenangelromance.com

facebook.com/GoldenAngelAuthor

twitter.com/GoldeniAngel

instagram.com/goldeniangel

OTHER TITLES BY GOLDEN ANGEL

Sci-fi Romance

Mated on Hades

Daddy Doms

Super Daddies: A Naughty Nerdy Romantic Comedy Anthology

Victorian Romance

Marriage Training

Domestic Discipline Quartet

Birching His Bride

Dealing With Discipline

Punishing His Ward

Claiming His Wife

Bridal Discipline Series

Philip's Rules

Undisciplined (Book 1.5)

Gabrielle's Discipline

Lydia's Penance

Benedict's Commands

Arabella's Taming

Venus Rising Quartet

The Venus School

Venus Aspiring

Venus Desiring

Venus Transcendent

Stronghold Series

Stronghold

Taming the Tease

On His Knees (book 2.5)

Mastering Lexie

Pieces of Stronghold (book 3.5)

Breaking the Chain

Bound to the Past

Stripping the Sub

Tempting the Domme

Hardcore Vanilla

Masters of the Castle

Masters of the Castle: Witness Protection Program Box Set

Tsenturion Masters with Lee Savino

Alien Captive

Alien Tribute

Big Bad Bunnies Series

Chasing His Bunny

Chasing His Squirrel

Chasing His Puma

Chasing His Polar Bear

Chasing His Honey Badger

Night of the Wild Stags – A standalone Reverse Harem romance set in the Big Bad Bunnies World

Poker Loser Trilogy

Forced Bet

Back in the Game

Winning Hand

Poker Loser Trilogy Bundle (3 books in 1!)

Printed in Great Britain
by Amazon